WHAT'S YOUR NAME?

MISS MAY

Fairfell Publishing

To my alleged mother who has done nothing but punish me for being born. You found the first book I wrote in the 6th grade, ripped it in half, and laughed in my face, telling me I'll never be an author. Well, here I am now and you'll never know. Removing you from my life, and writing my books, are the best things I've ever done.

SEPTEMBER 1 – FRIDAY

Midnight

It's the final stretch and I'm counting down the miles just past the nick of midnight. WELCOME TO BLACKRIDGE: THE NAMELESS CITY, the sign reads after seventeen hours. That's how long driving from San Diego to Blackridge, Oregon, takes.

There's nothing around us but darkness and trees on both sides of the road, standing tall and black. Then there's the sheet of fog, thick and offensive. Mom is barely ahead of us in her 2022 Honda Civic, but the fog is so dense her taillights have vanished.

A cluster of lights beam through the fog-like astigmatism, causing Atlus, my little brother, to sit up and remove his bare feet from the dashboard. His toes leave spots on the windshield. "Is that it? Mom said it was by a gas station," he says.

I look at my phone docked to my left. Seeing how much we still have to go makes me want to stomp on the gas and swerve into oncoming traffic … if there was any in this ghost town. "GPS says we still have another fifteen miles," I tell him.

Atlus slumps back down, and it doesn't take long before the gas station lights are behind us and engulfed by the fog.

I knew we were far from San Diego when a chill filled the car, and the heater replaced the A/C. It's dangerously comfortable. My eyes are heavy and when I blink, they stay closed for a bit too long before I have to throw my head back to wake myself up. I use the buttons on the steering wheel to turn down the music. "I can't see."

Atlus looks at me, the long drive taking its toll on him. His raccoon eyes are even darker, messy hair even messier, and attitude even attitud-ier. "What, you see with your ears?"

The bright red lights from Mom's car are in front of us and I slam on the brakes, jolting us forward. The contracting seat belt catches my body while an unbuckled Atlus almost has his legs bust through the windshield.

We're at a complete stall as some deer cross the road. One of the animals stops to look, its eyes glowing yellow as it stares into the headlights. They finish crossing and Mom starts to drive again with Atlus and me following behind. Just a few feet ahead, her taillights disappear once more beneath the fog.

That woke me up, at least a little bit. I need to stay this way until we get there.

We come across another section of bright lights through the fog and it's a gas station, the right one this time. Mom's car slows down to turn into a residential area.

"Turn left onto Misty Lane," the voice on my GPS says.

There's a break in the trees to turn into the neighborhood. The houses are squeezed close together into such a small development, but the homes are large standing at least two stories tall. Not a single light is on as we drive past through the night.

"Your destination is on the left," the robot in my phone speaks.

Here it is, our new home: 2958 Misty Ln, Blackridge, Oregon.

Mom pulls into the driveway of one of the houses made of brown brick and beige paneling and waits for the two-car garage to rise. Atlus and I pull up beside her, and we can finally get out of the car. Standing on my own two feet turns them into jelly and going out into the crisp, foggy air makes my skin prickle. It almost makes me want to get back to the heated seats of my 2020 Ford Explorer. Almost.

Mom stands in front of the garage with the headlights on behind her like her own personal spotlight, though she looks like anything except a star. Her thick dark brown hair is frizzy and tied into a ponytail, the band barely keeping everything in place, and there's more than one coffee stain on her sweater. She holds out her arms. "Home sweet home, kids!"

Atlus yawns. "Yay."

The movers are coming in the morning–later in the morning, I should say–so for now, all we have are the bags we could fit between the two cars. I throw my backpack over my shoulder and grab Squeak's carrier. Atlus has his soccer bag and some bull terrier mutt he found in the trash a few years ago and named, fittingly, Trash.

After packing, driving, hotels, and more driving, we enter our new home. Mom shoots on the lights for the living room, illuminating the ample space. The house is open concept, but without any of our things to make it into a home, it's just wood flooring casting off our reflections and bare walls. Directly past the garage door is a staircase leading to a balcony with several more rooms.

Mom drops her heavy duffle bag to the floor. "Well, what do you think, huh?"

"It's nice, Mom," I tell her as I put down Squeak's carrier and open the gate, but she's not ready to come out. She's a black cat so all I can see are her piercing yellow eyes staring at me. "It's okay, kitty. You can come out when you're ready."

Atlus doesn't say anything and instead takes his duffle bag to the bathroom directly across from the garage door.

Mom watches him, her face dropping before quickly perking back up. She claps her hands. "I'm gonna go get our beds. I don't know about you, but I'm pooped." She goes back through the garage and she's carrying two bags of rolled air mattresses when she returns. She sets them down on the floor and uses an electric pump to fill them both. The house is so empty that the whirring of the pumps bounces off all the walls.

I think air mattresses are the most uncomfortable thing on the planet, but once they're full I waste no time crawling into bed and under the blankets. The hardness feels good on my stiff back.

Since I've been driving for so long I haven't been able to

check my phone. I have a few text messages from my best friend Chloe back in San Diego:

Tuesday 3:58 PM

CHLOE: Tell me when u get there
Wednesday 4:10 PM

CHLOE: U still alive bitch????
Thursday 11:41 AM

CHLOE: ??????
12:56 AM

FIORA: I'm dead
CHLOE: Damm rip Fiora. can I have all ur shit?
FIORA: You might have to fight off the vampires and the werewolves.
CHLOE: This is the skin of a killer Bella

Mom lays beside me like she did the nights we spent in the hotels and runs her fingers through my thick, tangled hair. "Need some beauty sleep?" she asks.

I yawn and place my phone on the floor beside the mattress. "Why, you calling me ugly?"

She chuckles. "No, you're actually the most beautiful girl in the world." She covers her mouth as she yawns. "I'm exhausted. And tomorrow is another big day. I'll show you around all the places I used to go when I was your age. Well, more like Atlus's age. And the high school where you're going to graduate this year." She exposes her forehead and squints her eyes at me. "Right, Fiora?"

Mom made me pinky swear that I'll graduate this year after being expelled from my last school, but it's not like I can predict the future. "Sure, why not?" I say.

She continues looking at me with those large brown eyes but adds an extra emphasis of furrowed brows.

Atlus returns from the bathroom with his raven hair slicked back and face wet, but still looks as tired as I feel. He claims the other air mattress for him and his dog. "Hey Fi, I got another one, and this one is actually real," he says.

I'm lying on my stomach with my arm under the pillow. A strand of messy hair falls over my face and I blow it out of the way. "Bring it on."

"Okay, so there was this journalist who was investigating something big and was supposed to go out of town for whatever fucking reason. But days before he was supposed to leave, he started getting threatening messages warning him not to go. He did anyways. But before he could tell anyone what his research was about, he was found dead in a hotel bathtub. All his research was gone, his wrists were slashed dozens of times, and the room was completely covered in blood–"

Mom shoots her head up and wrinkles her face into a different look. One that has just as much disappointment as the looks she gives me but with an extra splash of *What the fuck is wrong with you*? "Atlus, what the hell are you talking about?"

"Oh, we were telling scary stories in the car," I explain.

"Um, how about some nice stories?" Mom suggests.

"Okay, but I'm not done," Atlus continues: "See, this dude was terrified of blood, something only his family knew about so–"

Mom holds out her hand, firm like a stop sign. "So am I, so let's stop." She lays back down on the rock-solid air mattress that barely makes a dent under the weight of her body. "Geez, the only time you two get along is when you're talking about weird stuff."

Atlus rests his head on his pillow. "Fine."

Mom supports her cheek in the palm of her hand. "I have a nice story. Did I ever tell you kids I was in Girl Scouts when I lived here before? We'd camp out in my friend Mary's backyard every summer and have bonfires. It was kinda like this except we were outside and in tents. We'd stay up late, sleep on air mattresses even cheaper than these, and wake up absolutely exhausted but we always got to make s'mores and roast hotdogs. I should take you kids camping. This one time–"

Atlus takes a long and deep breath, his eyes shut.

"Well, okay. Maybe not," Mom concludes.

I struggle to keep my eyes open and yawn. "I'm awake, Mom, but camping sounds awful."

Mom chuckles. "Yeah, I guess camping is one of those things

that's only fun in hindsight. I wonder what all the girls from my troop are up to these days. It's been so long since I've heard from anyone I used to know."

"You could always look them up on social media," I suggest.

"I have, but couldn't find anyone. Maybe they all blocked me. Well, goodnight sweetheart."

Finally, we can all sleep until the movers arrive first thing in the morning. Squeak comes out of her carrier to lie on my back, and I'm gone the moment my eyes shut. Her purrs soothe my tired and aching body.

Afternoon

The movers came early enough in the morning that after everything was set up, we could take a couple of hours to relax, sitting on the new couch and watching the new TV. Atlus wanted to watch *Dune*, but I won Rock, Paper, Scissors so we watched *The Greatest Showman* instead. *Rewrite the Stars* is stuck in my head as I hum the melody.

"Shut the fuck up," Atlus barks as he's rummaging through the barren pantry. "We don't even have any food." He pulls out a jar of spaghetti sauce and stares at the label as if it owes him money, the brutality of his Italian blood.

Mom enters the kitchen with a new dress on and a ponytail, though much neater than last night, with her hair freshly washed and blow-dried. She skips up to Atlus and tussles his dark hair. "That's because we're meeting my sister for dinner."

"No, it's 'cause you don't cook. I'm tired of takeout all the time," he complains.

"Geez, want some cheese with that whine? Fiora, you remember Aunt Addie, right?"

"Not really," I reply.

"Yeah, you were really young when we moved. Go get ready; we need to leave before the school closes."

I go for the front seat of Mom's Honda Civic when it's time to leave, but Atlus slams the door shut in my face. "No way in hell. You got to pick the movie so I get the front seat," he says.

"Fine, I'll rochambeau you for it," I say.

"Fuck off!"

Mom is in front of the steering wheel and leans over to speak to us through the open passenger window. "Fiora, let your brother have the front seat then you can have it on the way back."

Atlus sticks his tongue out before claiming his victory and the seat, slamming the door extra loud in my face. He opens it back up to slam it again.

Mom chortles.

Blackridge is a parallel universe from San Diego. It's daytime, yet everything is leaden and misty with the waft of salt. Though, it's not warm and inviting like the coast in California. It's eerie how quiet the town is, even during the middle of a Friday afternoon.

Mom's head grazes side to side as she looks around and drives simultaneously. "I can't believe how much of this place still looks the same," she says once we reach the resemblance of a town. However, many buildings appear abandoned, with boarded windows and showers of graffiti. "See that empty building right there? That used to be a skating rink where we'd all go to smoke weed in the bathroom." She snorts. "Then someone narced. I wish they'd open something else there instead of letting the building rot. Kids have so little to do outside of the house these days."

We drive some more and Mom continues to point out the places: "Nickels and Dimes! I can't believe it's still open. That's where I worked before I met Atlus's dad. I wonder if Amanda still works there. Fiora, you remember Amanda, right?"

"No," I answer, my head leaning against the window. "I'd have a better view if I could sit in the front seat."

Atlus looks over his shoulder at me in the back. "Shut the fuck up."

I stick out my tongue.

Mom ignores us. "Looks like the movie theater shut down too," she says.

Just out the window is the coast. The reek of salt and rotting fish is pungent while the water is so murky it's partnered with the drape of fog. "These docks are where we'd always go fishing," Mom says and then chuckles to herself. "Well, we called it *fishing*, but really we'd just drink and act like idiots. One time my old friend Ray actually jumped off one of the docks. Dude was lucky he didn't get swept away." We drive some more along the coast, the water clouded and gray, until Mom slows down the car. "This is new. I wonder what it is."

A cabin-style mansion high on the rocky ledge overlooks the ocean. Mom speeds up the car, and I watch the mansion disappear into the fog as if it were never there. Even the ocean has vanished.

Finally after going the long way through town, we arrive at Seal Coast Community High School. It's smaller than Promise Private Academy back in San Diego with only one building and two stories. The only thing that's similar is the security. There's a large red fence with the paint chipping surrounding the campus and in order to get through the gate, we have to pass through metal detectors first.

The security guard makes Mom open her purse before taking a glance inside. Then, we pass through the metal detectors that aren't on and enter through the front door. Straight ahead is an open space that leads to the foyer, but to the right is a room made entirely of glass. Administration Office, the tag says.

Mom hums. "This is new." She attempts to open the door but it's locked until the person behind the counter buzzes us through.

"Good morning. How can I help you today?" the woman asks. Her name tag says Paige Turner. Who the hell would do that to their child?

Mom reaches the front counter. "I'm here to enroll my kids. I have a senior and a freshman."

"Do you have the transcripts from their last school?"

"Yes, I do." Mom reaches into her purse, retrieving folded pieces of paper before handing them to the woman.

She hums. "Promise Private Academy? And these are excellent grades. Oh, and the soccer team? Tryouts for our team will be happening right after the semester starts. We'll certainly be lucky to have you." She smiles at Atlus. Upon flipping over to the next page, her smile fades. "Oh ... well, we're happy to have all kinds of diverse students." The woman grabs a few papers from behind the counter and hands them to Mom. "Alright, if you could just fill these out real quick, I'll get everything all set in the computer."

Mom takes the papers attached to the clipboards. "Thank you." We sit nearby at the row of chairs against the wall and Mom hands me one of the clipboards. "Here, fill these out."

"Why doesn't Atlus have to?" I complain.

"Because he's still a minor."

I sigh, but no amount of groaning and bitching is going to get me out of this. I sign my name: **Fiora Clairewater**.

Once we finish we return the papers to the unfortunately named woman behind the counter. She looks over them before nodding. "Welcome to Seal Coast Community High School. Here are your schedules and here is the student code of conduct. It's very important that you read these over before classes start, okay? We take our rules and traditions very seriously."

Mom nods before accepting. "Thank you."

After School

A smooth ride down the empty road ends when Mom slams the brakes. Atlus has his feet on the dashboard and almost smacks his face on his knees when he jolts forward. Mom scoffs and furrows her brows. "Geez, buckle up, will ya?" she scolds unseriously.

A line of traffic blocks the road with no one moving an inch, reminiscent of California. Mom strains her neck, attempting to see over the cars, and says, "That's weird. The mall is just up ahead so maybe there's some big Labor Day sale going on." She glances at the time on the dashboard. "We're going to be so late."

We start moving, albeit at a snail's pace. The closer we pull to the mall, the more clear are the red and blue flashing lights blocking the entrance. Uniforms stand guard as looky-loos wander.

"What the hell happened there?" Mom says.

A cop stands in the center of the road, directing traffic and letting one line of cars pass at a time. We're stalled in the perfect position for a view of the two paramedics packing a stretcher draped with a white sheet into the back of one of the ambulances. They slam the doors shut.

Atlus gasps and perks up from the front seat. "Did you see that? Was that a dead body?"

Mom's eyes are glued to the road, her face as stiff as stone. "Oh, ah … no. Don't distract me while I'm driving. A–And buckle up! I mean it, Atlus. You're going to get seriously hurt one of these days."

The cop standing in the road waves us through and we leave the scene–and traffic–behind.

Mah and Pah's is the pizzeria where we're meeting Aunt Addie for lunch and it's the only business left standing in yet another abandoned shopping district. There's more graffiti, FOR LEASE signs, and one of the empty stores broken into with glass scattered across the pavement.

Inside, Mah and Pah's is cozy and welcoming, as if Mah and Pah are the grandparents of everyone in Blackridge. Framed photos plaster the brick walls, each telling a story displaying the passage of time. Down the sequence of captured memories, they add wrinkles and speckles, and their hair grows white and thin, yet they still hold the same smile in every one.

Mom releases a heavy sigh. "This place hasn't changed a bit either. It was my favorite to go to on the weekends." She snorts. "But that was mostly 'cause they didn't card when you ordered booze."

Instead of a host, there's a sign instructing customers to sit wherever they like so we travel down the line of wooden booths until there's a woman sitting by herself. She looks like Mom with tan skin, brown eyes, and the traditional thick brown hair of the Navarro clan.

Aunt Addie stands from the booth to hug Mom. The two women barely touch before letting go, the distance between them being thicker than just how far they stand from each other. "I can't believe how long it's been." Aunt Addie says, her voice nearly identical to Mom's.

Mom sighs and smacks her hand on her thigh. "Where the hell has all the time gone?"

Aunt Addie takes a good look at Atlus and me. "Wow Fiora, I haven't seen you since you were in diapers. And you must be Atlus. I haven't seen you at all. And look how tall you are. Where the hell did that come from? I know it's not our side of the family."

It's awkward interacting with family members you barely know. They might as well be strangers, yet treating them as such is seen as rude.

We're standing in silence and staring at each other for a long, heavy moment. It's up to Mom to cut the tension: "Why don't we sit down?" she says.

Aunt Addie releases an audible sigh of relief. "Yes, yes! I already ordered everyone some water, if that's okay."

It's not long until a young waitress comes by and places down the waters in front of each of us. She has chin-length dark brown hair and a loose tie around her neck. "Hi, my name is Poppet and I'll be taking care of you. What can I get started today?"

Poppet?

Atlus looks at Mom. "Can we get wings?"

"Yeah, of course. Get whatever you want," Mom answers, then finishes giving the waitress our order.

The waitress nods without writing anything down. "I'll get that in for you right now. Feel free to help yourselves to the salad bar." She disappears into the kitchen around the back.

In the booth across from us sits two older women. One leans over the table like she's preparing to tell the other woman a secret, yet speaks loud enough for the whole restaurant to hear. "What a little skank. Put some clothes on. Wasn't it a boy just a few years ago?"

"That's what happens when they take God out of the schools," the other woman continues.

Some say you're never too old to enjoy the things you love, including gossip. And bigotry.

"We just came back from enrolling at Seal Coast," Mom is saying.

"Oh, I'm the senior social studies teacher so you might be in my class, Fiora," Aunt Addie says. "There's nothing wrong with needing a little extra help to graduate this year. Just remember to follow the rules and traditions and you'll be fine."

"Fi needs a lot of extra help," Atlus snarks.

"What about you, Atlus? What grade are you going into?" Aunt Addie asks.

"9th," he spits out with the angst only capable of a 9th grader.

"Oh, I remember the 9th grade," Aunt Addie reminisces. "It um ... gets better, it really does."

Mom has her elbow on the table and rests her chin in her palm. "God, I know. High school was such a nightmare. I can't believe you actually wanted to be a teacher."

Aunt Addie shrugs. "What can I say? Teaching is my life. My students are my life."

"How's that going by the way?"

"It's great. Starting a new year is always bittersweet. I miss my old students, but I get to welcome new ones. Plus, since it's such a small town I more or less already know all the kids before they even step foot in my class, including the troublemakers." Aunt Addie shoots a wink my way.

"No, not teaching. I know you're a dork about that," Mom says. "I meant your life in general."

Aunt Addie takes a much too-long sip of her water. Just when it seems she's done, she sips down some more. It's not until she is down to the ice that she answers. "Well, it's been going," she admits, avoiding eye contact and rubbing the sleeve of her knit sweater. "Money has been tight so I've been working a lot of overtime. I worked summer school, and then I'll be working detention through lunch once the semester starts. Not that I mind, though. The students who need a little extra help or guidance is what makes the job so fulfilling."

"Is money really that bad? I thought Mom's estate paid off the house," Mom asks.

Aunt Addie twirls the ice in her glass. "Yeah, it did. But necessities are still a lot. It's like everything is getting more expensive by the day. Plus, I'm trying to pay off my student loans before the interest fucks me up the ass." She gasps and covers her mouth. "Sorry."

Mom lets out a small laugh. "Oh, please. You should hear how these two speak. But we have an extra bedroom in the new house. You can always stay with us."

"You mean your office?" I point out.

"Family is more important than an office. I write dorky fantasy books, not launch codes. What do you say, Addie?"

Aunt Addie chuckles lightly, though also keeps her gaze down to her hands. "Oh, don't worry about me; I'm a big girl now. I can take care of myself. I'm lucky compared to most people. I don't know how anyone survives these days. It would be nice if I could afford a couple of kids before I turn 30, but it's good to finally have some family back in town. It's been lonely since Mom died. I've missed you, Bailey."

"Families are overrated," Atlus mutters, but I, sitting beside him, seem to be the only one who hears him.

"You know how Mom was," my mom says. "I wasn't allowed

to live under her roof pregnant. I've made a lot of bad choices, but that was never one of them." ... "Have you been seeing anyone? Two incomes certainly make things easier."

Aunt Addie blushes. "Bailey, is that really something to talk about in front of the kids?"

"Didn't you just say something about getting fucked up the ass?" Atlus asks.

"I'm all ears," I say.

Addie twirls her hair around her finger. "Well, there might be someone, but it's nothing serious."

I lean forward with my elbows on the table. "Oh, so just a booty call? Is he a teacher too?"

Her eyes widen and cheeks glow red. "No! It's nothing like that. It's just not serious yet, that's all."

"So, is he married then? Are you his dirty little secret?"

The waitress returns with platters of food and places everything on the table. Once her hands are free, she pulls a remote from her back pocket and ups the volume of the TV mounted on the wall. "Shots fired at the Blackridge Mall, leaving two dead and several others injured," the news anchor announces in a deep, over-enunciated voice. "Witnesses report the suspect entering the food court and then opening fire on staff and other customers. The shots were heard by security who reportedly shot and killed the suspect. Those injured are between the ages of forty and just seven years old."

Aunt Addie shakes her head. "Wh–What the hell? Wh–Who could possibly do something so evil?"

"That must have been what was causing all that traffic," Mom speculates. "Have things like this been happening a lot since I left?"

My head goes back and forth between the two as they talk. I like my pizza with ranch so I take off the pepperoni to eat by themselves then dip my pizza cheese side down.

Atlus takes notice and shoots me a signature death stare. "What are you, a fucking psychopath?"

Aunt Addie takes a long, deep sigh. "No ... No, not in a long time. I–I'm sorry this is what you moved back to."

Mom has a slight hint of a smile on her lips despite the conversation topic. Though, she's always been good at shifting and avoiding. "It actually almost feels like I'm right back where I left off." The waitress passes by our booth carrying a tray of drinks for the gossiping neighboring table and Mom flags her down. "Can I get a frozen strawberry margarita with salt on the rim, please?"

Aunt Addie throws up a shaky finger. "Make that two."

The waitress smiles and winks. "Two extra strong strawberry margaritas coming right up."

Finally this familial lunch is finished and we get to the car, but before we get inside Mom yells out to Aunt Addie at her 2008 Toyota Camry parked just a few spots down: "Bye Addie! Don't be a stranger!"

Aunt Addie waves. "Bye. I'll see you kids on Tuesday."

"Happy Labor Day! If anyone deserves to celebrate, it's teachers!"

While they talk, I'm quick to claim the front seat before Atlus's greedy ass can hog it.

Mom gets in the car with us and starts the engine.

Atlus rests his head against the window and uses the tip of his finger to draw in the condensation. "Aunt Addie is weird."

Mom pauses. "I think she's just stressed about everything. I mean, who isn't these days? Let's go home and watch *Dune*. This might be our last summer with the three of us." Mom sneaks glances at me, going back and forth between me and the road. "Because you're going to graduate this year and then go off the university, right, Fiora?"

I hold up my pinky. "I promised, didn't I?"

"Not if she fails again," Atlus snarks. I reach back in an attempt to smack him but he's not buckled and quick to duck away. "You're 18, I'm pressing charges!"

Mom shakes her head and chuckles.

The traffic is backed up for miles.

SEPTEMBER 5 – TUESDAY

Morning

Mom yawns as she pours coffee, the only thing she knows how to make, and only because it's instant. "How'd you sleep?" she asks.

I sit at the kitchen island and rub the crust from my eyes. "Like a corpse." I've been up for at least an hour since Squeak was yelling at me for her breakfast.

Mom chuckles. "Glad to hear that."

Atlus is sitting on the stool beside mine, flipping through the glossed pages of the student code of conduct. *"Seal Coast Community High School has a rich history of encouraging students to express themselves, creating a culture in which staff and students are exclusively referred to by monikers."* He looks up from the spiral notebook. "What's a moniker?"

"It's like the pen name I use for my writing," Mom explains, resting on the island counter with her cup of coffee between her fingers.

"Failing to address someone as their preferred name will result in immediate suspension and eventual expulsion for repeat offenders, prioritizing the safety of staff and students." Atlus picks out some of the bacon from his omelet and reaches down to give it to the mutt begging at his feet. "That's stupid. I can get not being a dick and just calling people what they want, but this sounds like everyone has to have a nickname. Why?"

Mom shrugs. "I dunno."

I snicker. "Going to school is gonna be like one big game of Guess Who."

"Is your character a loser?" Atlus asks.

"Yes, and he's you."

Mom has her elbows on the counter and sets down her mug to rest her chin in the palms of her hands. The tips of her lips curve just enough for a cheeky smile that says she's waiting for something. "You two done?"

Atlus and I look at each other. "Yeah, I guess," I admit.

Mom reaches into the pockets of her flannel pajama pants and takes out her phone. She taps on it a few times before turning the phone over and showing us what's on the screen. "Look, they wrote an article about me."

Atlus doesn't bother to look as he's too busy stuffing his face. "Who's *they*?" he says, cheeks full like a hamster. Trash stands up and scratches Atlus's leg before he reaches down and gives the pup more bacon.

"The Blackridge Online Newspaper. You'd know that if you'd look."

Bestselling Author Returns to Hometown of Blackridge

Nebula Clairwater is a bestselling fantasy author, but before there were contracts, book deals, and TV adaptations, Ms. Clairwater was privileged to call Blackridge, Oregon, her home. Ms. Clairwater and her family recently relocated back to Blackridge from San Diego, California, and *Blackridge Online* had the opportunity to speak with the busy author as she settles back into the town she again calls home.

What inspired you to move back to our quiet town of Blackridge from busy San Diego?

I was so young when I first left Blackridge, and even after being gone all these years, it was hard to find anywhere I could call home, and that's where I need to be right now. Blackridge is where I grew up and wish I could have finished growing up. Now, I need to be with the family I have left here. A quiet, peaceful coastal town is the exact place I have always wanted to raise my kids, but I have never been able to until now.

You grew up here, and I'm sure you have a lot of memories. What drew you away from home?

To be blunt, I was young and thought I was in love. Now, I'm in my thirties and going through a divorce. That's why Blackridge is the best place for my kids and me right now.

How are you settling in? Are you reconnecting with any old friends?

Nebula Clairwater is a pen name, and I've always been particular about my privacy, so I doubt anyone I used to know even knows who I am. But if anyone recognizes me, I would love to reconnect with my old friends, and I'm always happy to make new ones.

I know you mostly write fantasy, but would you ever publish a book in a setting similar to Blackridge?

You know, I thought about that once. It's so foggy here I was going to do something about a killer fog, but I'm pretty sure I played a game about that once and would hate to plagiarize accidentally.

Do you have any upcoming novels that will be released right here in Blackridge?

I always have ideas running around in my noggin, and I currently have a couple of books in the hands of my editor. I honestly can't tell you when they will be released. These things can take months or even years. At the moment, I'm not working on anything. I just moved and am going through a divorce, so right now, I'm focusing on settling in and taking care of my kids.

Mom wears a grin on her face as she tucks her phone into her pajama pocket. "Well, whatcha think?"

Atlus doesn't look up from his phone. "It's great, Mom."

Mom scrunches her brows and scoffs. "You didn't even look."

Atlus looks up. "It's great, Mom."

"Yeah, yeah, yeah."

"It was great, Mom," I assure her. "You almost sounded like a professional."

"Hey, I am a professional!"

Even though I've had my license for a few years now, it's tradition for Mom to drive us to our first day of school. I hurry out to the garage and beat Atlus for the front seat. "I get it on the way home," he complains as he packs himself into the back where he belongs.

Despite it being a small school, there's a long line for the drop-off queue, and when it's our turn at the curb, Atlus and I get out of the car. "Bye!" I say before closing the door. Mom waves through the window before pulling away from the curb and driving off.

Two students can go through the metal detectors at once and I cut past Atlus to get there first. A boy stands next to me, grabbing my attention. Most people are taller than me, though he is exceptionally tall with a sharp jawline despite other soft features. He has unkempt fawn, reddish brown hair and big brown eyes. His skin is silky smooth without a single blemish, and best of all, he's wearing a Bad Omens hoodie, the same one I have from their latest merch drop.

"Nice hood–" I attempt to say but get cut off when another boy in a letterman jacket cuts in front of me.

He's about the same height as his more attractive counterpart but much bulkier and has fluffy brown hair. "Slam," he says.

The cute guy looks at the jock and hums. "Hmm?"

The giant and brawnier guy shoulder-checks the boy into the fence. There's a loud clunk like the banging of a gong as his head connects with the metal bars. "I said *slam*, pay attention next time." The bully and his goonies in letterman jackets wander off, but one stays behind to laugh the hardest. He has light brown hair styled in a ducktail and, ironically, is shorter and skinnier than the boy who was just bullied. Duck Tail skips off to meet up with the other brainless clay eaters, but not before calling the boy a slur and spitting at his feet.

Other people also notice and only point and mock the boy on the ground. He remains down on the concrete, rubbing his face as they pass.

A short man stands above the boy on the ground, his legs stiff as a board. He's wearing a suit and tie and silver hair with a mustache while there's a briefcase tucked under his arm. "This is no time to be fooling around, Mr. Joey," he says.

The mark on the boy's face is already turning red. "Yes, sir. Sorry, Mr. Phillips."

With an unapproving mien, the geriatric marches away with the heels of his shiny shoes tapping against the pavement.

So many staff and students pass by, not paying him any mind other than a snark and a snicker. "What a loser." Several students take out their phones to take pictures as he sits on the cement, hanging his head.

I reach out my hand, but I'm met with a shove from behind. "Get out of the fucking way!" Atlus bitches.

I snap my head back at him like a lasso and cry out the first thing that comes to mind: "Kill yourself!" When I look back at the guy on the ground, he has gotten up and merged with the crowd.

Atlus and I enter through the main entrance and down the hall into the foyer. A girl sits at a table with a large red banner that reads Student Council in a bold white font. A few other students stop to write something, but many more walk past.

"Don't talk to me," Atlus says and parts away towards, according to my map, the freshman wing of the school.

"Like I'd ever choose to talk to you!" I yell at the back of his head as he pays no mind.

The morning bell has yet to ring, so I kill time by approaching the table. The girl sitting there has long dark red hair with some bangs covering one of her eyes. She wears a white blouse that lacks wrinkles due to her perfect posture. "What's up?" I ask.

"You must be one of the new transfer students. Welcome," she states. She speaks clearly, her voice deep, luscious, and effortlessly alluring.

"Am I already that popular?"

"I'm the student council president. It is my duty to be aware of all the students." She stretches out her hands to highlight the sign plastered to the table. "Hence, this fundraiser. O'Brien, our star hitter on the baseball team, was injured in the shooting several days prior. The student council is gathering volunteers for a fundraiser to help relieve the stress of his medical expenses."

"Oh hell yeah, a fundraiser? I'm awesome at those."

A strand of red hair falls in front of her face and she tucks it behind her ear. "Are you? That's wonderful. The student council would greatly appreciate it." She hands me one of the pens sitting in a plain white holder. "Allow me to introduce myself: I am called McCarthy. It's tradition for all students and staff to go by aliases."

Skimming down the list of names written on the sign-in sheet, most of them are obviously fake, even for a school with a culture of monikers. Dirty Sanchez? I.C. Wiener? Chlamydia? Cheese? I sign my name and phone number at the bottom of the list. "So, what kind of fundraising are we doing? Selling chocolates? Armed robbery?" I ask.

"Volunteers have the opportunity to do whatever they like," she closes her eyes and smirks, "as long as it's legal and approved by the administration. Some are mowing lawns or babysitting. One is starting a band. I am currently orchestrating a carwash but have yet to confirm a date or location."

"Oh hell yeah, I can totally do that. Except for babysitting. I hate those fucking things."

She hums a chuckles, almost like a song. "Duly noted. I will be making contact shortly."

The campus map guides me to the locker I'll be renting for the school year and a guy stands at the locker beside mine. He's bulky and wearing a letterman jacket, though I don't recognize him from the crowd of bullies this morning. "Hey, are you new here? What's your name?" he asks.

"Fiora," I answer.

"Oh, that's awesome! I love that show."

"No, I'm not named after the show. The show is named after me. What's up with–"

A girl approaches the locker on my other side and fiddles

with the dial. She's almost as tall as the guy, wearing knee-high black striped socks, shorts exactly fingertip length for the dress code, and a tie loosely wrapped around her neck. "Leave people alone, Griffin." Her eyes lock on me. "Hey, I think we've met before."

"Hey, you're the girl from the pizza place! Poppet, right?" I say.

She smiles. "Yeah, Mah and Pah are my grandparents. Did you just move here?"

"Yeah, a few days ago."

"Oh yeah? What brought you to the middle of nowhere?"

"*Leave people alone, Poppet,*" Griffin mocks with his best–worst–imitation of a feminine voice.

Poppet sticks out her tongue, a metal bar pierced through it, before returning her attention to me. "What's your first period?" My schedule is crumbled somewhere in my hoodie pouch so I dig it out and hand it to her. "Oh, you have English with Mr. Simpson? I can show you where his class is. Mine is just right down the hall from there." She puts a few things into her locker before I follow her down the hall.

"Wow, I can't believe it's my first day and I'm already being walked to class by a cute girl," I tease.

Poppet giggles and winks. "What can I say? I saw you and just couldn't help myself."

First Period

A group of girls sitting at the table closest to the door wave me down upon entering the classroom. "Hey, are you new?" one with pale skin and black hair with bangs asks.

"No," I say, and sit down at the empty seat the hand around my wrist leads me towards.

"You are so new here," a girl with straight, shiny brunette hair points out. She wears a large, gummy smile. "What's your name?"

"Fiora," I answer.

"No, like, what's your *real* name?"

I tilt my head and squint at her. "What are *your* names?"

"April, May, June," the aforementioned girl explains.

I restrain my giggles. "Wow, what a coincidence. Are you triplets or something?"

They look at one another, confused by the fact that they're not related and those names are nonchalantly abiding by this school's *rules and traditions*.

The one with dark skin and coily hair furrows her brows. I think she's June. "Um, no. Has anyone told you yet?"

"Yes, I'm familiar with most months."

"No, about the cur–" April never gets a chance to finish that sentence.

Like a viper, May is quick to strike at her next target, and that fake gummy smile reduces to a wrinkle-inducing scowl. "April shut up. You're embarrassing yourself. What are you, a child?"

April slumps back in her chair like it's made of acid and she's melting. "I'm sorry, May."

May makes a zip motion with her hand. "You're still talking." She turns to me with her smile reapplied "So, what's your real name? So we can be friends."

"You go first," I say.

May isn't backing down even as she struggles to keep on that smile. "You're being awfully rude right now."

I get up from my seat. "I'm actually gonna go make like a tree since everyone here is fucking crazy."

As I'm leaving, in comes a much larger, balding, red-headed man. "Oh, you must be the new transfer student. I'm Mr. Simpson," he says, gesturing to where I previously sat. "There's a seat right over there. Class is about to start."

I sit back down with a sigh and pouty face.

May leans in and whispers in my ear. "If that stupid name is real, you're next."

"What the hell are you even talking about?"

A chime signals through the speakers embedded into the

ceiling before the TV mounted on the wall turns itself on. That girl with the long red hair is sitting directly in front of the camera, chest out and posture perfect. "Good morning, staff and students. I am McCarthy, this year's student council president and these are your morning announcements–"

May leans closer to the other girls and pretends to gag as she points a wicked witch finger down her throat. "Of course the welfare queen got a boobjob over the summer." April and June look at each other, forcing giggles. "Doesn't she look ridiculous? It makes you wonder just how she became president. I know I didn't vote for her."

My eyes roll so hard they could fall from their sockets. "Mind your business."

"Um, no. Why don't you mind your business?"

"*I know you are but what am I?*" I mock.

"You better stop!"

Mr. Simpson hisses to gain our attention. "Girls." He places a single finger to his lips and blows air.

"–Let's start this year off right," McCarthy finishes with her announcements and the screen turns off.

Mr. Simpson takes to the front of the class. "Good morning, students! Everyone have a good summer vacation?" He waits for a response–any response–but gets none. "Alright, since no one wants to share their exciting adventures, let's start with everyone's favorite thing: reading the student code of conduct!" That causes a few groans from the class. "Come on, you know the routine. We do this every year."

He takes out the same glossy-covered spiral notebook Atlus was reading from this morning and leans against his desk. He clears his throat and licks his finger before opening the cover and starts to read: "*The Board of Education assures each student has a right to an education, and this is provided through a safe and orderly school environment...*

"*Seal Coast Community High School has a rich history of encouraging students to express themselves, creating a culture in which staff and students are exclusively referred to by monikers.*

Failing to address someone as their preferred name will result in immediate suspension and eventual expulsion for repeat offenders, prioritizing the safety of staff and students."

Second Period

Ms. Hoyos is scheduled as my social studies teacher, though upon entering the classroom, Aunt Addie is writing on the whiteboard. "Oh! How are you liking Seal Coast?" she asks. "I got so excited when I saw your name on my roster, but I need to ask you: What would you like to go by?"

"Fiora," I answer.

Her lengthy fingers clasp to my wrist like the talons of a hawk before I'm dragged out into the hall. A few students head towards the door and Aunt Addie waits until they've passed before saying, "You can't do that. Are you trying to get ki–in trouble again? It's really important that you fit in and graduate this year."

Red marks form around my wrist, and my first thought is suing. My second thought is: "You know, everyone keeps saying that, but I don't even know what that means. I happen to like my name, and it's special to my mom."

"Don't you think it's fun getting to be called whatever you want?"

"Fine. Then I want to be called Cunt Queen."

She stares at me, blinking her eyes several times. "Queen is a cute name. Have people call you that." Her hand presses against my back as she leads the way into the classroom.

I take a desk with no neighbor sitting beside it, though a group of girls gossip from the row of desks behind me. "He's not here," one says.

"Are you sure he's supposed to be in this class?" says the other.

"Yeah, he told me at orientation before the shooting."

"Do you think he's one of the people that died?" says a third.

"There's no way. We would have seen it on the news."

"But it's not like we know his real name."

"Wait, so do you really think O'Brien is actually dead?"

The bell rings and Ms. Hoyos takes her stance in front of the class. "Okay, quiet down, class. Good morning, everyone!"

"Good morning, Ms. Hoyos," the students chorus, and the class begins with more reading of the student code of conduct.

Third Period

The art teacher, Mr. Mark, according to my schedule, doodles on the board minutes before class begins. He has thick glasses, and his face doesn't look much older than his students, though his messy brown hair is starting to gray early. He is a seemingly normal-looking failed artist turned teacher ... if it weren't for the blue nitrile gloves on his hands and see-through raincoat over his button-up shirt and jeans.

Circular tables fill the floor of the classroom, many of them with seats filled by chatting friends. That cute guy who was pushed into the fence this morning sits at a table by himself and waves to a girl with long, mousey brown hair. "Hey Keaton, over here! I saved you a seat!" he says.

The girl looks at him for only a moment before continuing the conversation with the other students.

Ulterior motives aside, no other seats are available so I join the boy at his table. "She's just not that into you," I tease.

Upon closer inspection, the red mark on his face is swollen and will turn black and blue in no time. "Yeah she is. She's my girlfriend. She just ... needs some space, is all," he claims.

"Are you telling me or yourself?" I ask.

He rests his arm on the table. "I'm sorry, do I know you?"

"Um, no. I just moved here. I'm Fiora."

"Well, I'm Joey."

I shoot from my seat and slam my hands down on the table with more force than anticipated, causing a loud bang.

"Finally! Someone with a real name!"

He chuckles. "Well, no, it's not my real name. If you're new then I guess you don't really know yet, huh?"

I return to my chair. "I know it's tradition for everyone to go by fake names, but no one will tell me why."

"Well, maybe they're just trying not to freak you out since you're new." He leans in closer. "There's been this rumor for a long time that if someone finds out your real name, you die."

I nod and absorb the sound of his boyish voice, yet there's something rough around the edges about it. "That's stupid," I say.

He chuckles and shrugs. "Well, like I said, it's just a rumor. It's a small town. We don't have much going for us without a ghost story."

"What do you do, chant someone's name in the mirror three times? Write their name in a killer notebook while thinking of their face?"

"Haha yeah, that sounds about right. It's just some scheme to get tourists in, and I guess we grew up going along with it. Sometimes we still have to tell people that Salem, Oregon, is not where the witch trials happened."

"So that's why everyone has been so desperate to find out my real name? To see if I drop dead?"

"Well, don't take it personally. I doubt anyone is being malicious about it. It's just been a long time since we've had a new student. I don't think anyone actually believes it."

"I met the Calendar Girls in my first period. One of them said I was next."

He squints his eyes and smirks a little. "Calendar Girls? Oh, you mean April, May, and June? May might have been malicious, but April and June are nice when they're not licking her boots."

Mr. Mark takes to the front of the class with his doodle on the board finished. It's a beach landscape. "Hello class, it's so nice to be here on yet another beautiful day." No one agrees or responds. "What did everyone do during the summer?" ... He taps at his doodle on the board with the marker in his hand. "I took a trip to Miami with my partner. It was my first time being on the east coast, much different from our little town here in Oregon. There was so much to do and see. Then, of course, there's the beach. Can't go to Florida without checking out those beautiful beaches."

He goes to the box of gloves on his desk and puts on another pair before returning to the board to draw something else. When he finishes, he moves to the side so we can see. It's a jellyfish with surprisingly detailed tentacles for a quick sketch. "I did, however, get stung by a jellyfish. It turns out I'm allergic and had to spend one of the nights in the hospital rather than the hotel, so that wasn't fun. Does anyone else have any memories from the summer they want to share?"

The class is dead silent, his eyes gazing over each student until they land on me. "Hello. I've heard all about you. Would you like to introduce yourself?"

"No," I answer, and it gets a few chuckles from the class.

Mr. Mark shrugs and holds up his hands. "Hey, if nobody kills the time, then we gotta read the student code of conduct, and I don't think anyone wants that." A girl with thick blonde hair tied into pigtails raises her hand. "Yes, Cheese?" Mr. Mark calls on her.

"Did your partner pee on you after you got stung?" the girl called Cheese asks.

Mr. Mark reaches over and grabs that same glossy-covered book. "I knew I was going to regret sharing that. Alright, let's get started."

At least since it's the first day, we're getting out at lunch after the third period.

Lunchtime

"Hey, what are you doing after this?" I ask Joey as the class packs up.

"Oh, I already have plans. Sorry." He jumps from his seat and waves at that same girl from earlier. "Hey Keaton! You're off work today, right? Why don't we go bowling or something? I'll pay!"

She only gives him a single disgusted glance before leaving the class with the group of girls she sat with.

I come up behind Joey. "So, were those your plans?"

He sighs and slumps his shoulders. "Yeah, something like that. I'll see you tomorrow."

I can't get out of this damn school fast enough, and I'm excited to see someone normal finally, even if that person is Atlus. And even if he's already in my seat. I've never gotten into the back so fast in my life.

Mom looks at me through the rearview mirror. "How was your first day, Fiora?"

"These people are fucking crazy," I say.

"I'm sure it's not that bad."

"It's pretty bad," Atlus backs me up, his feet cozy on Mom's dashboard.

"Did you have Aunt Addie as one of your teachers?"

I shoot forward and cling to the back of Mom's seat like a cat who doesn't want to take a bath. "Yeah, and she's one of the crazies!"

"Oh come on. She's a little *eccentric* but this whole family is. Let's go get something to eat. I'm starving and I know you kids must be. I'm thinking breakfast for lunch."

Bread and Butter is a diner not far from the school, and we park the car and head towards the front entrance. "My friends and I would always come here after concerts. It'd be midnight and the only place open, but that's the best time to go," Mom says as she holds the door open for us.

A woman, at least in her late thirties, approaches the podium and grabs a handful of menus. "Three of you?" She looks up, and her eyes widen at the sight of Mom. Her face looks as if she's seen a ghost. "Bailey Navarro?"

Mom smiles. "Yeah, hi. Do I know you?"

The woman shakes her head and quickly returns her gaze to the menus in her hands, never taking her eyes off them. "No, no. You wouldn't know me. I was a few grades above you."

"Oh, but you know me?"

"I've heard some things. People have been wondering what happened to you after ..."

Mom wraps one of her arms around my shoulders and squeezes. "Eh, you know how it is. I got knocked up, dropped out, got married, moved to San Diego, and got divorced. This is my daughter Fiora and my son Atlus."

The woman looks up from her hands and her glance lands on me. Her name tag says her name is Emily, but I'm curious if people are doing that stupid fake name thing outside of school.

"Y–You look just like your mother when we were in school. Oh, but I'm sure y'all are starving. Follow me." Emily leads us down a line of booths and seats us at the end. "Your server will be right with you."

Mom sets her menu down on the table and stares at the hostess who has returned to the front of the restaurant. "I swear she looks familiar, but I can't remember an Emily."

As nauseating as today has been, I at least managed to survive the first day. All I have to do now is get through the rest of the year and graduate. June 7th, the last day of school; that's my goal.

SEPTEMBER 6 – WEDNESDAY

7:02 AM

FIORA: Good morning everyone. It is now 7 a.m. and nighttime is officially over time to rise and shine!

7:18 AM

CHLOE: god i hate u
CHLOE: ur such a fucking weeb
CHLOE: kill urself
FIORA: A body has been discovered!
CHLOE: i fucking wish
CHLOE: how r things in blackhell?
FIORA: Hell

Morning

The line for Seal Coast's security is longer than it was yesterday and Atlus and I secure our spot behind a group of boys. They're dressed in shorts despite the chilly and misty morning. "I heard there were a couple of new students yesterday," one of the boys says.

"New students? Who would move to this shit hole?" another says.

"Think they know anything about the curse?"

"We should totally find them and find out their names."

The security line passes, and inside the school, Griffin is at our lockers. He closes his as he calls out: "Fiona!"

"It's Fiora," I correct.

"Damn, still not budging. How about we make a deal?"

I give him a side-eye as I put in the wrong locker combination and have to try again. "I'm listening."

"I guess your name right, and you have to give me your phone number."

"You know I can just lie, right?"

He holds out his pinky. "Not if you pinky swear."

I shoot a cheeky smile at him and wrap my finger around his. "Fine, you're on. What do I get if you can never guess it?"

"My phone number."

Heat rises to my cheeks.

Another pinky wraps around ours and it's Poppet's. "What we swearing to?" she asks.

"It's a secret blood oath. You wouldn't understand," Griffin jokes.

"Are you kidding me? I'd bring my knives to school if I didn't have to go through so many metal detectors."

"The cafeteria already has butter knives."

The bell for the first period rings, and we disperse.

Third Period

The girl with the mousy brown hair Joey claims is his girlfriend sits at the same table in the back with the same group of people from yesterday. Joey seemingly pays no mind as he grabs the chair beside mine. "Hey it's Fiora, right?"

I nod. "That's right."

"How do you spell that?"

"F-I-O-R-A."

"Oh like the show?"

"Yeah, why?"

He smirks and winks as he rests his arms on the table. "No reason, don't worry about it."

As much as his smirk makes my heart race, something more noticeable catches my attention: the red mark on his face from yesterday has turned into a full black and blue bruise. "Hey, are you okay?"

He touches his face, aware of my concerns, though they could have been about anything, like his self-esteem. "It's nothing," he claims.

"What's their problem?"

"You mean Falco and Cappy? They're just a bunch of assholes. It's funny 'cause Cappy was their target before he joined the football team. But I guess now that he's one of them, their attention turns to me, and he thinks he's all hot shit for it."

"Why don't you beat his ass?"

He snorts. "Yeah, I'll get right on that."

I'm only half joking. Maybe if the other students around here stood up for themselves now and then, everyone else wouldn't be such dicks.

The bell rings at the exact time Mr. Mark races through the door. He chuckles. "Made it just in time. Almost had to give myself detention." He goes to his desk to put on his gloves and raincoat. "How is everyone today? I know yesterday was kind of a drag, but today we're ..."

Lunchtime

The bell signaling the end of the third period and the beginning of lunchtime rings, and Joey is one of the first out of his seat. "Hey Keaton! Wanna grab lunch? I brought extra money. I've been saving up my checks. I'll buy you whatever you want!"

She swaggers past him with her posse, leaving him without so much as a single glance. Joey takes a deep breath and hangs his head.

"I can sit with you," I tell him.

He scratches the back of his head. "I dunno. I don't think my girlfriend would like that."

I stare at him, steadying my breathing and blinking so he can't see the daggers my eyes are shooting at him. I hold back what I want to say and instead say, "Well, I don't really have any friends here yet, so I don't have anyone else to sit with. You'd be doing me a favor."

He winks at me, and it's so smooth and flawless. "Alright, I'll be your friend. You know, as a favor."

Joey takes the lead as I follow him from the classroom. Upon entering the halls, a husky, luscious voice calls out: "Excuse me." Pockets of students fill the surrounding area, meaning the voice could be calling out to anyone until it appears behind my back: "Excuse me, Fee-ora, is it?"

I turn around, and the student council president is holding a clipboard. "It's Fi-ora," I correct.

"Please accept my apologies," she says. "Also, please pardon my intrusion. I have been getting in contact with the students who signed up to be a part of the volunteer committee. The genuine ones, at least. We are gathering in the gymnasium and a complimentary lunch will be provided."

I nudge Joey with my elbow. "Hear that? Complimentary means free. Sign up with me, new bestie."

He stares off into space but perks up when I grab his attention. He looks down at me. "Huh?"

"Volunteer with me."

McCarthy offers him the clipboard and passes him a pen. "The student council is garnering volunteers to fundraise for O'Brien's medical expenses," she says.

Joey accepts the items. "Oh, yeah. I can do that if it doesn't get in the way of my work schedule."

"I can assure you, all events will be flexible and at your discretion." Joey signs his name and returns everything to the council president. She smiles and nods. "I will see you two in the gymnasium momentarily." She turns around, her hair dramatically flipping, and struts down to the other end of the hall. "Cheese!" she calls out, and the girl with the thick blonde pigtails sprints down the hall at full speed. The soles of her sneakers slap against the linoleum, and the echo bounces off the walls.

The gym is downstairs and at the back of the school. When we arrive, there are fewer kids in the building than names on the sign-up list. A few more students join us in the gym, including Cheese, McCarthy, and the Calendar Girls.

"Excuse me," McCarthy's powerful voice rings through the gym, causing everyone to shut up and look her way. "I would like to thank everyone who has arrived this afternoon. The reason why I have gathered you all this lunch period is because the administration has agreed to help with the fundraiser. In that regard, they have generously donated boxes of chocolate for which we can sell, all proceeds going towards the cause." She turns behind her to the Calendar Girls: April, May, and June. "Ladies, if you would be so kind."

The three girls go out to the storage room in the back and come out pushing dollies stacked with boxes. They pull them up to McCarthy who wears a proud, almost smug, smirk on her face as she closes her eyes and smiles. "As you can see, there are more than enough to go around. It is not expected to sell every single bar, though any and all efforts are appreciated. Three cases will be given to each student here and if more is required, please make a request with the student council.

"Now, as I said, lunch has been provided. Feel free to help yourself to the pizza outside on the field, and good luck, everyone. Happy selling."

That gets the crowd more excited than the actual fundraiser for a kid who was shot and could have died–or has already died, according to some of the gossip that flows through the halls at an accelerated rate. I can feel the excitement as well. "Fuck yeah, pizza!"

The pizza line forms fast, and Joey and I get stuck in the crowd. We end up at the end of the line behind the blonde girl from our art class. "Hi Joey," she says.

Joey slightly raises his hand. "Hey Cheese."

After grabbing our slices of pizza, the three of us sit together on one of the bleacher benches. Joey holds a slice to his mouth but stalls before taking a bite. "So, where did you move here from anyways?"

"San Diego," I say.

Joey has a teasing smirk. "Oh, so you come from money."

"Kinda. My brother's dad is a piece of shit so we left and had to downgrade." I fan out my arms to showcase the beautiful scenery of a high school gymnasium. "Hence, Blackridge."

"Ah, a tale as old as time itself."

"What about you? You from here?"

"Yeah, me and Cheese have been neighbors in the same shitty trailer park our whole lives, and I've been working at Nickels and Dimes since I was like, fourteen. It's the local dollar store."

"Yeah, I gathered that much just from the name. So you also come from money."

He laughs. "Just a much smaller quantity. My dad also sucks if that makes you feel any better."

My jaw drops and I put a hand to my chest as I gasp. I'm so shocked. With Joey's rock-bottom self-esteem and questionable sexuality, I never would have guessed, and that's what I say.

He gives me a gentle shove and a chuckle, that smile of his lighting up even the dankest and smelliest gymnasium. "Shut up."

Fourth Period

Mr. Phillips, an older, much older, yet significantly short man with pure white hair and a perfectly trimmed mustache, stands at the side of the door. The bell rings and he shuts the door, locks it, and takes to the front of the class. He scans the heads at each table before securing a target: "Miss Lemming, your grades are not good enough to be hiding from me." He sternly directs his finger to the floor, like ordering a trained dog. "Come to the front, now."

From the back of the class, a girl with messy brown hair barely tied into a bun scoots from her chair and meekly carries her things to the front. She sits beside me.

A Grinch-like smile appears on Mr. Phillip's face. "That's better. Now, did anyone notice what I did just a moment ago?"

He gestures to the door. "I locked it. I have no tolerance for tardiness. If you are not in your seat by the time the bell rings, then you will not be in my class. You will go to the principal's office, where you will be appropriately punished, as stated in the student code of conduct. You spent all day reviewing it yesterday so I'm sure you are well aware of all the policies by now.

"And it is not just tardiness I will not tolerate. It is cellphones, chewing gum, food, water, back talking, sleeping. Anything other than staring straight at the board and absorbing my lecture. If you do not wish to learn what I have to teach, then you are no student of mine." His eyes land on his target like a dart to the bullseye. "Isn't that right, Miss Lemming?"

She slumps in her seat beside mine. "R–Right."

"That's yes, sir."

"Y–Yes, sir."

He paces the desks like a prison guard with his hands behind his back and a stick up his ass. "Believe it or not, teachers hate seeing familiar faces back in their classes." He turns around towards the whiteboard. "You are all seniors now–some of you again–which means this semester we'll be working on ..."

I lean in close to Lemming's ear. "What's up his ass?"

Her gaze is glued to her hands cupped in her lap. "I failed his class last year, so now I'm repeating, and he just won't let me forget it."

"How could anyone possibly forget? He's a dick. That's why he's stuck being a high school math teacher. I'm repeating my senior year too and it's no biggie."

That forms the slightest smile on her face. "Really? I don't remember seeing you last year."

"Oh, well ... I went somewhere else."

That causes her smile to fade and her head to turn away. "Oh."

"But I can still give you some notes. I could actually pass my classes if I wanted to."

She taps on her folder. "That's okay. My friend Marki already gave me some. She's really smart and takes honors classes."

Mr. Phillips looks over his shoulder. "Do you think I cannot hear the whispering behind my back? No tolerance. If I catch you again, you will be made to leave."

After School

I don't realize I forgot to get the chocolates in my locker until I'm almost at the student parking lot. "Oh, hey. Fiora!" a voice calls out. It's Joey. He carries stacks of chocolate boxes.

"Hey Broey," I say.

His brownish brows furrow, and the ends of his lips curve into a slight smile. "Broey?"

"Yeah. What's up?"

He lifts the boxes in his hands just a bit. "I almost forgot these, so I had to go back."

"They'd still be there tomorrow, ya know."

"Yeah, I know. But I have a way to sell all of these, like, super quick."

"What, an MLM?"

His cheeks flush with embarrassment. "What? N–No. I have a girlfriend." He stammers.

"No, not like that, dork. Multi-level marketing. You know, pyramid schemes?" I explain.

He chuckles nervously and scratches his head but almost drops his box of chocolates. He quickly puts his hand back and catches the boxes before they tumble. "Oh, haha. Yeah, right. Um, but no. See, I work at the dollar store a few miles down the road so I can sell these at my register."

"Oh hell yeah, that's sneaky. I like it."

His eyes widen as he gasps. "Oh shit. I gotta go or I'll be late! I'll see you tomorrow!" He takes off ahead towards the student parking lot.

"Bye Joey!" I call out. "I love your hoodie, by the way!"

He keeps his back towards me but raises a hand to wave. One of the cases falls from his other hand, and he has to bend over to pick it up, causing the remainder to fall as well. "Yours too! INK rocks!" He scoops all three boxes from the sidewalk and hurries to the student parking lot.

What a fucking dork.

SEPTEMBER 18 – MONDAY

Morning

Three weeks have passed since I started attending Seal Coast, and Joey isn't budging. We goof off every day in art, and then at lunch, we hang out and talk about music. We like many of the same bands and share even more bands that the other hasn't heard of yet. He's either oblivious to my subtle flirting or fully committed to this delusion that he's dating Keaton. But that's okay; I'm like a cicada: patient, then annoying as hell when it's time to surface.

Knock knock. Mom enters my bedroom. "You about ready to go?" She approaches and brushes the part of my hair that hangs down. "You look so cute. I don't think I've seen you with your hair up since you were in elementary school."

"Well, you know, gotta make a good impression," I say.

Mom has a cheeky grin reflecting through the mirror and crosses her arms. "*Good impressions* are usually for the first day, not the third week. What's his name?"

I can't hold back a broad smile just imagining his face and saying his name: "Joey."

"What's he like?"

"He's tall and really cute. He's really insecure and has a girlfriend that treats him like shit, but I think he likes it."

Mom nods. "Sounds just like your type."

"Exactly! That's what I'm saying."

"Be ready soon … and I might not be here when you and your brother get home from school."

"What, why?"

Her eyes glance away as she shuffles a bit. "I have a job interview today."

I want to laugh. I attempt to hold it back but let out a snort instead. "A job? Are you not getting your royalties anymore?"

"Geez, what's with all these questions? I get bored while you kids are at school all day, is all. And I want you to actually show up, too. Don't just drop him off then leave like you usually do. You promised you'd graduate this year."

"Yeah, yeah, yeah."

She sticks out her tongue and wobbles her head back and forth. "Don't, yeah, yeah, yeah, me."

After breakfast, I wait for Atlus in my Ford Explorer. He comes sporting his new soccer uniform and tries opening the passenger door, but it's locked. He bangs on the window. "Open the door!"

"Say the magic words," I sing through the cracked window.

"Open the fucking door!"

"Those are not the magic words."

"You're going to make me late for practice!"

"I'm waiting."

He sighs. "I have no backbone. You're always right, and whatever you say always goes. Fiora Clairwater is the one and only queen. Now open the fucking door!" The door clicks as it unlocks, and Atlus sits in the passenger seat. "I hate you."

"I hate you more."

It's a drawn-out and dreary drive to Seal Coast before securing a spot in the student parking lot.

"Hey Fi?" Atlus asks as we exit the car. There are puddles on the asphalt leftover from last night's rain.

"What happened to *don't talk to me*?" I mimic.

"Fine, like I'd wanna talk to you anyway."

We walk a few steps before I ask, "Fine, what is it?"

"Do you like it here? In Blackridge, I mean," he asks.

I take a deep inhale of the misty air, the dampness clinging to my skin. "The weather sucks. It's either raining or foggy. We had to leave all of our old friends in San Diego while most of the people here are pieces of shit. But I have met some cool ones, so I guess I'll live."

Atlus is silent momentarily, watching his sneakers drag and scrape against the pavement as he walks. "Yeah, I guess I made friends too. And Mom seems happier."

"Well she grew up here. It's almost like she's a kid again before I came around and cramped her style."

That manages to get a chuckle out of him despite the melancholy atmosphere.

"Hey, Fiora!" a voice that causes butterflies in my stomach calls out. Speaking of *one of the cool ones*, it's Joey wearing orange framed glasses that match his hair. "What's up? Sweet hoodie."

Atlus walks ahead, his figure disappearing under the thick sheet of fog.

"How is it even possible to see in this Silent Hill ass place?" I ask.

Joey chuckles as he walks alongside me. "Yeah, the weather sucks. I have no idea how much longer my car will last before it turns into complete rust." He takes off his glasses and tucks them in his pocket.

"I haven't seen the sun since I got here. I miss it."

He does his signature wink and smirk. "Any plans to go back to sunny Cal-i-for-ni-a?"

"God, I fucking wish," I say.

We reach the security line and stand behind a group of gossiping freshmen girls. "God, I sit next to Farrah in second period and that bitch smells so bad I want to puke," one of the girls no older than fourteen complains.

"Puke would be perfume on her," another girl says.

Joey and I get through the security, and standing outside the main building is a girl handing out fliers. It's impossible to miss her, but most people walk past her while only a handful accept the fliers, immediately crumpling them up and dropping them to the floor. "Only pieces of shit litter!" the girl yells out. She has dark skin, all-black clothes, curly black hair, plump lips under jet-black lipstick, and several facial piercings.

"What's up?" I ask, curious about her solicitation.

She hands me one of the fliers. "I'm starting a band so we can play at the fundraiser for O'Brien's medical bills." She looks over her shoulder. "No thanks to these assholes! Don't everyone line up at once!"

"Oh, hell yeah. The hot redhead with the really big boobs told me about that a few weeks ago," I say.

"You mean McCarthy? She finally set a date for the fundraiser. It's a car wash on the 24th so there won't be a lot of time to practice."

I hand Joey one of the fliers and he takes a look. "A band?" he asks.

"Why not? We're already on the volunteer committee," I say.

He scratches the back of his head. "Well, I've been selling tons of those chocolates at my register. Ain't that enough?"

"Do you play, Joey?" the girl asks.

"Yeah, guitar and bass."

"Well, I already got a guitar, so you can try out for bass." She turns to me. "What about you? You're the new girl, right?"

"I'm Fiora; I play drums."

"Kick-ass, every band needs a good drummer. Especially a chick."

"Hey, I never said I was good. That's on you."

Her face is stone cold as she nods. "Then just show me what you can do. I'm gonna ask the student council if we can use the music room after school for practice."

Joey scratches his head. "Um, I kinda have to work today. Rain check?"

"When do you have off?"

"Saturday, maybe. In the afternoon ... maybe. I'd have to ask my girlfriend to cover my shift ... if she answers my calls."

"You have a girlfriend?"

"Yes, I have a girlfriend! I've been dating Keaton for six months."

The girl places a hand on her extended hip. "Whatever, but I need more than a maybe. I'll request the music room for Saturday, so make sure you get it off. Not like we're doing anything special. My Discord is at the bottom. Message me and I'll send you a list of songs to learn."

Joey and I walk away and he admires the flier in his hand. "Joining a band would be so cool," he gushes. "I need something to do outside of work now that Keaton is giving me the cold shoulder."

I want to throw myself on the floor and cry and scream like a spoiled child told no for the first time. "Break up with her!"

"No! I love her."

We keep walking until we get to the lockers and have to part ways. Poppet curtsies at the sight of me. "Entering Princess Fiora."

I go to my locker and fiddle with the dial. "Hey, you two losers want to try out for a band this weekend?" I ended up with a stack of the fliers and hand one to each of them. They look them over.

Poppet shrugs. "I have no musical talent."

"I don't believe you."

She leans her back against her now shut locker with a cheeky little grin on her lips. She shimmies her shoulders. "You calling me a liar?"

"I ain't calling you a truther."

Griffin hands me back his flier. "Sorry, Fitma, but I sound like a bullfrog."

I snatch the flier out from his hand. "You guys suck. And you're still wrong."

First Period

"But he's still alive, right? So that can't be it," I hear June whispering to the Calendar Girls as I sit at our table. Unfortunately, our seating arrangements from the first day of school are permanent.

"But other people died," April states, her voice higher than usual.

"Maybe that's 'cause nobody knows his name. The fundraiser is for him. McCarthy wouldn't do all of this if he really died, right?"

"I don't know. This whole thing is really freaking me out. What if it really is real?"

May groans and rolls her eyes. "God, who cares? Just shut up already." She notices me and scoffs in my direction. "Ew, what is that?"

"Your breath blowing back at you," I rebut.

"If anything smells, it's that *thing* in your hands."

I notice I'm still holding the stack of band fliers. I could be holding a dozen roses, bricks of gold, and a Persian kitten, and she would still have something bitchy to say.

The bell rings, and Mr. Simpson enters the room. He leans down to our table. "Hey girls, I know it's hard to keep quiet around your besties, but class is starting."

A chime plays through the speakers, and the TV turns on for the morning announcements ...

Lunchtime

The bell rings, and Joey's attention is drawn to Keaton. "Hey Keaton! Wanna sit together? My grandma made her shepherd's pie you really like."

Her only response is a disgusted glare as she leaves the room with her friends.

I hold my hand up to reach his shoulder. "Joey, you know what they say about the definition of insanity?"

"Yes, and that's not what it really means!" he cries.

"You know who knows the real definition of insanity? Insane people."

He sighs, defeated. "Come on, let's just go to lunch."

We walk out together, the halls filled with students along with their chatter and mutters of gossip.

"Oh god damnit," I complain.

"What?" Joey asks.

"My mom just texted me. My stupid little brother forgot his lunch, so now I have to bring it to him."

Mom's Honda Civic is parked at the curb outside campus, and she rolls down the window when we approach. "Sorry, he's not answering his phone." She passes his lunchbox through the window.

Joey waves. "Hi, nice to meet you."

Mom releases a schoolgirl squeal. "You must be the boy! Joey! I've heard so much about you! I'm Nebula Clairwater."

"Mom!" I cry.

She takes a long look at him, admiring every nook and cranny. "Your mother wouldn't happen to be Aubree O'Reilly, would she?" Mom eventually asks.

"Huh? Oh, yeah. She is," Joey confirms, taken by surprise.

"I knew it! You look just like her. How's she doing these days?"

Joey scratches his head. "Um, I wouldn't know. I live with my grandma."

"Oh no, I'm so sorry. She always was a big partier. Well, I gotta get going. You kids have a good lunch!" The window rolls up, and Mom's car pulls away from the curb.

Joey smirks and stuffs his hands in his jeans pockets. "So, you talk to your mom about me?"

"No, she just likes fucking with me," I say.

"Then how did she know my name?"

"Obviously 'cause she knew your mom."

"But my mom didn't name me Joey … I doubt she even knows that's what I go by now."

"Whatever. Come on, let's go. I'm hungry."

He winks at me with that stupid look that makes my knees weak. "Okay, whatever you say," he chimes. "I'll meet you in the cafeteria."

Atlus has PE in the gym before lunch, so I meet him at the bleachers. I approach and drop his lunch box on the floor before him. "Learn how to answer your phone, dork," I say.

"It's still in my locker, loser," he says, tying his sneakers.

"Only deadbeats who peek in high school care about PE."

"Only idiots who can't pass their classes have to repeat a year."

"I can pass my classes; I just didn't want to, leech."

"Yeah, okay. That's what all losers say."

"I already used *loser*, so you lose loser!" I stick my tongue and march out of the gym, almost losing my footing against something–or rather someone–loitering the halls. An underclass girl sits with her back against the wall and a stuffed tote between her knees. "Hey, are you okay?" I ask.

She wipes her face on her sleeve before she looks up. She has short dark brown hair and striking blue eyes that would sparkle even without tears. "Y–Yeah. I'm okay."

I kneel to her level. "What's wrong?"

"No, it's nothing."

"It's not nothing. What's wrong?"

She sniffles. "Y–You don't think I smell, do you?"

Honestly, she does. If the stench were a perfume, the name on the bottle would be *Emphysema*. "I don't smell anything."

"They gave me these in front of everybody in the gym." Inside the tote is an array of soaps, toothpaste, and deodorants.

"*They?*" I ask.

"My friends," she says.

"That's bitchy."

"I–It's okay, really. They said it was just a joke and that I shouldn't be so sensitive. I just wish … it could have been a little less embarrassing." She sniffles. "They even did it right in front of the boy I like. My dad smokes in the apartment. I can't help how I smell."

"And your *friends* did that?" She nods. "Have you tried punching them in the face?"

Her eyes widen as she gasps. "Wh–What?"

"They're not your friends; they're bullies. Jokes are supposed to be funny. What they did was just cruel. You don't let people treat you like that. No one is allowed to treat anyone like that. They can fuck right off."

She looks away. "I'm sorry."

"For what?"

"I just keep upsetting people."

I reach into my hoodie pouch and hand her one of the fliers from this morning. "Here, we're forming a band for the fundraiser on Sunday. You should audition and make some new friends who aren't so shitty. The Discord link is at the bottom."

She accepts the flier and gives it a good look. "Th–Thank you."

"I'm Fiora, by the way."

"I'm Farrah."

"Cool, so then I'll see you this weekend."

I leave her with that and go to the cafeteria to find Joey sitting by himself at a table. I come up from behind and place my chin on his shoulder, getting a whiff of his cologne. "You really have no friends, huh?"

He looks over at me. "I don't see you with any either." I sit beside him and open my lunchbox while he leans over to take a peek inside. "Oh, I want some," he says.

"It's just leftover takeout." In front of Joey is a plate of mush. "What the hell is that? Are you a baby bird?" I ask.

"*Chirp chirp*." He chuckles, "No, it's my grandma's shepherd pie. Here, try some." He takes a forkful and brings it to my mouth. It tastes much better than it looks. There's lots of creamy potatoes, gravy, and mixed veggies. He takes a bite with the same fork, some gravy getting left on his bottom lip before licking it away.

Fourth Period

Mr. Phillips makes no exceptions to the tardy rule, especially on test day. He pushes the door shut when the bell rings and locks it with mirth. Some poor soul who makes it just a second too late is at the window, and Mr. Phillips holds his wrist to the glass. He taps on his watch.

"What a dick," I comment under my breath.

Mr. Phillips struts across the front of the class. "You will have the rest of the period to finish your exam, and this could set the course for the rest of the year. It's too early to be falling behind. "Don't think that you can, *when in doubt, go with C,* your way into an A. You either know the material, or you don't. And if you don't, you don't belong in my class. Isn't that right, Miss Lemming?"

"Y–Yes sir," Lemming agrees, and some asshole students even snicker and whisper.

Mr. Phillips goes around the class, placing a stack of papers face down on each desk.

I lean into Lemming's ear. "Fuck 'em. They're dicks." She doesn't say anything, keeping her gaze on her binder. Stickers of microphones and musical notes decorate the cover. "Hey, do you sing?" I ask.

"I love to sing," she says. "I sing in my church's choir. At least ... I used to. This year, I have to spend all my time studying so I don't fail again."

"Fuck that. Join my band," I blurt out a little too loud and get a few heads to turn my way. I lower my voice to a whisper: "Fuck that. Join my band."

"You're in a band?"

"Well, not yet. I'm trying to get people together to audition this weekend. It's for the fundraiser car wash thingy."

"Oh yeah, my cousin told me something about that at lunch."

"Your cousin?"

"She's a freshman. You wouldn't know her."

"Farrah?"

Lemming's lips curl just the slightest tad. "Yeah, that's her."

"Oh hell yeah, I just met her. You should totally come with her. Show her what it's like to hang out with people who don't completely suck."

"That sounds fun. I'll think about it."

Mr. Phillips stands in front of the class and dramatically clears his throat. "Alright, that's enough. No more talking. I want to see pencils moving and eyes on your own paper. You have the rest of the period."

Math isn't my best subject, but I'm not awful at it either. Follow the formulas and input the variables. Easy enough, right? Apparently not, as Lemming stares at her scratch paper, sweat dripping from her brow. Halfway through the allotted time, students start bringing their tests to Mr. Phillip's desk while Lemming remains staring. The bell's about to ring.

Mr. Phillip's chair squeaks against the linoleum as he pushes it back and stands to his feet. "Alright, time's up."

Lemming continues to stare before breaking the silence with a croaky voice: "I–I didn't get a single one right."

"That's not possible. Even if you guessed, you should have gotten at least a few," I assure her.

She shakes her head. "I did every question, and none of my answers were even close." Her voice is shaking, hands trembling.

I peek at her scratch paper and can't understand anything she did. Did we even take the same test?

The bell rings, and Lemming is the first to shovel her things in her backpack, crumpled papers and all, before making a mad dash to the door. I call out to her, and she flinches before turning around. "What do you want?"

"Do you wanna hang out after school? Maybe we can go over our answers and see what went wrong."

"I can't. I'm sorry. I just can't." She hurries out the door.

What is wrong with this place? Why can no one stand up for themselves? April and June, Joey, now Farrah and Lemming. I guess when you live in a small town, bullying is the only fun you can have–that and seeing who drops dead from some rumored curse.

SEPTEMBER 23 – SATURDAY

Afternoon

Joey works today but said we'll go to band practice once he gets off, so I'm killing time by talking with Chloe on the phone while I play The Sims. "How is it out in buttfuck nowhere?" she asks.

"Exactly as you'd think," I answer. "Everyone is up in everyone's business. There's only three things to do: bully, get bullied, and get pregnant."

She giggles. "Oh yeah? Which are you doing?"

"I'm working on the *getting pregnant* one," I joke. "Gotta keep up the family tradition."

"Um, yeah, if you can get that twink to dump his beard."

"Hey, I'm working on it. Slow and steady wins the race."

"*Hey, hey, you, you, I don't like your girlfriend!*" she sings. "*I think you need a new one.*"

"Shut the fuck up. I never imagined myself identifying with a 2000s pick me anthem."

We talk nonsense for about another hour until it's time to leave. "I'm going now," I announce after knocking on the door to Mom's office.

She comes out and wraps her arms around me. She squeezes tight. "Good luck, sweetie! I know you'll do great."

"Thanks, I'll let you know how it goes!" I hurry down the stairs and into my Ford Explorer parked in the garage.

Nickels and Dimes is a cheap convenience store in the same district as the laundromat, a small dive bar, a salon, and a couple of closed businesses. I'm greeted when I get inside but not by Joey. "Welcome! Oh, hey Fiora." It's Keaton, her eyes bright, almond-shaped, and uncharacteristically happy. "Can I help you find anything?"

I drag my feet against the wiry carpet as I approach the counter, looking around the store as I do so. No one else is here. "Um, yeah. Joey?"

Keaton's face and tone drop, her almond eyes looking much more like a snake's. "Oh. He left about 20 minutes ago."

"Do you know where he went?"

"Why don't you just ask him yourself?"

"I don't have his number. He said it's wrong to give it to other girls while he has a girlfriend."

Keaton crosses her arms and sticks out a hip. "Well, that's his opinion. I never told him that."

Just the mention of Joey turns her into a different person. It's almost like I can see the wall she's building up brick by brick. "Break up with him," I say.

She sighs and drops her arms to her sides, chipping down only a tiny layer of that wall. "I'm trying to find a new job first, but no one is hiring. I only got this job 'cause of him, and I can't afford to get fired after dumping him. I've been hoping he'll break up with me first."

"You know he's not going to do that. He's really hoping you'll come to band practice. Then we're playing at the fundraiser tomorrow."

"I know, that's why I told Amanda I'll cover his shifts. I don't want to go. It's exhausting. We have class together, we work together, and then he always wants to hang out on our days off. I have countless text messages and voicemails from him. I can't even post stories on Snapchat or Instagram anymore 'cause he'll see it and know I was on my phone, then here comes another call."

"He clearly wants more than you do," I say.

She scratches her throat. "Clearly. He's never been able to handle being by himself ... Look, I'll give you his number."

"Thanks."

A voice I've never heard but strangely recognize calls out Keaton's name. Then, a plump, short woman with a lazy eye and ear-length hair joins her behind the counter. The way she speaks and the way her body wobbles back and forth is like she's on a boat struggling to keep her balance. "Keaton, did you ever find out where those new hand mirrors go?"

Keaton nods. "Yeah, they went next to the pocket sewing kits in the home goods department."

"Oh good, 'cause I was freaking out."

"They're just mirrors, Amanda."

Her head moves in weird directions like an owl. "You know what they say about broken mirrors." She turns to me and smiles. "Hello, did you find everything okay? ... Fiora?"

I cock my head. "Yeah?"

She lets out a shriek. "Ah! I remember when you were just a baby. Your mom Bailey used to work here." She takes another good look and then sighs. "You look just like her when she was your age."

"Yeah, I get that a lot."

"She was a good worker, and you were just cute as a button."

"Really?"

"Oh yeah. She always had your hair in little pigtails and–"

"No, I mean about my mom."

"Oh yeah. She was always here on time, would offer to stay late and help me close. Too bad we don't have any positions open or I'd hire you on the spot."

"Thanks, I'll keep that in mind."

Amanda brushes her hand against Keaton's shoulder. "I'm gonna go check my blood sugar." She grabs one of Joey's candy bars by the register and heads towards the back of the store.

Keaton looks at me and smiles. "Looks like she found my replacement for when I quit."

"Put in a good word for me?" I ask. She outstretches her hand and we shake on it. "So, about Joey's number ..."

I'm out of the store and now that I have Joey's number, I call him on the way to my car. He doesn't pick up, so I text him instead:

FIORA: Hey Broey, it's Fiora. I went by Nickels and Dimes looking for you but you weren't there. Keaton gave me your number.
JOEY: Hey Fi! I just got to the school. Me and Pandora will be waiting in the music room
FIORA: Pandora?
JOEY: The girl starting da band of course!
FIORA: Of course her fake name is Pandora.

* * *

Chairs are folded and lined against the music room wall to make space for the band and our equipment. There aren't as many people here as I'd like, but there are more than I expected. The only one I'm surprised to see is Poppet. "I thought you said you have no musical talent?" I tease.

She winks and throws up a peace sign. "Doesn't mean I can't dance."

Joey is here tuning a bass guitar, and Farrah is here, but someone is missing: our singer. "Is Lemming here yet?" I ask.

Pandora looks at her phone and checks a few different channels on Discord. "Um ... I don't think she ever messaged me."

I blow air. "I knew she was going to blow us off."

Farrah perks up and prances like a fawn to my side. She's carrying a silver flute in her grip. "Oh, she's been really upset since failing her last math test, so she said she's going to stay home and study. We can all play after she's feeling better."

"That's okay. We'll find a singer later," Pandora declares and claps her hands to gather everyone's attention. "Beggars can't be choosers, so we gotta work with what we got. I'm on guitar. Fiora, you're on drums. Farrah, you're on flute. Joey, you got bass. Poppet you ... I don't know, just keep doing what you're doing or something. Whatever that is." Pandora has her electric guitar and secures the strap over her shoulder. "Let's get started and see what everyone can do! We perform tomorrow!"

SEPTEMBER 24 – SUNDAY

Afternoon

Mah and Pah permit the student council to use their parking lot for the fundraiser and the trailer pulling the band's equipment has arrived.

McCarthy approaches as we begin to unload. "Good morning. I hope you are all doing well. I apologize for the inconvenience."

Joey carries the case to his bass guitar. "Inconvenience? You got us a truck! Like, a big ole real-life truck!"

McCarthy closes her eyes, absorbing the praise as a plant does sunlight. "Yes, I am aware of how tiresome it can be hauling equipment."

I carry pieces to my drumset. "Hell yeah, this kicks ass. It's almost like we're actually rockstars."

McCarthy smiles. "I appreciate the gestures. If you don't mind, I have other matters to attend to." Her hair is caught in the breeze as she turns around and approaches the restaurant.

Once she's out of earshot, I turn to my fellow band members. "Okay, I'm just going to say it: why does she talk like that?"

Joey shrugs. "I dunno."

"Great insight, Joey," Pandora teases.

I return to the trailer to grab the remaining bags for my drumset, making five in total, and Joey skips to my side. "Hey, do you need help with that?" he asks.

"Nah, I'm good," I tell him.

"You sure? They look pretty heavy."

I wink as I lift a bag in each hand. "What, don't think I can take it?"

"I'm sure you can take anything." He shakes his head like a

shaggy dog out of the bath. "Wait, no! That's not what I mean! I mean, I'm sure you can take anything you want. Wait, no–"

Pandora's shoulder-checks him as she passes by with her guitar case. "Stop being a perv."

"I–I didn't mean it like that, I swear!"

Poppet rests her chin in her palms with a teasing grin. "Joey, your fly is open."

In a panic, Joey drops his case and looks down at his jeans. "No it's not! Why is everyone ganging up on me?" His voice cracks.

"'Cause you're cute when you're flustered," I tell him.

His face grows redder. "Y–You think I'm cute?"

"Stop sexually harassing our token male," Pandora barks from the parking lot.

"Y–Yeah!" Joey agrees.

"Shut up. Come on Little Drummer Boy, stop flirting and help us set up."

"I'm not flirting, and I play bass!" Joey cries as he retrieves the case at his feet.

We set up our instruments under the awning, and Mah sticks her head from the restaurant's glass door. She's a short, very short woman with a hunchback and white hair as thin as a dandelion. "Poppet deary, can you help me make the lemonade before all the customers arrive?"

"Coming Nonna!" Poppet says, dancing a spin as she passes through the door.

Farrah is dropped off better late than never by an older and weathered car, and the driver does not stick around for pleasantries. "Sorry I'm late!" Farrah says with flute in hand.

"It's no big deal. We're just setting up," Pandora assures the underclassman.

Poppet returns with a tray of drinks, balancing them without a tremble in her arm as she hands each of us a glass. "Here you go. And yours. Oh hi Farrah, want something to drink? It's my nonna's homemade marionberry lemonade."

Students orchestrating the carwash are dropped off in

batches as they fill the parking lot, including Cheese. McCarthy approaches her with a large poster board and a handful of markers. "Ah Cheese, you're here. Would you mind making a poster? It needs to be large and colorful enough to gain the attention of passersby."

Cheese shrugs and drops her bucket, splashing soapy water across the asphalt. "Okay."

As time passes, more people arrive, volunteers and patrons alike. A table offers complimentary marionberry lemonade and pizza while vehicles form a line to be washed.

Cheese approaches McCarthy at the table and presents her sign. "What do you think?"

McCarthy stares, eyes wide and jaw dropped. "What the hell is that?"

"The fundraiser."

"Yes, I'm aware. I'm the one who asked you to make a poster. I mean, what is *that*?" She points at the stick figure with gushes of blood coming out of it.

"It's so people know this fundraiser is for O'Brien," Cheese answers.

McCarthy sighs. "I should have known better than to ask you, but there's no time to make another. Go stand by the road and garner the attention of more customers."

Spectators stand and watch with drinks and pizza in hand as the band performs. Joey scans the heads in the crowd as he plucks his bass strings."Nobody has seen Keaton yet, have they?" he asks.

Pandora looks over to the taller man standing on her right. "The girl with small eyes and wavy brown hair?"

"Yeah!"

"She's sucking face with that guy with the leather jacket and motorcycle."

"What?" Joey cries out and surveys the crowd, more scattered. "No she's not. She's not even here. You don't really think she'd be cruel enough to cheat right in front of my face, do ya?" None of us respond. "Do you?" he asks again.

"Yeah," I shout so he can hear me from my position on the drums.

He looks back at me fast as a whip. "What the hell, Fiora?"

"What? I just answered."

"I was needing assurance, not your actual honesty!"

"Then be more clear next time. How was I supposed to know? Geez."

Pandora rolls her eyes. "Oh yeah, makes perfect sense. *Give me your opinion, but only what I want to hear.*"

Farrah pulls the flute from her lips to join the conversation. "Who's Keaton?"

"My girlfriend," Joey insists.

"She doesn't deserve you, Joey," Poppet chimes as she shakes the tambourine Pandora gave her for something to do.

Joey's diction is defeated. "Well, this is our first show, so I was just really hoping she'd come. You know, at least pretend to support me."

A 2022 Honda Civic pulls into the parking lot, and Mom, Atlus, and Aunt Addie come out. I have to keep playing, but I call out to her anyway. "Hi Mom!"

She waves and gets a ticket number from McCarthy while Atlus goes straight to the pizza table. He grabs a slice before coming to see the band. "You suck," he says after he finishes his bite. I throw my drumstick at him, but he dodges it instinctually.

Farrah blushes. "Hi Atlus."

He takes another bite and slightly waves his hand as we continue to perform.

Evening

Everyone in town stops by before the night ends, including an apparent guest of honor. An older model Nissan Quest pulls into the parking lot, and a boy steps out from the passenger seat. He has short platinum-dyed hair, and his arm is stuck in a sling. The crowd erupts into applause.

"Who's that?" I ask.

"What? That's O'Brien. The dude all of this is for," Joey answers.

Poppet hums. "So I guess it wasn't the curse, right? 'Cause if it were, he'd be dead."

Pandora grunts, seeming annoyed at the very suggestion. "Of course it wasn't the curse. He was shot by some lunatic with a long history of domestic violence. Literally could have happened to anyone, anywhere."

"That's good, at least. I mean, it's not good that he was shot. But good that some killer curse didn't take him out."

"Whatever. Like anyone actually believes in that."

"I don't know, I've been hearing people talk about it a lot more since the shooting, ya know?" Joey comments. "It's like they've been waiting to see if he dies while in the hospital or not."

O'Brien approaches the student council table, close enough for me to eavesdrop. "Don't tell me you did this all for me?"

"It wasn't just me. It was all of us," McCarthy answers. "What would we be if not a community?"

"You're right, thank you. You know, with my arm out of commission, I can't play baseball anymore, so I'm going to need something to do with my time. I was actually thinking about joining the student council ... if that's okay."

McCarthy smiles. "Yes, I think you would be a perfect fit. I'll find a position for you by Monday."

Three girls in bikinis leave the car they're washing to prance towards O'Brien. "Hi Brien!"

His attention turns to them. "Oh, hi."

"Is there anything we can do for you?" the one in the yellow bikini asks.

The one in the pink bikini steps forward. "Yeah, can we get you anything? A drink? Some pizza?"

O'Brien uses his arm not stuck in a sling to point at the minivan he came from. "My mom is here for a carwash."

Many people from town stick around after the sun sets and their cars have been washed. Poppet hands out drinks, including beers and wine, while the rest of us pack away our instruments as McCarthy approaches. "I'm impressed with what you've been able to put together in such a short amount of time," she says.

"I could say the same to you," Pandora praises. "I've been wanting to form a band anyways."

"You certainly found yourself a group of talented individuals."

Pandora gestures towards me. "It wasn't me, actually. It was all Fiora. Honestly, I was struggling to get anyone to join. Even the band geeks."

McCarthy's attention turns to me. "I believed you when you said you were good at these types of functions. You have a certain aura about you." She tucks a deep red strand of hair behind her ear. "Would you be interested in joining the student council as our event planner?"

That gets my attention. "So what, I'd just throw a bunch of parties?"

"More or less. As long as they are school-appropriate and approved by the administration. Prom is the biggest event of the year."

Joey places a hand on my shoulder, causing a shiver down my spine. His fingers are long and sturdy. "You should totally do it! You can make this the best year ever!" he says.

Poppet throws up her hand not carrying a tray of drinks and waves it in the air. "Oh! Oh! Oh! I want a dance party!"

I furrow my brows. "Isn't that just prom?"

McCarthy smirks. "Well, what do you say?"

"Hell yeah, I'll do it!"

"Great. Then I will see you at the student council room on Monday."

Atlus approaches with yet another slice of pizza. It's his sixth throughout the night. "Only losers join the student council."

"Then your meeting is on Monday," I rebut.

Mom and Aunt Addie join us. "I didn't know you played the drums, Fiora," Aunt Addie comments.

"I put her in lessons when she was eight so she'd have something to beat on other than her brother," Mom explains before giving me a rib-crushing bear hug. "I'm so proud of you! You were so good and didn't blow anything up."

"There's still time," I struggle to say through my crushed lungs.

Mom releases her python grip hug. "Oh hush. Did you have enough to eat? Do you want something to drink?"

I turn to Poppet. "A margarita?" She only shakes her head, so I return to Mom. "I'm actually really tired."

I look back at all my friends. I'm amazed at this little group I've put together since coming to Blackridge. Everyone worked so hard today. I'm proud of them. "I'll see you guys on Monday."

We all say our goodbyes and then head home.

Night

I'm comfortable in bed with Squeak on my lap while I wait for Chloe to answer the phone. She picks up after the first few trills. "Hey bitch, I thought you'd still be partying!" she says

"You know me, the party never stops," I reply.

"So, how was it?"

"It was a lot of fun. We probably raised, like, at least a thousand dollars."

"Oh hell yeah! What are you gonna do with it?"

I scratch Squeak under her chin as she purrs. "Well, it was a fundraiser, so we don't get to keep it."

"Oh yeah, it's for that dude who was shot or something. As if a thousand bucks is gonna even make a dent for medical bills in this shithole country."

"Right? But it's whatever. He showed up and flirted with the student council president. Then a bunch of other girls were flirting with him all night."

"Whoa, is he cute?"

"Yeah, he's pretty cute. He dyes his hair and plays baseball."

"Ooh la la, Leon Kuwata."

A call comes in from Joey on the other line. "Ah, hey, Chlo, can I call you back? The twink is calling."

"Boo, you whore."

We hang up, and I answer Joey's call. "Hello?"

"Hey, do you follow Lemming on Instagram by any chance?" is the first thing he says.

"I don't think so. Why?"

"Her handle is WhenLifeHandsYouLemmings. Watch her story. It's … concerning, to say the least."

I minimize the call while keeping Joey on the line and pull up Instagram. I type in the name, and there's her account with a colorful ring around her profile picture. I press on it and a video plays: Lemming sits by her lonesome in a dreary room, her eyes red and swollen as they stare directly into the camera. "My name is Holly McGuire. I'm a senior at Seal Coast Community High School and live at the Pointe Grove Apartments, room 12 B." Tears stream from her eyes as she takes a deep breath. They leave streaks down her cheek and drip down her chin. "I can't take it anymore. Please, someone … anyone … do something." She takes a deep breath and the intake stutters. The story ends there.

I'm stunned, and it takes longer than I realize for me to say anything. "Did she just dox herself?"

Joey's voice sounds just as concerned as I feel. "Yeah. It seems like she's trying to kill herself with that rumor. You don't think it's actually going to happen, right?"

I rub my eyes to gain some composure. Why am I shaking? "Of course not. You said yourself it's just a gimmick to bring in tourists."

"Yeah … Yeah, you're right. I've been trying to call Farrah on Discord since I saw it, but she's not answering."

"Maybe she already saw and is getting her help."

"You're right. That was definitely a cry for help. I just hope she gets it in time. ... Hey Fi?"

"Yeah?"

"Thanks for convincing me to join the band. It was a lot of fun playing with everyone. I hope we can do it again. And have Lemming as our singer once she's okay."

"Yeah, that sounds awesome. You need to write us a super emo breakup song once you finally get the balls to dump Keaton."

He chuckles but ends with a sad sigh. "I'll see you tomorrow."

"See ya."

SEPTEMBER 25 – MONDAY

"The small coastal town of Blackridge is in mourning after the apparent suicide of Holly McGuire this past Sunday," the news anchor announces.

The screen changes to the face of a man with a graying beard, his eyes bloodshot and swollen. The banner says his name is Gregory McGuire. "I am living every parent's worst nightmare."

The screen returns to the newscaster, who sits unmoving with their back perfectly straight. "Holly was a senior at Seal Coast Community High School, and just hours before a family member discovered her body, she posted something troubling to social media. It was a video of herself, visibly crying and stating she *can't take this anymore* and begging for someone to *do something*."

The screen returns to Lemming's father. "I don't understand how this could have happened. She's been having a rough time, but it's not something to kill yourself over. I just don't understand." He pauses and shakes his head. "I just don't understand."

The newscaster keeps their composure stiff as stone. "If you or someone you know is struggling with suicidal ideation, please call or text the suicide hotline at 988."

Morning

There's something ominous in the air, even for Blackridge. It's another foggy morning as Atlus and I approach the campus of Seal Coast from the student parking lot. We're behind a group of girls. "But she told everyone her name right before she died!"

one of them says.

"Didn't the news say she committed suicide, though?" another asks.

"She also told everyone where she lives. Who knows if some crazy person came and shot her like O'Brien."

"Maybe it was the same person!"

"The guy who shot O'Brien was killed by security, remember?"

"Oh yeah."

"But nobody knows O'Brien's real name, right? So it was just a coincidence. But now everyone knows Lemming's real name, and she's dead!"

"Poor Lemming. I wonder what happened to make her do that."

Atlus drags his sneakers across the pavement as he walks beside me. "Did you know her?" he asks.

"Huh?" I hum, taken off guard.

"Did you know her? The girl who died."

"Um, yeah. Kinda. I had a class with her."

Joey jogs to catch up and walks with us. "Hey," he says, his voice melancholy as he takes off his glasses and tucks them into his hoodie pouch.

I look up at him. "Hey."

"How you holding up?"

"I'm okay. What about you?"

He sighs, his hands tucked in his hoodie pouch as we walk. "I had a really bad feeling. I wish there were something we could have done."

"You tried calling Farrah. That's the most you could do."

"I should have called the cops or something."

"Why, so they can see a girl having a mental health crisis and kill her before she can kill herself? Or even worse, have her kidnapped and institutionalized where she'll undoubtedly be tortured and just want to die even more?"

"Yeah, you have a point. Have you heard from Farrah since the fundraiser?"

I shake my head.

We get in line for security, surrounded by more gossip: "But she told everyone her name!"

"Stop being stupid. She killed herself; the news said so."

"She just wanted attention."

"No way it's real. I bet she ain't even dead."

"Hey, new kid, what's your name?"

Feedback plays from the speakers before McCarthy's unmistakable husky voice fills the halls of Seal Coast. "This is an emergency student council announcement on behalf of Principal Pal. All staff and students, please report to the gymnasium for an assembly immediately. Thank you." The speakers click off.

Joey looks down at me. "Do you think this is about Lemming?"

I shrug, and we report to the gym.

Students from all grades pack the bleachers, and Joey and I find Pandora and Poppet already sitting together. We join them on the bench. "Have either of you seen Farrah?" I ask.

Pandora's posture is the opposite of McCarthy's, with her back arched, shoulders slumped, and arms crossed. "If her parents have a heart, they'll keep her home. I heard she's the one who found Lemming's body."

My chest sinks and there's something bile sitting at the bottom of my stomach. "That poor girl."

Joey drops his head and leans over his knees. "I–I just can't believe this happened. There's just no way it's the cur–" He's cut off by more speaker feedback.

Principal Pal is an older balding man with a large gut and a long beard. He takes the center of the court with a microphone in hand. "Good morning, students and faculty. We are holding this assembly with a heavy heart. As I'm sure many of you know by now, we lost one of our cherished classmates over the weekend. The student many of you know as Lemming has passed away." He pauses as gasps and murmurs fill the gymnasium. "This is a great shock and tragedy for our little community. We have a strict anti-bullying policy, and under no circumstances will such behavior be tolerated. Please, if you are being bullied or see bullying in the halls, report it to me or a trusted faculty member. Anyone who is struggling with depression is encouraged to seek out help from a mental health professional." He gestures to a middle-aged woman standing behind him wearing a pencil skirt and glasses. Her chestnut hair is tied in a bun. "I would like to introduce you all to Laura Burke. She is a licensed professional counselor who has come from Salem to help us through this difficult time."

"Do you think that's her real name?" someone whispers behind me.

"Think she'll be next?" the other person whispers.

"If she is, then it has to be real, right? Now everyone knows her name."

"Yeah, if it's even real."

Principal Pal passes the mic to the counselor. "Hello, students," she greets, "it is a pleasure to meet you all, and I hope to meet those who need it on a more personal level. I will be stationed at the nurse's office if anyone wants to chat; no appointment needed. As long as I'm not currently with another student, I am always more than willing to lend an ear and offer any needed advice." She returns the mic to Principal Pal and takes a step back.

"Thank you. You may all go to your classes and continue today as any other. Even in the face of tragedy, life must move on."

Students rise from the bleachers while voices fill the gym. McCarthy fights through the overwhelming amount of bodies for such a tiny space. "Fiora, I apologize for the interruption, but we have an emergency student council meeting. Please meet with us as soon as possible."

"Gotcha," I say.

McCarthy pushes her way through the crowd. "Excuse me, official business. Excuse me. Pardon me."

Joey is at my side, towering over all of us shorter girls.

"What does the student council even do anyways?"

I shrug. "Guess I'm about to find out."

Instead of fighting through the crowd, I venture off to the nearby bathrooms. No one else is here. At least, that's what I think until I hear the sound of hushed sobs–familiar ones at that. "Farrah?" I inquire, peeking under each of the stalls.

She wipes her eyes. "Oh, I'm sorry. I'm okay."

I crawl across the disgusting bathroom floor to join her in the stall. Tears soak her face as she sits on the toilet, holding her knees close to her chest. "No you're not," I say. "What are you doing here? You should be at home."

She sniffles and wipes her face as she shakes her head. "No, no. I can't go back there." She gasps for air before breaking into sobs. "My ..." She struggles to get out the words. "My apartment is across from Lemming's." She sobs even harder.

I place a hand on my heart. I don't know what to say, so I act. I reach over and hug her. Farrah clings to me as tears soak into my hoodie. I let her stay there and cry as long as she needs.

After I don't know how long, she finally catches her breath and loosens her grip. She sniffles her snot nose. "I–I–I was in my room, and all of a sudden, I heard a loud bang. I went to check on her, but she was already dead."

The moment those words leave her lips, the violent sobbing returns. She throws herself back into my arms, and I let her stay as long as she needs.

I run my fingers through her short, silky hair. "I understand not wanting to go home right now. I can't imagine what you saw or how you're feeling. Do you want to talk to that counselor about it? I can go with you." She shakes her head as she's caressed against my chest. "I have a few things to take care of, but how about we hang out after? This place is too depressing."

She looks up at me, her face glistening and eyes red. "Really? Why are you always so nice?"

That makes me want to laugh. "Trust me, I'm not. Stay right here and I'll come get you when I'm done, okay?"

She nods.

First Period

"Sorry I'm late," I announce as I sit at the table beside O'Brien. The student council room is down the faculty hall and the size of a broom closet. It barely fits the six of us, causing the air in the room to be stuffy and muggy.

As president, McCarthy takes the head of the table. To her right is her vice, May. Next to her is April, the secretary. Sitting next to her is June, the committee representative. "It's alright. Now that everyone has arrived," McCarthy starts, cupping her hands atop the table, "we all know why we're here. Principal Pal has asked that we make an extra effort to ensure everyone's safety at the school. There is a strict zero-tolerance policy for bullying, and we must be diligent with the enforcement."

I let out a small snort. "*Zero-tolerance for bullying* my ass. That's all I've seen since I've got here, and I know everyone sees it too. You have girls too afraid to speak out against their queen bee. Other girls are being made fun of for how they smell. Dudes getting slammed into fences and called homophobic slurs. And people keep trying to find out my real name to see if I drop dead or not. Now, a girl really is dead. When does this *zero-tolerance* policy actually come into play? When we're the ones who have to do it?"

There's a moment of silence, and May is the one to break it: "Well, what did you do about it?" she asks.

My jaw drops. "Huh?"

"Did I stutter? You saw all of this; what did *you* do about it?"

"I don't know what you're saying. I don't speak Neanderthal. We're the students. What is there to do? Tell the teachers who see this shit too and already do nothing? They're just trying to put the blame on us as if this isn't all their fault. It was a teacher who was giving Lemming shit for failing one stupid test. He had it out for her from day one."

"No one even knows if she really was being bullied. She was just a big crybaby wanting attention, and now she has it."

I stand up and slam my hands on the table. "And you're about to get a punch in the teeth!"

"Enough," McCarthy declares in her queen voice and waits until May and I are back in our seats. "I must agree with Fiora, at least to a certain extent. Blackridge has a prominent culture of bullying that has been on full display but covered up since I was a freshman. Now, that is simply impossible. Bringing in a counselor for students is not enough. It is too little, too late.

"That's why I propose a candlelight vigil held here at the school. There is no going back, but we may still show our respects to the deceased and bring awareness to the situation, hopefully in the process preventing further tragedies. What are everyone's opinions?"

May scoffs and rolls her eyes. "Of course. It's always whatever you say."

"I just stated I am merely asking everyone's opinions."

"And what if they disagree?" May gestures to the table. "Anyone?" No one speaks up, so she shoots looks at her lackeys. "*Anyone?*"

I look April and June in the eyes and shake my head. They remain silent, their gazes glued to their shoes.

"So we're all in agreement," McCarthy confirms, then pauses for any opportunity for rejection, but there is none. "Very well. I will share this proposal with Principal Pal. We will regroup once we have an answer."

O'Brien slightly raises his arm not stuck in a sling. "As the new treasurer, I suggest the money raised from the last fundraiser be given to Lemming's family."

McCarthy gasps. "But that money is for you!"

O'Brien smirks. "It's alright. I'm alive, and I'll heal. But Lemming is gone. She deserves a proper funeral. They're expensive and hard on grieving families."

McCarthy looks around the table. "Does everyone agree?" Heads nod aside from May, who only scowls. "Alright, then majority rules. As for now, meeting adjourned. I will write everyone late slips so they may return to class."

As we rise from our seats, the door bursts open, and all heads turn. There's a girl with tears streaming down her face. "I–I'm so sorry!" she cries.

"Marki, what is the meaning of this?" Queen McCarthy inquires.

The girl slams her hand on the table, her tears and snot dripping onto the plastic. "It's my fault. It's all my fault. I'm the reason why Lemming killed herself!" There's a moment of silence where we stop and stare at one another before the girl continues. She takes a big inhale to pull the snot back to her sinuses. "I–I–I gave Lemming a cheat sheet with all the wrong answers. I thought she'd know they were fake and realize she's smarter than she gives herself credit for!"

May scoffs. "I think you mean *gave* herself credit for. Past tense; she's dead."

McCarthy keeps her composure. "May, now is not the time nor the place. Marki, have you told Principal Pal about this?"

Marki shakes her head, sending her long hair flying like a whip. "No! I don't want to be expelled! But I didn't mean for any of this to happen! I'm so sorry!" Tears stream from her face as she breaks into uncontrollable sobs. She struggles to catch her breath.

We're standing still, awkward and unsure. We watch and listen as this girl's heart shatters before us. Even May seems to be struggling to keep up her ice-cold scowl.

McCarthy seems unphased and lets Marki have her moment before abruptly ending the display: "Marki, would you mind giving us the room?"

Marki looks up, her face drenched in fluids. "Huh? Oh, um … yeah."

We return to our seats around the now-soiled table, and McCarthy waits until Marki is out of the room and the door clicks shut. "Well, what are everyone's opinions on this matter? Does that classify as bullying, and are we obligated to report it?" McCarthy inquires.

"Well, she didn't intend to be mean, right?" June asks.

May snaps her neck in June's direction. "Who asked you?"

"I–I'm sorry."

"I asked," McCarthy barks. "One more outburst from you, and I will dismiss you entirely from the council. Do I make myself clear?"

"You can't do that. I was elected," May snarks.

"No you were not. I was elected and chose you as my vice out of fairness. I reserve the right to revoke it at any time."

That shuts up May, who sits back with a pout and arms crossed.

"It doesn't matter what her intentions were; it matters how the victim feels," I voice. "And Lemming felt so bad she fucking killed herself over it. It's not like it's a secret that Lemming was struggling and insecure about her grades. Now Marki doesn't want the consequences of it, even if it was *just a prank, bro*. You don't do that to your friends."

"Her consequence is that her friend is dead," April says, then hangs her head. "I can't imagine living with that. What if the whole school finds out?"

"'Cause of her. She knew Lemming was struggling, but instead of helping her, she pulled this stupid prank. And now she's dead. Lemming studied her ass off so she could graduate this year, and everything she studied ended up being a joke."

I pause, that video Lemming posted etched into my brain like a brand; her face and her voice, the tragedy in it all. She felt so hopeless that she thought her only option left was to die. At least, that's what I assume. It's not like anyone can ask her now. "I don't know if Lemming found out about Marki's prank, but if she did, she must have felt completely betrayed," I eventually say.

There's another moment of silence, the air thick and heavy with grief and uncertainty.

It seems to be a theme for McCarthy to be the one to break the silence: "This is a democracy, so we'll have a vote on it. Everyone, have your answers by tomorrow. Meeting adjourned, and I mean it this time."

It takes McCarthy a moment to hand everyone their slips, and then we finally get to leave. I walk with O'Brien as we pass Marki in the hall, who sits on the floor with her knees in her arms. We pay her no regard.

The Calendar Girls come out from the student council closet and May shoulder-checks me as she passes. "I'm gonna kill her," I blurt out.

"You were really cool in there," O'Brien comments.

"I didn't do anything."

"I meant speaking up to everyone like that. May is mean, and McCarthy is such a stickler for the rules. Honestly, I didn't even know what to say. It's almost intimidating being in there."

A cheeky smile forms on my lips. "You like her."

"No I don't," he's quick to deny.

"You don't even know who I'm talking about."

"I don't *like* anyone."

"She's pretty hot too."

"It's not even just her looks. It's how smart and confident she is. She's had a rough life but never lets that stop her. If anything, it's what makes her so driven, no matter what those mean girls say behind her back. And I don't care about any of the rumors. The past is the past, and what matters is the person she is now."

My smile expands. "So you do like her."

"I never said that."

"You so wanna be handcuffed and stepped on."

He stops in place, his bushy brows furrowed. "What are you even talking about? Why would someone step on me, and why would I want them to?"

"'Cause–"

A girl from at least a few grades below us skips up to us while her friends stand off to the side, whispering into each other's ears and giggling. "H–Hi, Brien," the girl says.

"Oh, hi."

"Do you need help carrying anything? Um, you know … 'cause of your arm," she asks.

"No, I'm okay. Thank you. Though, shouldn't you be in class? Now that I'm in the student council, I think I have to report these kinds of things."

The girl gasps. "Oh, sorry!" She runs back towards her friends who are giggling louder than ever.

I come up and throw my arm over his taller shoulder. "You have a better chance with her than McCarthy. They've probably been standing there waiting for you this whole time. Not to mention the half-naked girls all over you at the carwash."

O'Brien shoots a look at me like a hawk. "Don't you have to be annoying somewhere else?"

I gasp, narrowly forgetting a prior commitment. "Oh shit, I do! Remind me to make fun of you later!"

"Why would I do that?"

Second Period

Instead of reporting to second period with Ms. Hoyos, I return to the bathroom where I left a crying Farrah. "Farrah?" I call out.

The stall door opens, and Farrah comes out. "I'm right here." Her eyes are red and bagged, but she's had a moment to calm down.

"You ready to go?" I ask.

"Where are we going?"

"I saw a salon over by Nickels and Dimes when I was there the other day. How about there?"

"Oh, you mean La-La Nails?"

"Yeah, you wanna go?"

Farrah sniffles as she nods.

We leave the bathroom and walk together down the empty hall. In the meantime, I take my phone from my back pocket and text Atlus:

FIORA: Leaving. Find your own way home
ATLUS: Eat shit n die ur so useless
FIORA: You're*

As I pass through the main gate, Farrah hesitantly stays behind. She fiddles with her fingers. "Um, are you sure this is okay? Won't we get in trouble?" she asks.

"You can only get in trouble if you get caught," I say.

She shifts her stance and there's even a skip in her step as we go to the student parking lot. "Wow, you have your own car?" Farrah gawks once we get to my Ford Explorer.

I touch the handle to unlock the car. "Oh, yeah. It was a present from my mom after I got my license."

"That's so cool! I can't wait until I can drive."

"Ha! Then you're just going to be everyone's chauffeur."

"That's okay. I don't mind. I like helping people. It's better than having my dad or cousin drive me around everywhere."

I groan and roll my eyes. "I have to drive my brother everywhere, and it's the worst."

Farrah's cheeks are glowing red as she fiddles with her fingers. "Atlus is ... nice."

We arrive in the same district as Nickels and Dimes, and I open the glass door to the salon. "Have you been here before?" I ask, my senses assaulted by the stench of chemicals.

"Once. A few years ago with my mom ... before she left," Farrah answers.

The walls inside La-La Nails are lined with shelves cradling an array of colored nail polish bottles. After checking in, Farrah and I each choose a color and follow our technicians to their stations in the back. I choose red, while Farrah picks a baby blue that matches her eyes.

Farrah sits at the station to my right. "H–Hey Fiora?" she says.

"Yeah?" I say.

She bites her lip. "Um, Lemming's funeral is on Saturday. We're keeping it private, but I'd really like it if you came."

"Yeah, yeah. Of course I'll come."

She smiles weakly. "Thanks. Not just for this, but everything."

I return the gesture.

After School

It's raining buckets as Farrah and I race to my car after getting our nails done. The downfall makes us drenched and shivering until the heated seats of my Ford Explorer save us.

Driving down the main road through Blackridge, there's a break in the trees and a sign for the Pointe Grove Apartments where Farrah lives. I pull into the lot and park at the curb in front of the complex. It's a three-story building composed of aged red bricks. "Hey, are you going to be okay in there?" I ask.

Farrah nods. "Thank you for distracting me for a while. I had a lot of fun." She holds up her newly done nails. "It's like having a big sister."

"We can do it anytime. I'm always down for skipping school."

She giggles. "Just as long as we don't get caught!"

I stop her just before she can get out of the car and into the rain. "Wait, Farrah!"

"Yeah?"

"I know we had fun today, but I'm not very good at this stuff. You should really consider talking to that counselor, okay?"

She nods at me. "I will. Thank you, Fiora. You keep helping me a lot. Maybe one day I'll be just like you."

"Trust me, you don't want that."

She takes off running to avoid the falling water, and I wait until she's safely inside the building and out of the rain before driving home.

The only thing I want to do is take a hot shower, so that's the first thing I do upon arriving home. I have the whole house to myself once I'm clean, dry, and dressed. Mom has a few more interviews this afternoon, and Atlus–

Shit. Atlus!

The front door bursts open, and Atlus is soaked from head to toe. "I had to walk home in the rain, you stupid bitch!"

I flick my wrist at him from the couch. "Oh, get over yourself. I told you to find a ride home. Go dry off then get the Switch so we can play Smash."

He scowls. "Fine. I'm beating your ass." He skips steps going up the stairs.

"Remember when you used to climb up the stairs on all fours like a dog? What a fucking weirdo!"

Atlus returns with a change of dry clothes and the Switch. He rests it in the docking station atop the mantel, then hands me a controller.

After a few hours, bright lights break through the rain and shine through the window. Mom enters carrying large paper bags. "Hey Fiora, why are you already ditching school?"

I'm like a lightning bolt as I turn around to look at Mom standing by the garage door, kicking off her shoes. "I can explain," I say, and Atlus takes that brief moment of distraction to come up from behind and hit me with a charged side attack. "Dick!" That was my last life, securing his victory.

Mom sneaks up behind the couch. "Well? I'm waiting. You said it was going to be different this year."

"It is different. I have a really good excuse. A girl at school killed herself over the weekend and another girl who found her body was kinda traumatized about it, so I took her to get our nails done." I hold up my hands. "See?"

Mom steps closer to get a look as if everything I just said is entirely normal and holds my hand in hers. "Oh those are pretty! I love the color. Red has always looked so good on you."

Atlus drops his controller to the couch, no longer needing it after his cheap victory. "She also made me walk home in the rain!"

"You could have gotten a ride from literally anyone else!" I argue. "Aren't you supposed to be some big shot on the soccer team, or do they not actually like you since you're so unbearable?"

Mom groans. "Fiora, the one thing I ask of you is to share the car with your brother." She holds up the paper bags. "I got Italian food!"

Now Atlus is the one groaning. "That's it? It was pouring and thundering and lightning! What if I got electrocuted?"

Mom takes the containers from the bags and places them on the kitchen island. "I'm sorry, hun. It won't happen again, or none of you will get to use the car."

"That's not fair!" Atlus whines.

"Yes, it is. Now come on, I got you both chicken Alfredo! I got the job, so let's celebrate!"

Atlus's brows furrow like when a girl back at Promise Private Academy told him she doesn't believe pilgrims existed. "*You* got a job?"

Mom retrieves plates from the cabinet and returns to the island. "Yes I got a job. I told you about my interviews last week. Why are you both so surprised?"

Atlus sits down on one of the stools. "Are your books not selling anymore? What about the show?"

"My books are selling great, actually." She slides a plate in front of Atlus and then hands me one after I sit down.

"Then why'd you get a job?"

She shrugs. "I'm 35 years old. Maybe I want something else to do with my life instead of sitting at home in front of a computer all day."

I twirl the noodles around my fork, the sauce clumpy. "So then what are you doing?"

Mom holds out her arms as if unveiling the next big invention until a new and better one comes out next year. "Well, you two are looking at the newest assistant manager for the garden department at Bedrock."

Atlus and I indeed are looking, alright.

"Too bad Nickels and Dimes isn't hiring right now. I saw Amanda the other day and she loves you," I tell her.

Mom sighs and leans over, resting her arms on the island. "Yeah, I saw her too, but I don't want to go back there–too many memories. Plus, Bedrock will let me bring plants home. Kinda like the cat distribution system, but for spider plants."

Atlus sniffs the Alfredo wrapped around his fork. "This sauce is from a can."

"Don't everyone congratulate me at once," Mom says.

We don't congratulate her.

SEPTEMBER 26 – TUESDAY

Morning

Atlus hogs the stove as he fries some eggs before school so I grab something from the fridge. Mom laughs once she sees what's on my plate. "Strawberry pie for breakfast, Fiora?" she says.

I finish chewing my bite. "What? I don't like eggs."

Atlus attempts to dig his dirty fork into my pie. "I want some."

I slide the plate away. "Get your own, ringworm."

He lunges again, securing a strawberry slice and some Jell-o onto the tip of his fork.

I throw up my arms in defeat. There's a clang when the metal fork connects with the glass plate. "Now it's just completely inedible."

Mom shakes her head, chuckling. "Fiora, stop being dramatic. Atlus, go get your own. There's plenty still in the fridge."

I scoop away the nearby strawberries that Atlus touched and drop them onto his plate. "Fine, more for me," he gloats.

"Can we return him?" I beg.

Mom shrugs. "Sorry, lost the receipt a long time ago."

Atlus sticks his tongue out.

A call from an unknown number bearing a Blackridge area code appears on my phone. I don't answer, and the mysterious caller leaves a message a moment later: "Fiora, this is McCarthy. I apologize for the lack of notice, but please arrive at Seal Coast as soon as possible. The student council has an emergency meeting with Principal Pal. I will see you shortly."

I sigh and grab my bag before throwing it over my shoulder

and taking a few more mouthfuls of pie. "I gotta go."

"We still have, like, thirty minutes," Atlus complains.

"Then you can stay here. But unlike you, I have responsibilities."

He blows raspberries.

"It's okay Atlus, I can take you today," Mom volunteers.

I almost forgot something. "Hey Attie, do you have class with a girl with blue eyes and a pixie cut?" I ask.

"You mean Farrah?" he asks. "Yeah, we have gym together. Why?"

"Perfect, that's what I thought." I reach into my backpack and retrieve a bag I stashed there last night. "Give this to her."

Atlus opens the bag and looks inside. "Clothes?"

"Yeah. Give those to her and tell her that she smells nice."

"But she doesn't. The opposite, actually. I think the chick is a chain smoker."

"Don't be a dick! Just do it."

The other student council members, except O'Brien, are waiting in the foyer when I arrive at Seal Coast. He comes rushing in. "Sorry I'm late," he says. "It's hard getting dressed with only one arm."

"You look well enough. Come, let's proceed," McCarthy orders, leading the way to the faculty hall. Paige Turner, sitting behind the reception desk, buzzes us into the glass enclosure and we turn down to another hall before reaching a door with the plaque Principal Pal.

Principal Pal holds open the door upon our arrival. "Come on in."

It's a small office with a desk and chairs and a few extra unmatching plastic chairs brought in to satisfy our numbers. The student council members sit on one side of the desk while Principal Pal takes the other, cupping his hands atop the wood. "So, I want to talk with you all about this newest proposal. This *vigil*," he spits the last word out like bile.

"Yes sir, that was my suggestion," McCarthy admits.

"I can understand where the sentiment is coming from,

but everyone is already well aware of suicide, especially after the recent *circumstances*. Matters are being taken care of, and students have the opportunity to speak with a counselor if needed. Instead of dwelling on the past, we must move on to better, more constructive things."

McCarthy clenches her composure. "Principal Pal, no offense and I apologize for speaking out of turn, but our community is in mourning. Students are feeling powerless and we can't *thoughts and prayers* our way out of this, this time. A girl is dead, sir. The student council came to a unanimous decision on the matter, believing this would be beneficial to our student body and prevent any further possible deaths. Bullying is an epidemic, and people need to be educated on the damages of it, sir. It plagues our halls like a virus."

"Which is precisely why we will not dwell on the matter. You want to make a difference and prevent more deaths? Report all instances of bullying like I already told you, and for Christ's sake, get students to stop talking about this ridiculous curse!"

"With all due respect, sir, the curse is embedded into the culture of Blackridge, and it's tradition for students to go by aliases. So much so that it's stated in the student code of conduct that noncompliance results in suspension or even expulsion. You can't blame students for speaking of the rumor that came about it."

Tension builds in Principal Pal, yet he prevents it from boiling over by releasing a deep breath. "I wasn't the one who put that there. If it were up to me, this whole charade would be put to an end. It never did any good for our economy. It has only created a generation of paranoia."

"Nonetheless, there have been several instances of bullying that I personally have reported but have yet to see any results," McCarthy argues.

"We're taking care of it."

"When? After another student takes their own life?"

There's a twinge in Principal Pal's expression. "McCarthy, that is enough. Your passion is appreciated, but I have the final say. The student council will have to find something else to occupy its time with. Focus on something more positive, like the prom. What we could really use right now is a pep rally. Lift some spirits instead of bringing them down. Now go. Classes will start soon, and I'm not writing you late slips."

McCarthy nods. "Thank you for your time, sir."

We pile out of the office in uncomfortable silence, relishing in our defeat, all of us except May, who bares a smug grimace on her face.

O'Brien stands with his good hand in his pants pocket. "What do we do now?" he asks.

McCarthy sighs as a strand of red hair falls in front of her face. "What else can we do? The student council cannot act without permission from the administration. We will simply have to develop another, more appropriate proposal."

"So that's it?" I ask.

"I'm afraid so," McCarthy confirms. "In the coming hours, I will mull over a new proposal for the student council to prevent."

"Principal Fascist only said the student council can't hold a vigil. He said nothing about us doing it as individuals," I refute.

"Fiora, I understand where you're coming from, but as president, I cannot allow any disturbances. It could put all of our positions in jeopardy. I may have already put the student council on the line by speaking out of turn just moments ago. I got too caught up in my emotions, which was unpresidential of me. I apologize." The bell rings. "We'll discuss this matter further at another time."

"Yeah, yeah, yeah."

Lunchtime

The bell signaling the end of third period rings and Joey, Cheese, and I head toward the cafeteria. "Oh god damnit," I blurt out when I see the missed call from McCarthy on my phone.

"What's up?" Joey asks.

"Let's find out."

I hold the phone to my ear and listen to the message: "Fiora, please bring your lunch to the student council room so we may continue our discussion from earlier. I'll be waiting."

"Student council shit," I tell him, and we finish our walk to the cafeteria. I may not be able to eat with them, but at least we can stand in line together.

After picking up my lunch of fried cheese sticks, I join the others in the student council room where everyone–except for O'Brien–is waiting. He arrives a few minutes after me with a packed lunch.

"Great, glad everyone could make it," McCarthy begins with her bagged lunch resting on the table. "I wanted to continue our discussion from earlier, but more importantly, I want to hear everyone's vote for the Marki situation. Remember, the student council was specifically asked to report any and all instances of bullying. Has everyone decided on their answer whether or not to report her to Principal Pal?" Heads nod. "Alright, show of hands: who votes yes?"

May is the first to throw up her hand, and that causes her shadows to raise theirs as well. O'Brien raises his hand. I'm the only one hesitating and McCarthy takes notice. "Fiora, is everything alright? You seemed so passionate the other day," she says.

"It's not just Marki," I answer. "It's that quack teacher, Mr. Phillips, too. If he wasn't such a dick pickle and actually, you know, taught, then Lemming never would have failed that test to begin with. Even with that stupid prank."

"Yes, surely that topic will be mentioned as well if and when we file a report."

I come to a decision, raising my hand.

McCarthy's hand is the last to rise. "Alright, then it is unanimous. I will discuss this matter with Principal Pal, and we will go from there. Any disciplinary action is in his hands.

At our next meeting, we will discuss what event we should organize to replace the vigil. For now, let us feast."

I roll my eyes.

After School

McCarthy said that students feel powerless, but that statement doesn't include me. I'm not powerless and will do something about it, starting with a visit to Nickels and Dimes.

Joey is behind the register wearing an apron and those glasses I like. "Hey Fi, what's up? Are you this busy every day?"

I lean against the counter. "I need candles."

"We got tons of candles, but they're not any good. There's a Bath and Body Works in Salem, though."

"They don't have to be good. I just need a lot of them."

He smirks and winks. "Why, burning something down?"

"No. I want to hold a candlelight vigil at school for Lemming during lunch tomorrow."

"I thought Principal Pal isn't letting the student council do anything?"

"The student council isn't doing this. I am."

His teasing smirk turns into a genuine smile. "That's–That's actually really cool of you. Come on, they're right over here." He walks out from behind the counter and I follow him down one of the aisles. "So we have a lot of these small scented candles for a buck, but down here, we have some of the nicer prayer candles. Then we have these plain candlesticks." He points over the displays to another aisle. "Oh, and of course we have birthday candles and stuff too."

"Okay. Awesome, I'll take all of them."

He looks down at me, furrowing his brows. "*All of them*?"

"Yeah. Do you have any more in the back too?"

"Um, yeah. We almost always have overstock."

"Awesome, I want those too."

"Seriously? You know you have to pay for these, right? I

can't just let you take them. There are cameras everywhere. I'd totally get fired."

"Yeah, I know. I need enough for the whole school. I'll get a cart and you get the boxes from the back."

I grab a cart from outside the store before returning to the aisle and packing it full of candles.

Joey approaches, carrying a couple of boxes in his arms. He sets them down and opens them. "So we have a lot of these prayer candles which are probably perfect for a vigil. Then we have these too." He pulls out a candle the size of a quarter with a metal rim encasing the wax and sniffs. "I really like these blue raspberry ones. One time, we got some strawberry and cream candles that smelled so good. I got one for Keaton, but she didn't want it, so now I just have it in my room to smell sometimes. I don't burn it, though, 'cause it's so cute."

Listening to him speak makes me realize how heavy my head is on my shoulders. "Are you queer?"

He fakes a laugh. "Wha–What? What does that have to do with anything?"

I smirk at him. "Nothing. And there's nothing wrong with it."

"I know there's nothing wrong with it. I just don't know where that came from."

"You sure are getting defensive for a hetero."

"I–I didn't say that either! Well, what about you? You go first."

I shrug. "I dunno. I just like to tease people."

He scratches his head. "Well, you're good at that, that's for sure."

Another customer is waiting at the register when we're ready to check out. As I stare at the back of his head, there's something familiar about his skinny frame and messy brown hair.

Joey returns behind the counter and greets the customer: "Hey Mr. Mark."

"Hey Joey. Hope you're doing well," Mr. Mark says.

"Well, I'm here," Joey says, scanning the item Mr. Mark is purchasing.

It's a quick transaction where Mr. Mark doesn't take a bag or a receipt. Before exiting the store, he notices me and my cart of candles. "Oh, hey Fiora. That's uh ... a lot of candles."

"It's for a school project," I say.

He squints at me behind his circular-framed glasses. "But I work at your school, and none of the other teachers–" He shakes his shaggy head and brushes it off. "You know what? I'm not even going to ask. Have fun with ... whatever it is you're actually up to. The less I know, the better." The single item in his hand is a box of blue nitrile gloves he wears every day in class.

"Yeah, you too," I say and place the items on the counter. "So this is where he gets those stupid gloves?"

Joey takes the first candle and begins what's going to be a long scanning process. "Yeah. Sometimes he gets other things too."

"What, like rope and duct tape?"

He chuckles. "Or Tums."

"Yeah, I don't need to know about my teacher's gastrological problems. Thanks."

"One time, he was going to get a box of condoms but he put them back when he saw it was me at the register and not Amanda."

I huff a laugh. "I needed to know that even less."

Joey continues scanning, but I fill any space he clears on the counter with more candles. He sighs and scratches his head. "This is gonna take forever."

"What else do you have to do?" I ask.

"Play on my phone."

"How many desperate texts have you sent Keaton today?"

He pauses as he scans more candles, each beeping before being placed in the bag to his right. "They're not desperate. Besides, I'm... I'm pretty sure she blocked my number ..."

I raise my brows at him. "And you still think you're

together?"

"I won't stop trying until she tells me it's over."

"Joey, if she blocked your number, it's over. Treating you like this is her telling you it's over. Just take a hint, geez."

He scans in silence for a moment and puts the candles in bags. After each one is filled, he takes it from the rack and hands it to me to place in the cart. "How are you affording all of these anyway?" he asks.

I try my best to wink at him like he always does at me, but I'm unsure if I look as cute. "How about hooking me up with an employee discount?"

He snorts. "Cute of you to think I get an employee discount in this dump. Most I can get is a free soda sometimes."

"Oh, so you think I'm cute?"

His grip loosens on the candle in his hand, but luckily, nothing breaks. "No! ... I mean, I don't mean *no*! But I don't mean–I don't mean! ... What I mean is, that's not what I said."

I giggle at his awkwardness. "My mom's a bestselling author," I admit. "She wrote the book series that the show *Tales of Fiora* is based on."

Joey calms down and returns to scanning. "Oh, based. That makes a lot of sense though."

"How so?"

"Well, I tried Googling your name once and all that came up was the show. It's cool to pick a name after a character your mom wrote. Man, that show is hella popular. You must be crazy rich ... you're right about moving here being a downgrade."

I smile, focused on the first part of what he said. "You Googled me? Stalker much?" I tease.

His face turns red again, but he keeps most of his composure. "No! I just didn't have your number at the time so I was tryna see if I could message you on Instagram or something."

"You were trying to message me?"

"Well, we're friends, aren't we?"

I smirk. "Nice save."

"It's not a save. It's the truth."

All the candles are scanned and placed in bags. Joey whistles at the total. "I've never seen someone buy so many ... well, anything. You're like that person we always hear about in math questions." A receipt prints out almost as long as Joey, who stands at least 6 feet tall. He hands it to me. "Don't you dare try to return anything."

I hum. "I wasn't planning on it, but I do like a challenge."

He smirks. "Need help bringing everything to your car?"

"You will do anything to get out of actually working, won't you?"

"Hey, helping customers is working!"

"I'll see you tomorrow, Joey," I tell him and push the cart out of the store.

SEPTEMBER 27 – WEDNESDAY

Morning

"Come on Attie, let's go!" I call out up the stairs.

"Hold on, I'm coming!" he yells back, exiting his room. He has practice today, so he's wearing his dorky soccer uniform. "Why are we leaving so early?"

"'Cause I have shit to do and Mom is still sleeping."

"Oh yeah, Mom's still sleeping so let's yell throughout the house like a crazy person," he bitches as he prances down the stairs.

"I will break your fucking ankles."

We go to my car in the garage where I start the engine while Atlus stands at the door, holding it open and staring inside. "What the fuck?"

Bags fill the passenger seat and cab.

"Get in the hatchback," I tell him.

"Why can't all of this stuff go in the hatchback?"

"'Cause it's more important than you." I press the control on the dashboard and the back rises. "Go, or I'll make you miss your practice." He slams the passenger door shut and mutters something under his breath. "And stop your bitching!"

He climbs into the cargo space and I press the button again to close it. "I hope you get pulled over and arrested for child endangerment," he growls.

"Child endangerment only counts for humans, not gargoyles."

We're the only ones here when we pull into Seal Coast's student parking lot. Atlus hops out from the hatchback. "Practice doesn't even start for another half hour. What am I supposed to do?"

"Help me."

"No, I hate you."

"Have a soul, ghoul. It's for the girl who died."

Atlus carries the ironing board since he's taller, and I have as many bags as I can fit around my wrists. We cross the street to set up on the sidewalk.

It takes a while for kids to start showing up, all jocks. I'm on my own after Atlus goes off with some of the kids from the soccer team, and not long after, the football team approaches, including Griffin. They stop at my ironing board table with the others in his flock. "Hey Felicia," Griffin greets.

I shake my head, partially offended by that one. "Absolutely not."

He snaps his fingers. "Damn, I thought I got you that time. What are you doing?"

"I'm holding a vigil for Lemming today at lunch, so I'm giving out candles."

"That's awesome. Yeah, we'll take some." I hand him candles, and he passes them down the line of letterman jackets. "We gotta get to early practice. I'll see you later, Francis."

"Still no!" I yell out as they walk away.

I garner more attention as the start of the school day approaches. Kids surround my table, each wanting a candle of their own.

Principal Pal marches from the front gate and crosses the street onto the sidewalk. "What is the meaning of this, missy?"

"The student code of conduct says you have to call me by my preferred name, and that is not *Missy*," I say.

"I made myself explicitly clear that the student council is not to press these matters any further!"

I gesture around the table–ironing board. "Do you see the student council?"

"You are the event planner, and this is an event, an unauthorized one at that."

"That's at the school. The sidewalk is public property."

"Fine, then you can stay out here. You're suspended for the rest of the week."

My jaw hits the floor as I release a scoff. "For what? I didn't even do anything. You can't punish me for doing something outside of school!"

"Yes, I can. For causing a distraction amongst the students and disturbing the peace."

I roll my eyes and cross my arms. "It was pretty peaceful until you came along with a stick up your ass."

"I'll see you in my office on Monday, and I expect an apology, Fiora." He walks away, and even with his back turned, I can feel his mirth.

Joey crosses the road and stops once he reaches the ironing board. "Well, he sure looked happy. How's it going? Looks like you're doing a good job. There's barely anything left."

"I got suspended."

He scrunches his face, looking just as confused as I feel. "For what? You're not even technically at school yet."

"For hurting his fragile little feelings, I guess."

He scratches the side of his head. "Geez, talk about being good at killing a mood. So, is the plan off then?"

"No it's not off. I'm going to need you to be my eyes and ears. Video call me once you get through the gate."

He winks and smirks. "I gotcha."

Joey crosses the street and queues for security. Once he's on campus, a video call comes through on my phone. I answer, and there's Joey's face. He holds the phone at an underhand angle and says, "Hey, so what am I actually supposed to be doing?"

"Just hang around for a while so I can see what's going on," I say.

"Okay, gotcha, I–"

"Joey," a masculine voice from off-screen sings tauntingly.

"Leave me alone, Falco. I'm busy," Joey states.

"Aw, but I can't help but feel that you're avoiding me."

"Yeah, 'cause you're an asshole."

"I bet you'd like that!" a higher-pitched, hyena-like voice comments. It's not Joey's or Falco's, so it must be that Cappy guy–aka Falco's shadow.

There's another voice, husky and stern. "Falco, please leave us. This is official business." That one I'm familiar with: It's McCarthy.

Joey laughs nervously. "Official business? Am I under arrest or something?"

"I would like to assume you're innocent in this matter. Where is Fiora?"

"She's suspended."

"That's not surprising. Principal Pal is not pleased with her actions, and now it is the duty of the student council to clean up whatever mess she has caused behind our backs."

"Is it really that big of a deal? They're just cheap little candles."

"According to Principal Pal, it is."

There's a moment of silence as the screen shows Joey's shoes scuffling against the pavement as he walks away. He returns the camera to his beautiful face. "Did you catch all of that?"

"Yeah, that's about what I expected," I say.

The bell rings. "Hey, I gotta go. When should I call you back?"

"When you get out of art."

He winks. "Gotcha. I'll see you then."

Most of the candles are gone, so I pack what's left in defeat and go home, parking in the garage beside Mom's car. "Fuck!" I blurt out. Of all the days she's off from her new job, today has to be one of them.

I bite the bullet and enter the house. There's a calm before the storm until a door opens from upstairs, and Mom looks over the banister. "Fiora?"

I look up at her. "Hi Mom. You know I love you, right?"

"Did you forget something?"

"Well, not exactly ... I kinda got suspended."

Mom scoffs. "How are you already suspended? It's barely been a month! Who are you fighting with this time?"

"One: kind of a few people. Including the principal. But two: I have a good reason!"

"That's what you said last time."

"And you agreed last time, so you can trust me on this."

She crosses her arms and stiffens her stance. It's rare to see Mom put her foot down, but her one rule for me–other than sharing the car with Atlus–has always been to graduate, and after fucking that up last year, I'm on thin ice. "Well, I'm waiting," she states.

"Remember that girl I told you that died?" I start to explain. "Well, the principal is being a total dick about it, so all I wanted was to give her a candlelight vigil at school today. I was giving out candles when school hadn't even started yet and I was on public property so I seriously did nothing wrong!"

"Did you mouth off to him?"

I pinch my fingers until my skin is almost touching. "Maybe like this much, but he started it."

Mom sighs. "Yeah, yeah, yeah. Everyone else always starts it. And how's that working out for you?"

"Well, I'm suspended for the rest of the week, and I'll probably have detention up the ass when I go back."

Mom loosens her stance. "I'm proud of you for wanting to do something for your friend, but you could have done that vigil anywhere, like outside her apartment or at the church. You only wanted to do it at the school so you could pick a fight. You don't have to like the guy. Hell, you don't even have to respect him, but choose your battles, Fiora."

"He started it. It was self-defense."

"He's also the one in charge of your education, and you promised me you'd graduate this year."

"Why do I have to do it? You still have Atlus to be your golden child," I plead.

"Because you're the one I gave up everything for."

Her words pierce through my heart like a bullet. "I'm sorry, Mom. I'll do better."

She doesn't say anything before returning to her study. The

door shuts and locks behind her.

Lunchtime

I'm taking a bubble bath when I finally hear back from Joey. I answer his video call, and he's with Cheese as they walk down the hall. "Hey, so–Oh!" he starts to say. His brown eyes gaze away while Cheese cocks her head and continues to stare at the screen. "Sorry."

"Calm down, you can't see anything," I say. My chest is submerged underwater and sheeted by bubbles.

He looks back at me. "Oh, right. Um, so we've kinda bumped into a few problems."

"Explain *a few problems.*"

"Principal Pal confiscated all the candles. He searched through everyone's lockers, backpacks. Everything."

"That fucking fascist! God forbid we get the school to show some respect for a girl who just died!"

Joey and Cheese reach the cafeteria, and Pandora joins the call after they sit down and join her at one of the tables. "I'm surprised they didn't do cavity searches," she adds. "They're cracking down on *contraband.*"

I want to laugh. "Contraband? They're candles. Some of them smell like blue raspberries."

"They've been flat out suspending anyone found with lighters, matches, vapes. Without the stoners, the school feels totally empty."

Poppet throws herself in front of Joey to join the call. "Hello beautiful Princess Fiora, I've missed you."

"I've missed you too."

Joey leans in to make himself visible to the camera again. "What, am I not a beautiful princess?"

Poppet gives him a big smooch on the cheek. "You're a very beautiful princess, Joey."

Joey continues and scratches the side of his head. "Anyways, what do we do now?"

"We shove this issue even more down Principal Pal's throat," I declare, my bubble beard giving me strength. "If he thinks I'm annoying now, then just wait until he sees what else I have up my sleeve … I just gotta figure out what that is first."

Pandora whistles. "Real smooth."

The screen cuts to black, and a few students cry out and yell. Voices with no faces murmur as people speculate about what could be happening. A speck of light breaks through the darkness and rises, holding itself steady in the air.

"Hey, check this out," Joey's voice says through the black, and his phone rises. There's a clear view of what fills the cafeteria: students using the lights of their phones and holding them to the ceiling, reminiscent of candles. All is silent, even just for a moment.

The cafeteria lights turn back on, and Farrah stands against the wall, her hand on the light switch.

A high-pitched, ear-shattering whistle collapses the silence. It's campus security. "Alright, that's enough! Everyone, hand over your phones right now!"

The screen is sporadic as it turns back to Joey and the others. "Oh shit, looks like we gotta go."

"Good job everyone," I praise before the call ends.

I lower myself back into the warmth of my bath, feeling a sense of accomplishment—or rather, a sense of pride in how the whole school came together for Lemming, even just for a brief moment. If only we could have done that for her before she had to die.

SEPTEMBER 29 – FRIDAY

Morning

Mom has always been cool, but not *let me sleep in when I'm suspended*, cool. I still have to wake up when my alarm goes off, shower, and dress like I would if I were going to school today. I finish brushing my teeth and go downstairs for our usual breakfast, but there's something strange. It's calming, like a nice deep breath of fresh air. Someone is missing. "Where's Atlus?" I ask.

Mom is in front of the stove, stirring unfluffy and unseasoned eggs. "Oh, good morning. He's sick, so he's staying home today."

I sit on a stool at the island. I don't like eggs but even I can tell that they are exceptionally awful. "He's totally faking it. He just wants a day off."

Mom chortles. "Atlus isn't like you." She takes the pan off the heat and tries to flip the eggs onto a plate, but a large chunk of them are stuck so she uses a metal spatula to scrape them off.

"Is … Is that for Atlus?" I inquire.

Mom holds out the plate and admires it like she's proud of it, while Atlus has been making better eggs for himself since he was five. "He's always complaining about how I don't cook, so I thought this would make him feel better." She takes a closer look, her expression dropping. "What, you don't think he'll like it?"

I take the plate from her and slide the eggs into the garbage disposal. "Ah, no. That's worse than not cooking. Want me to make him something and I'll just tell him you made it?"

She grabs my hands in hers. "Would you please? That would make you the best daughter ever."

"I'm already the best daughter ever."

"Yes, yes you are. Thank you!" She gives me a smooch on the forehead.

I take her place in front of the stove, unconfident in where to begin.

The whites from the cracked-open eggs leak across the counter and soiled dishes litter the sink. The pan resting on the hot burner is blackened, so I toss it in the sink to deal with it later. I also toss the bowls she used in there. Since I–and she– have no idea what she did, I will start from scratch. The end product is French toast, eggs, and bacon, all cooked to Atlus's known liking–and not by Mom.

Atlus is in bed when I enter his room, and he doesn't tell me to get the hell out. He's facing the wall and doesn't notice me placing the plate and juice on the nightstand. I raise my foot and use it to nudge his shoulders. "Wake up, loser. Mom made you breakfast."

He shuffles a bit under the blankets before turning over. His cheeks are bright red and his bangs are caked to his forehead with sweat. "Mom?" He pulls himself to sit up and covers his mouth to yawn. "Where'd she get that from? Bread and Butter?"

"No dick. She made it."

He stares at me with those cold, dead eyes. He doesn't break contact when he coughs into his elbow.

"Okay, fine. I told her I'd make it then tell you she did it. So tell her thank you when you see her."

"It's not that hard to make bread, eggs, and bacon," he complains.

I chortle, not thinking so either before seeing the disaster left in the kitchen. "Yeah, you'd think," I say. I straighten up. "Well whatever. I did my job. I don't want your sick plague germs."

Just as I'm about to leave, he says something behind my back: "Thanks."

I look over my shoulder. "You're welcome."

Afternoon

2:58 PM

JOEY: So is the band still a thing or was that just for the fundraiser?
PANDORA: It's still a thing
PANDORA: I've been working on writing original songs we can start practicing soon
JOEY: K cool cuz Lincoln saw us play at the fundraiser and just asked if we could play at the bar on weekends. Said he'll pay us in free food and drinks!
FIORA: Who's Lincoln?
JOEY: There you are Fi. How's your vacation going?
JOEY: He's the owner of Tipsy Beaver the pub right next to Nickels and Dimes
JOEY: He wants us there like right now
POPPET: I'm working :(
POPPET: We're always sups busy on weekends
PANDORA: You don't do anything anyways
POPPET: Ouch XD
POPPET: Your insults wound me like lightning
PANDORA: I can make it though. Be there in a few
JOEY: You coming Fi?
POPPET: Hehe Joey just asked if your coming
PANDORA: Grow up
FIORA: Of course I'm coming. I'll come right now if you tell me to
JOEY: I want out of the band Q_Q
JOEY: But yeah, come!

Thick fog replaces the morning rain when I back out from the garage. I stall before turning to the main road, noticing a figure barely breaking through the mist. Is that a person? A tiny one at that. Upon further inspection, it's Farrah.

I leave the car parked in the driveway and approach where she stands on the front porch. "Farrah? Did you walk here from school?"

"Hi, Fiora!" she greets, then fiddles with her fingers. "I've been here for a few minutes but was too scared to ring the doorbell."

"What are you doing here?" I ask.

"Oh, I'm sorry. Am I not supposed to be here?"

"Nah, it's cool. Did you see the band's group text? Joey got us a gig, so I'm gonna check it out. Want a ride?"

She takes her backpack from her shoulders and holds it in front of her. "Oh, Um … That's not why I'm here. I noticed Atlus wasn't at school today, so I brought him the assignments he missed." She pauses to look down at her hands. "He's been so nice to me that I wanted to return the favor."

I unlock the front door to get us out of the brisk and misty air. "His room is upstairs."

Her eyes widen as she gasps. "His room?"

"Do you not want to give it to him?"

"No, no! I do. Thank you." She scurries through the door. "Wow, your house is so nice. I love all the plants."

"Oh, yeah. Our mom just got a new job at the gardening department at Bedrock so she's always bringing shit home." I point to a particular door up the stairs. "That's Atlus's room."

"Oh, thank you!" She moves at a snail's pace as she climbs the stairs, even taking a few looks back down at me before she's on the balcony and knocks on Atlus's door. She goes inside, and I take my leave.

Instead of going to Nickels and Dimes, I go to the Tipsy Beaver next door where there is the intense reek of weed. From the entrance is a gaming area with a pool table and a couple of retro arcade games. Off more towards the side is the bar where blue-collared men nurse their middle of the afternoon beers, and sticking out like sore thumbs are Joey and Pandora. Pandora is the one with the blunt and she passes it to Joey who takes a long drag.

I approach them. "Care to share with the rest of the class?"

Joey exhales the smoke from his lungs and passes me the joint before turning towards the bartender. "This is us. Well, some of us at least."

The man behind the bar is shorter than Joey but probably quintuple the weight, most of it in his gut. He's older, with gray stubble on his chin and likely balding hair under his baseball cap. He comes out from behind the bar. "I could have sworn there was more of yous."

Joey scratches the side of his head. "Well, not everyone could make it on such short notice."

The gray man waves it off. "Nah, forget about it. Yous will do. I'm Lincoln. Let me show yous around." The stage is adjacent to the bar with everything we need set up: drums, bass, guitar, amps, and a mic. "This is where I'd like you kids to play," Lincoln explains. "I like to have live music on the weekends, but I had to let my last band go. They was taking advantage of the free drinks and would get too shit-faced before even going on stage. But all of yous are underaged, so I don't gotta worry about that. Free sodas all the way, am I right?"

Lincoln holds out his fist and a confused Joey bumps him. "Yeah, totally," Joey says.

"You know, I liked what you were playing at the car wash. I don't want any of that loud yelling shit, alright? I got an older clientele here. Give them something to rock out to without reminding them of their fathers after a few glasses of whisky." He laughs too loud at his own what I think was supposed to be a joke. "So, whatcha thinking?" he inquires.

Joey looks down at Pandora and me. "What do you say?"

Pandora takes another look around the dark and dank bar. "I can dig it."

Lincoln claps his own hands. "Fantastic. Think you can get everyone together by next weekend?"

"They better," Pandora says.

"Alright then. I'll see you kids next weekend." He punches Joey on the shoulder. "Except for you. I see your skinny ass all the time."

Joey massages where he was hit as he fakes a laugh. "Yeah, haha. I gotta get back to work."

Pandora gestures for me to hand her the blunt and she takes another hit. She blows the smoke from her metal-filled nose. "I just want to go home." She passes what little is left of the blunt to Joey who finishes it.

The three of us exit Tipsy Beaver together, but Pandora goes off into the parking lot while Joey and I go right next door to Nickels and Dimes. He returns to where he spends most of his time outside of school: behind the register.

"Where do you get your weed from?" I ask.

"I get it from Cheese," he answers.

I chortle. "I don't even know why I asked."

Joey chuckles and joins me leaning over the counter. Our faces are close and gazing into one another's eyes. "So, how's your vacation going?" he asks.

I run my hands down my face, pulling on my eyelids as I groan. "It's brutal. I'm so bored all the time."

"You? Bored? You mean you're not starting riots or lighting something on fire?"

"Oh, now you give me ideas when my suspension is almost over? I can't wait to go back to school."

"Wow. I never thought I'd ever hear someone say that. Well, if I didn't have school, I'd be stuck behind this counter every waking moment, so I guess I get it."

"At school, behind a counter, on your back, no matter what you're getting fucked."

Joey wears a cheeky grin as he looks into my eyes. "Are you a virgin?"

I blow raspberries. "Psst, maybe a born-again virgin."

Joey reaches into the collar of his shirt and exposes a chain with a cross on the end. "Oh, wanna go to church with me on Sunday?"

I jump back from the counter, feeling a sensation across my skin only described as burning. "No! You're a goddamn fucking Christian? The absolute betrayal! I thought you were cool!"

He watches my horror in amusement before tucking the chain back under his shirt. "Relax, I'm not. But my grandma is, and I like to have her believe I'm a good little Catholic boy." He finishes off the last part with a thick Irish accent.

I've never released a more enormous sigh of relief and return to the counter, my heart still pounding. "So, does your grandma know that you're–" my wrist goes limp.

Joey looks away briefly before returning his big brown eyes to mine, weighing whether to tell me or not. "No. She wouldn't disown me or anything, but she has dementia, so she'd just forget right after telling her, and who wants to come out to their grandma every day?"

"Come out as what, exactly?"

"I'm bi," he says.

"Okay yeah, I totally clocked that."

Now Joey is the one to blow raspberries. "You didn't clock shit. So you really are a virgin, right?"

The bell saves me when the glass front door pushes open and it's Keaton. She glances at me as she passes, but nothing towards Joey. She goes behind the counter and stands at the other register to clock in. The drawer opens and she counts the money inside.

"Time to get on your knees and start begging," I tease.

Joey always keeps eye contact. "Why? Do you want me on my knees?"

The amount of butterflies fluttering in my stomach makes me want to puke. Joey isn't usually like this. This has to be the weed talking. It's like he doesn't notice Keaton. "Hey, what's up? You're looking a little red," he says.

Keaton calls out his name and he finally looks. He straightens his back and scratches his head. "Hey Keaton! Are you doing anything after work tonight?" he asks.

"No, I'm closing," Keaton snaps. "Go to the back and do inventory."

The smile on Joey's lips shatters to bits. "Oh, um … yeah, right." He looks back at me. "Will I see you on Monday, or are you gonna get suspended again?"

I exhale through my nose, the air suddenly heavy. "I wouldn't miss seeing you for the world, Joey."

Joey responds with a deep breath and a forced smile as he slips from behind the counter and disappears down one of the aisles.

Keaton has a roll of dimes in her hand and counts as she drops the coins into the bin in the drawer. "He likes you, you know? If you make a move he won't say no."

"I don't want to get him like that," I tell her and tell myself. I want Joey to like me because he actually likes me. Because we have a lot in common, we have fun, and he finds me attractive. Not because I'm the only person giving him the time of day but because I make him feel worthy. "I'll see you around Keaton. Let me know when you get a new job."

The metal clanking against plastic breaks when she stops dropping the coins into the tray. "You'll be the first to know."

The bell on the door rings as I make my exit.

SEPTEMBER 30 – SATURDAY

Afternoon

Lemming's service is being held at the church; the air is suffocating. A woman softly plays the organ while the rest is silent. It's a private ceremony due to the attention surrounding Lemming's death, and at the back of the room is a podium where she lies in her coffin. It's closed with her family standing beside it. Cappy is hard to recognize without his letterman jacket. I've recently learned that he was Lemming's brother.

I leave them be with their grief and sit at the nave.

Griffin and I lock eyes and he dismisses himself from the other football boys to join me. "Hey," he says.

"Hey," I say back.

"I've missed you at school, but I heard everything that happened was 'cause of you. I was hoping you'd be here."

"Yeah, but I also kinda got suspended for it," I say.

"That just makes it cooler. If Principal Pal wasn't doing so much damage control, this whole thing would have blown over by now."

"Yeah, it's like he's actually scared that Lemming was killed by some stupid curse. He even told the student council to get everyone to stop talking about it." I sigh and slump my shoulders, ruining my posture. "I just wish there was more we could have done before she ended up dying. Maybe if she had just talked to someone, none of this would have happened. But I guess she felt like she had no one to talk to."

Griffin stuffs his hands in the pockets of his dress pants. "You never really know what someone is going through."

"No, you don't."

He smiles slightly and nods. "Will I see you at school

tomorrow?"

I smile back at him. "You will." He walks back towards the group of boys, but I call out to him: "Hey, what's my name?"

He turns back around with a fancy spin. "Francine?"

I shake my head. "Nope."

Farrah walks from the casket and passes Griffin on her way toward the church's nave. "What was that about?" she asks.

"It's nothing. He was just saying hi," I say.

"No, I mean about your name."

"Oh, every time he sees me he tries to guess what my real name is. It's just a joke."

Farrah gasps and slaps her hand against her mouth. "But jokes are supposed to be funny. That could get you killed! Lemming's body is right there."

"You don't really think she died over some curse, do you? She was suicidal."

"She told everyone her real name right before she died!"

Moments like this are what Mom was referring to when she told me to *choose my battles*. I won't argue with a child clearly in shock and mourning. Believing in a curse is more comforting than knowing your family member deliberately killed themselves, and then you were the one to find their body. "How are you holding up?" I ask.

She looks down and picks at her nails, the baby blue paint chipped. "I-I don't know."

The same man who was crying on the news after Lemming's death stands at the podium while the remaining guests join me at the nave. "I would like to thank every one of you for coming today," Lemming's father states. "We all know why we're here. It's because we know how much of a special girl my daughter Holly was. She was the most caring girl I've ever met, always putting others before herself. Maybe that's what her downfall was." He wipes his eyes with a handkerchief from his suit pocket. "At least after today, I know she's resting easy. Whatever it was that was hurting her so much can never touch her again." He gestures to the priest, who comes to take center stage.

"The Lord loves all his children," he begins his speech. "He gives us life, He gives us will, but He also knows that without hardship, we would have no growth. He gives His strongest warriors the toughest battles, but unfortunately, not all wars are won. The Lord is always with us all, but some need Him closer than others. We can trust that precious Holly is safe in His hands, protected where pain can no longer reach her. He is with you, He is with me, He is with all of us. There is nothing on this earth that you go through alone. Now, let us pray."

We hang our heads and the church is silent.

Evening

There's a break from the downpour when I pull into the garage and just sit. No music plays, and my thoughts are numb. I just … sit.

My body runs on autopilot as I hop out of my car and enter the house. Atlus is in the kitchen and something smells good. I put back on my game face. "What are you making me?" I ask.

He is kneeling in front of the oven and looking through the glass. "Nothing. I hate you."

"What is it?"

"Potatoes au gratin."

"And those are …?"

"Basically cheesy potatoes with onions."

"Oh hell yeah."

The timer on his phone goes off and he takes the potatoes from the oven, the cheesy smell filling the house. Steam flows from the baking dish as he uses a spatula to dish out the potatoes. "How was the funeral?"

I shrug. "Eh, it was a funeral. I didn't really know the girl. I was just there for Farrah."

"Why are you friends with Farrah?"

"I don't know. 'Cause she doesn't really have anyone else. She actually thinks I'm a good person."

Atlus snorts.

I lean against the counter. "So, what did you do when she was in your room?"

"I keep telling you, nothing!"

I fan the steam from the potatoes towards my face. They smell amazing. Definitely cheesy. "You didn't get your sicky germs on them, did you?"

"That's what I used for the seasoning."

He better be joking.

I take my plate to my room upstairs and place it on the nightstand to cool. Meanwhile, I wait for Sims to load and give Chloe a call. "Was it sad? Did you cry?" is how she answers instead of the standard *Hello*.

"Yeah it was sad, but I didn't cry," I say. "I didn't really know the girl. I was mostly there for my friend."

"Did she cry?"

"Of course she did. Then the girl's dad gave a little speech, and he started crying."

"Damn, that sucks. My dad always said his worst fear was one of his kids dying before he does. Then he went and died on us."

"I don't think he exactly did that on purpose."

A text message from Joey pops up on my screen:

JOEY: Hey how was Lemming's funeral?
FIORA: It was nice.
FIORA: Surprised you weren't there. Pandora and Poppet weren't there either.
JOEY: Poppet said she had to work and Pandora said she didn't care
FIORA: Ouch
JOEY: I really wanted to go but had to work too. And it's not like I can call Keaton and ask her to take my shift
FIORA: Break up with her!

Joey stops replying.

"So, last night I couldn't sleep so I was doing some exploring through the deep web," Chloe says.

"You mean Reddit?" inquire.

"Whatever. So, I was reading about how the British royals used to eat Egyptian mummies for, like, medicine and stuff ..."

Instagram suggests several counts to follow while Chloe word vomits, one of them being Griffin. His account doesn't post much, though the most noticeable photo is of him standing on the Seal Coast football field. He wears his uniform with his head drenched in sweat and beside him are two well-groomed men in suits and ties. Georgia Bulldogs get ready here I come! Go Dawgs! the caption reads.

"Ew, Georgia?" I blurt out.

"Georgia? No, I'm talking about British people eating mummies," Chloe says.

"No, not you. This guy who flirts with me at school. Looks like he got some big football scholarship to play all the way in Georgia."

"Oh! Get that big redneck football money!"

"I'd rather kill myself."

"Do you know what position he plays?"

"The only thing I know about football is that Kurt auditioned for the role of kicker on *Glee*."

"Ha! Well, find out. Not worth the effort if he's just on the bench or something."

"What effort?" I say that, but I'm already Googling the roster where I find a list of everyone's names. Except Griffin isn't his real name. The roster also has their heights, weights, grades, and hometowns. "Wait, here it is," I say. 6' 2, 190lbs, freshman, Blackridge, Oregon. "Zachary Moore." I click on the link, and it's the same picture of Griffin with those two men. Below is a brief bio about him:

Zachary Moore was born in the small coastal town of Blackridge, Oregon. He has been passionate about football and playing since the third grade. He currently lives at home with his mother and two bulldogs, making him the perfect addition to our team.

"Is he cute?" Chloe asks.

"Eh, not really my type. I like someone else."

Chloe snorts. "Yeah, that twink."

"I'm telling you, I can fix him. He just has to dump his girlfriend first."

Chloe and I talk about nonsense for the rest of the night.

OCTOBER 2 – MONDAY

Morning

Today is my return to Seal Coast, and after getting ready, I head downstairs to join my family in the kitchen. Atlus is making eggs benedict. Mom stands beside him and takes a big whiff of the ham he's frying. "Hmm, that smells amazing. Can I have a couple?"

"Yeah," Atlus answers and slides everything onto a plate before joining me at the island. "Are you even allowed to go to school today?"

I stick my tongue out. "Yes, dork."

Mom claps her hands together in the form of a prayer. "Fiora, stop getting into trouble. Please, I'm begging. Graduate this year. It's only the beginning of October and you're already ditching and getting suspended."

I slide my backpack off the counter. "Yeah, yeah, yeah."

Mom sticks out her tongue. "Don't, *yeah, yeah, yeah*, me."

* * *

It's another damp, foggy day, and a sheet covers the air when Atlus and I enter the student parking lot. Joey pulls up in his 2003 Ford Focus and parks in the spot beside us. He pulls on the handle from the inside, but the door won't budge due to the side of the door being caved in as if struck by a wrecking ball. The window rolls down and Joey slips out his thin, long body before falling to the pavement. He picks himself up and looks at his beaten-up car. "Ah man!"

"What happened?" I ask.

"He fell on his face," Atlus comments deadpan.

Joey groans with his lip curled. "A deer totally body slammed into my car. I was really hoping it'd be okay."

I chortle. "The deer or your car?"

"Well, both. But mostly my car. I mean, look at it!" He throws out his arms. "What if it's totaled? It took me years to save up for this piece of junk."

"You sure it was a deer and not a person through all this fog?" Atlus suggests.

"D-Don't even joke about that. That's, like, one of my biggest fears. You know, accidentally hitting a person. We got a lot of crackheads in Black-shit, ya know." Joey sighs and kicks at the front tire. "I'm gonna have to ask my grandma to help me deal with the insurance. I've never made a claim before." He sighs. "If she even remembers how to."

"Insurance is my biggest fear," I joke, getting a little chuckle from Joey.

We walk towards the front gate and line up for security. "Is it just me, or have things been super depressing lately?" one of the kids standing in front of us asks the group of boys he's with.

"Uh, yeah. Some thot killed herself," says another boy in the group.

"I heard that in college when someone kills themselves, like, the whole grade passes and doesn't have to go to class anymore."

"They should have that in high school, too!"

"I heard she didn't really kill herself."

"Don't tell me you believe that shit."

We finish passing through security. "Don't talk to me," Atlus says before parting.

"Wait!" I call out. I swing around my backpack and pull out a bundle of plastic daisies I picked up from Nickels and Dimes during my *vacation*, as both Chloe and Joey put it. "Give these to Farrah and tell her you're sorry for her loss."

He snatches the fake flowers from my hand. "Yeah, yeah, yeah." He goes off to join his friends on the soccer team.

Joey watches. "I didn't know Atlus was friends with Kellen."

Kellen is a boy from the soccer team who has visited our

house a few times. He has curly, light brown hair, almond-shaped eyes, and a long, pointed nose. "Yeah, so?" I ask.

"He's Keaton's little brother," Joey says.

"I swear, everyone in this town is related to everyone."

"Pretty much."

"You better not tell me your real last name is Whittaker."

He winks and smirks. "That's a secret."

"Oh yeah, that's right. My mom already said your name is O'Reilly, Irish boy." I stick my tongue out and gloat.

Joey pretends to tip an imaginary hat on the top of his head and speaks in a heavy Irish accent. "Top of the mornin' to ya."

We split ways upon reaching the lockers and Griffin is here wearing a freshly pressed suit and tie. "Poppet called; she wants her tie back," I tease.

Poppet approaches from behind and fiddles with her locker. She sways her shoulders back and forth like there's a song playing only she can hear. "Hmm, no. He can keep that one."

"Good morning to you too, Poppet," Griffin says. "Good morning, Francesca."

I shake my head. "Still no. What are you so snazzy for?"

He looks down at his suit and tie like he forgot he's wearing it. "Oh, McCarthy asked us to. Something about bringing school spirit to the halls before our next game."

"You play football in your suits? Talk about bougie. Must be where all of the school's budget is going 'cause it's sure as shit not books or quality teachers."

He laughs. "No, we change into our uniforms before we play, but it's just tradition to dress up before a game." He gestures to Cappy down the hall, dressed in the same suit he wore to the funeral. "We have an away game on Saturday, then Sunday is more of a pep rally after everything that happened last week."

"Wait, how do I not know about this? I'm literally the student council event planner."

Poppet has a girlish giggle. "'Cause you were suspended, silly milly banilly."

I groan. "Oh yeah. That's probably McCarthy's damage

control after my *display of juvenile delinquency* or however the hell that robot would put it."

"Yeah, pretty much," Griffin says. "I'd love it if you came, though. It kind of is your night of honor afterall."

"I know nothing about football," I say.

"You don't have to. There's greasy food, and you get to scream a lot."

"Oh hell yeah, count me in then."

Feedback plays from the speaker mounted to the wall before Principal Pal's voice comes on. "Fiora, to the principal's office. Fiora to the principal's office."

"Oooh, what did you do this time?" Poppet sings.

I close my locker. "What didn't I do?"

I cross the foyer and go down the hall, but I have to be buzzed in by Ms. Paige Turner to enter the glass room to go down another hall. Principal Pal's office has the door shut and I don't knock before entering. He's sitting behind his desk with a cell phone pressed to his ear and holds up a finger until he finishes. Finally, he ends the call and gestures for me to sit down. "I hope you've taken this time to reflect on your actions," he states.

"I played video games and took bubble baths," I tell him.

Principal Pal cups his hands atop his desk. "Your punishment is not over. For the next week, you'll be serving detention at the library during lunch hour. Maybe this will teach you some obedience."

"Lunch is absolutely not an hour."

"Two weeks then. And I will keep adding weeks until you learn to keep your mouth shut and abide by the rules. We still have all year."

"That sounds like a freedom of speech violation."

Principal Pal shakes his head and releases a long sigh. "Why must you make things harder for yourself than they need to be? Three weeks. Now, get to class. The bell is about to ring."

I leave the office where McCarthy is waiting out the door. She sits in one of the chairs lined against the wall but rises at the sight of me. "Fiora," she says.

I close the distance between us. "Okay, let me have it."

"Have what?"

"You're here to kick me out of the student council, right?"

She closes her eyes and raises the corners of her lips. "Quite the opposite, actually. I wanted to thank you for standing up to Principal Pal when I couldn't."

"For real?"

"Yes, *for real.*"

"What are you talking about? You totally kicked ass when arguing with him the other day. He's just a tyrant."

"I am glad there are people like you standing up on the students' behalf in ways I am not permitted." The first warning bell rings. "Well, we must be off." She starts to walk down the hall and towards the main lobby.

"Wait!" I call out.

McCarthy looks back, her dark red hair flowing with the motion. "Yes?"

"What ended up happening last week? You know, about the Marki thing."

"Marki has been expelled, and Mr. Philips is at a seminar for sensitivity training. He will not be returning for the rest of the semester and, in my opinion, should not be returning at all." She leaves through the glass door.

Lunchtime

Ms. Hoyos sits behind the front desk and waves when I enter the library. "Hello, Fiora. I can't say I was surprised to see you on the detention list. You can sit over there and help the other student check the returned books for damage."

"Other student?" I ask.

Keaton sits at one of the circular tables with a pile of books in front of her. She flips through the pages of one book, sets it down, and then grabs another to restart the process, taking bites of her sandwich in between.

I join her at the table. "Hey."

She looks up and smiles. "Hey."

I grab a book from the top of the pile. "So, whatcha in for?"

"Oh, ah … I'm not in detention. I volunteer."

"Why, so you don't have to have lunch with Joey?" She doesn't answer and picks up another book. "Break up with him," I say.

"You know why I can't."

"You're just torturing him and yourself."

She closes the book and returns it to the pile before leaning closer to me. "Can't you just convince him to do it? You're his friend … probably his only one."

A sound that mixes a scoff and a laugh releases from me before I say, "Trust me, I've tried. I kinda have my own ulterior motives, and he won't budge."

"Yeah, I know. I think the only one too dense to notice is Joey himself."

"Well, what about you?"

"What about me?"

"I've … noticed the way you look at Griffin when you pass us in the halls."

She shies away and smiles. "I mean, I dunno."

"That's a yes if I've ever heard one," I say.

She twirls a strand of her wavy hair around her finger. "I like Griffin. I never cared about football but I go to all the games just to see him play. I was really hoping we could have a chance together before he goes out of state, but …"

"Oh, just a heads up, I'm going to the game on Sunday and inviting Joey."

She smiles and nods. "Thanks for that."

We continue to work together for the rest of detention–just a few more hours to get through the day.

OCTOBER 8 – SUNDAY

Afternoon

The Seal Coast school colors are red and white, so I put on a high-waisted white skirt, a red harness crop top, and a red cardigan in case it gets cold. I tie my hair in a ponytail and put in some bobby pins to keep everything in place. In the meantime, I video call with Joey. "Hello?" he answers.

"Hey, I'm going to the pep rally tonight. Wanna come?" I ask. "Poppet, Farrah, and Cheese are going too. Pandora said she'd rather choke on her own tongue."

"The pep rally is basically just a football game, right?"

"I dunno. Prolly."

"Then yeah, totally I'll come!"

The excitement in his voice takes me by surprise. "Wait, *you* like football? I'm just going so I can yell at people."

"Well, no. I don't. But Keaton does. She never misses a game." Oh … "Um, Joey?"

"Yeah?"

"Keaton's missing the game tonight."

"How would you know? She was at the away game last night. I saw her in the stands on Falco's Instagram story."

"'Cause I talked to her."

"When?"

"Earlier in detention."

"Did she say anything about me?"

I sigh. "Joey, you know she's waiting for you to break up with her, right? She'd do it herself, but she's afraid of getting fired."

"I … I'd never do that to her."

"Break up with her or get her fired?"

"Well, both."

"You have to ... I mean, if you love something, let it go, right?"

He raises his brows "What did she tell you?"

"What do you mean?"

"*What did she tell you?*" he repeats sternly. "If we're friends, then you need to tell me. I ... I can take it, whatever it is. Even if she said she hates me."

I sigh before relenting. "She likes someone else."

"Th–That's somehow so much worse. Who?"

I pause and have to think this through. I don't like being a narc, but he needs this band-aid ripped off. "Griffin."

"Griffin? The linebacker on the football team?" he asks, breaking in his voice.

"I don't know what he plays, but yeah."

He sniffles. "Oh ... so that's why she goes to all the games. I ah ... No, I don't want to go tonight, Fiora. I'm sorry. I'll see you at school."

"Joey, I–" I can't finish before he hangs up. Great, now I feel like an ass ... again. Why can't I stop upsetting him?

I finish getting ready and head out the bedroom door. Atlus leaves his room simultaneously, causing us to bump into each other. "Nuh-uh, no way in hell, Fi. You don't even like sports," he says.

"Get fucked, Atlus," I say.

"I'll get fucked before you do."

"A ziplock bag filled with Vaseline doesn't count and don't you dare ask me for a ride."

"I'm not. I'm going with the soccer team."

I flick him on the forehead before skipping down the stairs and going to my car in the garage.

Evening

Seal Coast is filled to the brim like the morning rush, but the sun sets instead of rising. I meet O'Brien at the curb in front of the school after his mom drops him off in her minivan. "Hey Fi," he greets. "What scheme are you up to this time? Didn't think I'd see someone like you here. At least, not without some kind of plot up your sleeves."

"Geez, is that really my reputation now just 'cause of some stupid candles?" I say. "No scheme, fuck you very much. I was personally invited by the running back."

He raises a bushy brow "Falco invited you?"

"Ah no, Griffin," I correct.

"Oh, he's the linebacker."

"I know nothing about football. I just knew it was a something-back."

He chuckles. "That's alright, I'll teach you."

"Do you mind waiting for the other girls with me?" I ask.

"Other girls?"

"Poppet, Cheese, and Farrah, but she said she came with her cousin Cappy so she should be around here somewhere by now," I explain.

"Is Joey coming?" O'Brien asks.

I shuffle my feet. "He's kinda pissed off at me right now."

He chortles. "Why, what'd you do this time?"

"Told him what he didn't want to hear but definitely needed to."

"Oh yeah, Joey hates that."

We step back from the curb, standing and waiting as more kids are dropped off. Poppet comes from the student parking lot and joins us. "Hello, hello!" she sings.

Cheese is the next to arrive. "Hi Brien," she says.

O'Brien slightly waves his good hand. "Hey."

"Come here often?"

"Yeah I love sports. I would have loved to be on the team if I were bigger."

"You could audition for the role of kicker," I tease.

"I'm better with my arms." He slightly raises his arm in the sling. "Well, at least I used to be. Baseball and boxing are my vices."

"Oh hell yeah! Let's rochambeau!"

O'Brien furrows his brows that are much darker than the dyed hair on his head. "Ro-sham-bo? What's that?"

"It's when I kick you in the nuts–"

"No, just no. Stop right there."

The football field is in the back of campus and our little group finds a section to sit on the bleachers, thanks to Farrah saving everyone a spot. "Hey Farrah, how are you feeling?" I ask.

She nods. "I'm okay. I like getting out to keep my mind off things."

"I'm sorry about your cousin," O'Brien says.

"Thank you." Farrah looks around the crowd. "Um, is Atlus here yet?"

I shrug. "I dunno."

"I'm glad that he's feeling better. Class isn't the same without him."

I blow raspberries. "I'm still pretty sure he was faking. He saw me get a vacation and wanted in on it too."

"At least he did it without getting suspended," O'Brien snarks.

Principal Pal takes the center of the football field with a microphone, his voice beaming through the speakers. "Good evening, good people of Blackridge. It is a great honor to have you all here tonight and to feel the warm embrace of a community. Friends, families, loved ones. Now, put your hands together for our cheer team!" He steps off to the side.

A group of girls wearing short red and white skirts and carrying pom-poms take Principal Pal's place in the center of the field. Music plays as they dance. After their routine, they stand in front of each other in a line, leaving a gap between them as they shake their pom-poms. That's when the football players come running out down the aisle and the crowd starts getting excited.

* * *

The pep rally ends, and the boys on the football team remove their helmets. Griffin's head is drenched in sweat when he approaches us sitting on the bleachers. O'Brien is the first to greet him and the two boys fist bump. "Hey man, how you been?"

"I should be asking you the same thing," Griffin says.

O'Brien slightly raises his bad arm. "I'm not dead yet."

Griffin waves. "Hey girls." He turns to me. "Hey Fergie. What'd you think?"

I shake my head. "One: absolutely not. Two: I wanna say you played well."

"You wanna?"

"I have no idea what I just watched or who you were the whole time."

He laughs. "I get that. I–"

"Yo, Griffin!" Falco yells at the top of his lungs down on the field.

Cappy is with Falco, much smaller in comparison, and jumps up and down with his helmet gripped in his hand. "Party at my place tonight, fuckers!"

Griffin looks over his shoulder. "Hey, I gotta go and I'll probably be staying super late. You coming to the party tonight?"

"I wouldn't be caught dead," I tease.

"Then how about school on Tuesday?"

"I really have no choice but to be stuck with you, huh?"

He skips down from the bleachers, but not before looking over his shoulder and giving me one last smile.

O'Brien nudges my shoulder. "Was that a date I just heard?"

I shake my head. "Nah, he just flirts with me at our lockers."

"You so want to be stepped on."

"Yeah, but not by him." That gets a laugh out of the others. "Well, does anyone wanna go do something?"

O'Brien checks the time on his wristwatch. "My mom is probably already here to pick me up."

"I'm getting a ride with Cappy once he leaves," Farrah says.

I turn to Poppet. "What about you? You drove here, right?"

She hums and nods. "Mah and Pah's doesn't close until 11 so we can grab a pizza. I have to return the car anyways."

"Now that sounds like a date."

We get up from the bleachers and leave the others behind to go to the student parking lot. She gets to her rusted truck first. "I'll meet you there, okay?"

Night

Poppet stands at the door, professional and ready to greet me when I arrive at the restaurant. "One tonight? Right this way." She leads me to a booth, dramatically swaying her hips with each step, and then places the menu on the table. "What can I get started for you?"

"How about that margarita?" I inquire.

She smirks. "Mango or strawberry?"

"Strawberry."

"Good choice. Coming right up." Poppet returns a moment later with two margaritas and joins me in the booth. We both take a sip. The ice causes a shiver through my already chilled bones, courtesy of the Blackridge fog.

"I'm surprised Mah and Pah are up so late," I comment.

Poppet giggles. "Mah and Pah went to bed, like, five hours ago. It's mainly my parents and older brothers running the place; then I help out on weekends and during the summer."

"That's kinda a sweet gig."

She takes a big sip, sucking down the blended ice like it's nothing. "Yeah, I love it." Her cheeks are starting to turn red.

I twirl the ice around the glass. "Are you even Italian?"

Poppet pinches her fingers together. "*I cooka da pizza.*"

"Well, then get to it! That's what you invited me here for, right?" I roll my eyes. "Actually think you're gonna get something out of me without some wining and dining?"

Poppet scoots out of the booth and then curtsies. "Whatever you say, Princess Fiora." While keeping her stance, she tiptoes backward into the kitchen through the saloon doors.

This has been a damn fun night. It feels good to be back hanging out with everyone, and these margaritas make me feel even better.

OCTOBER 10 – TUESDAY

Morning

The fact that I have *Fergalicious* stuck in my head almost makes me regret going to the pep rally on Sunday, no matter how fun it was hanging out with everyone again. I hum it to myself while snacking on some microwaved frozen sausages for breakfast.

Atlus approaches the island with a plate of crepes he made for himself. "Can you shut the fuck up?"

"Can you stop breathing?" I rebut.

"Where's Mom?"

"Still sleeping. She's off today. Why?"

"I have something for her to sign."

I drop my fork and rest my chin in my hands. "Oh, are you suspended? What did you do?"

"Nothing. It's for sex ed."

"What do you need that for? You're involuntarily celibate. Or is it 'cause you fucked Farrah?"

"I keep telling you I didn't fuck Farrah! I don't even like her."

The more defensive he gets, the more I will pick on him about it.

For once it's not so foggy in the early morning, and we get a good look at the wooded scenery on the drive to school. It's almost peaceful with the empty, small Americana-town vibes. Leaves decorated in an array of colors have yet to fall. Browns, reds, oranges, and yellows. Without the fog, I can't believe this is Blackridge.

Several deer retreat from the woods and scamper across the road. I slam on the brakes and Atlus jolts forward, smacking his face against his knees. "Ow, fuck!" he cries as he holds onto his nose. A few drops of blood drip onto his white shirt.

I pull over to the shoulder on the side of the road. "Well, buckle up and keep your legs off the dashboard." I take out napkins from the compartment, and Atlus uses them to plug his nose. We get back onto the road. We're not far from the school. The contrast of red against white on his shirt is undoubtedly noticeable. "Wanna borrow my hoodie?" I ask after parking.

Atlus shakes his head. "I have a spare shirt in my locker."

We walk towards campus and Joey is at the bike racks. "I could have given you a ride, ya know," I tell him.

He tugs on the lock before standing up. "I don't want to be a burden."

"Who told you that?"

"Told me what?"

"That you're a burden."

He scratches his head. "Well, no one. Not in those exact words, at least. But you know what I mean."

"No I don't."

"I just don't want to be a burden."

"You're not, so don't even think that. I offered 'cause I want to."

He smiles and winks. "Thanks." We start walking towards the main gate. "So, how was the pep rally?"

"It was a lot of fun. You should have come."

"Why, so I can watch the guy who's stealing my girlfriend?"

I scoff and roll my eyes. "Oh shut up."

Atlus squints, pinching his bloody nose. "You have a girlfriend?"

"Yes I have a girlfriend!" Joey's voice cracks. "Wait, what happened to your nose? Are you okay?"

"Your girlfriend Fiora can't drive."

"Shut up, Atlus!" I bark. "Ignore him Joey. The umbilical cord was wrapped around his neck when he was born and it failed to finish the job."

A crowd pools in front of Seal Coast, the main gate

seemingly locked. "Whoa, I wonder what's going on," Joey comments.

"Are you sure there's school today?" I ask.

Atlus has his phone in the hand he's not using to plug his nose. "It's not a holiday or anything. Maybe you got the whole school suspended too."

"I didn't do anything … I think."

Principal Pal storms through the school's main building and marches to the gate. The keys swing and jingle in his hand as he unlocks the gate, but he opens it only enough for him and his big belly to pass through before locking it again. He fans out his arms, shooing away students. "School is canceled for the day. Everyone go home. Go back to your buses, to your cars, call family. Just–Just go home." He scoots back in through the gate.

Muttering fills the crowd, and the only sound louder is sirens. Flashing red and blue lights approach the school. Three cop cars and an ambulance park along the curb.

"Okay, now I really wanna know what happened," Joey states.

"Do you think someone else killed themselves?" Atlus asks.

"At school? Nah." Joey looks down at me. "Right?"

I shrug. "I dunno. It could just be an average school shooting."

"But before school even starts though? Doesn't that beat the purpose?"

Uniforms pile out of each vehicle. The guys from the ambulance are quick to go around back and pull out a stretcher while one of the cops is doing what Principal Pal failed to: disbursing the crowd. "Everyone go home!" the officer cries. "This is an ongoing investigation."

"*Investigation*?" Joey repeats. "So something did happen."

Pandora sneaks up to us. "Principal Pal is probably freaking out about something stupid like candles and lighters." She has Poppet, Cheese, and Farrah with her.

Through the crowd comes McCarthy, followed by O'Brien.

"What is the meaning of this?" she barks. "Fiora, what did you do this time?"

"Killed a person," Atlus comments.

I elbow him in the ribs. "Shut up, no I didn't."

"She didn't do anything. It was like this when we got here," Joey comes to my defense.

Poppet is standing behind me and on her tippy toes. She's tall enough to see over almost everyone in the crowd. "I can't see a thing."

If she and Joey can't see what's going on, then no one can.

"The only people on campus this early are the sports teams," O'Brien explains.

"You don't think someone collapsed, right?" Pandora asks. "You know, people will play sports with an undetected heart condition and then suddenly drop dead."

"That sucks," Cheese says in her usual monotone with her head cocked and pigtails hanging down to her chest.

"I said everyone go home, now!" the officer continues to shout. "A curfew is now in effect."

Poppet gasps. "A curfew?"

McCarthy sighs. "If school is canceled, then I must return to my bus. I will inform the student council as soon as I find out what is happening."

She and the other bustakers slowly make their way to the back of the school through the large, rubbernecking crowd.

"I'm gonna go meet up with the soccer guys," Atlus announces and disappears into the sea of bodies.

"Don't expect a ride home!" I yell out. I look up at Joey as we walk away from the gate. "Well, since there's no school today, let me give you a ride home. You can put your bike in the back. It has enough room to fit a fourteen-year-old."

He laughs, his shoulders shimming with every chuckle. "Know from experience?"

"Yes. Don't change the subject. I'm giving you a ride."

"I don't want to be a–"

"Shut up. I'm giving you a ride."

He winks. "Okay, okay. Let me get my bike. Thanks."

After unlocking his bike and rolling it to my car, he loads it into the hatchback. "This is a sweet car!" he says when he gets to the passenger seat.

"Thanks," I say. "So, where do you live?"

"Oh, go out to the light and make a left."

I drive back into the picturesque autumn view and follow his directions. It's been a month since I met Joey, and it's nice when it's just the two of us. We're always in class and surrounded by other people. We talk about many things, but this is my chance to get to know him outside of music and his Keaton-esque delusions. Who actually is Joey O'Reilly? "How long have you lived with your grandma?" I ask

"My whole life. I don't think I've seen my mom since I was like ... four years old, maybe."

"Damn, that sucks."

"Well you know. She had me really young and was into partying. She was leaving me with my grandma most of the time anyways. Then she just ... never came back."

"Do you care?"

He looks away and rests his head against the window, the colorful leaves passing us by. "Maybe a little. But it's for the best. It's better that she's not around if she can't get her shit together. I turned eighteen in June anyways, so it's not like she can come crawling back now."

"I feel you. My mom was a teen mom too, but she actually stuck around. She's still kinda childish though. She used to work at Nickels and Dimes."

He looks at me. "For real?"

"For real. Then she met Atlus's dad and moved us to San Diego. She was essentially a sugar baby, but it let her stay home to raise me and write her books. When they started becoming best-sellers, we could afford to be on our own so we were gonna leave, but then magically, suddenly, condoms stopped working and here's Atlus. Now they're in the middle of this big nasty divorce."

"That's fucked up," Joey says. "My mom was, like, 15, my dad was in his 20s. They had a secret relationship but had to come clean when she got pregnant with me."

"I hope you've kicked his ass."

He laughs, lacking the joy. "I know he was at the hospital when I was born 'cause I've seen pictures, but he's been dipped ever since. What about your dad? Was he at least the same age as your mom, or is he another piece of shit too?"

"Yeah, they were high school sweethearts."

"Do you still see him? Is he in Blackridge?"

I keep my eyes fixed on the road, an array of colored leaves passing by. "I never met him. He died before I was born."

"Oh shit, I'm sorry. How?"

"A shooting. I didn't know the guy. What am I gonna do, cry about it?"

Joey puts his elbow on the window and rests his jaw in his hand. "I can get that. I honestly have no clue if either of my parents are still alive or not. If someone were to tell me right now that they died, I don't know how I would feel. Not like it would affect my life in any way. I mean, strangers die all the time, then we move on."

"Just look at Lemming. She died barely over a week ago and everyone has already moved on. Seems like even Farrah is doing better. She was at the pep rally."

Joey chuckles nervously and scratches the side of his head. "Let's not talk about the pep rally."

He gives me more directions until we're on a dirt road deep in the woods, and at the end is a clearing in the trees to make way for several trailers. "Well, this is me," Joey says.

"You rode your bike from all the way out here?" I gawk.

"Yeah, well, you know."

"No, I don't know Joey. You're always trying to minimize things that are fucked up in your life."

"I ... I don't know how to respond to that. Thanks for the ride though. Do you wanna come in?"

I nod. "Yeah."

Joey retrieves his bike from the hatchback and I follow him to his trailer. An older woman with thin, light red hair sits in a reclining chair while watching *The Price is Right*. "Hi Grandma," Joey says, but gets no reaction. "Hi Grandma!"

Finally, she turns around. "Oh Joey!" She has a thick Irish accent. "Look at this. There's this fancy new thing called an air fryer. It doesn't need oil or anything; I dunno how it does it."

"We have an air fryer, Grandma."

The old woman flashes a warm yet gummy smile as she waves at me. "Hello, Keaton. It's been a while."

Joey scratches his head. "This isn't Keaton. This is my friend Fiora."

"Oh, how lovely."

"We're gonna go to my room now."

Joey takes the lead and we end up in a room down the hall. It's small and does not have much in it. He has a single mattress on the floor with no frame and unmade red plaid sheets. There's a dresser with a TV and framed picture of Joey and Keaton on top. One arm is around her as they smile. Beside the picture frame is a small pink and strawberry cream-scented candle. The drawers from the dresser are falling off the tracks and the floor is decorated with dirty clothes, including a couple of boxer briefs. The nicest things in here are his instruments leaning against the wall. There's an electric guitar, acoustic guitar, and the bass he uses for the band. Joey shuts the door behind us. "Sorry, she has dementia."

"Yeah, I kinda figured that when she called me Keaton," I say.

"Her caretaker thinks she should be put in a home so she can be taken care of full-time since I'm always at work or school. But ..." He trails off.

"But what?"

His eyes glance down as he chuckles softly. He kicks away one of the pairs of underwear on the floor. "I don't know where that leaves me. Pretty selfish, huh?"

My stomach sinks and the air feels heavy when he talks about himself like this. "When have you ever been selfish?" I ask.

He doesn't answer, the look on his face shifting between a slight smirk then to that of melancholy.

"Joey, I know you're not closing that door with your girlfriend!" A thick Irish accent yells out through the trailer.

He opens the door. "Sorry Grandma," he calls out down the hall. He returns to me, his cheeks florid and scratches his head. "Sorry about that. As if an open door has ever stopped me. Once her trashy reality shows come on, she doesn't hear a thing." It takes him a moment to process the words out of his lips. "Not like I'm gonna do anything! And you're not my girlfriend!"

"Yeah, yeah, yeah. I've gotten the memo." I wander around the tiny room, careful not to step on his unmentionables.

Joey laughs nervously. "Um, sorry. I wasn't expecting anyone to come over or I would have cleaned up a little." He bends over to scoop the dirty clothes in his arms and tosses them into a nearby cloth hamper. "After work, I get so tired I just take off my clothes and crawl into bed."

With the floor cleared, I'm free to pace around his room, not that there's much space. We might as well be in a closet. "I get it. You like to be nakey."

"Th-That's what you got out of that?" He sits down on the mattress, the springs crying under the pressure.

I join him. There's a moment where neither of us says anything as we stare into each other's eyes. His are big and brown, and I never noticed the specks of gold inside them. Everything about him is so cute. His nose and lips seem so soft and gentle, yet he has the sharp jawline of a man. His Adam's apple, his collarbone. Just these little things on him make my knees weak while I wouldn't think twice about them on anyone else. He even has small patches of freckles on his cheeks.

My heart pounds in my chest, and the blood through my veins boils. I need to say or do something so he doesn't realize I'm losing my mind. But what do I say? Since when do I not have anything to say?

Has it been as long as it feels?

"So, what got you into playing music?" I ask.

"Well, I love music," he answers. "When the pandemic hit, we were doing virtual school for a while and my hours were cut, so I said fuck it and bought a guitar. Watched Youtube videos to teach myself how to play my favorite songs and learned how to read notes."

I could watch him play music and listen to him speak for hours, especially when he's talking about himself without tearing himself down a few notches. "You're self-taught? That's so cool. I knew you were a natural talent."

He shakes his head. "No way. I'll never be able to compare to everyone else in the band ... Or anything, really."

Yep, there it is. There's Joey.

He stands from the mattress on the floor. "I want to show you something." He retrieves the acoustic guitar that rests against the wall before returning and sitting beside me. "I wanna teach you how to play."

"Are you serious?" I ask.

"Yeah." He sets the guitar in my lap and the springs in the mattress scream when he scoots behind me. My right-hand holds the neck of the guitar while my left is on the body. Joey places his hand atop mine. He's a skinny guy, but he's still a big guy with large, mitten-like hands and long, slim fingers. His skin is rough and calloused against mine, yet warm and alleviating. "Okay, so you have to press down on the strings pretty hard," he instructs.

Is this subtle flirting? Holding a girl and teaching her how to play guitar, that's musician flirting 101. Or have we just gotten so close as friends that he's comfortable with these things? This is Joey, after all ... Except, there was that moment back at Nickels and Dimes. Was that really the weed talking? I can hear Keaton's voice as clear as day: *He likes you, you know? If you make a move he won't say no.* Truth be told, those words have never left my mind.

My phone is on the mattress and the screen lights up. I sigh. "It's Atlus." I answer. "What do you want, twerp?"

"Don't you know how to answer texts, you illiterate swine?"

"Fuck you parasite, I'm busy."

"I need you to pick me up."

"So? Call Mom. She's off today."

"She said she has a meeting and you have to do it."

"Fine."

"We're at–" I hang up before he finishes.

Joey sits with his legs spread out and back against the wall. He chuckles. "I cannot believe the way you two talk to each other."

"Why? He's annoying."

He has that smirk on his face. The corner of his lips raised, teeth just slightly showing. "You love him so much."

"No, actually I don't. But I gotta go."

"I'll see you at school tomorrow. If there is school tomorrow." His lips are smiling, but his eyes are begging me not to leave, like a dog at the pound just begging to be adopted by someone–to be loved by anyone.

"No matter what, I'll see you tomorrow, Joey."

I leave his room and go down the short hall to find his grandma still watching TV. Her eyes are glued to the point of rot. "Bye Joey's grandma!" I say.

She holds up a shaky, wrinkled hand. "Goodbye, Keaton."

Choose your battles, Fiora, choose your battles. "If I were Keaton, I would have sucked off your grandson."

"That's nice, deary; come back soon."

That poor woman is in her own little world. A grandma with dementia, a girlfriend who can't stand the sight of him, and bullied by the jocks on the football team? No wonder Joey's so neurotic.

Out to the trailer park a group of people sit on one of the porches passing a blunt. A girl with long, flowing blonde hair makes eye contact with me. She wears a white spaghetti string tank top that would fit normally if her chest was proportionate to her body and gray shorts so short she might as well be wearing a thong. Part of a cherry blossom tattoo sticks out on her hip. "Hi Fiora," she says in a deadpan monotone.

My jaw drops to the floor as I question reality. "Cheese?"

She cocks her head like a confused pug. She's not in pigtails or baggy t-shirts, but there's no doubt this is Cheese. "Did you fuck Joey?" she asks.

"I'm still working on it."

"It's easy to fuck Joey."

"What does that mean?" She doesn't answer and returns to the porch to take her turn with the blunt.

I go to my car and follow the dirt road out of the trailer park.

Night

I'm playing The Sims when a video call from Joey appears on my phone. "What's up Fruit Loop?" I answer.

He scrunches his brows. "Hey, come on. I told you that in confidence. No name-calling. I already get enough of that at school."

"You're right. I'm sorry. Just couldn't get enough of me today, huh?"

"Oh yeah, I'm forever enchanted by your wit." His tone changes, and it's serious: "I just got a call from Falco, and he told me what happened this morning."

"Who's Falco? Oh yeah, the guy who bullies you. Wait, why do you talk to him?"

"Doesn't matter," he brushes off. "But someone did die. It's Griffin."

It's like the world stops upon hearing that name. The numbers on the clock cease to move, and there's no feeling in the air. Even my lungs can't inhale to take a breath. Joey keeps talking and these are definitely words, but I can't understand them. His voice might as well be muffled underwater. I might also be underwater the way I feel my chest gasping for air. A heavy dosage of white noise rings through my ears, blocking everything out until it slowly lessens, dying out like the drip of a faucet. I'm able to inhale sharply in a gasp as I find myself grounded back in reality.

Joey's voice has become clear. "Falco showed up for practice and Griffin was already there, shot in the head in the locker room. Said his body looked and smelled like it had been there for days. I bet it was sick."

The image is clear in my head. Griffin is dead. "Tha–That's not possible. I just saw him on Sunday."

"Yeah, it's true dude. Falco told me himself."

"Then who did it?"

"No idea. No one's been caught yet. I mean, you don't think someone found out his real name, do you? Ya know, after all that stuff that happened with Lemming, rumors have been flying all over the place."

Griffin's … real name?

Zachary Moore.

"What? No," I say. "What would that have to do with anything? That's not possible. It's just stupid gossip. I mean, I know my brother's real name and you don't see him dropping dead."

"Yeah, I get what you mean," Joey says. "I spent my whole life here so there are people who know my name and I know theirs, and none of us are dead. Well, except Griffin. But it was a big deal when he got that football scholarship. Literally anyone could have found his name."

"Football scholarship? … Never heard of it."

"The big hunky jock about to go pro and get rich? It was a big deal."

"So they killed him over it? If someone brought a gun to school then they were totally planning it, right? How would they not get caught?"

"I mean, I dunno. I'm just talking. I doubt it was the curse, but it's definitely something."

Definitely something, huh? "Hey Joey, do you know what

started the rumor in the first place?" I ask.

"Um, not exactly. I mean, it is just a bunch of rumors after all. I think it was something about the shooting that happened like 20 years ago. I can ask around and find out though."

"Yeah, that'd be cool. Let me know."

That smirk appears on his face. "Why, you're not scared, are ya?" he teases.

I scoff at the mere suggestion, or rather how trained he is at reading me. "Of course not, but it's just weird. First Lemming and now Griffin just in. like, a week."

"Yeah, it is. I can't remember the last time Blackridge had this much excitement. There was that shooting last month and now this? Things like this don't really happen in backwoods towns like us." That smirk is off his face as he releases a deep breath through his nose. "Now I'm starting to wonder if Lemming's death really was a suicide, especially how she told everyone her address like that. I mean, if Griffin was murdered then that means there could be a serial killer on the loose. Who knows who it could be? If he was killed after the pep rally that doesn't narrow it down at all. Practically everyone in town was there. The cops have already been going around and questioning everyone Griffin was seen with, so you should probably watch out."

"Thanks for the warning."

A faint hue of blue and red bleeds through the curtains' fabric. I pull them back to see the source: a patrol car parked in my house's driveway. The flashing colors light up the night. "Speak of the devil," I say, "they're here."

"Whoa, seriously? They're wasting no time getting to the bottom of this. They were just here earlier talking to Cheese," Joey says.

"I bet that went well."

He chuckles lightly. "Well hey, if you mouth off and end up needing bail money I have, like, two bucks in my checking account."

That puts at least a slight smile on my face. "Keep it on

standby."

Joey smiles as well. "Let me know how it goes?"

"You'll be the first to know."

We hang up, and without Joey's voice, I hear others through the walls. They're coming from downstairs, and one of them is Mom's. I leave my room and go out to the balcony where Mom is standing at the open front door. "–not without a lawyer," Mom is saying and starts to close the front door.

I lean over the balcony railing. "Wait!" That catches Mom's attention. "I want to hear what they have to say," I tell her.

There's surprise on Mom's face. "Are you sure?" she asks.

I nod and make my way down the stairs.

Mom holds the front door open. "Right this way."

Two men dressed in black slacks and jackets enter the house, each nodding at Mom as they pass. They approach me. "Are you Fiora Clairwater?" the one seemingly in the lead asks.

"Yeah," I confirm.

He offers me his hand and leaves it hanging momentarily before taking the hint and returning it to his side. "I'm Detective Angel, and this is Detective Damien. Why don't we take a seat?"

We gather at the kitchen table with the two suits and ties sitting across from me. "We wanted to ask you a few questions about your friend who goes by the alias *Griffin*," Bad Cop starts us off.

"I'm sorry to tell you this, but Griffin is dead. It most likely happened Sunday night," Good Cop explains.

Somehow, the words stab deeper through my heart than when Joey told me. I already knew Griffin was dead, yet this sets it in stone.

"Are you alright?" Good Cop asks.

I nod. "Yeah."

He reaches into his jacket's chest pocket and retrieves a notepad. "If you're ready, we would like to ask you a few questions."

"Shoot."

Both men look at me. That was not the appropriate thing to say. Bad Cop continues to stare me down, never breaking eye contact, while Good Cop clears his throat and clicks the butt of his pen. "When was the last time you spoke to Griffin?" he asks.

I recall the night of the pep rally and tell them about what happened, including who I was with. A night with all my friends that was so fun is now tainted. All I can imagine is Griffin stepping down those bleachers and how that was the last time I'll ever see him.

"Who was the last person you saw Griffin with?" Good Cop asks.

Yo Griffin! The voice plays in my head and I see the image clear as day. "I don't know his real name, but he goes by Falco."

The two cops nod at one another. "We've already spoken with this *Falco*," Bad Cop explains.

Good Cop presses on the butt of his pen and returns it and his notepad to his chest pocket. Both of them push back their chairs before standing. "Thank you, Miss Clairwater. We'll let you know if we have further questions."

Mom stands at the front door, ready to give the suits the boot. She fakes a smile. "Thank you for coming."

They nod at her. "Thank you. You have a lovely home," Good Cop says.

Mom wastes no time shutting the door behind them. "Fi, what was that about? Someone was killed at your school?"

"Um ... yeah, I guess so."

Mom approaches me with arms wide open and wraps me in them, my head resting on her shoulder. She holds me tight and sways back and forth. "I'm so sorry, baby."

Her embrace is warm and comforting, while her hair smells of lavender. "It's okay. I barely knew the guy. I'm gonna go to bed."

Mom lets go with one more brush on the shoulder. "Good night, sweetie."

"Good night."

Based on the questions they asked, the cops don't seem to

have any leads. How can they? Practically the whole town was at the pep rally, making everyone a suspect … if committing a murder under those circumstances is even possible. Bringing a gun to a school and committing murder is so easy it happens every day. But getting away with it? No evidence, no witnesses. How does that happen? There's no way I killed Griffin when I found his name, right? No, that's not possible. Joey makes it seem like many people have known his real name for a while. There's nothing different I could have done that would get him killed … Unless it's because I was on the phone with Chloe at the time. I skip up the stairs and open the second door on the right.

"Get out," is the first thing out of Atlus's mouth. He doesn't look up from the manga he's reading.

"You don't think that curse rumor is real, right?" I pant.

"Stop being stupid. Get out of my room."

"Like we both know each other's names and have our friends calling us by our names and neither of us are dead yet."

Atlus scoots to the edge of his bed and places his socks on the wooden floor. He crosses the room and gives me a heavy shove in my chest before slamming the door in my face.

That curse isn't real. There's no way. I didn't kill Griffin!

But if I didn't, then who did?

OCTOBER 12 – THURSDAY

Tales of Blackridge's latest death spread across the western coast like wildfire. The news covers the story extensively:

"The small coastal town of Blackridge, Oregon, is on lockdown after the killing of seventeen-year-old Zachary Moore. Another student found the victim's body in the locker room the morning before school. Police believe the murder occurred on Sunday after a football game at Seal Coast Community High School. When asked for a statement, the parents of the victim stated they did not know their son was dead and assumed he was spending the weekend at a friend's house after a party. No arrests have been made."

Morning

CHLOE: I'm so tired
FIORA: Samesies bestie
CHLOE: What do u have to be tired about? Ur on vacation
FIORA: I know and I should be sleeping right now!
CHLOE: We can totally trade places i have no prob falling asleep

She calls it a vacation, and it's partially my fault for letting her, albeit these past few days while Griffin's murder is being investigated at school have been anything but. Another one of my friends is dead and I can't get the inexplicable thought out of my head that I may be responsible. Admitting fault for Griffin's death is also admitting the authenticity that this curse may be more than a rumor.

After yet another sleepless night filled with tossing and turning, I lay in bed with Squeak at my side. I wrap my arms around her fuzzy little body and pull her closer to my chest. She struggles to get away and eventually squirms out of my grasp, but not without some head kisses first. She curls at my feet, winning the battle but not the war.

"Fiora, are you awake?" Mom's voice seeps through the walls.

"If I was, that would have woken me up," I yell back.

"Oh, sorry! Can you come down here?"

I kiss Squeak on her little forehead, and she stares at me with a look of betrayal and disgust before I crawl out of bed and go downstairs.

Atlus is making chocolate pancakes and bacon that smells so good. "I want some," I say, and steal a piece of bacon that is cooling on the rack.

"Then make it yourself!" he snaps and attempts to smack my hand with his spatula. It misses and whips the air instead.

I join Mom at the island. "What's up?"

"Well, instead of staying home all day playing video games, why don't you two come to work with me today?" she suggests.

Atlus places a plate stacked with pancakes on the island. "Why?"

Mom reaches over with a fork and adds the chocolate goodness to her plate. "Because I love you, and I miss you. And I worry about you two being home alone so much with all that's going on lately."

"I can kick some ass," I declare.

"Yeah Fi, go try to fight a gun," Atlus snarks.

He's lucky these chocolate pancakes are so good or I'd smack him upside the head. *"What's the difference between a god and a loaded gun?"*

Afternoon

Bedrock is the local hardware store, and Mom's new job is in the gardening department. Many of the plants are off-season, and it's a gamble to tell if the occasional water drip is from the gray clouds blocking the sky or the sprinklers hanging overhead.

A petite Black woman who would not look her age if it

weren't for her short silver coily hair works the register. "Good morning, Miss Navarro," she sings.

"Good morning, Peggy!" Mom greets. "I want you to meet my children. This is my daughter Fiora, and this is my son Atlus. They're gonna be helping out for the day."

"Oh that's just lovely. They look like a couple of heartbreakers."

"Fiora wishes," Atlus comments, and I elbow him in the ribs. "Child abuse!"

"Oh knock it off. Don't even start," Mom warns. An elderly woman stands at the register checking out her stuff: a couple of bags of potting soil. "Atlus, why don't you help this nice lady bring those bags to her car?"

The customer smiles. "That would be such a great help, thank you young man."

Atlus tosses the two bags over his shoulder and follows the woman, walking at a snail's pace to her car.

Meanwhile, I admire the flowers on display.

Atlus returns from the parking lot and holds two round stones against his chest. "Look Fi, boobs."

Geez, what is he, fourteen? "That's the closest you'll ever get to touching boobs."

"You have no stones to throw. Get it? Stones."

"I have boobs, wallaby."

"You'll never touch anyone else's."

"I can definitely touch boobs before you ever do."

Another voice speaks behind my back, deep and smooth like butter. "Whose boobs?" It's O'Brien's.

I notice something about him immediately. "Hey, your sling is gone!"

He barely raises his bad arm. "I know, I'm finally free."

"Barely recognize you without it."

He chuckles. "Do you work here?"

"Nah, just helping out for the day. My mom is the new assistant manager."

"That's cool." He points to a woman with two young

daughters going down one of the rows of plants. All three are in matching sundresses despite the damp and overcast day. "My mom and sisters want to grow some fruits and veggies."

"Atlus!" I call out to the little twerp who had walked away. "Go help that family."

"Why don't you do it?" he yells back.

"Can't you see I'm already busy?" I return to O'Brien. "You wanna go do something?"

He places a hand on his hip and smirks. "What happened to helping your mom?"

"Eh, I wasn't built for manual labor. Let's go fishing."

He looks over his shoulder in the direction of his family. "Alright, yeah. Let's do it."

* * *

It's much too overcast for a beach day. The sun holds no shine as it hides beneath a sheet of clouds, and the ocean has no sparkle as it's draped in fog. The air is as cold as the water when we step out of my Ford Explorer and into the brisk afternoon. The cabin mansion atop the cliff overlooks the murky horizon. "Hey, who lives there?" I ask. "Is it anyone from school?"

"Oh, nobody lives there," O'Brien says. "That's the Nameless Hotel."

"*The Nameless Hotel*?"

"Yeah. That's its ... name. In my opinion, it's always been in poor taste trying to profit off the rumor, but it's even more so now after what happened to Lemming and Griffin. I'm, um, sorry about that, by the way."

"About what?" I ask.

"About Griffin. I'm just not good at, like, talking about stuff ... and stuff."

"That's fine. I barely knew him," I say as I go around the back of the vehicle. The hatchback rises, and I retrieve our supplies from the trunk space: fishing rods and snacks, along with the bottle of tequila, which I keep hidden in the bottom compartment.

"Wh–What's that?" O'Brien and his bushy brows ask.

I hold up the fishing rods and tackle box. "Fishing gear."

"No, I mean, what is *that?*" He points at the bottle.

"Can't go fishing without something to drink."

"Vodka?

"No, tequila."

"J–Just how old are you, actually? How many times have you been held back?"

"Just once, fuck you very much," I answer and press the button to lower the hatchback. "I just have a really good fake ID."

"But you're short," O'Brien says.

We carry our supplies down the pier, the air getting cooler and salt clinging to our clothes' fabric as we venture into the ocean. Waves crash against the surrounding breakwaters.

I untwist the cap to the tequila bottle and gesture it towards O'Brien. "Like to do the honors?" He accepts the bottle and sniffs the tip of the neck, scrunching his face. "Don't smell it, just drink it," I say.

He brings the opening to his lips, and barely any clear liquid is down his throat before it's sprayed across the pier. "People drink this stuff?" he cries.

I laugh, thinking back to the first time I drank and how desperately I fought against showing my disgust to a much older crowd. "Try again, and just don't smell it first." He slowly raises the bottle to his lips. "And don't think about it too much," I instruct.

O'Brien takes a swig and keeps down every drop despite the contortions in his face. I toss him a bottle of juice from the cooler. "Here, wash it down with this," I say.

He swipes it from my hand and empties the bottle in two large gulps. He wipes his lips and rubs his sternum. "Is it supposed to feel all warm and tingly right here?" he asks.

It's my turn with the bottle. "Oh yeah, that's the good stuff."

We hold our rods as the lines sit in the ocean, swaying with the waves yet never catching a bite. The coast of Blackridge, similarly to the city itself, is caked in death.

O'Brien watches the ripple and crash of the waves, his cheeks red from the progress we've made down the bottle. "I shouldn't be here," he says.

"What, like have been born?" I ask.

"No, I mean here, Right now. With you."

"'Cause you like someone else? Well, don't worry about that 'cause me too." Though, O'Brien is cuter than I initially thought. I like his hair, his voice, and his muscles. He's popular among the girls at school, even if he doesn't realize it.

He shakes his head. "No, it's not just that. Do you remember my family at Bedrock? My little sister ..." he trails off and his voice chokes up, "she has cancer. She's had it before and was in remission for a while, but it's back and the prognosis isn't as good. That's why my mom wanted to plant some stuff. To teach her something about taking care of her body and sprouting fruit ... or something." He wipes mist from his face. "God, can I have some more?"

I pass him the bottle that's clearer than the ocean. "Help yourself."

O'Brien continues after downing another drink, skipping the chaser: "My mom, she's always in so much denial about anything bad happening. Me getting shot ... I could have died. Who knows if I'll ever be able to play baseball again, but she doesn't even let me think about that. And Peanut. What if she ..." The tears take over the mist.

He doesn't finish and I don't make him. I smile and chuckle. "Peanut?"

O'Brien wipes his face and curls his lips upon the shift in direction. "Yeah, Peanut. Our dad had nicknames like that for all of us when we were little. She's Peanut, my other sister is Pumpkin, and I'm–"

"O'Brien?"

"Potato," he corrects.

I snap my fingers. "How did I not see that coming? And here I thought you were just a good little Irish Catholic boy like Joey."

"Haha no, my family is from Venezuela."

I squeal like a puppy's plaything. "¡Por fin, alguien que no es gringo! Mi familia es mexicana."

"Oh, no. I don't speak Spanish. But I do think you just insulted me, oui?"

"Nah, it's a term of endearment."

He smiles before grabbing another drink. "But growing up like that is why I think my mom is so overprotective of us. I'm pretty sheltered for a kid who got shot. I've never had a girlfriend or even been on a date. That's certainly one thing I'd like to do before I die. I can't help but think we're surrounded by death lately."

Staring into the murky waters of the ocean, I can't disagree. "Then let's do it," I say.

"Huh? Um, no offense Fi but–"

"No, stupid," I cut him off. "I'm a girl, right? So that means I understand girls. And you're a guy, right? So that means you understand guys. I help you get a date with McCarthy, and you help me get a date with Joey."

"You like Joey? Why? He's … Joey."

"I like a challenge."

The side of O'Brien's lip raises along with one of his bushy brows. "Well, so do I. You're on."

We seal our deal with more tequila straight from the bottle before O'Brien empties the contents of his stomach into the ocean. "Alright, now give me your best pickup lines!" I say after he's finished wiping the bile from his lips.

OCTOBER 13 – FRIDAY

Evening

Seal Coast is closed during the investigation into Griffin's murder and there's a citywide curfew as well. No one is allowed out after dark, and the later the year grows, the earlier dawn sets in.

Thuds of water beat against the window's glass, followed by the occasional rumbling of thunder. Atlus and I sit on the floor in the living room playing a version of *Guess Who* where we've removed the original photos and replaced them with our favorite–and least favorite–anime characters. "Is your character the protagonist of their series?" Atlus asks.

"Yes," I answer and he knocks down tiles. "Is your character a grown-ass man having a feud with a teenager or young child?"

A snort pushes through Atlus's nostrils. "Yes. Is your character, like, cursed or a demon or something?"

"Um, no but kind of?"

"There is no *kind of*. These are yes or no questions."

"Fine. Demon, no, cursed arguably, yes."

He knocks down a few tiles. "If I lose 'cause you're stupid, I'm putting your toothbrush in the toilet."

"I'll freeze your jockstraps," I retort. "Is your character an incel?"

"Yes."

I knock down tiles until I only have a few left, but I'm confident in an educated guess. "Is it Adachi?"

"Yes."

Mom scoots past us and pulls back the curtain to look through the window. "I really hope Addie gets here soon. I'm getting worried."

Atlus and I reset our game. "You don't think she died, do you?" he asks.

"Attie, don't even joke about that," Mom scolds.

"I'm not entirely joking. You didn't do anything stupid again, right Fi?"

"Why the fuck are you asking me?" I snap.

"Seems to be all your friends that keep getting shot and killed. No secret who the common denominator is."

"You are so lucky I don't actually have powers to kill people 'cause you'd be next!"

"Both of you knock it off. That's not funny!" Mom snaps in a shocking turn of events. A bright light shines through the window, and Mom's mood quickly shifts. "Oh, that must be her!" she cries and rushes to the front door.

The pitter-patter of rain strikes against the pavement when the door opens, and there's a crack of thunder. "I'm so sorry I'm late!" Aunt Addie says as she scurries into the house. She wears a translucent plastic raincoat and shakes the water from her umbrella before retracting it.

"Don't worry about it. We're just glad you made it here okay," Mom says. "Do you need me to get you anything? A drink, maybe?"

Aunt Addie shakes her head. "I'm okay, Bailey. Really."

Mom nods. "I'll go get dinner ready." She excuses herself to the kitchen.

Aunt Addie steps closer into the living room. "Hey kids. It's been weird not seeing you two every day."

"Is that a hickey on your neck?" Atlus notices.

Aunt Addie shuffles and adjusts her collar. "No."

"I made dinner!" Mom calls out.

"You made dinner?" Atlus and I ask in unison as we sit down at the table.

Mom shoots us a look that tells us to play along. "Yes, of course I made dinner. I make dinner every night."

Atlus examines the piece of chicken on his fork. "This tastes suspiciously like takeout."

Aunt Addie takes a bite. "It's delicious; thank you, Bailey."

Mom scoots her chair closer to the table. "This is nice, having the whole little family here."

"How's the new job going?"

"It's great. I love being able to get out. I actually feel like a person again. You know Eric never let me have a job. He always hated my writing. How about you? Do you know when you're going back to work? We haven't heard anything about when the school might open again."

Aunt Addie scrapes her fork against the plate, trying to capture the few grains of rice that slip from the metal. She takes a deep inhale. "No, I haven't heard anything but ... but now I'm thinking of quitting."

"Quitting? But teaching is your life," Mom says. "You've wanted to be a teacher since we were kids. I remember I always made fun of you for it."

"A student was shot before the semester even started, and now two others are dead. One of them even died on campus. I just don't know if I can take this anymore. I still love teaching kids, and it's been nice seeing Fiora and Atlus every day, but I just can't stand the heartbreak." Her voice chokes. "These students are like my own children. And now having two of them dead ..."

There's a moment of silence.

"Is there any news on what happened to Griffin, at least?" I ask.

Aunt Addie shakes her head, her eyes avert. "No clue. The only thing the cops have to go on is the shell casing found in the locker room. But there's still no weapon or suspect."

Mom releases a heavy sigh. "I can't believe something so horrible like that could happen again. Is all the security just for show?"

"Yeah," I say.

"Pretty much," Atlus agrees.

Night

Mom and Aunt Addie are upstairs in her office while Atlus and I remain downstairs to do the dishes. He puts away the leftovers while I load the dishwasher. My phone lights up when I get a video call from Joey. I flick the water from my fingers onto Atlus's face then finish drying them on his shirt. He shoves me away. "Fuck off!"

"I gotta take this," I say as I swipe my phone from the counter. Water beats down on the window while the occasional thunder rumbles after reaching my bedroom. "Hello?" I answer and throw myself onto the bed with Squeak.

"Hey, it's me. Can you talk?" Joey says.

"I know it's you, Joey. I can see you. What's up?"

"Oh, right. So, I talked to Pandora and she knows what started the rumor. Her parents were there 20 years ago when it happened. So this is like, straight insider info."

"Well, what happened?"

"Okay, so, like, 20 years ago, this kid named Elliot Vaughn came to the school with a gun and a list of names. He killed every person on that list except for one before he was killed by the police. But then, just a few weeks later, that survivor ended up mysteriously dying. That's what started the rumor. Ever since then people have been saying that Elliot's ghost is haunting the halls, and he's still adding names to his hit list. And, like, this was all just a few years after Columbine, so it was a big deal. It finally put Blackridge on the map and they've been trying to cash in ever since about us being *the nameless city*."

I take a moment before responding, listening to the rain and wind and processing what I just heard. "But that's stupid. That has nothing to do with everyone going by fake names. Some dumbass ghost could just kill whoever he wanted."

Joey puts his hand up in front of the camera. "Hey, don't shoot the messenger–No pun intended." He continues: "Oh, and Fi, get this. Falco's dad is one of the detectives on the case and he said that the shell casing found at Griffin's murder matched the casing found after Lemming's suicide. Or I should say *alleged suicide*. They might start investigating it as a murder. I mean, she did tell the whole town her address and begged someone to *do something*. Totally sounds like an assisted suicide, right?"

I pause and swallow a lump in my throat. "Th-That's not possible. That would mean the same gun was used."

"Well, either this is the start of a serial killer, or there really is a killer ghost on the loose."

"Lemming was killed by her dad's gun, right? So what, she dies, then her dad uses the same gun to kill some random football player?"

Joey's shoulders bounce. "I dunno. The dad would be suspect number one, so there's no way they haven't already questioned him. I mean, I don't know ... at this point, it's all gossip anyways. O'Brien was shot in a failed robbery. Lemming was being bullied. Griffin ... I don't know. It's just kinda crazy that everyone has been a senior at Seal Coast, and Seal Coast is where the rumor started."

"You don't actually believe it, right?" I ask.

Joey pauses as his eyes study me. "Hey, are you okay? You're kinda shaky and pale."

"One of my friends just died! Of course I'm shaking!" I don't mean to lose control like that. It just slips out and the surface of my skin quivers.

Joey's eyes widen. "Right, right. I'm sorry! Um, but no, there's no way it's true. 'Cause like, why would the ghost wait 20 years before suddenly killing people? Something would have had to happen to trigger it, right? Besides, ghosts aren't real anyways. This is clearly just a crazy person or a bunch of crazy people. It's not like it's very far off with all the mass shootings and stuff, right? Or what about cults like the Manson family? It could be literally anything, so thinking it's a curse is just ... silly. Right?"

"Y-Yeah. You're right." I take a few deep breaths to calm my nerves. "I think I'm gonna go to bed early tonight. I'm pretty tired."

"Oh yeah, okay. And Fi? I'm sorry about Griffin, even if I didn't like the guy. Take care of yourself, okay?"

"Yeah, you too." I hang up and throw my phone onto the bed.

So for 20 years, this rumor has existed without anyone else dying, and now suddenly, two people from school are dead. Something had to have changed to trigger this, and I'm the change. How is any of this possible? It's not possible. I did not kill Griffin! I wouldn't kill anybody!

OCTOBER 14 – SATURDAY

Night

Our nameless band's first real gig is canceled due to the citywide curfew. Instead, I stay home and watch anime.

Atlus is making ramen in the kitchen, and I smell the pork belly he's frying. It makes my mouth water. Eventually, he comes out and brings both our bowls to the couch, and there are soft-boiled eggs cut in half resting atop the noodles. I look at it the same way I look at children, in complete and utter disgust. "I don't like eggs, Attie."

He reaches over with his chopsticks and picks out the eggs. "Then I'll take them."

"Or you could just give them to yourself in the first place instead of tainting my bowl with them."

"Or you can stop your bitching."

I grab the remote and play the next episode.

My phone lights up and it's an unexpected video call from Pandora. I slide the screen to answer. "Hello?"

"Have you seen the news?" she asks. Her background looks like she's in some kind of auto garage, and the loud banging and whirring of drills confirms this.

"No, we're watching *Buddy Daddies*. You should check it out. It's super gay."

"Forget about your gay animes for a second, Fiora. Turn on the news. They're arresting Griffin's killer!"

"What?"

The TV switches to the local news and there he is, Griffin's killer, and he's not me. The police escort him from the Pointe Grove apartment complex, hands behind his back and the press hoarding him like flies. Mics are shoved in his face, along with flashing photography through the rain, but Gregory McGuire keeps his gaze on his feet.

"So it was Lemming's dad after all? We gotta tell everyone," I say, expanding the call to the group chat. Farrah doesn't answer. Joey is in his room, Poppet is at Mah and Pah's, and Cheese is somewhere with god-awful grape and cherry wallpaper. "Cheese, are you on the toilet?"

"I'm on my period and it's really heavy so I'm just letting it squeeze out," she explains, her tone as dead as our buried friends.

"What the fuck?" both Joey and an eavesdropping Atlus gasp.

"Okay, but this isn't about that! They're making an arrest on Griffin's case!" Pandora intercepts.

"What?" the others cry in unison.

"Who was it?" Poppet asks.

"Greg Mcguire, Lemming's dad," Pandora answers.

"Wait, so it was him after all?" Joey sayss. "Did they say how he did it? Or why?"

Pandora shakes her head. "We probably won't find out any of those details until after the trial."

"Does that mean he killed Lemming too?" Joey continues to speculate.

"I don't know, guys. I'm just telling you what I saw."

Joey scratches his head. "Well, it was the same gun that killed both Lemming and Griffin, after all."

Cheese, still on the toilet, tilts her head. "How do you know that?"

"Falco told me. His dad is one of the investigators."

"Why do you talk to Falco?" Poppet asks.

"He just … drunk dials me sometimes. Griffin was his friend, and he's been really upset about the whole thing."

"Um, Griffin was my friend too," I point out.

"Oh right, sorry Fi. So um … what now?"

"This means no one else should die, right?" Poppet wonders.

"Guess we'll find out," Pandora declares.

OCTOBER 16 – MONDAY

Morning

School is back in session after Gregory McGuire's arrest. Students in line for security must empty their pockets into a bin, pass through metal detectors, and then have their bodies scanned by wands. Every compartment in backpacks, bags, and purses is searched religiously by having all contents removed and flipped inside out. Only once cleared can students step onto campus.

"Next," security says and waves the next person in. It's O'Brien and the process is repeated.

"This feels like being at the airport," Atlus comments.

After passing through security, I enter the foyer and catch O'Brien approaching McCarthy. Through his nervous twitching, there's a slight hint of a smile on his lips. "H-Hey McCarthy, you come here often?" he says.

She looks around the foyer. "To school? I've had perfect attendance for 11 years, and this year will be no exception."

He laughs nervously. "It's just a coincidence, is all."

"No, it's not actually. There's a student council meeting this morning, remember? I'm the one who called you here this morning."

"Um, I try not to give into *pier*-pressure."

McCarthy scrunches her single brow uncovered by the dark red flow of a curtain bang. She tucks it behind her ear. "Are you feeling alright? Do you have a fever?"

"O'Brien, no!" I cry out. I run forward to save him from himself by grabbing him and dragging him into the closest bathroom.

He pulls and tugs, trying to escape, but I refuse to let go of his wrist. "Hey, I can't be in here!" he says.

"What are you doing?" I bark.

"I'm shooting my shot like you keep telling me to."

"With *that*?"

"You liked it when we were on the pier. You were laughing."

I want to laugh again. "I was laughing *at* you, not *with* you! It was awful and cringey! And now we're not even on a pier so that pun doesn't even make any sense."

"Oh … Oh!" He smacks himself on the forehead. "I'm such an idiot. Now she's going to remember that forever!"

I flatten my hand and chop each of O'Brien's shoulders with my stiffened fingers. "I hereby dub you officially worse with girls than Joey."

He shakes his head and wiggles a finger in front of my face. "Hey, no, no, no. That is not fair. I am not worse with girls than Joey."

"At least Joey can get girls. He can't keep them, but he can get them."

"I can get girls. I'm great with girls!"

"Hi Brien." I know that monotone voice anywhere: it's Cheese, and with her are Pandora and Poppet.

O'Brien's face is red as if burning coals. He leans against the counter with his good arm, sticks out his hip, and strikes a pose. "Fancy seeing you ladies here."

Pandora raises a pierced brow. "In the girls' bathroom?"

Poppet has a devilish grin as she sways her skirt. "Is there anything you want to tell us, O'Brien, my Brien?"

He straightens himself out. "N-No! I gotta go!" he rushes out of the bathroom with all eyes on him.

"He's cute," Cheese comments and steps into one of the stalls.

Pandora takes a step closer to me and leans against the counter. "So, what did we just walk into?"

"A swing and a miss, a crash and a burn. Take your pick," I answer. "I'd love to stay and chat, but I have a meeting."

"Suspended again, Princess Fiora?" Poppet teases.

"Not yet. This time it's for student council." I stick out my tongue before going to the storage closet disguised as a student council office. O'Brien isn't late for once but refuses to make eye contact with any of the women, and that's everyone but him. His face is beet red.

"Good morning, everyone. Long time no see. I hope all has been well during that period of grief," McCarthy starts the meeting. "With school back in session, we have business to take care of: spirits are at an all-time low, and with Halloween coming up, it is the responsibility of the student council to plan the upcoming celebratory events. We must proceed with our duties and cooperate with whatever measures the new security asks of us. Do I make myself clear, Fiora?"

I'm leaning back in my chair with the front two legs off the ground. "Yeah, yeah, yeah."

June stands from her seat. "McCarthy, I'd like to say something … if I may."

"Yes, what is it?"

"Um, I'd like to announce that I am resigning from the student council."

McCarthy's single exposed eye widens. "Resigning from the student council? May I ask why?"

"My parents are going to homeschool me. They don't think it's safe here anymore. They're at the office getting my transcripts right now. I just wanted to come by and tell everyone … I'm sorry."

May releases a shocked puff. "You never said anything about this."

"I'm sorry. I didn't know how to tell you. I didn't want you to be mad."

"Of course I'm mad!"

"That's enough," McCarthy declares. "Preparing for this summer's prom without our committee representative is sure to uproot some problems, but we will manage and find a replacement. Thank you for being with us while you had the opportunity."

Feedback plays from the wall-mounted speakers before Principal Pal's voice exudes. "All students report to the field. All students report to the field. Thank you."

"Alright, the meeting is adjourned for now. June, take care of yourself and move on to bigger and brighter things. I know you can do it. Just believe in yourself and have some confidence. Be safe."

We exit the student council room together, but June goes in the opposite direction while the rest of us make it toward the back of the school and out to the field. These bleachers were the last place I saw Griffin alive. I join my friends who have saved me a spot. "Make room," I say and fan at them so they can scoot closer to make enough room for O'Brien and me. I lean into his ear. "Be careful not to talk to any of the girls."

Principal Pal takes the center of the field with a microphone and that counselor woman at his side. His voice reaches all ears. "It is unfortunate we are having to hold something like this yet again. As you all know, last week we lost another one of our students. Griffin was an immense talent and joy to have around. He was destined to go far and accomplish many things before someone took it upon themselves to take that from him. As we wait for justice to be served, I officially dub this the Griffin Memorial Field!" Applause ignites from the staff circled around him on the grass. "Please, treat this field and your fellow students with respect as we navigate these difficult times. Thank you. You may all report to your classes or the nurse's office if you have business with Mrs. Burke."

Teachers guide students back to class, starting with the freshmen. But one stays behind and waits for the seniors to step down from the bleachers: it's Farrah. "Fiora!" she calls out. She pushes herself through the crowd. "Fiora, you have to do something!"

"Like what?" I ask.

"My uncle didn't do it! You have to prove it!"

"Look, I believe in ACAB just as much as anyone else with a defiant personality disorder and conscience, but I don't know what you want me to do. I'm not *actually* a lawyer. I just talk a lot of shit ... like a lawyer."

Pandora steps forward. "If he really didn't do it, then you're going to have to get a good lawyer. We don't know what evidence they have other than it was his gun in both deaths, but that's pretty substantial. Even if he didn't pull the trigger, he'd still be facing something for not properly storing his weapons in the first place."

Joey intercepts. "H-Hey! I don't know if that's even true. I just told you what I heard. For all we know, they have no evidence at all and are just taking him in 'cause there's no one else. Right?"

O'Brien nods. "Right. Not to mention for a murder conviction they have to prove intent. I can't imagine any business he had with Griffin or for murdering his own daughter."

"Did anyone even see him at the pep rally?" Pandora asks around. Heads shake except for Joey's. "See Farrah? So if a couple of teenagers could poke some holes, I'm sure this would be a piece of cake for a good lawyer."

"My family can't afford a lawyer!" Farrah cries. "Can't the student council do something? Like hold another fundraiser?"

"The student council is at the mercy of our ruthless overlord, Principal Pal, and I can guarantee you he's not gonna wanna touch this with a ten-foot pole," I explain.

"That didn't stop you last time!"

"Last time was ... different. Lemming died and Principal Pal was trying to act like it wasn't his fault. But now ..."

Tears stream down Farrah's face. "But my uncle didn't do it! They're going to ruin his life!" She wipes them on her sleeve just for more to take their place. "I'm tired of being so powerless." I hug her and she clings to me like she did in the bathroom.

I hold her tight. "It'll be alright. No matter what happens, we'll be here for you. I'll see what I can do about a lawyer, okay? I kinda have a lot of experience in that department."

Pandora snorts. "I wonder why."

Joey is standing beside me, nodding his head. "We need Saul Goodman."

A loud whistle blows in my ear. "That's enough, ladies! Get to class!" the security guard barks through the buzzing bouncing around in my skull.

We join the rest of the crowd cramming into the main building and continue with the rest of our typical, uneventful day. Life continues to move on.

OCTOBER 24 – TUESDAY

Lunchtime

"Good afternoon, Fiora," Aunt Addie sings when I enter the library for my detention. If we hadn't had that break during the investigation, I'd be almost done with detention by now.

My lip twitches in my attempt to smile. I join Keaton at one of the tables while she stacks books alphabetically by author's last name. "I watched that K-drama you told me about," I say.

Her almond eyes light up. "Really? What did you think?"

"It's so stupid. I loved it. What does bread have to do with anything?"

She giggles, bringing something infectious to the musty library. "I have no idea, but I died at that part." She covers her mouth as she stifles some more giggles. "Hehe, I'm dying just thinking about it. Ahaha!"

"The ending was sad though. Do you know what you're going to do yet?"

"I was thinking about watching *Vincenzo*."

"No, like after you graduate. Like at the end of that show."

"Oh, I've been applying to universities but I probably won't hear anything back until after spring break," Keaton explains.

"Oregon State?"

She smacks her lips and shakes her head. "I applied in every state except for Oregon. I'm getting out of here one way or another."

"Ew, even the south?"

Her smile fades as she slowly nods her head. "Even the south."

"You know you'll have no basic human rights there, right?"

"Yeah, I know." She tucks her wavy hair behind her ear. "Part of me was hoping I'd get into UGA with Griffin, but ..."

"Geez, imagine never missing a game in that type of place."

A slow breath hums through her nose. "Yeah, it would have been crazy. But I think Griffin liked you. That's why he asked you to the game and not me."

I shake my head. "No way. We were just friends. Maybe he just thought you were off-limits. You know, since you're still technically with Joey."

Keaton stacks a few books atop each other. "Not like we can ask him now. But you obviously have a knack for sporty boys. You hang out with O'Brien too, and that freshman I see you walking with."

"You mean Farrah?" I ask.

"No ... no. Not Farrah. I know Farrah. I mean the emo one who's on the soccer team with my little brother."

My lip is twitching again. "That's my little brother. His name is Atlus."

"Oh, wow. You two look nothing alike."

"Yeah, different dads. He looks like him and people always tell me I look like my mom."

"I get it. I have two older half-sisters." An unknown rumbling fills the library and Keaton places her hand on her stomach. "S-Sorry. I forgot to pack my lunch this morning."

"Wanna go to the cafeteria?"

She returns to stacking books. "No, I can't."

"'Cause of Joey?" I ask and she nods. "I'll make sure he leaves you alone. It'll just take a second."

She looks at me and nods. "Okay."

Before we leave, we get permission from Ms. Hoyos and walk together to the cafeteria. Since lunch is already half over, there's no line so we go right up to the counter to grab some food. Today, they're serving fried cheese sticks and marinara, but Keaton, the vegan, takes a boxed salad.

I give the sauce a sniff. It's the generic stuff from a jar that makes Atlus pissed. "Hell yeah, I love these things."

"You can buy these in bulk online for your house," Keaton

tells me.

"You have to send that to me. My mom doesn't cook so we're always eating frozen shit or takeout."

Joey is at a table with the rest of the gang but has the eyes of a hawk and notices us. He jumps from his seat. "Keaton! Over here! Come sit with us! I-I can give you some chocolates!"

"Sorry Joey, we have detention!" I yell out, and that gets him to sit down and sulk. He holds his face in his hands while Poppet, sitting beside him, reaches over and pats him on the back.

Keaton sighs. "Thank you."

"Don't worry, I gotcha." We walk back to the library carrying our trays. "So, like, nothing happened between you two, right? Like, Joey isn't a bad person, right?" I ask.

"Oh no, not at all. Nothing happened," Keaton explains. "It's just like I said before: he's clingy and insecure. I try to make some distance, and he calls me crying. He acts as if his entire self-worth revolves around me, and it's exhausting."

"Yeah … I can definitely see that. You're the only one that gave him a chance."

"It's not my job to fix him, but he won't take a hint and move on, so I just don't know what to do. I break up with him, and his self-esteem gets worse. I ignore him, and his self-esteem gets worse. I try to be his girlfriend; I turn into his mom."

"Oh yeah, we were talking about his mommy issues the other day. He was brushing it off like he doesn't really care."

"He cares. He cares a lot, actually. He needs some therapy before he's ready for a relationship."

"Have you told him that?"

"*I only want to talk to you,*" she imitates in her best needy Joey voice.

I know I have a crush on Joey, but even I cringe at that. She captures his essence perfectly.

After School

I wait in the foyer for Atlus to return from the field so we can go home.

"Fiora," a husky voice calls out after the final bell. It's McCarthy.

"Please, whatever student council needs, can't it wait until tomorrow?" I ask.

"Actually, I'm here of my own accord."

I raise my brow. "For real?"

"A lot has happened since school started so I have not had the opportunity to ask how you are accustoming to Seal Coast."

"Well, I've been here long enough for people to stop asking my name trying to kill me, so that's dope, I guess. But then there's the whole *two people are now dead*, thing which kinda sucks."

Some of her red hair spills in front of her face and she brushes it behind her ear. She wears heavy winged eyeliner while her lashes are so long she doesn't need any false ones. "On behalf of the student body, I apologize profusely." She clears her throat. "It has come to my attention that I failed to inform you that in order to foster a position on the student council, one must maintain a 3.0 grade point average. Yours however, is significantly lacking."

"This is still sounding an awful lot like student council stuff."

"On the contrary, I was wondering if you would accompany me in the library for a study session."

"I like the idea of *with you*, just not so much the *studying* part."

McCarthy blushes, her cheeks igniting almost as red as her hair. Her bangs fall in front of her face again and are promptly returned behind her ear.

Atlus struts out from the freshman hall. "I'm hungry. I wanna go home," he whines and keeps walking.

"Forget the library, why don't you just come over?" I suggest to McCarthy and point my thumb like a hitchhiker towards

Atlus's back. "As you can see, I have a cranky little goblin to bring home."

She closes her heavily lashed eyes. "I apologize but I must decline. An unexpected extracurricular extrusion would interfere with my tight bus schedule."

"*An unexpected extracurricular extrusion*? Shut the fuck up. I have my own car so I can bring you home later."

McCarthy picks up her head, and her eyes widen. "You have your own car?"

"What's so surprising about that?"

"No, nothing. Nothing at all. Yes, I would love to accompany you. Thank you for the invitation."

I roll my eyes and she's good at pretending she doesn't notice.

It's easier leaving school than getting in these days. Cars line at the curb, and a few kids are still waiting to be picked up. We pass them and reach the bike racks, where we bump into Joey.

"Hey Broey, want a ride home?" I offer.

He looks up from the bike lock. "Oh, sorry. I have to work today."

"So? I can drop you off there."

"I don't want to be a–" he stops himself and replaces his stupid words with a smile. "You sure? You'd really be a life saver. I've been late a lot lately taking this stupid bike."

"How many times do I have to tell you that I'll give you a ride?"

Joey winks and smirks. "What would I ever do without you?" He finishes unlocking his bike and rolls it over to join us. "Oh, hey McCarthy."

"Good afternoon, Joey."

"I feel like I never see you after school."

"Yes, I am usually on the bus by now, but Fiora has invited me over for the pleasantries of an afternoon study session."

Joey jolts his head. "Huh? Fiora? Study? I must've hit my head too hard or something."

I stick out my tongue at him. "Shut up."

He winks. "Make me."

My knees buckle and my legs turn to jelly, but I quickly catch it and keep walking. Usually I'm up for the challenge of a pissing contest, but this time the words are sucked from my lungs. Is it just me, or has Joey been getting a lot ... riskier?

We arrive where my car waits in the student parking lot and Atlus is waiting by the passenger side door. I hold the keys but don't unlock the car just yet. "Nuh uh, get in the back loser. I have friends," I say.

"No you don't," he says despite my coterie.

"It's no bother," McCarthy insists and sits in the back while Joey packs his bike into the hatchback.

It's only a few minutes' drive to our first stop: Nickels and Dimes. Joey gets out and pokes his head into the cab. "Hey Fi, can you come in with me for a sec while I clock in?"

"Oh, yeah. Of course," I say, leaving the engine on for Atlus and McCarthy while I follow Joey into the store. First, he pulls out his glasses from his pocket and then puts on his work apron from behind the counter. He reaches his hands behind his back to tie the knot. "So, what's up Broey?" I ask.

He fumbles with the register for a moment before finally speaking. "So, you've been getting close to Keaton, right?"

I want to roll my eyes but keep my face still. I'm already getting sick of everyone's shit today, between McCarthy being a robot and Joey being ... Joey. Flirting with me one minute, then engrossed with Keaton the next. "Not really. We just have detention together," I say.

"But she talks about me, right? What does she say?"

I let out a long breath, releasing some frustration. "Not anything you don't already know."

"You said before that she liked Griffin, but now ..."

"What, you think now that her crush is dead she'll come crawling back to her second choice?"

He pauses. "Not ... not so bluntly, but kinda ... maybe."

I slam my hands down on the counter and stare him dead in the eyes behind those orange-rimmed glasses. "Joey, this is going to hurt your feelings, but I'm telling you this 'cause I love you. Griffin dead or alive, she doesn't want you. She thinks you're needy and clingy and obsessing over her constantly is just proving her point. She doesn't even have detention. She volunteers at the library every day just to get away from you."

He's silent as he opens the cash register and shuffles the bills as he counts before putting them back and retrieving another stack. "Thanks Fiora," he eventually croaks out. Tears glisten behind his lens.

"Oh come on, Joey! I'm not trying to always upset you, but you have to move on. People break up. Most people break up!"

He sniffles and lifts his glasses to his forehead to wipe his eyes. "No, you're right. I-I'll... break up with her when she comes into work today." No matter how much he wipes his eyes, too many tears flood the gate. He buries his face into his elbow crease. "It's all my fault she never got to be happy with Griffin. I keep fucking things up for everybody!"

"Joey, come on!" I walk around to his side of the counter, and the taller man towers over me. I wrap my arms around his body and my head rests against his chest.

"H-Hey, what are you doing?"

"I'm trying to support you, dork."

Initially reluctant. he stands there straight and stiff, but eventually, he hugs me back and rests his head on my shoulder. He lets me hold him.

After a moment, he pulls away and wipes his eyes. "I think I'm all cried out for the rest of the year." He chuckles a little. "I need to finish counting the drawer before any customers come in."

I return to the other side of the counter and reach over to place my hand atop his, reminiscent of the night he taught me to play guitar. His hand is larger than mine, and veins push against his skin. "Be strong. You can do this," I tell him.

He pauses before nodding his head. "Yeah, thanks Fi. That's all I wanted to ask. You can go have fun with your brother and McCarthy now."

I huff. "Trust me, it's not going to be fun."

I leave Joey in the store, not quite sure how I feel. He's finally going to break up with Keaton, something I've wanted since I first learned about them and something she's wanted for much longer. But seeing Joey so upset makes my chest feel heavy, like when he held me close to his heart he transferred some of his hurt into me. I'm tired of always upsetting him and never want to see him cry again.

My car is where I left it, with Atlus and McCarthy still inside. If someone wanted to steal my car and kidnap him, I don't think I'd complain. "About time. I want to go home," Atlus bitches.

"Quit your bitching." I put the car in drive and we finally head home.

"You have a beautiful home. I admire all the plants," McCarthy says as we step inside.

"My mom works at Bedrock so she's always bringing home something," I explain.

"She must be an exquisite caregiver. Look how they all flourish."

"No."

"Only to plants," Atlus comments and squirms into the kitchen. He retrieves some raw chicken tenders from the fridge that have been marinating in buttermilk while Trash sits at his feet, eyes following his every move. That spoiled mutt knows Atlus always gives him scraps.

McCarthy and I place our bags on the island and she pulls out the textbooks. "Your grades are relatively average with social studies being your worst subject, so I thought we should start there," she explains.

"What were you doing going through my grades?" I confront.

"I did not look at them of my own accord. The issue was brought up to me by Principal Pal," McCarthy explains.

"Oh fuck me. Can that guy get off my ass?"

She smirks. "Make him by proving him wrong and excelling

in all your classes. I have learned from experience that the one and only Fiora Clairwater is capable of much when she dedicates the effort."

Atlus chortles while battering his chicken tenders. I grab an eraser off the table and throw it at the back of his head. It bounces off his rock-hard skull and falls to the floor. Squeak quickly runs up and starts batting it back and forth between her paws.

McCarthy smiles wider as she opens up her social studies textbook. It's different from mine since she's in all honors classes while my grades are hanging on by a thread. "Let's start with the chapter on civics and American government," she says.

Atlus approaches the table and slides us a plate of some of the chicken tenders he made in the air fryer. "Thanks dork," I say, and grab one.

McCarthy sniffs. "These smell divine."

"Then have one."

She scans the table. "Are there any utensils?"

"No dude, just pick them up with your fingers."

"But aren't they messy?" She pinches one of the tenders, some of the sticky sauce coating her fingers, and studies it before biting. She covers her mouth with her hand as she chews. "This is delicious. What is this heat I'm tasting?"

Atlus squints. "It's honey sriracha."

"You've never had honey sriracha before?" I ask.

"Unfortunately my palate is limited," she explains, still covering her mouth like a dainty princess.

"Who are you?" Atlus asks.

"I'm McCarthy, the student council president," she answers seriously.

Obviously, Atlus knows who she is. A better question is, *What's wrong with you?*

Evening

McCarthy closes the last of her textbooks and looks at me with her arms crossed, an expression I'm used to seeing. "Fiora, you seem to be already well versed in all of your subjects. So, why are your grades not a reflection of this?"

"Oh, Ms. Hoyos is my teacher and I don't like her," I explain.

McCarthy raises a brow. "You're purposely failing a class because you dislike the teacher? Who does that depriment other than yourself?"

"It's just high school, McCarthy. It doesn't mean anything."

She takes another look around the house and releases a long sigh. "Yes, I can see how you would have developed that sentiment."

The screen from my phone lights up when a video call from Joey comes in. I answer, and he's on my screen in his glasses and red work apron. "Hey Broey. So, did you do it yet?" I ask.

He scratches his head. "Not exactly. Can you actually do a favor for me real quick?"

"Yeah, what's up?"

"Can you call Keaton for me? She hasn't shown up for her shift yet and I can't leave until she does. I'd do it myself, but you know … I'm kinda blocked."

"Yeah, no problem."

"Thanks."

"So does that mean you're getting off soon?" I ask.

"I was supposed to get off like, 30 minutes ago," he answers.

"What us to come pick you up? We can go get Philly cheesesteaks and smoothies at the mall."

His lips barely move in an attempt to smile. "That actually sounds really good right now, I'm starving. I also need to kinda eat my feelings away. Just standing around here bored is making me think way too much about things I shouldn't."

"Great, it's a date then."

That causes a cheeky smirk on his face before looking away from the camera. "I never said that. I gotta go, there's customers."

"Remember to break up with Keaton when you see her!"

"Yeah, yeah, yeah." He hangs up.

McCarthy's gaze is on me. "We're going to the mall?"

"Yeah, we need dinner right? Or did you fill up on too many chicken tenders?"

She closes her eyes and looks down. "I apologize profusely. I have never tasted anything like that before. It is only fair that I owe you dinner, but unfortunately, I did not bring any money."

"So? Joey probably doesn't have money either. I'll pay." I dial Keaton's number and listen to the phone thrill for a moment. There's no answer before the beep to leave a message. "Hey Keaton, it's Fiora. Just reminding you that you have work, like, right now. Oh, and I talked to Joey. You're gonna be a free woman, so congrats. See ya." I hang up and then turn to McCarthy. "We should invite O'Brien."

"O'Brien?" she inquires.

"Yeah, he's my friend."

"Yes, that is an exquisite idea. As treasurer, we can discuss the budget for our seasonal fall event. We surely are at a disadvantage due to June's resignation."

"No! No student council shit! We're all going to the mall to eat, hangout, have fun, and convince the boys to win us something at the arcade."

She hums. "Why would we want or need the boys to win us something? I believe I am more than capable of acquiring something so pedestrian if I so pleased. However, I fail to see the need."

I can only stare at her and blink as I dial to video call O'Brien. When he answers, he's in a room surrounded by white. "They finally lock you in the loony bin?" I tease.

"Close enough," he says, his voice as smooth as butter. "I'm in the waiting room of the cancer ward."

"Oh shit, I'm sorry. How's Peanut doing?"

"She's doing well so far, but the hard part hasn't even started yet."

"I was gonna ask if you wanna go to the mall with me,

McCarthy, and Joey. You know, for our deal."

He sighs. "Normally I would, but I should really be there right now."

I pound on my chest. "Godspeed, soldier." He smiles and shakes his head before hanging up.

McCarthy is staring at me with those large, dark, winged eyes and her arms crossed. "What are you scheming?"

"Me? Scheming? No way."

"You, as the event planner, have a deal with our treasurer?"

"Believe it or not, I actually don't care that much about the student council. It's just something stupid we're doing."

"I'm skeptical, but I have no reason to disbelieve you at the moment."

"Hell yeah, then come on. Let's go pick up Joey."

When we pull up to Nickels and Dimes, the usually empty parking lot is filled with flashing lights and uniforms. The front of the store is blocked off with yellow caution tape. I race out of the car. "What's going on?"

The same officer that was holding people back at Seal Coast after Griffin was murdered blocks the area. "Please stand back, this is an active investigation."

"Another one?"

One of the cops holds open the door to Nickels and Dimes, and out comes another officer, escorting Joey, who has his hands cuffed behind his back.

"Joey!" I scream. His eyes, glistening with tears, glance at mine as he's led to one of the flashing cars and thrown in the back. "Joey!"

McCarthy rushes to my side. "What is the meaning of this?"

"I don't know! Joey did nothing wrong!" Through the window, he sits unmoving, his head low. "Joey! Joey!"

The car drives off with Joey inside.

Both of McCarthy's hands are on my shoulders. "You need to collect yourself, Fiora." Her nails dig into my skin as she holds me back.

"No, we have to save Joey!" I plead.

"And how do you propose we do that?"

"We follow them! Do you know what the pigs like to do to little twinks like Joey?"

"That is merely a speculation. We lack any knowledge of what has transpired in these few minutes since you last spoke to him."

"We know enough, so are you coming or not?"

She closes her eyes and releases a sigh. "Not. You may drop me off at the bus station. I will be able to guide myself home from there."

It's a silent drive as we head to the bus station. McCarthy doesn't comment on how much I'm speeding, and when it's time to drop her off, I can see the disappointment in her eyes as she closes the door. The amount of restraint she shows to not slam it is admirable.

Night

Inside the police station is a small waiting room with a wall lined with metal chairs. A woman sits inside a fishbowl of bulletproof glass, very much like the administration office at Seal Coast. My heart is racing, and I'm huffing and puffing when I reach the counter. "I need to visit someone!" I cry.

The woman behind the glass rolls her eyes. "Name?"

"I don't know his real name, but he was just been brought here. Um, he's tall and has reddish brown hair. Last name should be O'Reilly."

"If he was just brought here then he would still be at intake, which can take several hours."

"Several hours?"

"If you wish to visit, you'll need to wait until after he is processed and come back with a name."

I wanna smack something, but I know better when I'm in a building surrounded by the enemy. I go to one of the chairs in the corner and pull out my phone. Someone else must have died, right? And now Joey is being blamed, right? First things first, I pull up Blackridge Online. The last article was posted two hours ago about a new county librarian being hired. Whatever is going on must be recent. Next, I check Instagram and everyone is posting their standard content. O'Brien posted a picture of himself with his sister, congratulating her on being such a fighter. Pandora posted a recording of a new rift she wrote, and Poppet shared a video of her pet rabbits hopping in a backyard. Even Joey has a story from a few hours ago and it's him panning the camera around an empty Nickels and Dimes, complaining about wanting to go home.

Joey is in jail and someone could be dead, yet no one else knows.

The door leading behind the bulletproof glass opens and a cop comes out. I jump to my feet. "I need to see Joey!"

"A curfew is now in effect. If you wish to see your friend, you'll have to come back in the morning."

"Another curfew? So someone did die! What happened?"

"Nothing can be released until after the initial investigation. For now I'm going to have to ask you to leave."

I roll my eyes. "We both know you're not asking." His hand is down by his belt, ready to grab any of the multitude of weapons.

I leave the station but don't go farther than that, sitting my ass down across the street on the cold public sidewalk and continuing the cycle of switching between apps and refreshing. Still, nothing.

A different cop comes out from the station and crosses the street. "Ma'am, you need to leave."

"It's public property."

"There's an active curfew. You're not allowed to be anywhere other than home."

"I'm homeless, actually."

"You can't be outside. You need to go to a shelter."

"There are no shelters in Blackridge. All the funding seems to have been directed somewhere else." For a town full of rundown businesses and rampant poverty, it sure has an extensive and fancy police station.

He pulls the handcuffs from his belt. "Stand up and put your hands behind your back."

I roll my eyes. I'm going to be the most immense pain in the ass and waste of taxpayer money, second to the police budget itself, that Blackridge has ever seen. I put my hands behind my back and the cuffs are squeezed tightly around my wrists. Even though he didn't say it, I have the right to remain silent, and I plan on using it for once. Whatever it takes to get back into that building and discover what's happening to Joey.

I'm back in the waiting room, but not for long as I'm escorted through the heavy metal door. There's another woman behind the counter. "Name."

"Lawyer," I say.

The cop behind me puts his hands all over my body, patting me down. He pulls my wallet from my back pocket before tossing it onto the counter, along with my phone, car keys, and a tube of Chapstick. "I'm going to need you to take that thing out of your face and any other piercings you have," he orders.

I remove my nose piercing and put it on the counter with the rest of my stuff, but I won't remove my belly button piercing unless it gets caught.

The woman behind the counter puts my nose ring, Chapstick, and phone in a plastic bag, but before putting in the wallet, she opens it up and loots through the contents. She pulls out coins, my cards, and my driver's license. She looks it over front and back. "Leila Drake."

Oh fuck.

She retrieves another driver's license. "Fiora Clairwater." She looks at me with a brow raised and a scowl. "So, which one are you?"

"Lawyer," I repeat.

"Fiora Clairwater," she says upon typing on the computer. Something prints out and she places the paper in front of me. "Sign here stating these are your belongings."

After signing, the cop latches onto the chain around my wrists before leading me like a dog. There are several metal doors down the hall not far from the reception desk and I'm led to the one in the middle. The cop finally removes the cuffs from my wrists and the blood rushes back to my fingers. I'm finally free and when the cop leaves, the heavy metal door slams shut.

The room is made entirely of concrete with nothing in it except for rows of metal benches welded to the walls and bright fluorescent lights hanging from the ceiling. The air is chill and suffocating. There are a handful of other women here, most of them much older and several of their faces are covered in scabs. But there's another girl around my age, and seeing her makes my jaw drop. She stands out like a sore thumb with thick blonde hair long enough to reach her navel and an everlasting blank expression on her face. "Cheese?" I cry.

She lazily holds up her hand as she sits on one of the metal benches. "Hi Fiora."

I sit beside her and the metal is cold on my ass. "What the hell are you doing here?"

"I got into a fight with my stepdad's girlfriend."

"Wow, you actually felt enough emotion to get into a fight?"

"She was in my face and kept telling me to hit her, so I hit her." I laugh and get a few bombastic side eyes from the older women in the clink. "What about you?"

My short burst of happiness comes crashing down. I hunch over and rest my arms on my knees. "The pigs arrested Joey and I wanted to see if he's here."

She cocks her head, her long and heavy hair falling to one side. "What did he do?"

"Nothing. Joey wouldn't do a damn thing."

"Wouldn't or didn't?"

"Both!"

"Did someone die?"

I pause. If even Cheese can catch on this fast, then there's no doubt that's what happened. "Probably."

"Was it Keaton?"

"Yeah, probably. Joey said she didn't show up for work and asked me to call her for him. She didn't answer."

"Makes sense."

I shoot her a look. "Makes sense?"

"Girl gets murdered, boyfriend is the suspect."

"Okay yeah, but this is Joey we're talking about. He was going to break up with her today."

She tilts her head, her lengthy hair falling. "By killing her?"

"No!" I squeal, causing me to get more nasty looks from the other women.

"Didn't Griffin get murdered the night you told Joey that Keaton had a crush on him?"

"Okay yeah, but that was totally a coincidence."

"There seem to be a lot of coincidences surrounding Joey."

"Well that's all they are."

"Okay."

"They are!"

"I said okay." Even still the monotone in her voice does not change.

There's no point in trying to convince Cheese. She doesn't care. But whatever happened, there's no way I can let Joey go down for it. Especially if another person was murdered.

OCTOBER 25 – WEDNESDAY

???

There's nothing to do but sit on these hard benches. I have no phone, and there's no clock to know how much time has passed during every soul-crushing second. It has to have been at least a few hours by now, but for all I know, it could only be a few minutes. I sigh loudly and look back at Cheese. "How long have you been here?"

"I don't know," she says.

"What time did you get arrested?"

She cocks her head as she hums. "Probably like at four."

"Four?" I yell out, further annoying the other women locked in here with us. "It was around eight when I was brought in. Who the hell knows how long it's been since then!"

"Really? It's been that long already?"

"*Already*?"

One of the scabbed-faced women leans forward on her bench. "I was here over twelve hours the last time I was here. It was worse than labor. At least in labor, you get an epidural."

I slump back on the bench, the hardness of the metal slapping against my back. Time stands still locked in a cell. It could still be the evening, the middle of the night, or morning by now, and I'd never know.

After who knows how many hours, that heavy metal door opens, and a cop is at the entrance holding it open with his shoe. "Trailey Thompson."

Cheese stands from the bench and takes a look back at me. "See ya, Fiora."

"Wait for me, okay?" I call out. I know it's a lot to ask since I could be here for many more hours, but Cheese seems to always do what she's told, even if it's in her own Cheese way. She nods before leaving with the officer, and the metal door slams shut.

The last thing I want right now is to be locked in a quiet room with my thoughts. Who died, and what does it have to do with Joey? It probably was Keaton, but why? Well, the same thing could be asked for everyone who has died. Lemming's suicide is getting more suspicious by the day, and I can't imagine anyone wanting Griffin dead. If it is the curse, does that mean Keaton's name got leaked somewhere? I still don't want to believe something so ridiculous could be possible. But as long as I'm locked in here, I can do nothing about it.

Every time that heavy metal door opens I shoot my head up, but they call a different name and eventually I'm the only one left. The metal door opens again and there's no doubt it's my turn. "*Feeora*–" the cop pronounces my name wrong. It's *Fiora*. Like Fire. I join the cop, and the metal door shuts behind us, leaving no one in the locked room.

Instead of returning to the front desk, I'm brought around to the back toward another station. "Hand," he orders. There's a scanner on the counter and I put my finger on it. It lights up green, and after a moment, the cop rolls my finger around. "Other hand." The process repeats.

A few more feet down, they place me in front of a camera and take my mugshot. It's one thing after another until I'm looped back around to that main receptionist counter. This time, it's a man behind the counter, so I've been here long enough for at least one shift change. "Name," he says.

"Fiora Clairwater."

He doesn't say a word as he types into the computer, and shortly after, something is printed out. He places it atop the counter. "You are charged with disorderly conduct in the second degree, ORS 166.025, resisting arrest, ORS 162.315, and unlawful possession of fictitious identification, ORS 165.813, which is a class C felony." He has a pen in his hand and presses the button on the butt before placing it on the piece of paper. "This is a release form stating your agreement to appear at your court date. Failure to appear will cause an immediate warrant out for your arrest. Sign here."

I'm not going to ask any questions or say anything smart. I sign the paper as fast as I can and hand it back. The receptionist accepts the paper and places it into a file. In the file is the same baggie of my stuff that was taken. That's the next thing he places on the counter and hands me another form. "These should be all of your belongings. Make sure everything is there then sign here," he says. I sign the paper and slide it back to him. That paper is placed in the same file. "You are good to go. You'll receive a letter with your court date to the address on your license–your real one."

Oh fuck you. That's what I want to say. But I also want out of here so bad I keep my lips sealed.

Morning

It's a fresh new morning stepping out of the police station, meaning I must have been in there for at least twelve hours. The sunrise is barely showing through a sheet of clouds, and thicker than that is the fog. "No bail for a felony? Fuck yeah!" I cheer once I've confirmed my freedom.

Cheese kept her word and is sitting on the station's steps. She looks up at me. "Oregon doesn't have a cash bail system anymore. As long as you're not dangerous or a flight risk, you get to go home."

"Fucking based."

"Why do you care? You're rich."

"Like I want to give these pigs my money."

"Fair."

I sit beside her and the pavement covered in dew. "Hey, since you've known Joey a long time you don't happen to know his real name, do you?"

"I do."

"Go ask if we can see him."

Cheese shrugs and gets up from the steps before entering the station. It doesn't take long for her to return. "He's still in questioning." She sits back down.

"Questioning? It's been hours."

"They'll either charge him with something or let him leave."

"But there's nothing they could possibly charge him with so he should be out any minute then." I retrieve my phone from the bag containing my personal items.

Cheese stares at me with those green vacant eyes of hers. "What are you doing this time?"

My phone is off, so I wait for it to boot up. "I want to find out what happened."

It takes about a minute before the phone turns on and opens the latest article from Blackridge Online:

Blackridge Murders Continue: Teenage Girl Slain!

BLACKRIDGE, Or. –Tuesday evening, just before 6 o'clock, the body of Milena Freeman, 17, was discovered by a coworker behind the Nickels and Dimes convenience store off Highway 62. A cause of death has yet to be released, though police describe an injury that appeared consistent with a gunshot wound to the head.

A male suspect with a past romantic relationship with the victim has been brought in for questioning. This is the third murder this year in the small town of Blackridge, with football star Zachary Moore, 18, murdered two weeks prior after a high school football game and dance instructor Kian Kennedy, 21, murdered during the shooting at the Blackridge Mall back in September just before Labor Day weekend. The case is still developing.

Cheese has her head on my shoulder, the morning breeze enhancing the scent of her strawberry shampoo. "The coworker and male suspect is obviously Joey," she says.

"That sure as shit isn't what I saw," I growl. "They were already treating him like a criminal. Had him cuffed with his hands behind his back and everything."

"So what, are you going to sit here and wait for him?"

I sigh before standing up and tucking my phone in my back pocket. "No, who knows how long it'll be. Even if they don't charge him, they can still hold him for up to 72 hours. It would just be a repeat of last night if I stay here. Do you need a ride?" I ask.

"No, I'll ask my stepdad to pick me up," Cheese says.

"After you spent a night in jail for fighting his girlfriend?"

"He hates her too."

I'd laugh if I were in a better mood. Another one of my friends is dead, and it's after we started getting to understand one another. I wait until Cheese's stepdad picks her up before leaving myself. At least this way, I'll know one of my friends is safe–for now. Not even two months since moving to Blackridge, and three people I know are dead.

* * *

Mom is in the living room when I get through the door while Atlus, the little snake, is upstairs watching from the balcony. He holds onto the wooden bars and presses his face against the gap like a prisoner, ironic enough. Mom meets me at the door with her arms crossed and hip extended. "Fiora, what the hell? You were out all night and didn't even call? I was worried sick! I called the police to file a missing person report and they said you were already in their custody!"

"Okay, but I have a really good reason," I attempt to reason with her.

"You keep saying that. You promised this year would be different, but you keep doing the same stupid things. Ditching, getting suspended, now even getting arrested. When does it start being different? The one thing I ask of you is that you graduate high school but it's seeming like I can't even keep you out of prison!"

"It is different! You keep agreeing that I have good reasons."

Mom isn't budging. "Then what's your excuse this time?"

"Another kid from our school was murdered."

That makes her uncross her arms. I can still feel how tense

she is, yet there's something different about the air around her. She stands there, almost like the words–and even anger–have been pulled from her body.

Atlus breaks the awkward silence by asking, "Do you know who it was?"

I look up to him on the balcony. "It was Keaton, your friend Kellan's sister. The online newspaper just posted about it."

His brows furrow and that shit-eating grin on his face drops to a frown. "Keaton's dead?"

"Yeah. She was murdered last night."

Mom releases a deep breath. She directs her eyes toward the ceiling to hold back tears. "Fiora, that could have been you," she croaks out, sorrow replacing anger. "What did I tell you about choosing your battles?"

"I did choose this battle," I declare. "The pigs are trying to frame my friend. I tried to visit him in jail, and they arrested me instead."

That's when Mom shoots me a look, her eyes gone dry. "Were you giving them an attitude?"

I pinch my fingers close together. "Maybe just a little bit."

"Fiora! You can't do that. They could have killed you."

"Was it Joey?" Atlus's voice asks from above.

I look up at him. "He didn't do it."

"How do you know? You've known this guy for like a month. Don't tell me you're already whipped, you pick me."

"He didn't do it."

Mom pulls me close, wrapping her arms around me. "I'm just glad you're okay." She lets go but keeps her hands on my shoulders as she stares into my eyes. "What did you end up getting charged with?"

"Nothing I can't get dismissed," I promise.

Mom takes a step back and sighs. "Maybe we should look into homeschooling."

"What? No!" Atlus cries. "You can't! I'm on a team!"

"And I have friends!" I whine.

Mom shakes her head. "It's obviously not safe there. I can't believe I actually thought that after all these years, things would change."

"Nowhere is safe! That doesn't mean you get to deprive us of our childhoods."

Atlus scoffs. "Childhoods? You're practically a hundred."

"Will you shut up? I'm trying to help your case too! Plus, yeah. I'm 18. I get to choose where I go to school," I argue.

Mom slaps her palms against her legs. "I don't want to have to be worried sick about you two all day."

"During the day we're at school then there's a curfew. We'll do the buddy system if we have to."

"But you keep not going to school."

"Okay, but I will. No more ditching," I promise.

"And no more getting suspended," Mom bargains.

"No more getting suspended."

"And no more getting arrested."

I hold up my hand to swear. "No more getting arrested."

Mom gives me one last suffocating hug. "I'm just so glad you're okay. I have no idea what I would do without you or your brother. Last night I was so worried sick about you I could have thrown up."

"I'm sorry Mom. I'm gonna go take a shower."

She lets go and wipes away the few tears that escape from the dam. "Right, right. Go, take a shower. Don't worry about school today and go get some sleep. I know how uncomfortable that county jail is." She ends her sentence with a snort and shake of her head. "Boy do I. Then I wonder why you're always getting into so much trouble. You're just like your mother."

People always tell us how much we look alike, but I never considered us acting alike. I skip up the stairs and shove Atlus on his forehead as I pass by. I shut the bathroom door behind me and turn the switch to lock it.

"Can I skip school too?" Atlus's voice asks.

"No. Get ready. I'll drop you off today," Mom's voice says.

"That's so not fair. She gets to stay home and she got arrested! She should be punished, not rewarded."

"You are more than welcome to catch up with the Navarro clan criminal record. Until then, get your butt up and go to school."

The shower faucet switches on, and hot water has never felt so good. The steam fills the bathroom and fogs up the mirror. It's the one thing that's able to calm my nerves. After getting dressed, I throw myself to my bed and give Squeak some much-needed back scratches. She stays by my side while I do more digging on my phone.

Joey has been getting information about the case from Falco, so I find him on Instagram. His username? DaBigWillyzz. The last picture posted is that of himself and Griffin sitting together on some bleachers, holding bottles of light blue-tinted Gatorade. Rest in power, my brother. May you rest in peace after you get the justice you deserve, the caption reads. I wipe away a stray tear that falls from my eye. When Joey suggested Griffin might have been murdered by someone jealous on the football team, Falco was the first one to pop into my mind. But now … I know how hard it is to have a friend die and I didn't know Griffin nearly as long, nor were we teammates. I send him a message request.

My eyes are heavy as I lay here staring. I find myself dozing off to sleep before shooting awake. I need to keep myself occupied in the meantime. I go to Keaton's Instagram page where the last thing she posted was a picture of some vegan fish and chips. You can't even tell the difference! she captioned the post. Yes, yes you can. But none of the comments care about that. They're all people from school telling her how much they love her, as if she'll ever see it. It's strange scrolling through the pages of people who have died. They lived life normally like everyone else. There's a selfie of Keaton smiling. She was so beautiful and had big dreams for herself. This girl right here had no idea that all of those were going to be taken away from her. And the same with Griffin.

I have to wipe my eyes again. What am I doing? How is this helping? I return to Falco's Instagram page and not only has he

not replied, but now it says he has no posts.
The fucker blocked me!

OCTOBER 26 – THURSDAY

Morning

My body is floating and the black engulfs me, like the fog that blankets Blackridge. It's suffocating and endless. But through the fog, just on the tip of my tongue, are three figures standing, waiting. The one standing in the middle is significantly taller than the two at his side. Their faces are masked through the murky cloud of gray, yet I know who they are simply from their silhouettes: Lemming, Griffin, and Keaton.

Keaton's wavy hair gently blows as she takes a step forward, holding out her hand, but the darkness holds me back like a rope tied to a train track. Here comes the rumbling of the train and the sound blaring in my ears.

The next thing I know, my alarm is going off for school. "Fuck me," I groan and press the snooze button. Pulling that all-nighter in jail kicked my ass, and I ended up sleeping all day and night. When I check my phone, there's nothing from or about Joey.

Mom and Atlus are in the kitchen as usual. I jump down the last few steps down the stairs. "Come on, we gotta go," I bark.

Atlus's jaw moves back and forth as he chews. "I'm not done with my muffin."

"Then just bring it. Come on!"

Mom leans over and checks the time on the stove. "Geez Fiora, it's still early. You don't have to leave just yet."

"Well you know how serious I am about my education." I say.

She doesn't laugh and only gives me a skeptical look.

Atlus brings a container of blueberry muffins into the car. He finishes another muffin and then looks at me with crumbs still on his lips. "So did they make you cough and bend over?"

"I'll plant drugs in your locker so you can find out."

Upon arriving at Seal Coast and passing through the tightened security, I wait in the foyer as more and more students arrive, none of them being Joey. The first bell will ring soon so at this point I have no choice but to go to my locker. Poppet is already at the lockers when I get here. "Princess Fiora. I was worried you got suspended again," she says.

I play with the dial on my locker. "Close. I was arrested."

She releases a high-pitched breath. "What? You too?"

"Me too?"

"Well I guess you wouldn't know if you've been in jail. Keaton was murdered and Joey was arrested for it!"

"Oh, yeah. I know that much," say. "I was kinda there when he got arrested then I got arrested when I wouldn't leave the police station until I saw him."

Poppet closes her locker and leans against the metal. "So what happened? How did he do it?"

"He didn't do it."

The warning bell rings so I grab what I need and close my locker. "We need to gather everyone later so we can talk about it."

Poppet salutes as we start walking since our first periods are down the same hall. "Got it. We can rendezvous at lunch."

"No lunch. I still have detention. I'll send a message in the group chat for everyone to meet at the music room after school."

Poppet wiggles her finger. "Oh, music room is a no-go. McCarthy said we can only use it for–" she sticks out her chest and changes her voice, *"authorized official student council obligations."*

Poppet does a good impression, I have to admit.

"Why is this the first I'm hearing of it? I'm literally in the student council," I say.

"Well, probably 'cause you're always in detention, or suspended, or in jail."

"Just, like, the past month."

"You've only been here, like, a month."

First Period

The Calendar Girls are down one after June's transfer to homeschooling. She may be the first, but with everything going on, I doubt she'll be the last. Even my mom threatened us with homeschooling. May scowls so hard that her face looks like a crumpled sheet of paper. "Ew," she says.

I ignore her. I'm so not in the mood. If something starts with her today, it's going to end with her teeth shattered on the floor.

The bell rings, and class is ready to begin. The TV mounted on the wall turns on, and McCarthy on the screen demonstrates perfect posture. "Good morning, students and staff, I am McCarthy, this year's student council president, and these are your morning announcements." She speaks as clearly and professionally as a news anchor. "A new policy will be implemented at Seal Coast Community High School, starting today. Any form of gossip or spreading of rumors is hereby forbidden. Any students caught will be immediately suspended, and repeat offenders will face expulsion. Lunch today will be a choice of spaghetti with garlic bread or a fresh side salad …"

May groans right on cue. "I don't know what makes me want to gag more: the thought of school spaghetti or having to see that thot every morning."

I have my elbow on the table and rest my chin against my knuckles. "Don't you get tired of bitching about the same thing every goddamn day?"

She turns her head at me like a chicken pecking the ground for bugs. "Don't you? She's so, she's so, she's so–" May tries to continue, but when she lacks the words, she just grunts and snorts.

"So poetic," I comment.

"You shut up. No one asked you. McSlutty already has a stick up her ass from becoming president and now she thinks she's some messiah here to save us or something just 'cause a couple of people died."

That makes me lift my head and fix my posture. "Three. Three people have died."

May flicks her wrist. "Whatever. Keaton was a cunt anyways."

"Look who's throwing stones. Every time you open your mouth all that comes out is leukorrhea."

"This is America and we speak English. Hablas ingles?" This fucking bitch and her microaggressions. "All I'm saying is Keaton got what she asked for," May continues. "You of all people should be glad she's dead. She treated your little incel boy toy like shit. That's why he killed her."

"She didn't ask for it and Joey didn't do it. Nor is he an incel!" I defend. "At least Joey can actually get picked, unlike a certain bitter bitch I know."

April's voice is mouse-like as she attempts to intervene. "Um, maybe we shouldn't be fighting. Mr. Simpson will get us in trouble."

She might as well have said nothing the way her words go in one ear and out the other for both of us.

May stares me down. "I'd rather be a virgin than a man-whore. Make sure you get him tested for AIDS." That word sprays from her mouth like vile.

It's a miracle Mr. Simpson interrupts when he does. If not, all of May's teeth would be shattered on the linoleum. He sits at his desk but uses his big voice to shout across the room. "May! Did you not just hear the morning announcement? That kind of language is absolutely unacceptable. Go see Principal Pal."

May's jaw drops as she scoffs. "Me? Did you not hear her foul mouth?"

I slam my hands against the table and stare her dead in the eyes. "I wasn't gossiping. I said that shit straight to your face."

"Enough!" Mr. Simpson declares. "I'm ending this. Fiora, sit down. May, principal's office. Now."

May throws back her seat, the legs screeching against the linoleum. It's almost as loud and annoying as the screech and growl that comes from her own mouth as she stomps her way out of the room, making a special effort to make sure everyone knows she's mad when she slams the door behind her. A deafening silence fills the class.

Poor April, the witness to our epic battle, sits across from me with her hands in her lap and eyes gazed down.

Second Period

O'Brien was at the hospital when Keaton was murdered and Joey was arrested, so I doubt he knows anything, but I want to hear what he has to say nonetheless. Even if he doesn't know anything, he can at least be a distraction for the next forty-five minutes.

Ms. Hoyos enters the classroom with O'Brien by her side right as the bell to start class rings. She shuts the door behind her while O'Brien goes down the row of desks to his beside mine. "Fiora, can I see you outside for a moment?" Ms. Hoyos forms in a question, but of course, it's an order.

O'Brien leans over from his seat and whispers in my ear. "What did you do this time?"

"What didn't I do?" I say as I rise from my desk.

I follow Ms. Hoyos out of the classroom, who closes the door behind us. Once there's the click of the latch she throws herself onto me, embracing me and squeezing me similarly to Mom. "You don't know how worried I was when your mom told me you never came home the other night. Then when we heard there was another murder, we could have sworn it was you."

Damn. I was too worried about Joey to even think about how much I must have worried everyone else. "It was Keaton," I say.

Ms. Hoyos's eyes are heavy and drained, almost like the life in them is dripping out from an IV. She releases a defeated sigh.

"I know. That's the third student in two months. Four if you count O'Brien. Thank God he survived."

"But there were two people who didn't, right?"

Ms. Hoyos stares through me, blinking occasionally. "Yes. The killer and another victim. Let's get back to class." She places her shaky hand against my back and guides me back into the classroom.

I return to my seat beside O'Brien. As expected, he knows just as much as everyone else about what's going on: nothing but rumors.

Third Period

It's strange sitting at our table with an empty seat where Joey's ass belongs, but Cheese is his neighbor so she would be one of the first to know when he's out of jail, and that's exactly what I ask.

"No," she answers in her typical Cheese fashion, and that ends that.

Lunchtime

Ms. Hoyos is behind the desk in the library, and it's almost like Keaton is waiting at our table. She has a stack of books in front of her, and she's busy at work until she notices me. Then she stops and waves at me, excited to tell me about whatever new K-drama she's watching. But the image disappears just as fast as I hallucinate it, and nothing is there but an empty table and empty seats.

So many people keep disappearing from my daily life. Lemming is no longer in my math period. Griffin is no longer at the lockers. And now Keaton is no longer in detention. I still have so much of this and now it is actually starting to feel like a punishment.

After School

With the band forbidden from using the music room, we meet at the pickup curb outside of the security checkpoint. Poppet, Pandora, Cheese, Farrah, and I stand off to the side and away from the others waiting for their rides. Still, there's no sign of Joey. "Great, everyone is here," I start off.

Farrah looks left, then she looks right. Then she shifts her body around to look behind her. "Where's Joey?"

"That's what I wanted to talk to everyone about."

Pandora snorts. "We're not going to see Joey for a very long time."

"Why not?" Farrah asks.

Pandora raises a pierced brow. "Ah, 'cause he killed a woman?"

I clench my nails into the palms of my hands. "No he didn't!"

Cheese cocks her head. "We didn't see him at all in booking so I bet he's been in questioning this whole time."

Pandora rubs her eyes, bringing some of her lower eyelids down with her hands and exposing the red inside. "What?"

"Cheese and I sorta kinda spent Tuesday night in jail," I explain.

Poppet can't hold back her girlish giggle then saves herself by covering her mouth. She calms herself and clears her throat. "That's right. You mentioned that this morning but you didn't say what you did." Her head turns towards the girl with the thick blonde pigtails. "And you didn't mention that Cheese was there too."

"I punched my stepdad's girlfriend," Cheese explains emotionlessly.

Even the ever-stern Pandora cracks a smile at that. "I'm sorry, did you say your *stepdad's girlfriend*? Are you even in the band? Where the hell do you keep coming from?"

"No, this is just Cheese," I slice through the discussion so we can get back to the topic. "The article said they brought Joey in for questioning. They can only keep him for seventy-two hours unless they charge him with something, so he should be released either today or tomorrow."

"How do we know he hasn't been charged yet?" Pandora challenges.

Farrah gasps. "This is just like my uncle! He's being falsely accused too!"

"Well no, not exactly. They had enough evidence to actually charge your uncle." Sparkling eyes and a quivering lip take over Farrah's face, and Pandora quickly revokes her statement. "But that doesn't mean he did it! That's what court is for. Once all the facts are determined he'll be released, just like Joey." Despite our argument, Pandora turns her head towards me. "Right Fiora?"

"Yeah, definitely. The pigs have no leads so they're just throwing shit to the wall and seeing what sticks."

Poppet strikes gold when she says, "If it turns out Keaton was killed by the same guy then there's no way her uncle could have done it. 'Cause he's been in jail this whole time."

"But only if Keaton was killed by the same gun," Pandora states to the group. "It could be a random shooting like what happened with O'Brien. It's not completely out of the question."

Farrah's lip is still quivering like she's holding something back until it's finally released: "Why do you keep mentioning people being killed by the same gun?"

Cheese cocks her head. "They were all killed by your uncle's gun, weren't they?"

"Yeah, wasn't it Joey who said both Lemming and Griffin were killed by the same gun?" Poppet points out.

"I don't know!!" Farrah cries. "There wasn't a gun when I found Lemming's body!"

Those words fill the courtyard with a deafening silence. We all look back and forth between each other, the next person just as confused as the last. Cheese is the one to break the silence: "How do you shoot yourself without a gun?"

Pandora reaches over to place a hand on Farrah's shoulder. "Are you sure you didn't just miss it from the trauma?"

Farrah looks down to her hands in her lap. She's picking at her nails. "M-Maybe."

Poppet shrugs her shoulders. "Yeah. Like, there's no way her death would have been ruled a suicide without a weapon. Otherwise that's clearly a homicide. I mean, with that video she made it would have been super easy for some crazy fucker to come and bang, bang, bang." She gestures her fingers like guns.

Pandora nods. "Right." She says that, but there's something uncertain in that usually confident demeanor of hers.

Farrah keeps her gaze on her hands, picking at her nails more than ever. "Lemming wouldn't kill herself. I-It was the curse."

Nobody says a thing and the air around us is thick as lead.

It's my phone ringing that breaks the silence this time and it's a call from Atlus who must be done with soccer practice by now. "I gotta go get my little brother. I'll update everyone with what's going on with Joey, not that anyone cares," I say.

Poppet scoffs. "I care!"

Pandora looks directly into my eyes. "If Joey is innocent then he has nothing but my sympathy. If he did it, I hope he gets everything he deserves."

I'm as immovable as stone. "Joey didn't do it."

OCTOBER 27 – FRIDAY

CHARGES DROPPED FOR MAN ACCUSED IN KILLING OF HIGH SCHOOL FOOTBALL STAR ZACHARY MOORE

The Blackridge County District Attorney's Office has dropped charges against a man accused of the murder of high school football Zachary Moore, 18.

Gregory McGuire, 41, was arrested just shy of a week after the murder of Zachary Moore and was charged with murder in the first degree. Authorities now say additional evidence and information received by investigators do not support the charges.

Officers were called to Seal Coast Community High School the morning of October 10th after the body of Moore was discovered in the boy's locker room by a fellow student and teammate. The body appeared to have been there for several nights and suffered wounds consistent with that of a gunshot to the head.

After School

Wednesday 8:31 AM
FIORA: Joey, please text me back when you get this
Thursday 1:13 AM
FIORA: Whatever happened, please let me know. I'll believe whatever you tell me
3:28 PM
JOEY: I'm ok
JOEY: We can talk later I have to get ready for work
3:29PM
FIORA: Your girlfriend was murdered and you just got out of jail and you're already going back to work??
JOEY: Were understaffed
JOEY: I need to keep myself busy
JOEY: Or I'll fucking lose it
FIORA: Can I at least give you a ride?
JOEY: Yeah thnx
JOEY: Someone stole my bike while i was in jail

FIORA: I'll be there asap

Joey is sitting on the front porch with Cheese when I arrive at the trailer park. He pulls his hood over his head and steps into the rain before hopping into the passenger seat of my car. Small beads of water drip from his bangs when he pulls down his hood. "Thanks," he says and rests his head against the window.

"You're welcome," I say.

For days, I've wanted nothing more than this moment, to see him again and know he's okay, but now I don't know what to say or if he even wants me to say anything. It seems like whenever I'm with Joey, I'm always saying the wrong things. Several times during the drive, I catch him sniffling and wiping water from his eyes. Neither of us says a word until we reach the Nickels and Dimes parking lot, and I find a spot.

Joey pulls his hood back up before stepping out. "Thanks. Do you wanna come in so we can talk? I doubt there will be many customers today."

I nod. "Yeah, I do."

We run through the rain until reaching the awnin above the store. There's a HELP WANTED sign on the door and Joey holds it open for us. He goes behind the counter and pulls out his glasses from the pouch of his hoodie and then wipes the lens dry.

The elephant in the room is so large it hogs all the air in the store.

"You don't have to talk if you don't wanna," I tell him.

He pokes at the screen of the register and releases a heavy sigh. "Cheese told me what you did so I think you deserve to know."

"She did?"

"Yeah. It feels good to have someone in my corner. I know what everyone at school already says about me, but now I don't want to know. Not if they think ..." He pauses. "...Not if they think I killed Keaton."

"Anyone who actually knows you knows you would never lay a finger on her."

"Thanks." He opens the drawer of the register and is silent as he counts the money inside.

I give him a moment before asking the million-dollar question: "So what happened?"

He takes another deep breath. "She never showed up for her shift, so that's when I called you. Then while I was waiting, I thought I'd take the trash to the dumpsters out back. That's ... that's when I found her." He pauses again and takes another deep breath, the only thing stopping him from breaking out into tears. It's in his face, his eyes, and his voice. Joey continues: "She was shot in the back of her head, a lit cigarette still between her fingers ... That's when I called the police and they took me right into questioning."

I wasn't there, but I feel like I can see the image in front of me as clear as day. It's almost like I can smell the tar of the cigarette. "They didn't hurt you, did they?" I ask.

He shakes his head. "Not intentionally, at least. They put me in this conference type room and left me there for hours. Thought I was gonna go crazy. Then these two detectives came to ask me a bunch of questions. One of them was Falco's dad. They asked a lot of the same questions but always worded them differently to see if I'd slip up and change my story. They didn't let me go until they saw the footage from all the cameras around the store that proved I was here when ... when it happened."

My jaw drops. "Wait, that's it! So the cameras show who the killer is!"

Joey scratches the side of his head and chuckles a little. "Well, not exactly. I kinda ... turned off the cameras by the dumpsters."

I can only stare at him, blinking my eyes several times. "You're a terrible employee. You realize how suspicious that makes you, right?"

"Yeah, I know. That's why it took so long for me to be let go.

But before Keaton started hating me that's where we'd always go to smoke and hook up. I didn't need my boss seeing that. We'd totally get fired. But maybe … maybe if we got fired, Keaton would still be alive."

I feel like I can see that image clear as day too. Very romantic. "Keaton never hated you." I assure him.

That's what finally causes tears to fall from his eyes, and he quickly wipes them from behind his glasses. "Thanks. Maybe if I wasn't so selfish, she and Griffin could have been happy together before they…" He trails off. He doesn't need to finish. Behind the glare of his glasses are all his self-deprecating thoughts.

"Oh thank God, there you are!" a ditsy voice calls out, and Amanda appears from between the aisles. "You are a lifesaver. We've been in shambles these past few days." Thunder rumbles at the perfect moment and Amanda bobbles her head. "Well, not today." She notices me. "Fiora!" She outstretches her arms and goes in for a hug. "How are you, baby? Look at you, poor thing you're soaked!"

"I'm alright," I say.

"How's your mom?"

"She's good."

"Well if you or her need some part-time work you gotta let me know. We're dying over here."

"Thanks, I'll keep that in mind."

She brushes her hand against my damp shoulder before returning to the back of the store.

I'm left alone with Joey and the sound of the beating rain, but there's still something else that's bothering me. "Hey Joey, you think we can talk outside for a few minutes?" I ask.

"Outside?" He looks around the vacant store. "Yeah, I guess that should be okay. I don't see any customers."

He slides out from behind the counter, and I lead the way out of the store. We stand out here for a moment, listening to the patter of rain against the asphalt and watching the water fill the parking lot. A bolt of lightning strikes, and seconds later, thunder hits. Neither of us are saying anything yet, but I keep sneaking glances at Joey. He's leaning against the wall with unmistakingly a lot on his mind. He's holding himself tightly in his arms. "It's freezing out here," he says.

"Hey Joey?" I say.

He looks down at me with those big brown eyes. "Yeah?"

This is something I need to finally get off my chest, but I can't bear the thought of him looking at me differently. I take a deep breath and just spit it out: "If this curse actually is real, I might have been the one to kill Griffin."

And there it is, the change of the look in his eyes. "What?"

"A week before he died, I found that article about his scholarship and saw his name."

"Nah, the whole town had already seen that article long before you moved here. If it was going to kill him, it would have a while ago. Right?"

I shake my head. "I think my case is different. I was on the phone with my friend back in San Diego and I told her his name. I didn't mean to. It just blurted out."

"So, are you saying it's more than just knowing someone's name, it's spreading it? Then that's why Lemming ..."

I take a deep breath. "Keaton really wanted out of Oregon and told me she was sending applications to universities in every state."

Joey crosses his arms. "So to get out of here she spread her name around the country ... and now she's dead."

"Yeah, that's what it seems like. And remember what you told me about the survivor who mysteriously died? I bet their name was spread all over the news after the shooting."

"So their name was spread all over the country, then the curse finished the job. Yeah, yeah. That makes sense. I didn't look much into it and just assumed that maybe the survivor's guilt got to them. It would be easy to jump off the pier and never be seen again."

"You say that like you've thought about it," I say.

He looks down to his sneakers and shuffles his feet against

the pavement. He chuckles a little bit. "Yeah."

"Well knock it off. You're not allowed to do anything stupid until we get to the bottom of this. The police are obviously too busy framing innocent people and we have friends to avenge."

"This isn't going to be another reckless scheme is it?" he asks.

"No. We're going to find out how the survivor died and compare it to our friends ... 'cause there's something else that's been bothering me."

"Other than people getting killed?"

"Yeah. It's something that makes all of this even weirder. Farrah insists there was no gun when she found Lemming's body."

Joey's eyes widen. "That's not possible. She was shot and there was a bullet casing left behind. It was the same type that was found after Griffin's murder."

"I mean, unless someone took the gun?"

"There's no way her death would have been ruled a suicide if there was no weapon, even with how incompetent the cops in Black-shit are. Hell, even if she was murdered it would still be ruled a suicide if someone placed the gun in her hand. And after that video she made ..."

"Yeah, I know. That's what I don't understand. That's why once you get off, we're going to find out how that survivor died. It might give us some answers."

Joey scratches the side of his head. "Or just leave us with more questions."

"Yeah, but oh well. Come on, it's cold. Let's go back inside."

He holds the door open as we return inside the store.

Night

The storm has reduced to a light trickle by the time Joey gets off work and we exit the store. It's pitch black out aside from a flickering street lamp, and with it being over halfway through

October, it gets dark much too early, and there's that curfew after dark. "Maybe we should do this tomorrow," Joey suggests.

I look up at him as we stand under the awning. "What, why?"

"Well, 'cause there's that curfew and I don't want either of us to get in trouble again."

"So? Just come over and spend the night."

"Is that really okay? Your mom won't get mad?"

"No she won't care. Come on, let's hurry. It's freezing out here."

The first thing I do after turning on the engine of my car is flicking on the heater. The car is quick to heat up and pull onto the main road. The rain may be lighter than before, but the fog certainly is not. It's a dense sheet covering the road and the moon is nowhere to be seen. All that surrounds us is black and gray, and the feeling of dread tethered to the night.

I stop in the driveway as I wait for the garage door to open, then park beside Mom's car. After that, we can finally go inside. The first thing Joey does is drop his jaw. "*This* is what you were talking about when you said your family downgraded? This place has to be worth more than every trailer in my park," he says.

I hum. "You should have seen our last place. It was a mansion right on the beach in San Diego."

"What the hell? Then what did you pay for this place?"

We're making eye contact, and Joey is waiting for an answer. "1.4 million. And it's completely paid off. Cash," I say.

His normally smooth voice raises several octaves. "1.4 mill– in this economy? I hate you so much right now. Man, if I had that kind of money the last place I'd be living is Black-shit."

I reach over and grab his hand. "Come on, let's go to my room." I pull him up the stairs.

"Fiora, is that you?" Mom's voice calls out from behind her office door then she comes out to meet us at the balcony. "Oh, hi Joey. So good to see you again."

Joey waves with his hand not held in mine. "Hi Ms.

Clairwater."

"Oh please, call me Nebula. Or Nebbie."

I squeeze Joey's hand tighter. "We're gonna go to my room now." I lead him into my nearby bedroom and shut the door behind us.

"Wow, you're right. Your mom really doesn't care. My grandma would have a heart attack," he says.

"You said yourself that an open door never stopped you before."

"I may have been overselling myself." Joey says. Squeak is on the bed and he reaches his hand out for her to smell. "Hi. Aren't you a pretty kitty." She trills when he strokes her down her back.

My body is chill and my skin pricks under my hoodie. "Do you mind if I put on something warmer?" I ask.

Squeak, the traitor, has helped herself to Joey's lap. "No go for it," he says. I keep my back towards him so he doesn't see anything and pull off my hoodie with nothing underneath. Joey immediately reacts. He turns away and covers his eyes with his hands. "Oh! I'm sorry! I didn't mean to look."

"Who cares? Relax, I'm not going to steal your precious little virginity, Catholic boy," I say.

"Oh, right. I just didn't think you'd look like that."

I pick out The Plot in You hoodie I got from one of their concerts. "Why? What would I look like?"

"I dunno. I guess I never thought about it."

"Well you can open your eyes now, I'm covered."

He removes his hands from his face and opens his eyes. "So, ah, what are we doing in your room again?"

My laptop is on the nightstand connected to the charger. I unplug it and join Joey on the bed. "We're gonna do some research on that survivor who mysteriously died twenty years ago."

"Oh, yeah. Right."

I pass him the laptop. "I don't know what to look for."

"There should be a Wikipedia page or something."

Joey opens up the internet browser and types the keywords into the search engine to find the article. I lean over so we can read it together. He scrolls down to the part that lists the victims, and with it is a picture of a piece of paper. There are nine names crossed out, with only one at the very bottom remaining:

–~~Jameson Cane~~
–~~Caden Schmidt~~
–~~Angel Rogers~~
–~~Danni Greer~~
–~~Logan Clarke~~
–~~Sam Ryan~~
–~~Rene Martin~~
–~~Addison Gill~~
–~~Tyler Newman~~
–Bailey Navarro

"That's the surviving victim: Bailey Navarro," Joey reads.

I have to take a second glance for myself. I heard what he said and see it right in front of me, but I still can't believe it. "My mom?"

Joey shoots me a look. "Your mom? She just said her name is Nebula."

"That's obviously not her real name. You think there's a real life person on this planet named *Nebula Clairwater*? That's her pen name for her writing."

"But I don't get it. Why would people think your mom mysteriously died, and to the point where they invented a whole curse about it?"

"Well, she dropped out when she got pregnant and then moved to San Diego with Atlus's dad not long afterwards. That was about–" it hits me, "–twenty years ago."

Joey scratches his head. "So the survivor who mysteriously died from the curse after the shooting is actually your mom who is very much alive and just … moved to another state?" He rubs his eyes. "This is hurting my head."

I look back to the list of names displayed on the screen and there's only one other I recognize. It's crossed out, but I'm still able to make out what it says. "See that name? Tyler Newman? That's my dad."

"For real? The one who died before you were born?"

"I've never had any other dads. I knew he died in a shooting, but didn't think there was some whole conspiracy around it. My mom never liked to talk about it. She's always been the type to dodge things."

"I mean, I can only imagine the trauma. You and your baby daddy are targeted in a mass shooting. But if she changed her name and moved away, she has to know something about the curse, right?"

"I can try asking her but I can't guarantee any results. She did … she did try to convince Attie and I to transfer to homeschooling though. She even said something about thinking Blackridge would be safer after all these years."

Joey looks away and scratches his head some more. "You don't think … no, forget it."

I lean in closer to him, placing my hand on his knee. "No, say it."

"Well, we thought it was weird that it took the curse twenty years to kick in. What if it was triggered by your mom moving back to town?"

"That thought crossed my mind too, but it's not like there's anything we can do about it."

"So this is it? We're at a deadend?"

I take the laptop from him and close the top. "Yeah, it seems like it. We just have to hope no one else dies. And if they do, maybe we can get some information out of it."

"So all we have to go on is someone's name being spread, then they die huh?"

"That's really the only thing I can think of, at least for now until the pigs get more leads."

Joey rubs his face. "I'm really tired. I've had a rough few

days." He gets up from the bed and walks across the room. "I'm gonna head to bed. Good night."

I reach out to grab his hand. "Where are you going?"

"Um, downstairs to the couch?"

"No, fuck that. You're sleeping in here."

He looks around the room. "In your bed? With you?"

"Yeah, if that's okay with you," I tell him.

Joey smiles just a little bit, but after all he's been through, I'm sure it's the closest thing he can muster. He steps forward towards the bed but stops before crawling in. "Do you care if I take off my pants? I have underwear on, I just hate sleeping in jeans. And they're still kinda wet. I promise I won't do anything creepy."

I've already made myself comfortable under the covers. "Go for it."

He undoes his belt and button before pulling down the zipper. When he steps out of his pants, he's wearing a pair of black boxer briefs. Finally, he crawls into bed. The lights are off and I use the remote to turn on the TV for some white noise while we sleep.

I have a boy in my bed, and I'm so close that I can smell the scent of his shampoo. It's sour apple. I wish I could curl up close to him and place my head on his chest. I want his arms to hold me close and keep me warm on such a frigid, rainy night. Most of all, I want him to tell me that everything will be okay, if I can even get myself to believe that.

"Hey Fi?" Joey's voice says.

"Yeah?"

"Thanks for letting me come over. I don't know what I'd do if I were alone tonight."

"You're welcome. You're always welcome here."

Finally, I close my eyes.

OCTOBER 28 – SATURDAY

Morning

Joey is still fast asleep by the time I wake up. His eyes are closed, showing off those luscious lashes. I want to keep looking at him. I want to keep listening to him breathe. I wanna run my fingers in his hair and snuggle up close to him. But I don't do any of that. He said that it's nice knowing he has someone in his corner, and I want him to know I'll always be here in whatever way he'll let me.

He shuffles under the covers before waking up and yawning, covering his mouth with his hand. "Hi morning breath," I say.

"Oh, sorry," he says.

"Don't be. It's my fault. It was a spur of the moment thing and you don't have a toothbrush."

"I have to help Amanda open today so I can get a brush when I go in."

"What time do you have to be there?"

"Nine."

"Wanna grab some breakfast then I can drop you off?"

"I don't wanna be a–"

"Don't even finish that sentence."

He blows air through his nose and smiles. "Yeah, okay. Thanks." He covers his mouth as he yawns again. "What time is it?"

I reach over to check my phone. "A little past eight."

Joey groans. "Oh fuck me. Okay." He rubs his eyes some more before standing up and looking around the room. "Where did I put my pants? Oh, here they are." He bends over to grab his jeans and puts in one leg, then the other. He finishes buttoning them before grabbing his belt and putting it through the hoops.

I'm still lying in bed and resting my chin on the palm of my hand. "What, you don't wanna go downstairs and see my family in your underwear?"

"Uh, absolutely not."

After getting ready we exit my bedroom where we're struck with the sweet aroma of cinnamon. Joey inhales. "Oh wow, something smells super good."

"I bet Atlus made breakfast," I say.

We go downstairs where Mom and Atlus are in the kitchen, both sitting at the island. Mom has a plate of French toast in front of her and smiles with the fork still in her hand. "Good morning sleepyheads."

Atlus can simply only stare, his mouth gapped.

"Good morning Ms. Navarr–I mean Nebbie," Joey is quick to catch himself.

I scope out what Atlus has in front of him. He has a bowl of cereal as well as a helping of his famous baked French toast. "Oh, what'd you make us for breakfast?" I tease.

He grabs the plate of the cinnamon-coated bread and holds it away. "Nothing. You can eat shit." Trash jumps up and places his two front paws on his legs to beg.

There's still some of the French toast in a baking dish on the stove so I grab a couple of plates for Joey and myself. We join my family at the island and it's awkward, no one making a sound except for metal clanking against glass.

"You about ready to go?" I ask when I notice Joey's plate empty and he's drinking the rest of the milk from his cereal.

He has a bit of a white mustache on his lip but wipes it away on his sleeve. "Oh, I called for an Uber. I don't want to make you put out more than you already have." He spins his stool to look at my Mom. "Um, but I don't mean it like that, Ms. Navarro! Nothing happened, I swear!"

Mom snorts and raises her spoon to her lips, some of the milk dripping onto the marble of the island. "What do I look like, Mother Teresa?"

A car honks from outside, and Joey releases a breath of relief. "Oh thank God." He gets up from his stool and scratches the side of his head. "Well, thanks for having me over. And Fi … I'll call you."

"Yeah, you better," I tell him.

Joey places his dishes in the sink before rushing out the front door like the floor is made of lava.

"So you're fucking Joey now even after he killed Keaton?" Atlus wastes no time bitching once the front door is shut.

I flick him on the forehead. "I'm not fucking him and he didn't do it!"

"He was arrested for it!"

"No he wasn't! He was questioned then released 'cause he didn't do it."

"Oh so what, 'cause of some pretty boy you're a bootlicker who believes everything the pigs tell you now?"

I stick out my tongue. "So you agree, you think he's pretty?"

"Fi, I hope you're still taking your pill every day. And make sure you take it at the same time every day too," Mom chimes in.

"I'm not fucking Joey," I repeat.

Mom shrugs and holds up her hands. "Okay, but *if you do*, don't rely on just a condom. Guys like to poke holes in them, lie about them not fitting right, purposely put them on wrong, or flat out take them off when you're not looking. Then that's how you end up with Atlus."

Atlus drops his spoon down to his bowl, causing a loud clank and some milk to spill. "What the fuck?"

I can't help but laugh.

Evening

Mom is home from work and shut in her office. "It's unlocked," her voice calls out after I knock on the wood.

I open the door and go inside. Mom's office is simple and

calming. She's the type who needs tranquility when she works with the walls painted a nice blue-ish gray and her desk is tucked in the corner. She also has some more of her favorite plants, a couch, a TV, and a fountain to create the effects of running water. "Whatcha doing?" I sing.

"Writing," Mom sings back.

I prance up to her at her desk. "How's that going?"

Mom gestures her hand to present her screen. "What's it look like?" She has a document open, but the page only consists of white space.

"Looks like another bestseller."

Mom chortles and twirls her chair around to face me. She crosses her arms. "Alright, I'll bite. What do you want? Is your credit card maxed out again? Did you crash the car? Are you pregnant? Are you going back to jail?"

I plop my ass down on the couch. "Geez, what I'm not allowed to want to talk to my own mother?" She continues to stare at me with her arms crossed and raises a brow. "I've just been kinda wondering about my dad lately. You know, what he was like and how he died," I say.

That causes her to uncross her arms. "Your dad? You never ask about your dad. Honestly, I didn't think you cared."

"Well not really, but I've been thinking about him. Like, you're divorcing Atlus's dad and some of my friends have dads. I'm going to the same school where you met him and where he died. I can't help but think about him."

She takes a deep breath and lets out a small chuckle. The memories recite through the glistening in her eyes. "Your dad, huh? Tyler …" She trails off and smiles. "Your dad was the type of kid you'd probably beat up. A total dork, all the way down to the bone. He played the saxophone in the school band and wore buttoned up Hawaiian shirts."

I chortle. "You let someone like that knock you up?"

She nods, snickering. "Well it wasn't on purpose. He was a great artist and wanted to make comic books. I can't draw to save my life so I stuck to writing. He was actually the one to come up with the name Fiora."

"So what happened to him?" I ask.

Her smile fades. "He died."

"Yeah, I know that much. But why? There was a list. He had to have been targeted for a reason, right?"

Her eyes change, recollecting different memories. Instead of innocent nostalgia, her gaze is as if staring down the muzzle of a gun. "It was just a couple weeks after I found out I was pregnant with you." The ghastly look remains on her face before being directed to a cheeky smile, the same one she wears when there's something up her sleeve. "Alright, since we're playing the million questions game, I have a question for you." She playfully spins her chair back towards her desk and sorts through some of the papers. She picks out an envelope and, displaying it pinched between two fingers, she turns back towards me. "Do you have a lawyer yet? This came for you today."

I take the envelope from her. It's from the Blackridge County Courthouse. "Oh fuck me."

"I think you got enough of that already. Make sure to shut the door on your way out." She spins back towards the monitor, staring at the blank screen.

Well, that's the end of that. I shut the door behind me and return to my room. Squeak is on my bed, and I sit beside her to rip open the envelope. Inside are folded pieces of paper and scan through the walls of text until I finally get what I'm looking for: my court date, December 4th, 2023.

It's a few months away. I still have plenty of time and other things to worry about. I video call Joey. He answers, wearing his glasses, and stands in front of a glass cigarette case. Even this late into the evening, he's still at Nickels and Dimes. I guess he's forced to work doubles without Keaton around anymore.

"Fiora! My pal, my buddy! So did you talk to your mom?" he asks. "I've been on the edge of my seat about it all day."

I nod. "Couldn't get anything out of her we didn't already figure out ourselves."

His expression drops as he sighs. "Oh. So she doesn't know anything about the curse, huh?"

"Nah, I think she at least knows something the way she was quick to change the subject."

"Well, at least it wasn't a total waste. We were at least able to confirm something."

We were? That's what I ask.

"Yeah, we confirmed that the survivor from the shooting didn't die. So that means there really isn't a curse, right?" Joey says.

"But Lemming ..."

He sighs into the camera. "Yeah, I'm still stumped on that too. But if the curse isn't real and Keaton and Griffin really were murdered, then it has to be someone they knew."

"It does?"

"Well yeah. This is a small town. Remember how everyone was all up in your business when you moved here? There's no way a stranger would go unnoticed, especially if they were out here killing people. They'd be suspect numero uno."

"Yeah, you're right. And the pigs arresting you and Lemming's dad is just proof they have no leads. They're just throwing shit at a wall and seeing what sticks."

A bell rings from Joey's side and he looks away from the camera. "Hey, I gotta go. There's a customer. We'll talk about this some more later. Someone needs to get to the bottom of this, and I think it can only be us knowing what we know now ... for Keaton. There's no way I'm stopping until the killer gets what's coming to him."

"Ditto."

Joey hangs up, and I'm left looking at my own reflection from the phone screen. Are we really going to be able to solve this when even the police have no leads? If it really is some curse, then I have to accept the fact it's my fault Griffin is dead. If it's not a curse, then that means this could be the start of a serial killer throughout Blackridge, and it could be anyone.

OCTOBER 30 – MONDAY

Morning

"I don't get why we have to pick up your stupid boyfriend," Atlus bitches, unbuckled with his feet on the dashboard.

"I don't get why you weren't the twin absorbed in the womb," I bite back.

We reach the trailer park and I pull off to the side to park on the wilted grass. "Has Joey left yet?" I yell out through the rain.

Cheese is sitting on the porch of her trailer with a group of people too old to be from our school. They're rotating a blunt. Cheese shrugs through the beads of water and fog.

I march up the steps to Joey's porch and knock on the door. When there's no answer, I knock again. Joey eventually opens the door. His hair is messy, and he is wearing checkered pajama bottoms. "Fiora? What are you doing here?" he asks.

"It's Monday. I'm giving you a ride to school, duh," I answer.

Joey leans his shoulder against the door frame. "Oh. Ah … I'm not going today."

"What? Why not? You're the only thing that makes that place even remotely bearable."

That causes a slight smile to appear on his face, but it's quick to drop. "I can't go back there. Not while … not while everyone thinks I killed Keaton."

"Nobody thinks that." That's a lie. "I won't let them think that. We're going to get to the bottom of this. This is for Keaton and for Griffin … and for you, Joey."

Joey holds the door open wider. "Here, why don't you come in for a sec. Get out of this cold."

I step inside, away from the crisp wind and rain.

"Oh, is that Keaton?" a thick Irish accent calls out from in front of the TV. The elderly red-headed woman pulls herself to her feet, relying on a cane to slowly inch herself to the door. "Keaton, you looked so beautiful on the TV the other day."

Joey blows a breath through his nose. "Grandma, Keaton died, remember? That's why she was on TV. This is Fiora."

His grandma stretches out her neck and squints her eyes at me. Her hand shakes as it presses down on her cane. "That's right, I do see a difference."

I wave, unsure of what else to do. "Hi Joey's grandma."

"It's so nice to see you again, Keaton. You looked so beautiful on the television."

"I-It's nice to see you again too," I say.

She returns to her recliner in front of the TV, arm shaking and back hunched.

"Um, let me put some pants on then we can go, okay?" Joey says and goes to his room at the end of the hall.

I stand behind the lounge chair where Joey's grandma is sitting, and I watch TV with her. *Jerry Springer* is on and two women with their shoes off are pulling each other's hair while the audience cheers and chants.

Joey returns from down the hall, his hair groomed and pajama pants changed to joggers. "You ready to go?"

I nod and we go back out to the rain. The water is falling faster and we hurry to my car parked in the grass, puddles splashing with every step we take. I hop in front of the steering wheel while Joey sits in the back seat. The car is nice and toasty.

I turn the wipers onto a faster setting, and it's a quiet drive to Seal Coast Community High School. Atlus doesn't say anything, but I can see every thought in his smug face.

There's a line for security once we arrive at campus and the three of us are at the end. There's a group of boys in front of us, making no effort to mask their snarks and whispers. "Holy shit, is that him?"

"I can't believe they'd let someone like that back at school."

"Yeah, seriously. Who knows who he'll kill next."

"It's that stupid bitch's fault. I'm tired of listening to those stupid fucking feminists. You jump into the lion's den and you get eaten."

"Yeah, stupid cunt should have stayed in the kitchen."

"Or on her knees."

"On her knees in the kitchen."

"Yeah, I'll get her face covered in mayo."

Joey's body tenses, his nails digging into the palms of his hands. "Sh-Shut up …"

The group of boys laugh something sickening.

"I said shut the fuck up!" Joey snaps, causing a multitude of heads to turn. "You don't know shit about Keaton! Yeah, she hated me. I knew that. So what? She didn't deserve what happened to her and you don't get to talk about her like that! Say what you want about me, I can take it. But have some goddamn respect for the dead!"

The group of boys snicker. "Yeah, we know you can take it, faggot."

I tug on Joey's sleeve. "Fuck them. They're not worth it."

Joey breathes through his nose. "A couple of them I already have."

We get past security and it comes time for us to split. "Don't talk to me," Atlus says and excuses himself.

I look at Joey, his face stoic. Maybe it was wrong for me to convince him to come back to school so soon. "Are you gonna be okay?" I ask.

Joey winks and fakes a smirk. "Yeah, I'll be alright. I'm a big boy."

* * *

The student council closet is less cramped and stuffy after June transferred to homeschooling, and May isn't here, so I can only assume she's still suspended. Serves her right. All who remain are April, McCarthy, O'Brien, and myself, sitting around the plastic table.

"Tomorrow is Halloween," McCarthy points out. "I had a discussion with Principal Pal concerning the matters of what is and is not appropriate for the occasion. As you know, for many years it has been tradition during Halloween to take advantage of the rumors that fill our little town, but due to the current circumstances, such topics have been prohibited. Even tomorrow, the rule of forbidding the spreading rumors and gossip is in full effect and we are to report any students breaking said rule. That especially includes the talk of curses." April raises her hand. "Yes, April?" McCarthy calls on her.

"Principal Pal seems really scared about the curse. It's not real, right?" she inquires.

"There has been no evidence of such matters."

"May said–"

"I have no interest in what May has said."

"But Lemming–"

"Was an unfortunate tragedy, but we must move on."

"Okay, so what is allowed?" I inquire.

"Nothing associated with death," McCarthy explains. "Students are still permitted to dress in costumes of their choosing, granted that they are school appropriate. There are to be no ghosts, no ghouls, no vampires, no zombies, no mummies, no Jason, no Michael. There are to be no tricks, but treats are, however, permitted. There are also to be no haunted houses or stories related to death, whether fact or fiction."

I have my elbow on the table and rest my chin in my hand. "Geez, taking the fun out of Halloween."

"Fiora, you are the event planner. What did you have in mind?"

"Well, last time I brought a bunch of candles to school Principal Pal got all pissed off, but I was thinking this time I could use my power for good and bring a bunch of pumpkins."

"Pumpkins?"

"Yeah, everyone can get a pumpkin to carve and maybe have a contest during lunch or something. And someone else can bring candy and make pumpkin shaped cupcakes to sell, or something."

O'Brien slightly raises his arm that spent many weeks trapped in a sling. "That sounds fun and all, but also really expensive. I doubt that's in the council's budget, especially this last minute."

McCarthy nods, then tucks a strand of deep red hair behind her ear. "Yes, unfortunately I must agree."

"No biggie, I can get us a discount," I tell them.

"Fiora, as student council president, I cannot authorize any activity relying on *five finger discounts*."

I scowl. "What? No! My mom is the assistant manager at Bedrock. I'm sure she can give us an employee discount or something."

"Oh, I see. I apologize. That does sound permissible. I will submit an emergency proposal to Principal Pal and let you all know as soon as I receive a response. Meeting adjourned."

OCTOBER 31 – TUESDAY

Lunchtime

With the approval of my proposal, pumpkins are spread throughout the gym, each with some newspaper or a piece of cardboard underneath to catch any of the scraps. Anyone who wants to carve a pumpkin is free to participate. My friends are around me with large fruits of their own in front of them, but someone is missing. "Where's Joey?" I ask.

The others look around. I missed third period to help set up the gym, so he could have gone off anywhere after the bell rang. I can only imagine how hard being here has been since what happened to Keaton. Nonetheless, I'm saving him a pumpkin that no one else is allowed to touch.

Poppet shrugs. "I dunnos," she sings and continues eviscerating her pumpkin.

"I'm surprised he's even coming to school, I'll give him that much," Pandora says.

I point the tip of my scalpel at her. "Yeah, and you better fucking apologize for thinking he was the killer. You can only imagine the horrible shit people have been saying."

"I told you, he has my sympathy."

The red metal doors are pushed open, and Joey enters the gymnasium. He looks around the room for a moment before spotting us and sitting next to me. "Wow, this is great. Tons of people showed up."

"Hey, maybe you should join the student council, Joey," O'Brien suggests.

A wild McCarthy appears from behind us with April at her side. "We do currently have an open position we need filled. We are in desperate need of a committee representative."

Joey scratches the side of his head. "Um, I'm not so sure about that."

"That might be for the best," April agrees. "Student council can get … messy."

"Yeah, that's what I was thinking."

McCarthy stands tall with her back straight and chin held high. "Nonsense. I have come to find the student council has been rather peaceful these past few days. Nonetheless, the offer remains."

Cheese cocks her head. "McCarthy, are you going to the hotel tonight?"

"Unfortunately I must decline, but I wish the rest of the class to have a fun–and safe–evening."

"Oh fooey, you never do anything with us, McCarthy," Poppet whines.

"Those are simply my circumstances."

"Hey McCarthy," I call out, and the standing girl looks down at me. "We should go to the mall this weekend since, you know, we didn't get the chance to last time. April, you can come too."

McCarthy smiles. "Yes, I would enjoy that. Thank you for the invitation. Hopefully this time there will be no disruptions or criminal charges."

Cheese tilts her head to the other side, her long blonde pigtails draping over her shoulder. "What about you, April? Are you coming to the hotel?"

April waves both of her hands. "No way. Things like that freak me out. I have plans with May tonight anyways."

I want to gag. I hate being reminded of her existence. McCarthy is right; the student council has been peaceful these past few days.

"What about you Brien, are you going?" Cheese asks. "We can share a room."

"I'm sure rooms will be decided once we get there," the oblivious silver-haired doof responds.

Farrah's head switches back and forth between those talking in the group. Her carving looks like a dog. In fact, it's reminiscent of Trash. "Wait, what's this about a hotel?"

"Originating several years prior, it has been an unofficial tradition for the seniors of Seal Coast Community High School to test their bravery upon spending the proverbial Halloween night at the Haunted Hotel," McCarthy explains in a very *proverbial* McCarthy manner.

"Oh … I dunno if I'd want to go to something like that." Farrah huffs. "Isn't it going to be scary?"

Cheese stabs her scalpel through the shell of her pumpkin like it's a non-virgin in a slasher film. "Are you going Joey?"

Joey is elbow-deep in his pumpkin, scooping out the seeds, but pauses before answering: "I-I don't think that's a good idea, sorry."

"No, I think it is a good idea," I say.

Joey looks at me. "Huh? What happened to *I actually don't give a fuck about Black-shit and its traditions*."

"I think it's a good idea. We should go. It could help with what we've been talking about."

"What we've been talking abo–Oh! Yeah, that. You're right. Yeah, okay. I'll tell Amanda I can't come in today. She owes me a day off with all the over-time I've been doing. Besides, it's Halloween. I doubt we'll get any customers tonight."

Poppet shimmies her shoulders and does a little dance. "Oh, what have you been talking about? Something about being alone? In a hotel?"

I stick my tongue out. "Stuff."

Cheese stares at Joey sitting right across from her, tilting her head back and forth as she does so. Joey takes notice. "Wh-What?" he asks.

She tilts her head in the other direction. "Is your sweater backwards?"

Joey looks down at himself and pulls at his collar to look inside. "Oh shit!" He pulls his arms inside the sweater and turns it around before poking his limbs back out through the holes. "Um, thanks."

The bell rings, signaling the end of the lunch period and

many groans and whines fill the gymnasium. Guess that means people were having a good time despite the student council's limited resources.

Evening

FIORA: Tonights the night
CHLOE: that u lose ur virginity?
FIORA: No cunt
FIORA: That I get fucking murdered
CHLOE: o shit good luck bestie
CHLOE: remember that i get all ur shit
CHLOE: i especially want ur spiritbox shit
FIORA: You don't even like metal
CHLOE: i dont need 2
CHLOE: i like her thighs

But if the curse isn't real and Keaton and Griffin really were murdered, then it has to be someone they knew ... There's no way a stranger would go unnoticed, especially if they were out here killing people. They'd be suspect numero uno. If there really is a killer, they're likely someone we know, and tonight, practically the whole senior class is spending the night at some creepy hotel that profits off the very killings haunting Blackridge. What could possibly go wrong?

The stench of salt and rotting sea carcasses pervade enough to burn my eyes, signaling my pending arrival to the coast. I keep driving and through the thickness of the fog develops a figure: the Nameless Hotel. It rests atop the ledge overlooking the ocean and is surrounded by a barrier of tall trees, masking it from the heart of Blackridge.

It's warm and cozy inside the lobby of the hotel, unfitting of the ambiance it protrudes. The flooring and walls are made of wood to match the cabin aesthetic and off to the side there's a seating area in front of a large, crackling fireplace. Off to the other side of the lobby is an area blocked off with a sign that reads COMING SOON.

Many faces from Seal Coast permeate the lobby, and I find

the ones belonging to my friends. Poppet is wearing a red and black plaid fleece nightgown. She pinches the bottom and curtsies at the sight of me. "Princess Fiora."

I gesture for her to stand. In the group, there's Cheese, Joey, Pandora, and Poppet. O'Brien approaches from the front desk and joins our little group. He holds up a couple of plastic cards. "I got us our rooms. We're all on the sixth floor," he says.

It's a bumpy ride up to the highest floor of the hotel and with a ding, the metal doors slide open. We walk on wiry carpet with a red diamond design that's almost nauseating. There are lamps plastered to the taupe painted walls as we travel to our rooms all the way at the end of the hall. When we get there, the bulbs from the lamps on the walls are flickering, making this end of the hall much darker than the others.

"Yep, this isn't spooky at all," Joey comments.

"What, you're not scared, are ya Broey?" Poppet teases.

"N-No!"

O'Brien takes the keycards out of his pajama pocket. "Each room should have two double beds, so some people will have to double up."

Cheese puffs her cheeks like a hamster. "I want to share a room with Brien."

"I figured I would share a room with Joey."

Hearing his name garners Joey's attention. "Huh, me?"

"Yeah, to separate the boys and the girls."

The boys go to room 607 while us girls are across the hall in 606. It's a small room with the bathroom to the side, then past that is an open space with a couple of double beds and a TV. Poppet is the first to toss down her things and jump onto the nearest bed. There's barely any bounce when she lands. "Well, that sucked." She rolls over onto her back and pats the spot beside her. "Come on, Princess Fiora. You can bunk with me."

I come up and sit beside her on the bed. It's nice to take off my shoes.

There's a knock on the door, and Pandora answers. It's already Joey and O'Brien. "What happened to separating the boys and the girls?" Pandora questions.

"Come on, that's just for when we go to sleep. We don't wanna be bored by ourselves all night," Joey explains. The two boys step inside and the door latches behind them.

"So, you don't want to be bored, huh?" Pandora says and retrieves something from her bag stationed on the floor. It's flat and sturdy, a board of some kind, and she presents it to the boys.

Joey shakes his head immediately. "Nuh-uh, no way."

"Pandora, don't you think there's a time and a place?" O'Brien asks.

"What's a better time and place than here on Halloween?" Pandora defends.

Poppet is sitting beside me and leaning back with her arms stretched out behind her. "What is it?"

Pandora turns around. In her hands is an Ouija board. "What, are you scared? don't tell me any of you actually believe this crap."

The air in the room grows heavy.

"Well … It's just that three of our friends have died," Poppet says. "Isn't it a little too soon?"

"Okay, so you don't wanna try to talk to them?" Pandora asks. "Hey, maybe we can ask them who the killer is."

I know it's Halloween and the idea of using an Ouija board in a cursed town sounds cool as hell, but something about this just isn't right, and I know I'm not the only one who feels it. There's a somber look on Joey's face. "Fine, you can do what you want. I'm gonna get some air." Leaving those words, Joey is out the door.

Speaking of time and place, this is neither the time nor place for someone to be going off on their own. I follow Joey out of the room and call out to him when I find him in the hall. He's at a vending machine purchasing a soda. "Let's go down to the bar," I suggest.

There's a hiss when he twists open the cap of the bottle. "The bar?"

"Yeah, you know, to talk. Away from everyone else."

"Y-Yeah. There's no way I'm going back in there right now. I know Pandora can be brash and that's the type of stuff people do on Halloween, but that was … too much."

"No, I totally get it. I know Pandora doesn't care about Lemming, or Griffin, or Keaton, but that was totally insensitive."

"…Yeah," Joey breathes.

We enter the elevator at the end of the hall and wait as the metal box descends. Joey takes another sip of his soda before holding it out to me. "Want some?" he asks, and I accept.

The elevator reaches the ground floor and the metal doors slide open. We're back to the thin wooden corridor where to the left is the main lobby, but to the right and towards the back of the hotel is the bar. The bar is a decent size with a bartender behind it and no one else on the stools. Joey and I sit down. Staring right into my soul is the head of a deer mantled on the wall.

The bartender is an older man with a gray and styled mustache. "What can I get for ya?"

"Can I get a gin and tonic?" I order.

"I'll need to see an ID little lady."

I pull out my wallet from my pajama bottoms. "Oh fuck me." That's right, the pigs took my fake ID. "Never mind. Can I just get a Coke then?"

The bartender knocks on the wood surface of the bar. "One Coke coming up. And you sir?"

Joey looks up and waves his hand. "Oh no, I'm okay. Thank you."

The bartender walks off to the side towards the drink fountain.

Joey rubs his finger around the smooth edges of his plastic soda bottle. "Hey Broey?" I say, and he looks at me. "You were saying that Keaton and Griffin were most likely murdered by someone they knew, right? If they really were murdered after all."

Joey looks back at the bottle cupped in his hands. It's a little over half empty by now. "Yeah, I did say something like that, huh?"

"Do you think it's someone here with us right now?"

He takes a moment before answering and releases a deep breath. "Dunno. I've been thinking about that a lot, and the only thing I can come up with is that it has to be someone on the football team. The football team is mostly seniors, and everyone who died so far has been a senior. But it definitely has to be someone who would be in the locker room with Griffin and ..." He pauses again, and I already know what he's thinking. He always has that speckle in his eye when Keaton is on his mind. It's a mix of heartbreak and yearning, now with a dose of disclosure. "And someone who knew Keaton's work schedule. I'm sure she got along with the other football guys trying to get close to Griffin."

What he's saying makes sense, but there's something still bothering me: "But how would they get the same gun that killed Lemming?"

"I–I don't know."

I'm looking at Joey, but through the corner of my eye, I see someone strutting down the hall. "Speak of the devil," I say.

Joey looks over his shoulder, and Falco is at his side.

"There you are," Falco says and pulls a plastic card out of his pocket. He tosses it onto the bartop. "I'm in room 501," is all he says before heading back towards the elevators.

Joey picks up the key card and studies it. "Um Fi ... I'll see you in the morning, alright? We can talk more about this later. You said yourself we're at a deadend, right?"

I cannot believe what I'm witnessing. "Are you serious? You're gonna leave me to go fuck Falco?" It's that last part that really makes my head spin. "You've been fucking Falco? Why are you fucking Falco? He treats you like shit!"

Joey doesn't look at me; he just fiddles with the room key in his hands. "He's been having a really hard time since Griffin died."

I adjust myself so the front of my body faces Joey, and I place my hand on my chest. "What about me? Griffin was my friend too. Do you know how much I've been freaking out thinking I might have got him killed? And what about you? You were obsessed with Keaton. You're the one who found her body and the pigs tried to frame–"

He cuts me off. "I'm aware of everything that's happened." He takes his bottle from the bartop and slides out of the stool. "I'll see you in the morning, 'kay?"

I'm left with no one but myself and my Coca-Cola. I don't bother finishing the carbonated sugar and leave the full glass at the bar. Part of me wants to run into Joey on the way up, and another part of me doesn't want to see his face for a while. I'm in the elevator by myself as it climbs to the top floor, listening to the sound of working gears and my own thoughts. I hate both of these.

The doors open up on the 6th floor and I drag my feet all the way to the end of the hall. Might as well go back to the room and put an end to this night.

NOVEMBER 1 – WEDNESDAY

Morning

Last night was the worst Halloween of my life. No trick or treating, no getting drunk, and the guy I like is fucking someone else. At least it's finally over. We girls sit in the hotel lobby in front of the cackling fire as we wait for the boys to make their debut. The heat comforts me after a night that was everything but.

Cheese is in one of the armchairs with her knees to her chest and head resting in the palm of her hand. She's fast asleep. Lucky for her, while the rest of us are stuck in a chorus of yawns.

By and by, O'Brien appears from the elevator corridor, still in his pajamas and seemingly disgruntled. He stops to look around the lobby before he spots us and approaches. "Guys, something bad happened! It's Joey. H-He never came back to the room last night and I've been looking for him all morning!"

I sigh. "Oh, Joey spent the night with Falco."

O'Brien appears more disturbed by this than the possibility of Joey being murdered. "Joey and Falco? What does Joey have to do with Falco?"

"Oh you haven't heard? They're fucking," Pandora shares the news.

"Oh wow. I didn't know Falco's gay. I didn't know Joey's gay either."

"Don't worry, Joey's fine," Pandora states. "Falco wouldn't do anything to his walking, talking fleshlight."

I scoff and whip my head towards Pandora. "Do not call Joey a fleshlight. I'd never expect slutshaming and biphobia from you, Pandora."

"Look, I'm all for empowerment and sexual liberation, but what Joey needs is a backbone. I was sick and tired of listening to him bitch about Keaton, and now what, we're supposed to keep coddling him when he cries about Falco?"

"Hey, lay off Joey," Poppet defends.

"Joey might need a backbone, but you need a fucking heart," I snap. "Maybe he wouldn't be so insecure if the people who are supposed to care about him weren't constantly treating him like shit."

"You guys can stop talking about me now," says a voice. It's Joey's.

Pandora waves her hand. "Oh shit Joey, I'm sorry. You know I wouldn't have said any of that to your face."

"Th-Thanks? Um ... Fi? Can I talk to you for a sec?"

I rise from the comfort of my seat in front of the fire. "Yeah," I say, though I'm not exactly happy to see him right now. I follow him to a more private part of the hotel. We end up near the area under construction.

Joey scratches the side of his head. "Um, I'm really sorry about last night."

"It's water off a duck's back," I tell him, but it's not. I know that I'm not Joey's girlfriend so I have no right to be jealous or bitter, but I am. It hurts watching him choose someone else–someone else who doesn't deserve him.

Joey doesn't look me in the eyes and keeps his arms crossed. "It's just that ... My life sucks, okay? And sometimes it's nice to ... feel good."

"Yeah, I get it." I don't get it. "Come on, I'll drive you to school."

But first, I have to call my mom and let her know I survived the night–we all did.

NOVEMBER 3 – FRIDAY

After School

FIORA: Time for our plan to be set into motion?
O'BRIEN: Plan?
FIORA: Yes. I help you get with McCarthy, you help me get with Joey
O'BRIEN: You're still chasing Joey? Doesn't he have a boyfriend now?
FIORA: Whatever
FIORA: Meet us at the mall in about an hour and bump into us like it's a coincidence
FIORA: Then I'll make some excuse to go do something with April and leave you alone with McCarthy
O'BRIEN: It's almost scary how much you plot behind people's backs

Speak of the devil: "Hey, whatcha doing? Texting your boyfriend?" Joey teases, looking over my shoulder as I wait for McCarthy in the foyer.

I lock the screen for my phone. "No, I found a credit card on the floor so I'm buying a bunch of plane tickets so no one else can have them."

Joey furrows his brows. "Th–That's the most randomly malicious thing I've ever heard. You're not actually doing that though, right?"

"No, of course not."

He chuckles. "Man, I've got to learn not to take everything you say seriously."

"I'm serious sometimes. That's the fun part. Gotta keep you on your toes."

I hear McCarthy before I see her, her steps sounding like a draught horse prancing her hooves down the cobblestone of England. "Good afternoon Fiora, good afternoon Joey. Am I to assume our plans are still agreeable, or should we prepare for another cessation?"

I pucker my lips and take a good look at Joey, who is

currently not in jail and hopefully won't be again anytime soon. "Nah, I think we're good."

"Oh, are you guys going somewhere?" Joey asks.

"Yeah we're gonna try again to take that trip to the mall together. April is coming too. Wanna come?"

Joey scratches the side of his head. "That sounds fun and all, but I have to work. Amanda finally hired a new cashier so I have to help with training. But after this I should have more free time."

"Then we should go to the mall together sometime, just the two of us."

Joey smiles. "Yeah, I'd like that."

April skips from down the hall to join the parade. "Sorry for being late!"

I wave my hand. "It's no biggie." I look up at Joey. "Do you want a ride to work on our way to the mall?"

"Yeah, that would be great. Thanks. Honestly Fi, you're a lifesaver."

I wink at him. "Just make sure to make it worth my while."

Red rises to Joey's cheeks as he chuckles.

The group of us walk towards the end of the foyer when an irritating and nasally voice calls out: "April, there you are! I've been looking all over for you." It's May. Her suspension is up, which means we have the pleasure of her company. "Come on, I wanna get the hell out of here."

The personality I've been seeing of April without May around crumbles, and she can barely lift her gaze from her shoes. "Oh, I'm sorry May. I sort of already have other plans ..."

May's jaw drops as she looks between Joey, McCarthy, and myself. It's hard to tell which one she's disgusted the most by. "Are you fucking kidding me? You're ditching me for these skanks?"

McCarthy brushes a strand of loose red hair behind her ear. "If you are not going to be mature enough to handle this in a respectful manner then we will not be obliged to tolerate this conversation further."

"I'm sorry May. We can do something this weekend," April pleads.

May scoffs. "Don't even bother." She turns her back and struts away.

Cold sweat forms on April's brow. "Wait!" She looks over her shoulder at me. "I'm sorry Fi." She takes off running after her master.

"Well, that was quite the experience. Shall we get going then?" McCarthy asks.

"Yeah, I want to get the hell out of here too," I say, and we leave for Nickels and Dimes.

"Do you wanna come in for a sec?" Joey asks after we pull into the parking lot.

I look at McCarthy in the backseat through my rearview mirror. "I'll be right back."

She's sitting upright with perfect posture. "No matter, take your time. I'll be here."

I leave the engine on to run the heater and follow Joey into the store. Amanda and Cheese stand behind the counter. Joey seems just as surprised as I am, if not more so. "Cheese, what are you doing here?" he asks.

"She's my new hire!" Amanda is excited to announce.

Cheese lazily waves her hand. "Hi Joey, hi Fiora."

Joey leans against the counter. "I didn't know you needed a job. You should have told me. Are you–uh–not making enough with your side gig?"

"I need a job for my plea deal," Cheese explains.

"Wait, what? Plea deal?" I say. "You pleaded guilty? Why the hell would you do that?"

Cheese tilts her head. "'Cause I did it."

"So? That's what criminal defense lawyers are for."

"I don't really care."

Yeah, that's about as much as I was expecting.

Amanda rolls her head like her neck is a ball and socket joint. "I don't care what she needs the job for, I just know she's my savior. Joey, you teach her the ropes, alrighty?"

Joey salutes. "Yes ma'am."

"You two have fun, and Joey, good luck," is all I can say.

* * *

The Blackridge Mall is mainly abandoned. We enter through the food court and only two stands remain, one for pizza and one for Philly cheese steaks. All the others have since been left to collect dust. Walking deeper into the mall, many stores are out of business with their metal gates drawn and faded outlines of the signs that used to be there. Even the businesses that have survived don't have a single customer inside. Most places still standing are military recruitment offices, no doubt taking advantage of the rampant poverty.

McCarthy stops in place and deeply inhales as we pass one of the few stores open. It's decorated with pink and bright fluorescent lighting. "This smells divine."

She's right. There's an aroma protruding from the store that's fresh and fruity. It's not in an overpowering way but in a more inviting way. "Let's check it out," I say.

There's no one else inside except the cashier behind the register texting on her phone. She doesn't look up when we enter the store. The shelves are stocked with what attracted us here: candles, soaps, and scented lotions. McCarthy picks up a pink bottle of lotion and untwists the top to give it a whiff. While her back is turned, I pull out my phone:

FIORA: We're at some store called Tilly's. McCarthy is looking at lotions. You should buy her some!
O'BRIEN: On my way!

McCarthy turns her attention to me, holding out the bottle and tucking her loose hair behind her ear. "You have to smell this." I lean in close and give it a sniff. It's strawberry and sweet.

A tall, lean man with unmistakable short platinum-dyed hair enters the shop: it's O'Brien. "Hey McCarthy, do you come here often?" he asks.

McCarthy holds a pumpkin spice-scented candle in her hand. "No. In fact, I do not. Fiora invited me."

O'Brien tucks his hands into the pockets of his jeans. "That's nice. I'm looking to pick something out for my sister. Maybe you could help me? I'm not good with this kind of stuff."

"I cannot proclaim myself as an expert in these matters, but there is nothing I will not at least apply my best efforts to."

While those two attend to their matters, I take the moment to slip from the store. I wait at the food court, killing time by nursing a slice of pizza that's more oil than flavor.

O'Brien joins me carrying a pink bag, but no McCarthy walks alongside him and holds his hand like I was hoping. "Hey, where you've been?" he says.

What the hell happened? And that's what I ask him.

He pulls up the seat across from mine and sits down. He releases a held-in breath. "She likes someone else."

"What? No way! Who?"

"Well, you actually."

"No fucking way."

"Yes way. She just told me herself. So looks like you're just as bad with girls as Joey too."

"Shit, if I wasn't so committed to chasing Joey I would totally go for her. She's gorgeous."

O'Brien looks at me with his olive-green eyes and dark bushy brows. "Why *are* you chasing Joey of all people? Like, surely you can do better."

"I can fix him," I boldly declare.

O'Brien smirks and chortles. "Good luck with that."

"Hey, you're supposed to hold up your end of the deal and help me!"

"Face it Fi, operation: You help me, I help you, like most of your plans, is a bust." He holds up the pink bag in his hand. "I'm gonna go give this to my sister so at least today's not a total waste. I'll see you at school."

O'Brien scoots from his seat and is out the glass sliding doors.

Just minutes after O'Brien disappears, there's another voice. It's McCarthy's. "Ah, Fiora. So this is where you ran off to. I am to assume this is yet another one of your schemes?" She approaches the table, standing in front of me.

"Oh, um … yeah. Sorry about that," I say.

McCarthy closes her eyes and smiles. "It's of no matter. It's a side of you I've come to expect, and frankly admire."

"Oh yeah, totally dude."

"Before we take our leave, there's somewhere else I would like to visit if it pleases you. There is a store that sells lovely dresses I would like for the two of us to try on together."

"Oh yeah, totally dude," I repeat.

She tucks a strand of hair behind her ears and bats her eyes. "Well then, shall we be off?"

Trying on dresses with McCarthy? That actually sounds really nice.

Night

An account by the username E.L.L.IOT.VAUGHN requests to follow me on Instagram. Add a name to my list, the bio reads, and only a single photo has been posted to the account so far. It's April, looking directly into the camera and smiling. There's a forest background behind her with multicolored leaves as if it's possibly a yearbook photo. Below is a caption that only says one thing: Eloise Horton.

Holy shit, this is precisely what Joey and I talked about. Someone is spreading April's name in an attempt to kill her. I have to call him and let him know.

"Hello?" he answers.

"Joey! Have you checked Instagram recently?"

"Oh, no. Believe it or not but I haven't been on my phone much. Training Cheese is an–uh–experience. But why? What's up?"

"Just check Instagram. You should have a follow request. Cheese too."

Joey's voice is further from the phone. "Hey, it's Fi. She wants us to check Instagram." His voice comes back. "Okay, yeah. Here it is. Wait, Elliot Vaughn? Holy shit! And there's April. Someone's doxxing her!"

"This is exactly what we talked about! About how spreading someone's name can get them killed! Someone else figured it out and is trying to kill April!"

"Do you have her number? You know, since you're in the student council together. You should call her and make sure nothing has happened yet. If we can save her, this might be our biggest clue yet."

"Yeah and you know, the whole stopping someone from being murdered part."

Joey stutters and mumbles. "I-I mean yeah, that's a given."

I sigh. April and I may be in the student council together, but we're not friends. "I'll call McCarthy and see if I can get April's number from her. She's always calling all of us for meetings an shit."

"Okay yeah, let me know how it goes."

"Totally."

I hang up Joey's call and immediately dial McCarthy. After only a few trills, she answers. "Good evening Fiora. For what do I owe the pleasure?"

I swallow to try to hide the dread in my voice. The adrenaline pumping through my veins causes my hands to shake. I can barely hold the phone to my ear. "It's no biggie, but real quick could you send me April's number? Like, as soon as possible. As in, right now."

She hums through the speaker. "Oh? And may I ask why?"

"Well ya know, since she didn't come to the mall with us today I wanted to call and ask what's up."

"Ah. Very well. I will text you her number momentarily."

"Thanks McCarthy, you're a lifesaver." In more ways than she knows.

Upon receiving McCarthy's text, I dial April's number. It's only a few trills in my ear, but it feels like a million. What the hell am I supposed to do if she doesn't answer? *"Your call has been forwarded to an automated voice messaging system."*

"Fuck!" I scream out and dial again. Is it already too late?

After the fourth call, there's an answer. "Hello?" says a voice that's unmistakably April's.

I don't even attempt to hide my sigh of relief. "Hey Ape!"

"Ape? Who is this? Why do you keep calling me?"

"It's Fi. You know, from student council and Mr. Simpson's class."

"Oh, um … hi Fiora. Now's not really a good time."

There's a further away and unmistakable voice. "Ew, hangup on that cunt." It's May. I never thought I would be so grateful to hear that nasty bitch's voice. At least this means April's not alone.

"Sorry Fi, can I call you back later?" April asks.

"Or not at all. Hangup!" May snarks from the background.

Now it's time for my excuse for calling: "I was just calling to let you know that O'Brien met us at the mall and we had a little unofficial student council thing. Just wanted to tell you in human-speak before McCarthy tells you in beep boops."

There's a small giggle through the speaker. "Good to know. I'll see you on Monday."

"Yeah, see you Monday." But before I hang up, there's something else I need to say. "Just be careful and don't panic, 'kay?"

Now, to make the final call for the night and let Joey know everything is fine.

NOVEMBER 6 – MONDAY

Morning

It's become part of my morning routine to pick up Joey for school, not that I mind it. "Man, the fog is so thick today I could barely see you. But these heated seats are a lifesaver," he says after hopping into the back seat. He holds himself in his arms as his teeth chatter.

"Glad I could make your ass happy, Joey," I say.

"Th-That's not what I meant."

Atlus chortles.

Despite the fog and long security line, we arrive at school on time and before I part ways with Joey, he has something to say: "Um, hey Fi? Later can we talk about something–alone?"

I nod. "Yeah."

Atlus gargles deep in his throat and pretends to gag. "You two make me sick."

"Shut the fuck up Of Mice & Men."

The three of us disperse, separating down different school wings. I meet with Poppet at our lockers, almost swearing I can see Griffin's image standing beside her. They laugh and bicker. But upon getting closer, the mirage fades, and his locker is left abandoned, the red-tinted metal collecting dust. I wonder what names he would have guessed if he was still here. Faith? Fay? Frankie? Franny? Even if he had the whole year, would he ever be able to guess it's actually Fiora, and would it kill me?

Poppet curtsies, and the loose tie around her neck dangles to her knees. "Princess Fiora."

We get what we need for our first periods and close our lockers before taking our usual route to class. I reach mine first, and then Poppet goes further down the hall to hers.

First Period

"Where's April?" I ask when I take my seat.

May is texting on her phone under the table and doesn't bother to look up when she responds: "How should I know?"

"Ah, 'cause she's your friend?"

She looks up from her phone. "Doesn't mean I'm her mother. Have you ever minded your own business before?"

"My fist is about to mind your face."

Mr. Simpson sits at his desk on the other side of the room. "Girls, that's enough. We're about to get started in just a minute," he says.

After the bell, the TV turns on for the morning announcements: "Good morning, students and staff, I am McCarthy, this year's student council president, and these are your morning announcements. A new policy will be implemented at Seal Coast Community High School: Starting today, the use of cell phones, social media, and other wireless communication devices will not be permitted on campus. Cellphones and other devices are to remain in students' personal lockers during school hours or left at home. If outside communication is approved, you may do so at the front office under supervision of staff. Students caught with a cellphone or other wireless communication devices are subject to confiscation where such items must be retrieved from the front office by a parent or guardian. After three strikes, the punishment is a week's suspension. Any more violations after that are grounds for expulsion. Students are reminded to abide by Seal Coast's rules and traditions. For lunch today …" The TV shuts off when the announcements are finished.

Mr. Simpson takes the front of the class. "Alright, you heard the boss lady. I know you all have your phones on you. Go put them up."

May still has her phone in her hand and her horse mouth

drops, exposing her gums even more. "That's not fair."

Mr. Simpson shrugs. "Sorry, those are the rules. If you don't put it up I'll have to take it from you."

May grinds her teeth and neighs before kicking back her chair.

I get to my locker and Poppet is already here. "So we meet again so soon, Princess Fiora. How are we supposed to survive without our *wireless communication devices*? Surely her majesty must have some kind of royal decree?"

"We'll have to write letters with ink and feathers then send them through carrier pigeons," I play along.

"Better yet, I will send mine through doves and teach them to sing songs. Loud screaming ones."

Feedback plays from the speakers mounted to the wall. "Fiora, to the principal's office. Fiora to the principal's office."

Poppet closes her locker and giggles. "Wow, this has to be some kind of record."

"What the fuck?" I whine.

"What did you do this time?"

"Nothing."

It's true.

Principal Pal stands in front of his office, holding open the door. "Take a seat," he orders and gestures me into the room. We enter and both take our seats. It's an exaggerated and confining moment of silence. The mechanical watch strapped to his wrist ticks with every passing second. "I told you not to bring anymore attention to the matter," he finally breaks the silence.

"I didn't do anything," I proclaim. The oppressive heaviness in the air makes me feel I should use my right to remain silent and retain a lawyer to speak on my behalf.

He releases a deep breath, trying to remain calm, but all I see in front of me is a bull ready to lunge. A loud snort puffs through his nostrils as he paws at the ground, and I stand in front of him with a flowing red cape. "Fiora, do you know why so many people are disappointed in you? It's because you have so much potential, and all of it is wasted. You have all of these great qualities that could lead to so many accomplishments, yet here you are time after time again."

"I didn't do anything," I'm adamant.

He releases another breath that signals he's ready to get to his point: "You're a smart girl. Have you heard of *suicide contagion*?"

"What?"

"It's when suicide rates increase after a highly publicized suicide. Almost like a chain reaction, if you will. I told you not to bring any more attention to what happened to Lemming, then you went and did it anyway."

"That was over a month ago! I served my suspension and my detention."

"I encouraged students to seek help for their mental health and banned the student council from bringing more attention to the matter. Yet because of your antics the matter is still on everyone's minds and now–"

"Yeah, 'cause a girl is dead!"

"And now another one is too."

I slump back in my seat, an array of emotions bouncing through me. Everything from frustration, anger, and now confusion. "What?"

"April. She died by suicide over the weekend." His tone is a mixture of no emotion and all the emotions, a purgatory between numb and distraught. "Investigators are keeping the matter silent for now, as am I, but word will spread fast if it hasn't already. Please, I am begging you, do not act impulsively. Let the professionals handle this."

"Oh … um, yeah. Okay."

"You're not in trouble. You may go back to class."

I rise from the seat I've been in so many times it must have my imprint by now. My feet are so heavy I can barely drag them across the linoleum, the soles of my sneakers occasionally squealing as I step. I need to tell Joey. I can't text him without my phone, and this can't wait.

The bell has yet to ring so Joey remains in his first period: math with Ms. Colman, who has been subbing since Mr. Phillips got transferred. I open the door without it being locked, and all the students turn their heads towards me. Joey sits in the back at a table with O'Brien.

"Fiora, can I help you?" Ms. Colman asks.

"I need to see Joey real quick. It's student council stuff." I fib.

I glance over and see the look on Joey's face. He looks just as confused as Ms. Colman. The teacher nods. "If it's for student council then I guess it's alright. Joey? Can you come here please?"

Joey pushes back his seat, as well as O'Brien, and both boys follow me out of the classroom. I wait until the door clicks and latches before speaking. "O'Brien, what the hell are you doing?"

"You said it's for student council," he says.

"Why would I need to talk to Joey about student council?"

Joey scratches the side of his head. "Yeah, that's what I'm kinda wondering too."

"Whatever, fuck the student council!" I cry. "It's April. She's dead."

"What?" both boys exclaim in unison.

"Yeah, Principal Pal just told me himself. He said she killed herself over the weekend," I explain.

Joey leaves his jaw agape. "Huh? This weekend? But–But we. Everything was supposed to be okay!"

"Obviously it's not okay! It's that fucking account! This is exactly what we were talking about!"

O'Brien waves his arms back and forth in a crossing motion, his right one clearly lacking the mobility of the other. "Wait, wait. What are you guys talking about? What happened?"

"It's that fucking account!" I repeat.

"What account?"

"On Instagram!"

Joey takes the words from my mouth when he explains what happened Friday night about the Instagram account and the post exposing April's real name.

O'Brien noticeably loses his stance, his knees buckled and palm pressed to his forehead. "Th-The curse? It's actually real?"

Joey has his arms crossed, wearing his thinking face. "Hey Brien, after you got shot, your name wasn't in the news or anything right?"

It takes a moment for him to react, but O'Brien gains enough composure to shake his head. "No, I'm still a minor so they never released my name."

Joey nods. "Okay, so then if this thing is real, then you should be in the clear." He turns his attention to me. "Have you talked to May about this yet? She might be the last person to see April alive."

I shake my head. "I got out of Principal Pal's office and came right over here to tell you."

"Oh yeah, I heard them call you on the intercom and wondered what the hell you got yourself into this time."

"I didn't do anything. And I doubt I'd get a straight answer from May if I went right back to class anyway."

"Yeah, she's not the biggest fan of either of us. Does she even know yet? Was she acting sad or any different at all?"

O'Brien shakes his head, hands trembling. "How can you guys talk about this so calmly when another one of our friends is dead? You're not actually trying to solve this, are you?" Joey and I look at each other. At this point, is this even solvable? April's death seems to confirm our biggest fear: the curse exists, and now someone is using it to kill. "I need to sit down," O'Brien says, dismissing himself to the classroom.

Is there even anything left for us to discuss? Is this how it ends? Is the only thing we can do now is wait to be killed by something we can never see?

"Hey Fi?" Joey says. I look up at him, his head hanging. "If we're all gonna die anyways, there's something that's been on my mind lately. Would you mind coming over after school? It's about what I wanted to talk to you about. And um … bring an overnight bag."

Evening

"Oh hey, you made it," Joey says when he answers the door. It's just before curfew, with the sun setting and fog thickening. It drapes us in a brisk embrace.

"Yeah, I say." Why am I stalling? I've been to Joey's countless times, but this is the first time I feel physically sick to my stomach. My knees are weak and my palms are sweaty. The wooden panels of the front porch are damp and falling apart, feeling like they're going to crumble beneath my feet. Or is that from my legs shaking?

Joey holds the door open. "Here, come in. It's freezing." I step inside, and Joey shuts the door behind me.

The TV is on, but Joey's grandma is missing from her traditional lounge chair, leaving only a perfectly molded imprint behind. Instead she's at the kitchen counter and her hands tremor as she tries her best to spread red jam across a slice of bread with a butter knife. Joey comes to her side and takes the butter knife from her fragile fingers. "Here, let me get that for you, Grandma." He's much more proficient at spreading the jam, then comes the peanut butter. After slicing it in half diagonally, he places the sandwich on a paper plate and hands it to the old woman. "Come on, Grandma, let's turn on your show." He places his hand on her arched back and guides her to her chair.

Joey's grandma stalls when her attention lands on me. The paper plate quakes in her hands. "Oh Keaton, you look so lovely. I love what you've done with your hair. Did you dye it? It looks much darker."

Joey's face is sullen, more so than usual. "Grandma, Keaton is dea–" he tries to explain before surrendering. "Never mind." He supports the elder with both hands while her gait is barely mobile. Her feet can hardly separate more than an inch apart as if bound by the chains of an oppressive arthritis.

Finally, she makes it to her favorite chair in front of the TV and is steady enough to sit down, thanks to the support from her grandson. Once she's seated, he takes a thick fleece blanket from the couch and drapes it over her lap. "Thank you, Charles," she says in her thick Irish accent, and Joey has a sad smile on his face.

Joey moves much faster when not being used as a crutch and comes to join me. I've known Joey for months now, and I've gotten many good looks at him and imagined many more. But no matter how much I try, I cannot wrap my mind around the possibility of him being a *Charles*. "Your real name is Charles?" I ask, slightly teasing but primarily curious.

"Oh, no. Charles was my grandpa. She just gets confused and calls me that sometimes."

"Damn. So she doesn't even know who you are either." I frame it as a joke, but the longer it sits in the air, the more disheartening I realize it is. Why am I never saying the right things?

He releases a low sigh. "Yeah, sometimes. Come on, let's go to my room. There's something I want to show you."

His room is down the hall, and the TV's blare grows more distant until we reach it. The framed picture of him and Keaton is face down on the dresser.

Joey stands in front of his mattress on the floor and reaches for the front of his pants, but his hand ends up in his front pocket. He pulls out his cellphone and taps on the screen before turning it over and showing me the display. It's that same Instagram page, and another post has been published. It makes my eyes immediately widen. Miles Joseph O'Reilly.

A scream escapes from my body. "No! Who the hell is doing this?"

Does this mean Joey is next to die?

Joey tucks the phone back into his pocket. "I did it." He lowers himself to the mattress. "I messaged the account and told them my real name. Less than an hour later, that post was up."

I sit down beside him. "But why? Why would you do something so stupid?"

A slight snicker brushes Joey's lips. "Do you know how many times I've wanted to ask you that?"

"Don't change the subject. Why would you do that? What if you die?"

There's a conviction in his voice that's unprecedented for Joey. "I said I'm going to get to the bottom of this no matter what, and I meant it. After this, if I drop dead, then we'll know this curse is real. If I don't, then there's a serial killer running loose in Blackridge and using these bullshit *rules and traditions* everyone is so scared of to get away with it."

I can't stop shaking my head. I don't get it. How can someone possibly on the verge of death be so willing to accept so many impossible *ifs*? "How are you getting to the bottom of anything if you're dead?" He stares me in the eyes. He's determined but desperate, and even through this ruse, I can see the fear the shining gold specs his iris give off. I get what he's saying. His mouth may not tell his thoughts, but those eyes do. He's always been so sensitive, so desperate just to be accepted. "Is that why you invited me over?" I ask. "So if you die, I can see how it happens?"

He nods. He removes his gaze from mine and hangs his head. "I know that Keaton and I were over long before she died, but that doesn't mean she deserved to be murdered. I can't just sit back and do nothing while a killer could be out there doing things that Keaton will never get to do again." There's a quiver in his lip and dew filling his eyes. He flutters his eyelashes before the water has a chance to fall. "Seeing a dead body in real life is crazy. You can just sense the lack of life like you would a doll. ... Every time I close my eyes, all I can see is Keaton. But she's not happy and smiling, or even snarling like she hates me. S–She's dead ... face down in a pool of her own blood. Now I'm just supposed to move on after seeing someone close to me like that? Well, I can't. I wake up everyday, I go to school, I breathe, I eat, but I'm not living. It's not fair. Keaton wanted to live too! She wanted out of Blackridge so damn bad. And the thought of it killing her … If I could take her place, I would. I … I need to know why Keaton had to die. It's not like I have anything to live for anyways."

"Joey," I say; the name I've been calling him for so long brushes through my lips in a whisper. There's a heaviness in my chest, an overwhelming sense of grief and sadness. It's intoxicating the way the weight fills my body like lead. It's an avalanche. I feel as if I'm witnessing him with a noose wrapped around his neck, and now I'm waiting for him to kick the chair. Is this the last time I'll ever see Joey alive and breathing?

He likes you, you know? If you make a move he won't say no.

I lean in closer to Joey and place my hand on his knee. That gets him to look back at me. Do I say something, or do I just do it?

I do it.

I push my head forward until my lips press against his, and he doesn't move away. In fact, he kisses me back. Our simple pecks turn into so much more, and I scoot my body closer to his. I want to sit in his lap, so that's exactly what I do as we never take our lips from one another. Both his hands are wrapped around my back and hold my body close to his, but slowly, they inch lower.

Since moving to Oregon, I've thought I would never feel warmth again, but this is the hottest I've ever felt. Joey has his hands grabbing my ass while his tongue is in my mouth, licking mine. I clench his jaw with both my hands, and he leans back, lowering us down to the mattress while we continue kissing. I'm lying on top of him with my chest pressed against his. Can he feel me? I want to feel him.

I pull myself away and straighten my back, staring into Joey's eyes. First I pull out the band for my ponytail and shake my head, causing locks of hair to fall. They're thick and wavy from being tied up for so long, wanting to break free. There's something else that wants to break free, too. I grab the rim of my hoodie to pull it over my head, wearing nothing underneath. There's a chill when my flesh is exposed, but my skin was already prickled from his touch.

I'm presenting myself bare to Joey and this time he doesn't look away or shield his eyes. He bites at the bottom of his lip and releases a breathy sigh. "Holy shit." One hand is on my ass, and the other reaches up to cup my breast. I'm not the biggest girl in the world, so I fit perfectly in his palm. His finger traces the edges of my nipple, causing it to grow even more sensitive.

Now it's Joey's turn. He wears a black and white striped long-sleeve shirt and leans up from the mattress to take his arms from the holes, then pulls it over his head. It messes up his hair and I latch onto the strands to draw myself closer. Our lips meet again, our bare chests pressed together. He holds me and dips me as I sit in his lap. My legs are spread, and I can feel a hard pressure against my pelvis.

I need my tongue to speak so I break. There's something I want more. "I want to see it," I breathe into his mouth. It's been nothing but teasing as it rubs against me.

Joey pulls away and shoots me that look with a smirk and a wink. "*It?*" he asks, knowing exactly what I mean. He just wants to hear me say it.

"Take off your pants."

"Yes ma'am."

Joey stands in front of the mattress and starts with his belt. He meddles with the metal buckle before slipping it from the loops and tossing it to the floor. Next comes the button on the front of his jeans, then comes the zipper. His pants are pulled down to his ankles, leaving him in nothing but his boxer briefs where I can see the imprint of his hard dick pushing against the black fabric, desperate for its escape. The underwear comes off and Joey jumps out from under the elastic like a spring.

He's hard as a rock and it's staring right at me.

Joey is standing over me, his body bare and demonstrating how much he wants me, so I wrap my fingers around his shaft. It's my first time feeling a boy's penis, and calling it *hard as a rock* is a genuine description. However, the flesh is springy and flexible. It's so easy to move up and down, which I know makes him feel good.

He's not circumcised and I like that, but this is Joey. No matter his status, length, or girth, I'd still want every bit of him. It's merely a coincidence that his dick is perfect. I move my hand up and down his shaft, and though I'm inexperienced, I know his tip is his most sensitive part. He breathes through his mouth and a clear, springy liquid emerges from his tip. I must be doing something right.

Joey turns his chin to the ceiling and exasperates a moan. "That feels so good."

My life sucks, okay? And sometimes it's nice to ... feel good.

I want to make Joey feel good. At this point, I think I'm supposed to put it in my mouth. He moans some more and holds back my loose-hanging hair.

"Wait," he says.

I take his dick out of my mouth but keep working his shaft up and down in my hand as I look up at him. "What?"

He bends down and our lips touch. "It's your turn," he tells me and pushes me down so my back lays flat on the mattress. Joey crawls on top of me, his dick pointing like a compass. He starts kissing my lips, and when I think this moment can't get any better, he kisses my neck. My skin rises in excitement as his touch sends a shiver down my spine. All of this feels so good. He keeps kissing me as his hands explore my body. I know he likes my breasts and my ass the way he keeps touching them, but he also knows how to run his hands down my stomach and caress my thighs. How could he possibly already know my body well enough to know all the simple things to make me crazy?

Whenever I want Joey to stay where he's at, he moves lower. But then it only gets better. He kisses my sternum then travels south until he reaches my navel. He bites at my piercing then licks all the way up my body. That sends a shiver all throughout me and he's watching my reaction. His eyes are locked with mine. "Do you want it?" he asks.

Water beats against the window and a bright flash of lightning illuminates the room. It causes the gold in Joey's eyes to glimmer. I love looking into his eyes, and I cup his jawline in my hands. "Of course I want you." I pull his face towards mine so we can kiss some more.

He licks my tongue with his, then he's back on my neck. He teases me as he goes lower and lower. His mouth sucks one of my nipples while his finger traces the other. Then, he goes lower and lower. He's touching me in all the right ways and places–places I've never allowed anyone to touch me before. Anything for Joey.

I've wanted this since I saw him being pushed into the fence on the first day of school. My first thought was how cute he was, but then it turned to becoming that one person who will always be there for him. He's always being picked on, called names, talked about behind his back, and even rejected by someone who, at one point, was the love of his life. But not anymore, not with me. I accept all of him, and I want all of him. I want his insecurities and his clinginess. I want his self-doubt and loathing. There's nothing wrong with you, Joey, and he proves it while my legs dangle over his shoulders and his head is between my thighs.

I run my fingers through his hair, soft and luscious–the only thing soft on Joey right now. I look down to watch him. I like seeing how it's *him* who is touching me and making me feel this good. One of his hands reaches up my body and I lock my fingers with his. We're so connected, but I want to be connected even more.

I tighten my grip around a cuff of his hair and pull his head back up towards my level. He has that signature Joey smirk, his lips wet and glistening. "Doth thy lady protest too much?" he says.

He talks too much, so I stop him by kissing him. "I want you." I'm surprised I have to tell him twice. I appreciate the expedition down south, but I want the main voyage.

His shoulders shimmy as he chuckles. "So, you really are a

virgin, right?"

"Shut up."

"There's nothing wrong with it."

I don't want to say it out loud. We're both naked. I had his dick in my mouth, and he had his head between my thighs, yet somehow this is the most exposing part.

He's back to kissing my neck and, in a breathy whisper, says, "I want to take care of you." He starts with his fingers, and I'm so sopping wet they slide right in. They go in and out several times, loosening me up, and then he takes them out, and there's something else pressing against me. Something much thicker and harder and something sharp pierces through my body like a bolt of lightning when he enters. Quite literally, I tear and release a high-pitched screech I never thought I was capable of, almost like a boiling tea kettle.

Only the tip could make it in before Joey takes himself out. "You alright?" I'm covering my mouth out of pure embarrassment and only nod. "I'll be gentle," he tells me, and we try again.

The tip gets in. I grit and take it, and then there are several more inches to go before his entirety is inside of me, and the most vulnerable parts of our bodies become one.

NOVEMBER 7 – TUESDAY

Morning

The alarm goes off and Joey shuffles under the covers before reaching over and silencing it. He looks down to see me resting against his chest. "Good morning," he says.

I look up at him, still unable to believe everything that's happened the past twelve hours. I'd think this is a dream if everything didn't feel so real, the pain and the pleasure. I take in everything about him. The mix of brown and gold in his eyes, the faint freckles in his pale complexion, the shape of his nose and jaw, and I remember the softness of his lips. I smile. "You look like a Miles."

He smirks. "Oh yeah? You look like ah ... hey, what is your real name anyways?"

"Fiora Clairwater."

Joey bites the bottom of his lip, and his eyes gaze away. "Oh."

I sit up. "Oh what?"

"No, it's nothing. I get it."

"Get what?"

"I mean, I get it. We still don't really know what's going on and you gotta protect yourself."

"You don't believe me? When have I ever lied to you–that you know of?"

He gives me a peck on the forehead. "You don't have to tell me if you don't wanna."

A sharp chill caresses my bare body as I throw the covers off me and find my backpack on the floor. I dig through the front pouch to find what I'm looking for and then display my open wallet to him. His eyes are elsewhere, gazing up and down my body. I clear my throat to get his attention–his proper attention.

He sits up from the mattress to grab the wallet from my hand and seems to have difficulty reading the small print as he holds it close to his face, squinting his eyes. Eventually, he reaches over to the glasses on the floor beside the mattress and puts them on. "Holy shit." He looks at me, my naked body baring over him.

"Told ya," I gloat. "And you called me a liar."

I'm quick to crawl over Joey and back under the covers.

He lays back down beside me and wraps an arm around my shoulder. He holds me close to his body and says, "Wait, I thought you said Clairwater is fake and that your real last name is Navarro."

"Navarro is my mom's maiden name," I start to explain, "but she changed her name and my name to Clairwater after she got published. A lot of professionals do it 'cause it makes paperwork easier. Atlus and I don't have the same dad, so he's actually not a Clairwater. He has his dad's last name still, but he wants to change it to Clairwater after their divorce is finalized. His name is Cerulli."

Joey twirls a loose strand of my hair around his finger. "Wow, so kinda busts our theory from the very beginning, huh? You've been going by your real name this whole time and you're still here."

"And you're still here," I say.

I'm so glad he's still here.

I give him a kiss, and he kisses me back before I rest my head against his chest. I wish we could stay here forever, but there's always something getting in the way. Joey brushes his fingers through my hair and groans. "Ah, fuck. School." He looks down at me. "I needa take a shower. Wanna join me?"

After showering and getting ready, we join Joey's grandma in the living room, where she rests in her usual chair, hopefully sleeping. He leans down to put his ear towards her mouth and waits a moment before giving me a thumbs up. "She's asleep." We venture towards the kitchen and he shuffles through the cabinets. "Um, breakfast. I should make you breakfast."

I lean against the counter, watching him panic. "You don't need to make me breakfast."

"Well, I kinda feel like I do after … I can make you toast." He finds a bag of bread with only the butt ends left.

"Why don't we just go through a drive thru on the way to school?"

Joey gleams at the bread bag, which spins as he holds it up. "Well, I wanna make you something."

I can't say no to the boy I like making me breakfast, even if it is toast made with the butt of the loaf. I guess Joey does know how to wine and dine a girl–in his own way, at least.

* * *

There's a student council meeting with May and I as the only ones here so far. We shoot each other daggers as we sit across from one another. The door opens and in comes a rushed O'Brien, late as usual, as if the watch he wears on his wrist is just for show. "Sorry I'm la–," he trails off. "Where's McCarthy?"

That's what I'm wondering as well. It's a Seal Coast rule and tradition for O'Brien to be late, but McCarthy? That's unheard of. … Unless something has gone horribly wrong. I push back my seat. "I'll go find her."

I search the hall and see her when I check the staff bathroom. She's in front of the mirror, hands pressed to the counter and head hung low. Her red hair drapes over her shoulder while dark lines of mascara stain down her cheeks. "Hey McCarthy, what's wrong?" I ask.

She doesn't look at me and closes her eyes. More black makeup smudges her face, and she takes a deep breath, puffing out her chest. "My mother was a drug addict, and I was born addicted to it too. I was taken away the second I was born and have been in the group home ever since. Nobody wants to adopt a crack baby … Then May went and told the whole school and everyone started looking at me and treating me differently. That's why I need to be better than everyone expects of me. I need to get out of here and be better than how

I was born." She slams her hand against the resin counter. "I'm not going to die in this fucking nothing of a town!"

I've never heard McCarthy talk normal, never seen this much emotion from her, never seen her as human. She continues: "I'm sure you've seen it ... that Instagram account. The one that doxxed April before her death. Joey was added to it last night ... and me this morning. You should pay him a visit while you still can–if you still can. I know you have feelings for him. I ... I ..."

I lean against the counter beside her. "It's not real."

That causes her to look at me, her eyes red and swollen. They match her hair. "What? But April ..."

"I can't explain what happened to April or Lemming. Maybe they both really did commit suicide, but Joey is the one who put himself on that page as an experiment and he's still very much alive. I think there's a killer in town just using the curse to cause mass hysteria."

McCarthy is silent as she looks at herself in the mirror. She tucks her hair behind her ears. "I'm a mess. Today's student council meeting will be postponed." She turns her gaze to me. "And Fiora, this never happened."

I nod. "Yeah, bet."

First Period

"It was you," I'm quick to accuse, sitting across from May.

May flips her hair. "What are you talking about, Enrique Iglasis?"

"It's you. You're the one behind that fucking doxxing Instagram account. April, Joey, McCarthy. They're all people that you hate!"

May sticks up her finger. "I did not hate April!"

"You sure acted like you did. You were horrible to her. You're horrible to everyone!"

"Why not? Everyone else is horrible to me."

"'Cause you deserve it. You fucking suck."

"You fucking suck!"

"Girls," Mr. Simpson barks from his desk. "That's enough."

The bell for class to start rings, and McCarthy is on the screen wearing a brand-new stainless blouse. She looks as beautiful as ever. It's almost impossible to believe she was in the bathroom crying just moments ago.

Second Period

"Class, we're going to be watching a video today on the different branches of government. I want you taking notes and no talking," Ms. Hoyos announces. A video projected onto the whiteboard begins to play.

O'Brien has a piece of paper in front of him with his pen moving. Eventually, he folds the paper and lowers his arm under the desk to hand it to me. I take it from him and unfold the paper to read it: "Have you and Joey figured anything out yet?"

I write my reply: "We'll tell you later. Can't talk about it at school." I fold up the paper and pass it back to him without Ms. Hoyos noticing a thing.

There are, however, murmurs that cause her to look up from her desk. The gossipers notice and shut up before she can identify who it is. The second she looks away, they continue: A girl a few rows ahead of me leans over to whisper into another girl's ear. "I don't believe for a second that she killed herself," she says.

"Why is it being covered up?" says the other girl.

"I'm gonna post a name on that Instagram page and see if they die. Who should we kill?"

"How about that bitch Cheese?"

There's a loud screech as Ms. Hoyos shoots from her chair and stands like a bull ready to lunge. Hot air flares from her nostrils. "That is it! You two, principal's office, now! If I hear another peep out of anyone I will expel you immediately!"

O'Brien and I don't make a sound as we look at each other.

Third Period

Seeing Joey for the first time since his morning puts butterflies in my stomach, my heart to my feet, and bile to my stomach. He's already sitting with Cheese and I play it cool as I join them at the table.

Mr. Mark takes the front of the class and he clears his throat. "Has everyone got a chance to finish their projects from last week? I've noticed some students haven't turned theirs in, but uh, that's not entirely unusual. I think we're ready to move on." He starts pacing around the tables. "I've noticed there are a lot of music lovers here. I mean, who doesn't love music? That's why for our next project, I want everyone to design an album cover. It can be your own interpretation of an album that already exists, or it can be of your own imagination." He makes it back to his desk and leans back. "Cool right?" Nobody answers him and he adjusts his glasses. "Alright, you know the drill. Paper and materials are in the back. Help yourselves."

Joey has his elbow on the table and chin resting in his palm. He's looking at me. "Hey Fi, there's something I need to talk to you about after school. It's about … you know. Something we definitely can't talk about here. Think you can drop me off at work and we'll talk about it there?"

I don't have an opportunity to answer before Cheese returns to the table after retrieving our supplies. She tilts her head. "Don't you usually fuck people in the bathroom?"

Joey is flushed and sits up straight. "G-Get out of my business!" He turns back to me. "Look, Falco won't be our informant anymore, but he did tell me something important. We can't talk about it at school or we'll get in trouble."

"Yeah, two kids were suspended already in my last class," I tell them.

Cheese tilts her head. "Being at school never stopped you before."

Joey slams his fists to the table. "That's not what I mean, Cheese! Geez, we just started going out and you're already trying to get me in trouble."

Wait, did he just say what I think he said? "Going out?" I ask.

He leans across the table and looks into my eyes. "Well yeah, if you want to. I just kinda figured after last night … and this morning. Oh shit, I'm not already being too clingy, am I?"

"No, no. I do want to. And yeah, I'll drive you to work."

After School

"Oh my fucking god," Atlus is already complaining as we meet up in the foyer after the final bell. He's wearing his soccer uniform with his duffle bag over his shoulder.

"What, did your balls finally drop?" I snark.

"No."

"So they haven't dropped then?"

He ignores me and goes straight to the point: "You fucked Joey."

"How is everyone finding out? We haven't even told anybody yet."

"You're sleeping with the enemy!"

I scoff. "There are a million and seven enemies in Black-shit and Joey is not one of them!"

"He murdered Keaton!"

"No he didn't! She was his girlfriend!"

"She hated him!"

"You only think that 'cause you hangout with that prick Kellan."

"He's not a prick, his sister was murdered!"

Someone clears their throat behind us. "Um, hey guys …"

"Joey!" I exclaim. "You ready to go?"

He scratches the side of his head. "I think I'm gonna take the bus today. I'll ah … see you later." He leaves it at that and is out the main entrance.

I shoot Atlus a death stare.

After dropping Atlus off at home I arrive at Nickels and Dimes, but there's no one behind the counter. Looking around, there's not a soul in the store. "Joey?" I cry out, my heart racing.

Joey appears from one of the aisles wearing his red work apron. He waves me down. "Sorry! It's stock day. Come over here, no one's around."

Seeing his face and hearing his voice sends an instant sense of relief through my body. I join him down the aisle with shelves lined with canned meals and fruit on one side, then boxes of cookies and crackers on the other.

"So, you talked to Falco?" I start off. "And he's not going to be our informant anymore?"

He nods as he stocks the shelf. "Yeah, I actually went to talk to him to break things off, but I knew he'd be pissed so I wanted to ask him something first."

"Well, what'd you ask?"

The box he's using to stock the shelves is empty, so he puts it down and sits on the wiry carpet. I join him. "About April. How she died. Falco said she wasn't shot. Her body was found hanging, and she left a note and everything. She was so terrified of being hunted down by the curse after being doxxed that she …"

My stomach drops. "So that confirms it then. Though, I guess we already figured that out," I rest my head on his shoulder, "since you're still here."

He brushes his fingers through my hair. "Yeah, that's what I think too. I also think it's safe to say that Lemming's death really was a suicide too."

I lift my head to look at him. "But that video."

He shrugs. "I don't know why she made that video and it's not like we can ask her now. Maybe she wanted to cause a panic around town as one last hurrah, or maybe she actually believed the curse was real and hoped it would kill her. Who knows?

Then I guess when nothing happened, she killed herself. Turns out the gun wasn't Gregory's at all. I was Lemming's. She got it from a pawn shop, so this whole thing was premeditated."

"But then what happened to the gun? How could the same gun that Lemming used to kill herself also kill Griffin and Keaton? Shouldn't the police still have it? Or destroyed it?"

"I-I have a theory," he chokes on his words. Once he tells me, there's no taking it back. "I did some research and when a gun is used for a suicide, it's usually returned to the family once the case is closed. It's not destroyed like it would be after a murder. But that can take a long time and there wasn't much of a gap between Lemming's suicide and Griffin's murder."

"Yeah, it was only like a week or two."

Joey bites at his thumbnail. "That's what I want to look into. I wanna go over the dates of all the deaths, including suicides, to see if there's a pattern. Maybe after Lemming's suicide, the real killer saw the paranoia throughout the town and took it to their advantage. Now people are more freaked out than ever. Who knows how many more people will kill themselves, especially if people keep getting posted on that doxxing page."

I shake my head. "I can't even count how many times I've reported that page."

"Yeah, me too. But every time it gets taken down another one pops up."

"Okay, and your theory? About the gun?"

He hesitates. "I could be wrong, but I think it's too soon for the gun to have been returned. So, that means it must have been taken by someone connected to the police, right? And that's why they're not making any progress on the murders. So it has to be someone being protected by the police, right? ... And I suspected earlier that it has to be one of the football players." His shoulders relax as he releases a sigh. "I think it's Falco. I've thought it's Falco for a while now."

"And you still fucked him?" I don't mean to say that; it just blurts out.

He looks at me with his head tilted in an almost Cheese-like fashion. "You still fucked me."

"I never thought for a second that you did it. I was the one defending you when they took you in for questioning."

He pecks me on the forehead. "Thank you for that."

"So, what now? If we have a suspect, what do we do about it?"

"We need to look more into this. Just 'cause Falco is the most suspicious doesn't mean he did it. I mean hell, just look at me. If the killer really is Falco, then his only victims were Griffin and Keaton, two people I can see him having motives for. There's no doubt he was jealous of Griffin for getting that football scholarship. And Keaton … he might have killed her 'cause we were together." He pauses, eyes staring into the fluorescent lighting like a moth to a flame. It hurts to see how much he still cares and thinks about her. She was his girlfriend, after all, and now she's gone without any sense of closure. He continues: "She was the last murder that we know of, and that was a little over two weeks ago … Wow, has it really only been two weeks?"

"A lot has happened in those two weeks."

"Tell me about it."

"So how do we look into this without getting busted by the cops and Falco?" I ask.

"First, I think we should make a timeline of all the deaths, see if there's some kind of pattern and maybe find out if we can establish any alibis. Do you remember the date when Griffin died?"

I shake my head. "I don't, but I can look at articles online and collect all the dates from there. I can do that tonight."

He smirks. "You're a lifesaver."

I smile back at him. "You know, that's not the first time you've called me that."

We take a moment to enjoy each other's company.

NOVEMBER 8 – WEDNESDAY

The facts:

- Holly McGuire–aka Lemming–died from a self-inflicted gunshot wound to the head the night of September 24th after posting a video to her Instagram story telling all of Blackridge her name.
- Zachary Moore–aka Griffin–was found dead in the locker room from a gunshot wound to the head by Falco the morning of October 10th, but he is assumed to have died the night of October 8th, after the football game that Sunday.
- Milena Freeman–aka Keaton–was found dead by a gunshot wound to the head by Joey on October 24th.
- Eloise Horton–aka April–died by suicide sometime between November 3rd and November 6th after her name was posted on the doxxing page.

Midnight

I make myself comfortable in the kitchen with a bowl of ramen. I'm not an aspiring chef like Atlus with fancy things like eggs and pork belly, and we're not on speaking terms due to his outburst about Joey. He may be innocent to the law, but the court of public opinion is another matter. I need to clear his name and proclaim justice for our fallen friends.

I slurp my noodles, careful not to get drippage on my paper, and study the dates until they're branded into my memory. September 24th, October 8th, October 24th, November 3rd. I massage my temples, my head aching, and my eyes strained. I'm not smart like Joey to distinguish a pattern.

Footsteps barrage themselves down the stairs. They're heavy, sloppy, and unfamiliar to the ear. I rise from the stool at the island to catch the assailant, but it's no other than my own mother. "Fi, ¿qué haces despierta a estas horas? (Fi, what are you doing up this late?)" she asks. She speaks clearly, enunciating her words after the apparent drink or two.

I fold the paper and tuck it in my pocket. "Quería un bocadillo. (I wanted a snack.)"

"Qué bueno, no quería despertarte. (Oh good, I didn't want to wake you up.)" She joins me at the island. "¿Quieres un trago? (Do you want a drink?)" A strong aroma of wine leaks from her breath. Her wobbliness brings me worry yet also admiration as she climbs the kitchen counters and opens the cabinet above the fridge, pulling out a bottle of tequila and a couple of shot glasses. She jumps from the counter and lands in a way that would hurt her knees if she wasn't buzzed.

"¿Cómo es que no sabía que eso estaba ahí? (How did I not know that was there?)" I ask.

Mom taps me on the nose. "Porque eres chaparrita. (Because you're short.)"

We sit down on the stools at the island and she pours us each a shot, careful not to waste even a single drop. She slides my glass across the countertop.

We clink our glasses. "¡Salud!"

Mom returns her empty glass to the island top. "Sabes que te quiero, ¿verdad Fiora? (You know I love you, right Fiora?)"

"Claro. ¿De dónde viene esto? (Of course. Where's this coming from?)" I ask, knowing exactly where it's coming from.

Mom looks down at her glass. Only a minuscule amount of clear liquid remains at the bottom. "Solo siento que no les digo eso lo suficiente. Normalmente les estoy diciendo a ustedes dos que dejen de pelear. Pero ahora está todo en silencio. Lo que me dice que ustedes dos realmente están peleando. (I just feel like I don't tell you kids enough. I'm usually telling you two to stop fighting. But now it's been quiet. Which tells me you two really are fighting.)"

I pour myself another shot. "Atlus llamó a Joey un asesino y Joey lo escuchó. (Atlus called Joey a murderer and Joey heard.)"

"Atlus solo tiene catorce años. Mientras no se atrape a un verdadero asesino, va a repetir lo que escucha de sus amigos. Kellan es un buen chico, solo está enojado y necesita a alguien a quien estar enojado. (Atlus is only fourteen. Until a real killer is caught he's going to parrot whatever he hears from his friends. Kellan is a good boy, he's just angry and needs someone to be angry at.)"

Mom pours herself another shot and downs it in one take. Her finger traces the edge of the glass. "Los traje aquí porque pensé que era el nuevo comienzo que necesitábamos, pero ahora siento que nunca me fui. (I brought you kids here because I thought it was the fresh start we needed, but now it feels like I never left.)" She slides my glass across the counter top and pours me a shot before sliding it back. Then she pours another for herself. She takes the shot of liquid courage. "Entonces, estabas preguntando sobre tu papá y el tiroteo el otro día. (So, you were asking about your dad and the shooting the other day.)"

I nod, hoping and praying she keeps talking.

"His name was Elliot Vaughn–the shooter, not your dad," she explains.

"Yeah, yeah I know that much."

Mom sighs. "I need a drink." She knocks on the glass bottle of tequila. "And not this type of drink. I need some water."

Jumping down from the stool makes my head spin. The drinks hit me fast and after fixing both of us a glass of water, I return to the island.

Mom takes several large sips, her throat moving and making audible gulping sounds. She sets it down like a shot glass before continuing her story: "His name was Elliot Vaughn, and he was my best friend. Or, at least, I thought he was. He was your favorite word: an *incel*. A *nice guy*. And that was what I told everyone anytime they said he wasn't good for me: that he was nice.

"He always told me how I did or didn't deserve to be treated. Every time I had a boyfriend, he always found some excuse to convince me to break up with him. He was a douchebag, he was talking to other girls, he was just using me for my body. It was no different when I started dating your father." Her gaze faces down while she shakes her head, a dim smirk on her lips. "Which is funny because your father was the only boy to ever treat me right. But that infuriated Elliot. Then when I told him I was pregnant, he told me to get an abortion and that I'd regret it if I didn't. I thought he meant I'd regret being a teen mom." She shakes her head. "But he didn't. He meant I'd regret making his list.

"The day of the shooting, I had awful morning sickness and ended up going home early, but I guess Elliot didn't know that. He went from classroom to classroom to kill everyone who he thought wronged him, including your father. He killed nine people before the cops finally showed up and killed him. Getting pregnant with you literally saved my life, Fiora. That guy was a ticking time bomb. If it wasn't that to set him off, it would have just been something else later.

"That's why I changed my name when I started writing, to distance my books from the shooting as much as possible. I want to be known as an author, not the girl on Elliot's list."

I don't know what to say, which I tell her. Every day all we do is read and watch the horrible things happening around the world, but it's a different experience hearing it from a victim. The world is fucked, and we've been desensitized to it.

"You don't have to say anything, Fi," she tells me. "I've made a lot of mistakes, but having you and your brother was the only thing I've ever got right."

She reaches for the bottle and pours us more shots.

"You both were so surprised that I wanted to get a job. Do you want to know why?" she asks.

I nod. To this day, I still don't believe–or remember–what excuse she gave us. "It's Eric, Atlus's dad. It's almost comical. The bastard marries a teenager with a baby and makes her sign a prenup, but now that I make more than he does, he wants money." She releases a heavy sigh. "Every single last penny I've made from my books and shows is going to you and your brother, so I needed something else to give him."

"Money?" I gasp. "So you started working at Bedrock to pay that son of a bitch?"

She nods, not a single tear in her eyes. Only determination. "He gets his money, I get full custody of Atlus."

"But that piece of shit hated Atlus!"

Mom presses a finger to her lips. "Shh, don't wake him up. But yeah. Even though I was leaving, he still found another way to use Atlus to hurt me. The money's not much, but I'd never be able to live with myself if he got even a drop more out of me." She sighs. "I moved you kids here because I thought it's what would be best for our little family, but I've made another mistake in a lifetime of many."

I can't believe I'm about to admit this, but, "Moving here wasn't a mistake."

Mom shoves me on the shoulders. It's not hard, but I wobble more than I should since I'm a little tipsy. "Atlus doesn't know and don't you dare tell him, not even when you're bickering." She gives me another light shove, and this time, I have to grab onto the edge of the island just to catch myself. "I want you to bicker with him. If you're both going to be stubborn about this, it'll never end. He's your brother and he loves you."

"Yeah, yeah, yeah."

Mom sticks out her tongue. "Don't you *yeah, yeah, yeah* me. Now get to bed. I know you have your lawyer meeting tomorrow."

"Good night Mom. I love you too."

Morning

JOEY: Good morning :)

That helps get me out of bed after staying up too late and drinking too much. Not only do I want to see Joey because he's my boyfriend now, but also because I have the list he asked for. I crawl out of bed and touch my feet to the hardwood floor.

A hot shower helps wake me up, and then I skip down the stairs to the kitchen. Atlus is in front of the stove frying some eggs, and neither of us says a word to each other as I walk past him and to the fridge. I press the fridge's button to dispense a single ice cube before dropping it down the back of Atlus's shirt.

He freaks out and squirms, trying to get the frozen cube out from under his shirt but cannot reach it. "What the fuck?" he cries as he dances in circles before finally brushing it out. He shoots me a death stare while holding the spatula like a weapon. "What the fuck is wrong with you?"

Mom comes down the stairs, her steps much lighter and steadier than when she drunkenly joined me in the kitchen last night. Her eyes are sunken, and her skin is visibly dry as she rubs her temples. "Can you two please not do this this morning?" She scoots herself into one of the stools at the island.

"Mom!" Atlus whines. "She put an ice cube down my back for literally no reason!"

"Fi, you have your whole life to pick on your little brother. Let's have one morning of peace?"

"That's all you're gonna say? And no, don't ask if I want any cheese with my whine."

"Oh good, so you already know what I was going to say."

Looks like everything is back to normal.

Third Period

With Joey's car totaled, I don't see him in the student parking lot. I don't get to see him at the racks with his bike stolen. He takes the bus with Cheese when I don't pick him up. Our lockers are on opposite ends of the school, so I don't get to see him before first period, either. The first time I get to see him is in third period, and I smile when I do. He's at the table with Cheese, and the bell rings shortly after I sit down. "Hey, I have something for you," I announce and dig into the pouch of my hoodie. I pull out the folded paper.

Joey accepts it with a wink and a smirk. "Is this a love letter?" he asks without opening it.

"Why, do you like love letters?"

He rests his arms across the table to lean in closer towards me. "I like whatever you wanna give me."

"How about a list of a bunch of dead people?"

That makes Joey sit up straight. "Oh yeah, I asked for that."

Cheese tilts her head. "You guys have a weird relationship."

Joey is unfolding the piece of paper. "Butt out of it Cheese. We can talk more about this after school." He leans back in closer to me. "Um, speaking of after school, why don't we go out? I mean, we hangout all the time and … stuff, but have never been on a date."

I hope I don't look as stupid smiling as I feel, but my smile quickly fades. "I have to meet with my lawyer after school."

Joey taps me on the nose. "Right, I almost forgot you're a criminal."

"Hey, innocent until proven guilty, baby."

Cheese tilts her head to the other side. "Why are you seeing a lawyer?"

I squint at her. "To fight my charges?"

"But you did it."

Joey and I shoot her the same look and say, "So?" in unison.

He turns his attention back to me. "Alright, how about lunch? We can't leave the campus so it won't be anything fancy, but we can at least eat out on the field."

Fuck I hate having to reject him so much. "I have detention at lunch."

He furrows his brows. "Still? Frome candle-gate? How?"

"'Cause school keeps getting canceled and a lot of times I have to spend lunch at student council so that cuts into my time served."

He winks. "You don't think Ms. Hoyos would be opposed to letting me join, do ya?"

"Don't even think about purposely getting in trouble so you get detention."

"Isn't that what you did for him?" Cheese butts in despite being told the opposite by Joey.

"Yeah, and look how well that turned out for me," I say.

Joey breathes through his nose and crosses his arms. "Man, this sucks. I finally get a girlfriend who actually likes me and we can barely spend any time together."

I put my hand on his shoulder. "But after I'm done we can have lunch together every single day. I'll tell student council to get bent if I have to."

That causes a smile on his soft and supple lips. "Really?"

"Yeah, really. Oh! And O'Brien wants to talk to us about you know what, but that'll have to be sometime after school."

"He asked me about that too. I told him I'll have to check my work schedule. Or maybe ..." His gaze turns to Cheese. "You wouldn't be willing to take a few shifts for me, would'ya?" She shakes her head. "What, why not? What's the point of being co-workers if we don't *co*-opperate?"

I cringe. This is the guy I let take my virginity?

Cheese has a pouty look on those plump pink lips of hers. "I want to talk to O'Brien too."

Joey claps his hands together in a plea. "I promise, just cover a few shifts for me and I'll help you get with O'Brien. Guy's kinda slow. He just needs a little extra push, is all."

Finally, Cheese relents and shrugs. "Fine."

After School

Dianne DeBoar, the lawyer I hired for my case, invites me into her office. We've talked on the phone, but this will be my first time seeing her in person. She shakes my hand and says, "Hi Fiora, I'm Dianne DeBoar. It's nice to finally put a face to the voice." She gestures to a leather-lined chair in front of the desk. "Why don't you take a seat?"

She sits and opens the binder, giving it a quick look over before presenting me with a professional smile. Either there's good news about my case, or she sees a big payday in her future. "Let's go over the lesser charges first," she says. "Second-degree disorderly conduct and resisting arrest. Those charges–" She makes an X shape with her fingers. "They're gone. They're dropped."

"Sweet!" I cheer.

"Don't celebrate just yet. The felony is the big one. I need you to be honest with me, were you being belligerent with the police?"

"I mean, that's the more professional way to put it, but only a little bit! I have freedom of speech."

She closes the binder in front of her with a hefty slap and gust of wind. "Well, you're in luck."

"Luck? I actually have a case? I was quite literally caught red handed. I could not have been more caught if I tried."

"You're in luck that you hired me and I don't let the police get away with brutality."

I slam my hand on her desk. The wood is cheaper than it looks. "Fuck yeah!"

"Because of your big mouth, you were overcharged. You were charged with unlawful possession of fictitious identification, which is only a felony in Oregon if caught in the act. Say, using it to purchase alcohol, marijuana, a firearm. You were not doing any of those things–at least not at the moment. You got overcharged, I argued, the charge got dropped. You are officially charge free."

I jump from my seat. I've never wanted to kiss a middle-aged woman so badly. "You are a lifesaver!"

"Get into any more trouble and you know who to call."

"Yeah, Saul."

I'm practically skipping when I leave the office and head out into the fog. The first thing I do upon getting in my car is turn on the heater, and the second thing I do is call Joey through Bluetooth.

"Hello? So how did it go? Are we gonna need to schedule some conjugal visits soon?" his voice asks through the speaker.

"Nope! And you are officially no longer allowed to call me a criminal! My charges were dropped."

"That's awesome! W-Wait, but aren't you still a criminal though? Didn't you go to jail before you moved to Oregon?"

"That's a nonfactor."

"What'd you do?"

"Oh you know, this and that."

"Th-That doesn't mean much. *This and that* for you could mean anything from petty theft to nuclear bombing."

"Geez, why do you all think so low of me? But it doesn't matter! I'm free!"

"So ... free as in, right now free?"

"Yep."

"Free for a date?"

I'm glad he can't see how wide my smile is. I love how much he keeps asking me. I don't care if other people might see it as clingy. Maybe I'm clingy too. "Yeah, totally. We need to celebrate."

"Cool! Come to Nickels and Dimes."

"Nickels and Dimes? What happened to begging Cheese to take your shift for you?"

"Well, without you I didn't have anything better to do so I figured I'd get some overtime in. I can't get my mind off certain things whenever I have a spare moment." *Certain things*, huh? "But you should still come. I have an idea."

"Oh yeah? What kind?"

"That's a secret."

"Well, I'll trust you. You've become our idea guy lately."

I pull into the familiar parking lot of Nickels and Dimes, and Joey is waiting under the awning in front of the store. He has a plastic party popper in his mouth and blows it at me. "Congratulations on not being a felon. If I had more time, I would have had a cake made."

He hands me one of the plastic toys and I blow it before pulling it from my teeth. "So, what's your secret idea?"

"You're getting treated to dinner and a movie: Miles O'Reilly style. That's kinda my way of saying I'm broke and Blackridge doesn't have a movie theater. Nickels and Dimes doesn't have much, but we at least have a frozen section. We can pick a few things out, get some snacks, some drinks, then go back to my place to watch Netflix."

I reach out to grab his hands. They're cold to the touch. "Or not watch Netflix."

A smirk appears on his lips. "Or not." He leans down to kiss me. "I'm so glad we're finally doing this."

Holding my hand, he leads me into the store for another example of Joey's wining and dining.

Evening

A movie played, but Joey and I certainly didn't watch. "Get home safe," he wishes me, then gives me a peck on the forehead on the way out. By the time I pull into the garage, the storm has set in and it's pouring rain.

Something smells good.

The troll commonly inhabiting the kitchen is in front of the stove, and that's where the delicious smell comes from. In the pan are pork chops, some cream sauce, and plenty of onions.

I attempt to stick my finger in the sauce, but Atlus quickly smacks the back of my hand with his wooden spoon. I pull back. "Ow, fuck."

"Keep your filthy fucking monkey paws out of my sauce!" he fee-fi-fo-fums.

"What is it?"

He returns the spoon to the sauce to stir it. It's nice and thick, and he uses it to top the pork chops: "Onion smothered pork chops. It's almost done."

"Where's Mom? We can't eat takeout *and* your pork chops."

"Fuck takeout. She's not here yet."

I glance over to the time displayed on the stove. It's pretty late for a night Mom doesn't close, but it took me triple the time to get home from Joey's between the fog and the rain. There's a quick flash of lightning, and a few seconds later, thunder comes.

The curtains cover the windows in the living room, but the fabric is thin enough for a beam of light that shines through. It stays for much longer than lightning. It's a car.

"That must be Mom," I note, but there's something strange about how the lights stare at the front of the house.

It gains Atlus's attention as well. "Is she not gonna pull in the garage?"

"Maybe she forgot her clicker. She was pretty hungover this morning."

The lights shut off with the car remaining in the driveway.

A lump I can't swallow forms in my throat. "Attie, go to your room," I order.

"No way," he protests. "I want to see what's going on."

I'm not so sure I want to see what's going on. We exchange looks before I step forward and check the front door. Standing on the porch are two people, neither of them Mom. They're detectives Angel and Damien, the good cop, bad cop duo. The water is loud as it beats down against the pavement. "Oh hell no, my charges were dropped."

"Fiora, may we come in please?" Detective Angel asks.

I shake my head. "Come back with a warrant, the doormat says so."

Just when I'm about to slam the door, he says something that stops me. Something I'll never forget for the rest of my life: "It's about your mother." Then, he repeats the question.

I never thought I would find myself holding open the door and inviting the police into my home. The dog continuously barks upon their entering.

I don't hear Atlus's heavy feet sneak up behind me. It's like everything around me has stopped. Even the rain ceased to fall. "What happened to our mom?" he asks.

Good cop gestures to the couch ahead of us in the living room. "You're going to need to take a seat."

He doesn't need to spell it out. That right there tells me everything.

Atlus and I sit beside each other on the couch, and Good Cop kneels down to our level. "I'm sorry to tell you this, but your mother is dead," he says.

The second he said it was about Mom, I already knew, and somehow, in the short amount of time it takes to go from the front door to the couch, I already processed and accepted it. Mom is dead. Just like that, life flashes past me in an instant. I think about last night and how it was the first time we sat down and talked. It was the first time she treated me like an adult without it turning into a lecture about how much of a fuck up I am. Now, I'll never talk to Mom again.

"M-Mom's dead?" Atlus chokes. His dark, sunken eyes have no tears, and his face is simply stoic. He's in shock.

It's hard to describe how it feels when time stands still.

Detective Angel nods. "I'm sorry lad, but she's gone. A passerby found her body on the side of the road barely a mile away from Bedrock. We've already notified the victim's sister and we will stay with you until she gets here."

How can so many things be running through my mind and nothing at all simultaneously? But no matter where my mind wanders, there's always something it returns to: "Was she shot?" I ask.

Both detectives look at each other, and Detective Damien decides to answer: "We can't disclose that information at this moment. It's an active investigation."

"It's pretty obvious whether someone was shot or not."

Detective Angel tries to reach for my hand, and I quickly pull it away. "Fiora, would you maybe like to step outside and get some air? I know this is hard news to hear."

It's strange how much of their attention is on me when Atlus is the minor here. "Where is she?" he asks.

"*Where is she?*" Detective Damien repeats. "I'm sorry, but she's gone."

As if that hasn't been made clear already.

"No, I mean where's her body," Atlus explains. "Can we see her?"

That causes the detectives to exchange another look.

Detective Angels shakes his head. "No son, you can't see her. Her body was taken by the coroner."

"I'm not your fucking son," Atlus's angst is triggered.

We sit in the living room in a moment of silence, listening to nothing but the rain beating down on the windows and the occasional rumble of thunder. It sounds like the storm is drifting further away.

Beams of light shine through the fabric of the curtains and a car stops in the driveway. Only moments later does the doorbell ring. The detectives start to act as if they're going to answer the door, but this is my house so I get up from the couch and do it instead. At the door is Aunt Addie. She's soaked head to toe from just a few minutes in the rain. "Fiora. I'm so sorry," are her first words.

I don't say anything and hold the door wide for her to enter.

"Ms. Hoyos, thank you for coming out on such short notice," Detective Damien greets and holds out his hand.

Aunt Addie reaches her hand out towards his, her shaking clearly visible. "Th-Thank you for telling me. I-I-I just can't believe this."

"We're working on this case to the best of our ability," Detective Angel declares in his best fake tone. He reaches into his coat pocket and pulls out a couple of business cards. He hands one to a shaking Aunt Addie and the other to me. "If you have any questions or information, please do not hesitate to give us a call." The card is a repeat of the one they gave me after questioning me about Griffin's murder.

"H-How will we know when someone is caught?" Aunt Addie asks.

Detective Damien nods. "The family will be the first to know. Please, take care of yourselves and be safe."

With that, the two detectives take their leave.

The three of us stay in the living room, not saying a word. I can hear Aunt Addie's breathing and Atlus's heart beating.

Atlus gets up from the couch. "I'm going to bed."

Aunt Addie pokes her head up like a prairie dog out its burrow. "G-Good night Atlus!"

He doesn't say anything and goes up the stairs, his socked feet barely making a sound.

I need to go to bed too. Maybe once I do, I'll wake up and realize this has been one big nightmare. I'll wake up to the smell of bacon and eggs, then go to the kitchen for breakfast and find Mom at the island drinking a cup of coffee like always. Right now, I only smell Atlus's pork chops burning on the stove.

NOVEMBER 9 – THURSDAY

NEBULA CLAIRWATER DEAD AT 35

Nebula Clairwater, bestselling author best known for fantasy trilogy The Tales of Fiora, has died. The author's publicist, Victoria Doyle, confirmed Clairwater died Wednesday night. It is unclear how Clairwater died or the circumstances surrounding her death. Sources with knowledge tell the media the author moved back to her hometown of Blackridge, Oregon, that has been involved in a recent string of murders.

ANOTHER ONE BITES THE DUST: THE LATEST VICTIM OF THE CURSE OF BLACKRIDGE

BLACKRIDGE, Or. –Detectives are conducting a homicide investigation after the body of an unidentified woman was found off South Shore Street Wednesday night. A motorist found the woman, who was unresponsive, just before 7:30 p.m. police said. She was pronounced dead at the scene.

Morning

I wake up and last night still happened. Mom is still dead. Squeak lies on my stomach, unaware of what's happening. I scratch her under her chin, and even the rumbling of her purring can't soothe this aching deep into my chest.

A multitude of unknown calls plague my phone's notifications, the press wanting information on Mom's death, no doubt. Every time a new call appears on the screen, I swipe it away. I only answer when the incoming call is from Joey. "Hello?" I say.

"Oh, morning voice. You just wake up?" he asks. "I've been trying to get a hold of you all morning."

I rub my eyes. I slept all night, yet have never felt so exhausted. "Yeah, kinda had a rough night last night."

"You're not the only one! Have you checked Blackridge Online? They found another body last night! And get this, a cause of death isn't mentioned at all. I remember in Lemming's story, her death was ruled a suicide right away. Then the articles about Griffin and Keaton specifically said they had *apparent gunshot wounds to the head*. This one doesn't say anything about that, or even identify who the victim is. What could this mean?"

Oh yeah, that's right. Joey and I have been investigating the killings. I guess Mom's wouldn't be any different. "Hey Joey?"

"Yeah? Oh, good morning by the way."

That causes a brief smile on my face that quickly fades. "Good morning. Can you do me a favor real quick?"

"Yeah, what's up?"

"Google *Nebula Clairwater*."

"Your mom? Um, okay." He's silent for a moment, and then I hear him start coughing like he's drinking something and choking. "Wh-What? What the fuck? Is this real? What happened?"

"Yeah, it's real. Good Cop and Bad Cop came by to tell us last night."

"Good Cop and Bad Co–oh, you mean Detective Angel and Damien. But–But–But. Fi I'm so sorry. The bus just got here, but I'll skip and get over there as fast as I can."

"No, get on the bus. School is so boring without you."

"School? You're not serious, right?"

"Of course I am. I still have the rest of my detention to serve so we can start having lunch together."

There's a pause.

"Oh, um … yeah, right. Yeah, I'll see you at school then."

I get off the phone with Joey before showering and getting dressed. The pouring hot water is exactly what I need to wake up, and my skin is soft and smooth after a nice shave and lather.

Downstairs, there's no aroma of anything cooking, and Aunt Addie lies on the couch. A blanket covers her body and the crease of her elbow is used as an eye mask. "Aunt Addie?" I ask.

She moves her arm away and sits up. "Oh, Fiora. Good morning."

"Did you sleep down here last night? You know you could have slept in Mom's bed. Not like she's gonna be using it anymore."

Aunt Addie has her gaze on her socks on the hardwood floor and continuously shakes her head. "N-No. No way I'm ever going in her room after what happened last night."

I hear Atlus's mutt's collar jingling before I see him, and the clinking gets more repetitive as he hops down the stairs. Atlus is soon to follow, his eyes darker than ever and hair messy. He says nothing as he passes us and leaves through the back door. I wait until Atlus and Trash are outside and the sliding glass door is shut. "What's going to happen to him?" I ask. Aunt Addie hums at me, so I repeat the question. "Now that Mom's gone, who has custody of him? What about his dad?"

She takes a deep breath. "Well, the courts will decide who gets custody of him."

"What the hell is that supposed to mean? You mean Mom died without a will?"

Aunt Addie shakes her head. "No, your mom had a will. She asked me a long time ago if I would take custody of you and Atlus if something were to happen to her but a will is merely a … suggestion. Custody is decided by the courts."

"So what, court just says *fuck you dead lady, we do what we want*?"

"Well …" she pauses. "That's one way to put it. CPS will always contact the father first. Then if he won't take custody they go down the line of next of kin."

I scoff. "His dad is a piece of shit! You mean just like that he can take Atlus away? All he ever did was use Attie as a punching bag."

Aunt Addie places her finger in her mouth, but the nails are so bitten down that she gets nothing but a nub. "I-I really don't know Fiora. Th-there's a lot of paperwork after someone d-dies. I didn't think that far."

"You're fucking useless."

She stares at me with those bulging eyes. There's nothing she can do about it when we're not in class.

The glass door slides open and Atlus and Trash enter.

Aunt Addie throws herself off the couch and rushes to the kitchen so fast her socks almost slip on the hardwood floors. "Atlus! You know, I hear you're quite the masterchef."

Aunt Addie's prying and bulging eyes are met by Atlus's defunct eyes. "Who told you that? My dead mom?" he said.

She's back to picking at what's left of her nails. They're bitten down so bare there's no space for even a speck of dirt under them. Quite literally, she's bitten off more than she can chew. "Um ... well, yeah. Y-You like cooking. You should make breakfast." She's quick to catch herself. "No! I'll make breakfast." She rummages through the cabinets like a rat looking for a smorgasbord. "Let's see, let's see. Um ... I can make ... uh ..."

Atlus sits down at the island. "I want takeout."

Aunt Addie spins around, thankful for her saving grace. "Yes! Takeout. I'll go get takeout. I can go get donuts and sandwiches from Coffee Grounds." She pats herself down around her pockets. "Now where did I put my keys?"

It's our mother who just died, yet it's this woman who is a mess.

I don't want to be a part of this so I grab my keys hanging by the door and go to the garage. I pause, needing a moment to process what I see–or rather–don't see. Mom's car isn't here. Somehow rain got on my face so I wipe it away before hopping in my car. The engine turns on, and the Bluetooth connects to my phone. *Take Me Away* by The Plot in You starts to play from the speakers and I turn it off. It's a silent drive to school, listening to nothing but the rain beating on my windshield.

* * *

Poppet is closing her locker by the time I arrive at mine. "What, you're not going to bow in the presence of royalty?" I ask.

There's no cheeky smile in her face or shimmy in her movements. She barely dips down to curtsy. "All hail Princess Fiora … Um, are you okay?"

"Why wouldn't I be okay?" I ask.

"Um … no reason I guess."

"Fiora!" Joey's voice calls out.

I finish grabbing my stuff and close my locker. I'm so glad to see him. "You've never visited me at my locker before," I say.

The first thing he does is embrace me, holding me close to his chest and giving me a chance to smell his cologne. "I just really needed to see you."

I hug him back, wrapping my arms around his thin yet toned frame.

The first warning bell of the morning rings.

"You're going to be late to your class, Joe," Poppet points out.

Feedback plays from the speakers mounted to the wall. "Fiora to the principal's office. Fiora to the principal's office."

Joey scratches the side of his head. "You really can't catch a break, huh?"

"You know me, always living the life of crime," I say.

My back is turned as I create distance down the hall, and Poppet and Joey talk behind it. "Why is she … okay?" Poppet asks.

"I dunno," Joey answers. "Guess it just hasn't hit yet. Let's give her some time."

I pretend I don't hear them and keep walking.

"Good morning, Fiora," Principal Pal greets me when I reach his office. He holds open the door and we both enter his office and sit in our usual seats. "Fiora, I would like to wish you my greatest condolences," he starts off. "Losing a loved one, especially a parent, is never easy. I am proud of your strength. Please, you and your brother take as much time as you need to grieve this tragic loss. With that said, I think it's time we put an end to this."

I'm slumped back in my seat. "What, you're finally expelling me?"

"No, I mean your detention. It's been long enough and you've paid your dues. I see no need to prolong this any further."

That causes me to straighten up. "You mean I can have lunch with my friends again?"

Principal Pal nods. "I've been watching you closely and you have made some great and supportive friends. Surround yourself with them. And take advantage of Mrs. Burke's resources."

"Yeah I'm not gonna do that, but I will have lunch with my friends."

I get up from the chair and excuse myself from his office.

Third Period

Mr. Mark arrives at class just before the bell rings and looks around at all the students present. His eyes stop once they get to my table. "Oh, Fiora. Um … we're glad to have you."

I squint my brows at him. "Glad to have you too, Mr. Mark."

That manages to get a few awkward chuckles from the class.

Joey rests himself against the table. "How you holding up?"

I groan, sigh, and roll my eyes. The holy trinity. "Can people please stop asking me that?"

Joey backs off. "I get it. Wanting things to go back to normal … keeping yourself distracted so you're too busy to feel what you're feeling. I won't bring it up again, not unless you want to."

"Why, 'cause her mom was murdered?" Cheese blurts out, and we both look at her.

Lunchtime

Our album cover assignments are almost finished, but the bell rings and we have to put them back on the drying rack until tomorrow. Afterward, we're out of class and in the halls. Joey reaches over and grabs my hand. "Don't suffer too badly in detention, okay?"

"Actually, I'm off the hook," I say.

"For real?"

"Yes, for real. In fact, Principal Pal specifically told me to hangout with all of you."

"Um … I can imagine why. But that's good. If I had known I would have packed something special."

"Shit, don't worry about it. I didn't even know until this morning. That's what I was called into his office for."

"Oh yeah, I was meaning to ask about that. Guess I just … forgot."

"It's hard to keep up with everything going on with you," Cheese says.

It's been so long since I sat in the cafeteria, and everyone is together: Joey, Poppet, Pandora, O'Brien, and Cheese. Someone approaches from the lunch line and attempts to join our little group. It's May. She sets her tray on the table and helps herself to an empty seat.

"What the fuck are you doing?" I confront.

"I don't exactly have any friends anymore," she answers.

"Yeah, and whose fault is that?"

May grabs her tray, and just as she's about to get up, someone else arrives and attempts to lead Joey away by the arm. "Come on, I have to show you something," Falco says.

Joey breaks his arm from his grip. "Fuck off. I'm with my friends."

Falco tries grabbing at him again. "It'll just take a second."

"No. I told you, I'm done with that."

"Hey!" Pandora snips. "No means no, ass face rapist. Go fuck off and die."

Couldn't have said it better myself.

May stands from her seat holding her tray. "Come on Falco, I'll eat with you." The pair walk off.

At least after who knows how long, I'm finally getting to have lunch with my friends again and things feel normal.

After School

After the last bell, Joey and I reach the curb in front of the school to meet with O'Brien. Except, he's not here. Joey scratches at the side of his head. "He hasn't been picked up yet, right?"

"Um ..." I pull my phone out from my back pocket and scroll through the mountain of notifications I've been ignoring to see if there are any from O'Brien. "Not that I know of."

"Fiora!" someone calls out. It's Farrah, and her sneakers slap against the damp pavement as she runs up towards us. "Fiora, I didn't think you'd be here after ... after–"

I present myself. "Well, here I am."

Farrah shakes her head. "It's not fair. First Lemming and now your mom? Neither of them deserved any of this."

"Yeah, and add Griffin, Keaton, and April to the mix. Whoever is doing this is going to fucking pay."

Farrah shuffles her feet and picks at her nails. "Um ... I noticed Atlus wasn't at school today so I was wanting to drop off his homework again. I wanted to talk to him too. I ... I know how it feels to lose a mom."

I look up at Joey and then back to Farrah. "I'd give you a ride, but we're kinda doing something right now."

Farrah perks up. "Oh, that's okay! Since it stopped raining I can take my bike. Your house isn't very far from here." She waves at us as she walks off towards the bike racks.

Joey hums. "Didn't her dad used to drop her off?"

I shrug. "I dunno."

"She's been smelling better lately too ..."

"Oh, that's 'cause of me. I've been giving her clean clothes since her dad chain smokes in the apartment."

"Wow, that's nice of you. I bet she's getting bullied less 'cause of it."

"What can I say? I'm a saint."

"Sorry I'm late!" O'Brien cries as he rushes through the campus's front gate. "Hey guys," he says when he catches up to us and points to the 2011 Nissan Quest in the pick-up queue. My mom's right there, but I haven't had a chance to ask her if you guys can come over yet."

"Aw, you still have to ask your mommy?" I tease. "I never have to ask my mom for anything ever again." The boys look at me, the silence deafening. "What? You can laugh. It's funny."

They fake some awkward and forced laughs, making the air feel heavier than if they had not laughed at all.

O'Brien leads the way to the silver minivan a few cars down the line and opens the passenger door. "Hey Mom, these are my friends Joey and Fiora. Is it okay if they come over for a little while?"

His mom waves from behind the steering wheel while the two little girls I recognize from Bedrock are in the back. One of them hides her head with a hoo-rag. "Hi Joey! I see you at the Nickels and Dimes all the time. I didn't know you were friends with my little Potato," O'Brien's mom says.

"We've become friends this year," O'Brien explains.

His mom isn't done examining us. "And Fiora, what a beautiful name. I don't think I've met you before but you look so familiar."

"My mom used to work at Bedrock," I tell her.

She snaps her finger. "That's right. Oh wow, you look just like her. How is your mom doing?"

"She's better than ever."

"Oh that's great. But yes, of course you can come over."

"I actually have my own car so is it cool if I just follow you there?"

"Oh yes, that's *snatched*."

"Mom," O'Brien grits through his teeth and hops into the passenger seat.

"Oh, apparently I'm being embarrassing now," his mom teases. "I'll go slow so you don't lose me through all this fog." The passenger door slams shut and the minivan pulls away from the curb.

After retrieving my car from the student parking lot, we catch up to the silver minivan waiting at the traffic light. The light turns green and I follow until reaching the suburbs of Blackridge which rests in a clearing of the dreary woods. The houses are all single-family with a large amount of space between them and seemingly at least an acre of backyard, all surrounded by trees and the same black metal fence. The minivan pulls into the driveway of one of the houses but doesn't park in the garage. Joey and I park behind it. The house is another single-family home made mostly of brick with some aged white wood trimmings.

All of us get out of our vehicles. "Oh good, glad you found the place okay," O'Brien's mom says, then invites us inside.

There's a fireplace with a TV mounted above it, and the sectional couch is dark brown, no doubt meant to hide the stains of disgusting little kids. However, there's no hiding the small and dirty hand prints that cover the white-painted walls. It's an open-concept house with the kitchen just a few feet away from the living room, and it has the ugliest green countertops I've ever seen.

"My mom doesn't allow girls in my room so we can talk in the garden," O'Brien says, leading past the kitchen and to the backyard.

His backyard is enclosed by a black-painted metal fence, and the area is filled with yellow and crispy turf. However, there is a small section made of stone that holds the plants they got from Bedrock. They appear to be thriving. There's a fire pit with camping chairs around it, and that's where we take our seats. "So, have you guys figured anything out yet?" O'Brien starts off the discussion.

Joey scratches the side of his head. "Well, yes and no."

"Oh?"

"Well, first we were able to confirm that the curse is 100% not real."

O'Brien releases a breath and relaxes his shoulders. "Oh thank God. You know, I never believed in that thing but then once people started dying, I had my doubts. Especially with no one getting caught yet."

Joey looks at me sitting beside him and places his hand atop mine. "Yeah, us too. But we had to be sure. We don't know why Lemming made that video and it's not like we can ask her, but her death was definitely a suicide."

"I-I feel kinda bad that relieves me so much."

"Yeah, me too. But that's also what I've been stuck on. There's no doubt that the same gun Lemming used to kill herself was used to murder Keaton and Griffin. It's just a matter of how." Joey inhales, then blows the air through his nose with a sigh. "I think our killer has to be someone the victims knew, that's why they let their guards down. Griffin was killed in the locker room after the football game, so I really think the killer has to be one of the jocks."

"You mean someone from the football team?" O'Brien asks.

Joey nods. "Yeah, someone Griffin would expect to be in the locker room. Both he and Keaton died never expecting a thing."

"Wow Joey, you're smarter than you look."

Joey scoffs. "You know, people are really starting to piss me off sometimes. Why wouldn't I be smart? I get straight A's and you cheat off me in math!" He brushes it off. "Whatever. Anyways, that's what I wanted to ask you about. I know you're not on the football team, but you at least have an innings with the jocks. So, we need you to be our eyes and ears on the field and in the locker rooms. Someone has to know something that they're not letting on."

O'Brien uncrosses his arms and nods his head. "Yeah, yeah

okay. I can do that."

A crisp breeze blows in and rustles the surrounding trees as the sun sets, causing the fog to glow with an orange hue.

The glass door to the house slides open, and O'Brien's mom pokes her head out. "Potato, don't you think you should walk your friends to their car?"

I smirk at him. "Is that your mom's way of telling us it's time to go?"

"Yeah, sorry about that," O'Brien says.

Joey and I get up from our chairs. "No need to walk us, I remember where I parked," I tell him.

As we walk out to the driveway, I replay Joey's theory, trying to find a way to fit all the pieces together. We get into the car and I start the engine to get the heater going, but I stall before backing out to the road. I realize he missed something. "You didn't tell him about Falco."

Joey shakes his head. "I want to see if O'Brien comes to the same conclusion I did. Then that way it's not as baseless."

"Wow, you are smart."

"Hey! Why are you acting surprised too?"

I back out and pass a few houses before we're on the main road. Joey is silent and resting his head against the window. The glass is murky with fog. I take a few glances between him and the road. "What's on your mind, idea guy?" I ask.

He doesn't look at me. "Nothing."

"Come on Joey, don't do this. I'm gonna keep asking you what's wrong and you're going to keep saying *nothing* until you finally cave and tell me. So just cut out the middleman. You're thinking about something. I can see it on your face."

He breathes out through his nose. "I don't care if Keaton hated me and I don't care if I hated Griffin, they deserve justice and whoever murdered them deserves to rot in prison for the rest of their miserable life." His voice trembles. "I-It's not fair that they're gone and some killer is still out there eating three meals, spending time with his friends and family, getting to sleep in a warm bed. It's not fucking fair." He pauses, and the air is heavy. I hear him take another large breath. "Then there's your mom."

Son of a bitch. He promised not to bring that up again. "What about my mom?"

"This is just a theory …" He chuckles to himself. "All I have are theories, huh? How pathetic." I almost thought Joey's self-esteem was getting better. But no, he just got better at watching what he says around me until he occasionally slips. "I don't think your mom was killed by the same guy we've been chasing."

I look at him, but it's only a quick glance before I return to the road. Through this thick fog, anything could jump out at a moment's notice, and we wouldn't know until it's busted through the windshield.

He continues: "The article about her not mentioning a cause of death just doesn't sit right with me. All the others said the victims were shot in the head, so why would this one be any different?"

My face is sullen as I stare down the long, seemingly endless road. I count the yellow dashes dividing the road to keep my mind from wandering to places it shouldn't, yet it does anyway. I see the image as clear as the night it happened and hear their voices as if they're right in front of me again. *It's about your mother.*

Maybe none of this would have happened if I had never opened that door last night. "I don't know," I croak. Joey doesn't say anything. His head is still pressed against the window. "Well?"

He looks at me and hums. "Well what?"

"*Well what*? You can't just say something like that then stop!" I don't mean to yell at him. I stare back at the road and count the yellow dashes as they pass. One. Two. Three. Four. Five …

Joey rests his head back against the window. "I-It's too soon. Just forget I said anything."

Right, like I can forget something like that. If I don't keep myself distracted, it's the only thing I will think about. "Hey

Joey?"

"Yeah?"

"Can I spend the night at your place?" I pause. "I-I don't want to go home. It's too … different."

There's glistening in his eyes. Joey is always holding back and worrying about being a burden to anyone, so sometimes I forget how hard this is on him too. He also lost someone he loved. "Yeah," he answers. "Better than sitting around and pondering things that can't be helped anyways."

I turn onto the dirt road and follow it until we reach the trailers. Once we get close enough, they appear through the fog.

NOVEMBER 10 – FRIDAY

Morning

This is the normalcy I crave. Waking up naked next to Joey, snuggling close to his body to beat the cold. He shuffles a bit before pulling his arm out from under the cover and silencing the alarm on his phone. He looks down at me resting on his chest and says, "Good morning." I appreciate his morning texts but much prefer to hear it in person, even if it does come with his morning breath.

"Good morning," I greet back.

When I'm with Joey, it's like nothing has changed.

Breakfast is a couple bowls of off-brand cereal while his grandma is fast asleep in her usual recliner chair. We're in the kitchen leaning against the counters when the trailer door opens and a woman enters. She has dark hair and skin so perfect it's hard to tell how old she is. Her teeth are chattering as she places paper bags on the counter. "It's so cold out. Good morning Joey."

Joey still has some milk on his lips but wipes it away on his sleeve. "Good morning. Oh, this is my girlfriend Fiora." Hearing him say that sends the butterflies fluttering in my stomach. "Fiora, this is Alice, my grandma's caretaker."

Alice nods at me. "Nice to meet you."

"Nice to meet you too," I return.

She's right about it being freezing. Joey and I exit the trailer and can't get to the warmth of my car fast enough. He rubs his hands together and breathes on them before placing them in front of the vents once hot air flows. He's so cute and I've never liked anyone like this before. Part of me was worried that after I finally got him, I'd get bored without the thrill of the chase like other boys I'd dated, but now I like the thrill of having him around my arm even more. He's the one I get to call mine. I lean close to him and place my hand on his jaw while kissing his neck.

Joey chuckles, and I feel the vibration in his throat. "Whatcha doing?"

"Heating you up." I breathe onto his neck. "You know, we fuck in your bed and we fuck in the shower, but we've yet to fuck in a car."

Joey looks around the interior. "Your car does have a lot more space than my old hooptie." He lifts himself up a bit to pull his pants down to his knees, his dick hard and pointing to the roof. "I saved you a seat."

I'm just going to pretend he didn't say that. I pull my leggings off and crumble them before tossing them to the back of the cab. It's a bit of a tight space shifting to Joey's lap in the passenger seat, then it's even a tighter space to slip him inside.

"Oh fuck," he moans once he's all the way in.

My hands are on his shoulders for leverage and his hands cup my ass, guiding me up and down as I bounce. I like it when he lets me do all the work and I watch the looks on his face as he sits back and enjoys. He bites his bottom lip and points his chin to the car's roof as he sighs.

There's a knock on the window and we stop. The silhouette of a figure masked by the fog stands on the other side of the glass. I wipe away the condensation with the sleeve of my hoodie, exposing Cheese. She points her finger downwards, and I roll down the window. A cold blast of wind breaks through the heat we've created in the car.

"Ah Cheese, we're kinda in the middle of something," Joey says.

Cheese tilts her head. "But you're always having sex with at least someone."

"D-Don't say it like that! You make me sound like a whore!" She tilts her head to the other side, and Joey stops her before she can open her mouth. "Don't even say it."

She says something anyway: "Can you give me a ride to school? I got suspended from the bus."

"Yeah, when we're done," I answer. "So fuck off."

"Joey doesn't last long anyway."

I press the button and the window slowly rises. Cheese is standing there, not leaving until the glass has risen completely. My attention turns to Joey. "Prove her wrong and make us late." I press my lips against his and continue to bounce in his lap.

Joey doesn't prove her wrong, and a few minutes later, the three of us are driving to the school.

It's a foggy walk from the student parking lot to the security line at the school's gate, and a familiar silver minivan sits at the drop-off curb. The passenger door opens and O'Brien steps out. "Oh, hey guys," he says.

Cheese waves her hand. "Hi Brien."

Something clicks in Joey, and he skips up to O'Brien before wrapping an arm around his shoulders. "O'Brien, buddy! How's it going? Just the man I wanted to see, actually."

"Have you figured anything else out about the case?" O'Brien asks.

"Not yet," Joey answers. "But sometimes we need a break from all the shitty things in our lives with something fun."

O'Brien grabs Joey's hand and unwraps it from his shoulders. "Sorry Joey, but I'm straight."

"Wh-What? No! I don't mean that! I mean Cheese! Just now she was asking what's the difference between softball and baseball, and you know me. I'm no sports guy so I have no clue."

Cheese tilts her head, her blonde pigtails draping over her chest. "No I wasn't."

Joey grits his teeth. "Yes you were." He turns back to O'Brien. "You should explain it to her while you walk her to class. Come on Fi." Joey leaves those two be and holds my hand as we grab a place in the security line.

I look up at him. "Wait, that was your big match making

plan?"

"I'd like to see you do better."

I wish I could say I did, but trying to set him up with McCarthy was a disaster. But at least it worked out for me in the end. It's cold standing in this line, barely moving, so I lean closer to Joey and rest my head against his arm.

First Period

May already has a stank look on her face before I even sit down at my seat across the table. "What?" she clucks.

I squint at her. "I didn't even say anything."

"I know, that's the problem."

She's right. I usually jump at the opportunity to get into a pissing match with her. I guess this is me finally maturing and picking my battles like Mom always told me to. "I guess I'm just bored of arguing with people all the time."

There's a moment of silence, and May lets her guard down. "I heard about your mom," she says. "I'm sorry."

So many people have been telling me that, and I never know how to respond other than, "Thanks."

"My dad is one of the detectives on the case. You could talk to him if you want."

That grabs my attention. "That–That actually would be great." With Falco no longer acting as our informate, everything we've been going off has been nothing but guesses and speculations. Am I really making a truce with May?

The bell for class to begin rings and the TV mounted to the wall turns on. McCarthy is on the screen, presenting herself as professional as ever. "Good morning students and faculty. I am McCarthy, your student council president, and these are the morning announcements ..."

The TV shuts off, and Mr. Simpson remains seated at his desk. "Alright, I want you all to use the first half of class to catch up on reading for your book reports if you haven't already," he instructs. "I know some choose longer books than others. If you've already finished your book, you can get started on the report or sit quietly and read something else."

If there's one thing high schoolers don't do, it's sit quietly and read when told to do so. "Hey May?" I whisper.

She hums. "Yeah?"

"Did you make that doxxing page?"

She shakes her head. "No, I didn't. And I didn't add April's name to the page either, if that's what you're thinking."

"Hmm? You didn't? But McCarthy ..."

"Okay I admit, I submitted McCarthy's name. I fucking despise her. But that was only after ... everything that happened, happened."

"What ended up happening?" I ask.

"April saw she had been posted on the account and was freaking out. I was there trying to calm her down ... then you called."

"No, you cannot pin what happened to April on me," I declare. "I only called 'cause I saw her on that page and you know, there's kind of a serial killer on the loose."

"Ah, yeah Sofia Vergara. I'm well aware. I just told you my dad is one of the detectives on the case."

"Sofia Vergara isn't even Mexican. At least get your racism right."

"I'm sure you can find out more when you ask him yourself, but my dad thinks the killer set up the doxxing page to get a list of victims like the killer 20 years ago had."

I scoff. "So you knew that and submitted McCarthy's name anyway?"

That also means Joey isn't as safe as we assumed. Sure, he didn't drop dead from some made-up curse, but now he could be the next target on the killer's hit list. I have to tell him–if he hasn't figured it out already himself.

May slumps back in her seat and crosses her arms. "She deserves everything she gets."

"Okay, I get that you're just a bitch and a pick me in general, but seriously, why hate McCarthy so much of all people? You can't even figure out what she's saying until you decode all the beep boops."

May glances at the TV mounted on the wall, though it has been turned off for some time now. "Before she was McCarthy, she went by July and was my best friend."

My jaw drops. "You're shitting me."

She shakes her head. "No matter what, anything I've wanted McCarthy has always had to take from me. Last year it was captain of the volleyball team, and this year it's the presidency. We got into one little stupid fight and she went and slept with the boy I like even though she's a lesbian."

I try to hold it in, but my laughs burst through my nose in a snort. "Wait, wait. Let me see if I got this straight: You tell the whole school she's a crack baby so she goes and fucks your crush?" I sit back and cross my arms. "I gotta say, she gets props for that one. It's like you finally met your mean girl match."

May leans in closer over the table. "Do you want to know who the guy was?"

"Don't even say it," I warn.

"Joey."

"Fuck!"

Mr. Simpson looks up from the desk he's much too large for. "Girls, you're supposed to be reading," he says.

There's a complacent grin on May's horse face. "But don't worry. I'm over him. He's actually not that special. You guys are together now, right?"

"Yeah," I confirm, claiming my prize.

"You–You actually make a cute couple. He deserves someone who will finally treat him right. And … you have a lot of friends. People seem to really like you. Even April. I hate to say it, but I was jealous when she was going to choose you over me." She looks down at her hands, that cocky grin wiped from her face. "But that doesn't mean I wanted her dead. Maybe if I was more supportive she wouldn't have …" She sniffles.

"Hey May?"

She looks back up at me sitting across the table from her. "Yeah?"

"If it's not too awkward, you can sit with us at lunch."

"Thanks, but no thanks."

After School

The car is parked in front of Nickels and Dimes when Joey pulls his hood over his head and steps out into the rain, the water falling as a gentle mist. Specs of moisture cling to the dark fabric. "I'm closing tonight so I'll be late, but you're more than welcome to hang out at my place," he says.

My fingers tightly grip the steering wheel. "I–I think I should probably go home for a little while. I miss my cat, ya know?"

"Oh, yeah. Squeak. She's cute. If you need anything, call me okay?"

I nod.

He closes the passenger door, and I don't drive away until he's safely in the building.

The rain is light, but the water builds on the windshield as I stay here, numb and staring at nothing. The water fills the glass just to be brushed away by the wipers. I watch as the process repeats several times. Over time, the rain starts to fall harder. I increase the wipers' frequency until the windshield is clear and put the car in reverse.

There's no music nor a thought in my mind, and before I know it, I'm in my driveway, waiting for the garage door to open so I can pull inside. Mom's car isn't here, and neither is Aunt Addie's.

Stepping into the house resembles the night we first moved here. It feels empty and foreign. There's furniture like a family lives here, yet I sense no sign of life. I'm on a set with studio lights blinding me, and where there should be a fourth wall, there's a studio audience waiting for me to recite my lines. I say something witty and snarky, then queue the laughing track.

All of Mom's plants are still here, but the leaves appear plastic and the mulch is nothing but wire. I rub my finger against one of the fronds and it's smooth and damp like it has been freshly watered, but it couldn't fool me. It can be green and growing one second, then withered and rotted the next.

A pillow and some blankets are left on the couch, meaning Aunt Addie must have spent another night camped out in the living room.

Trash barks from upstairs and it gets louder with the sound of an open door. The small mutt continues to bark as he prances down the stairs, but once he sees it's me his butt wiggles and his tail wags. I kneel down to pet him.

Atlus is still upstairs, leaning over the balcony railing. "Fiora?"

I look up at him, and he's a mess. He's wearing the same sweatpants, hoodie, and even the socks he wore the last time I saw him. His eyes are dark, red, and puffy, like this is his first break from crying.

"Who did you think I was going to be?" I ask, and he doesn't answer but doesn't need to. We both wish I was Mom coming home after a long day with bags of takeout. "Where's Aunt Addie?"

"Who cares?"

A rumble comes from the garage, followed by a closing car door. Aunt Addie enters the home not her own carrying a box of pizza from Mah and Pah's. She almost bumps into me like I'm a ghost she can't see. "Oh, Fiora. I didn't know you were coming home tonight," she says. "Um … how was school?"

I stuff my hands in the pouch of my hoodie. "It was school. There's a sub in your class."

"Yes, I know. I'll be back as soon as I can. Everything will be okay now, so there's nothing to worry about." She yells to the balcony, "Atlus, dinner's here!"

"I'm not hungry," he boldly states.

Aunt Addie holds up the box. "But I got pizza. It's what you said you wanted."

"We always had takeout with Mom!" he bellows and returns to his room. The door slams with so much force it raddles the house and shakes the portraits on the walls like an earthquake.

Aunt Addie turns back to me, the box shaking from the murmurs in her anxious hands. "It's... it's been like this for a while. I-I don't know what to do."

I should have taken Joey's advice. I could be watching *The Price is Right* with his grandma right now. "What, you mean your fancy community college didn't make you take Sorry Your Mom's Dead 101?"

She sets the pizza box on the kitchen island and blinks her bulging eyes at me. Beneath them, the skin is dark and saggy. She may be camping out on the couch, but she's not getting any sleep. "Fiora, I– ... Everyone deals with grief differently."

I brush her off. "Yeah, yeah, yeah. I'm not hungry either so I'm gonna take a shower."

Trash follows me upstairs and I open Atlus's door just a crack to let him inside the room. Atlus is on his bed, face down into his pillow and never turns away. Slowly, I close the door so as not to make a sound.

After my shower, I find Squeak lying on my bed who gets up and stretches when she sees me enter the room. I scratch at her arched back. "Big stretch," I tell her and join her on the bed. She helps herself to a spot on my lap, closes her eyes, and purrs.

Atlus's sobs break through the drywall connecting our two bedrooms.

Music has always been a big part of my life, whether for fun or distraction, and I need both of these things right now. My headphones are charging on my nightstand so I unplug them from the cord to place them atop my head and connect the Bluetooth to my phone. With Squeak still on my chest, I lean back to rest my head on my pillow and let the music play.

Any and all attempts at distractions or avoidance are futile. This pain is just too real, and that's all I feel: pain. It's so heavy in my chest that I can't breathe. It's heavy throughout my entire body as I'm crushed by the weight of something that I can only describe as an overwhelming sadness. It's burying me alive. It makes my eyes swell, and my hands shake. I wish I had cuts. I wish I had bruises. I wish I had something to place and something to heal.

I roll over and close my eyes, the tears soaking into my pillow.

NOVEMBER 13 – MONDAY

Morning

How are people supposed to get out of bed in the morning? Yet, I do. I brush my teeth, take a shower, and get dressed. While I'm here in my room doing my routine, everything is the same. I give Squeak a can of wet cat food before going downstairs. There's no difference until I open the door.

I don't smell anything cooking and Aunt Addie is on the couch while Atlus is nowhere to be seen. He's been crying so much and must have finally cried himself to sleep.

"Good morning," Aunt Addie greets.

Is it? "Good morning."

"You're up early … right?" She reaches for her phone on the coffee table. "Yeah, you're up early."

"Joey has the flu so I'm making him some homemade soup."

"Aw, that's so sweet. You're going to make a nice little wife someday."

"Shut the fuck up. Now you make me not want to do it."

I do it anyway, and just as I'm about to leave with a banana and a hot thermos of soup, Aunt Addie calls out to me from the couch. "Um … remember to come home after school so we can pick out an urn," she says.

I don't say anything and take my banana to my car in the garage. Aunt Addie's is parked beside it. I pinch at the top of the fruit to pull down the peel, but I can't bring myself to take a bite. My stomach feels so heavy and full of lead that taking a single bite will make me pop.

There's no rain this morning, but the fog is so dense it couldn't fool me. The mist fills my windshield and I turn on the wipers.

The windows of Joey's trailer are dark as I pull up and park alongside the grass. I knock on the door and wait a few minutes. I knock again, still with no answer. The soup is warm in my hand as I use the other to grab my phone from my hoodie pouch and dial Joey.

He answers. "H-Hello?" His voice is hoarse and groggy.

"Did I wake you up?"

"Um, yeah. Kinda."

"Sorry but I'm at your door."

"Huh? My door? Did you get my text?" He coughs. "I'm not coming to school today."

"I know. I gotchu something but the door is locked."

"You got me something?" Springs creak from the other end of the line and Joey lifts the blinds from his window. It's not a clear image through the fog, but he's standing before the glass. A moment later, the padlock clicks and the door to the trailer opens. I get a better look at Joey. He's wearing gray sweatpants and a black Korn hoodie; his flesh is clammy while his cheeks glow crimson.

I hold out the thermos of soup. "Here ya go."

He accepts and lifts up the lid. Steam rises. "I can't smell it. What is it?"

"Homemade tomato soup."

His lips raise and expose his teeth. The two in front are slightly buck. "I can't believe you made me soup and brought it all the way here. Thank you, Fi. You're so cute I'd kiss you but I don't want to give you my germs."

I stand on my tippy toes to reach his lips and kiss him anyway. Lately we've been exchanging more than germs. "Like I said, gotta keep you on your toes."

"How about my knees?" He smiles but breaks away to cough into the crease of his elbow.

I chuckle. "I'll see you later. Feel better."

He sniffles. "I'll try."

* * *

I leave my car in the student parking lot and head towards the front gate, where a familiar pair stands at the drop-off queue. I get closer, but they don't notice me through the thick sheet of fog. One is tall with an athletic physique, while the other is short with thick, long hair. Cheese has her head cocked. "Does she know?" she asks.

"I don't know," O'Brien answers. "We shouldn't tell her. She's been so calm since her mom died, it's kinda scary. You just know there's a bomb waiting to go off in that head of hers."

"Talking shit about me behind my back?" I say, grabbing their attention.

A cool sweat is quick to form on O'Brien's bushy brows. "Hey Fi, where've you been? Where's your shadow?"

"Joey's sick. Don't change the subject. Do I know what?"

"Um ... well ... You remember the Nameless Hotel? Well, their new exhibit opened and it's about the shooting 20 years ago and ... there are some things about your mom."

I scoff. "What the fuck? What were you doing there?"

"We were having sex," Cheese explains.

I punch O'Brien on the shoulder, avoiding his bad side. "Normally I'd praise you for finally getting it in if it weren't for this betrayal!"

"I–I didn't betray you," O'Brien defends. "We didn't know about the exhibit until we got there."

"That whole hotel is fucked. It's whole point is to profit off deaths, even when there's an active serial killer in the city."

"Yeah, I've never seen Blackridge so busy. The line at the hotel was out the door. We almost couldn't get a room."

"Well?" I ask.

"Well what?"

"*Well*, what did the exhibit have to say about my mom? That she survived a mass shooting just to get murdered by some fucking psycho 20 years later?"

"I–I don't think you want to know."

"We didn't go," Cheese explains.

"Thank you, Cheese," I say. "At least I can get a straight answer from somebody."

The warning bell rings, and we enter the school.

Lunchtime

"Fiora to the principal's office, Fiora to the principal's office."

Just when I was getting used to having lunch with my friends again.

Principal Pal is waiting by his office and he holds the door open for me. We sit in our respective seats. I'm slumped back with my arms crossed. "So, what did I do this time?"

"Good afternoon, Fiora," Principal Pal starts off. "First, I would like to announce that I have dismissed you from the rest of your classes for the day."

That causes me to sit up. "For real? I like the sound of that."

"Yes, I thought you would. Now for something you won't like: Mrs. Burke, would you come in please?"

The door opens, and the woman in a pencil skirt enters the office. Principal Pal excuses himself from the room while Mrs. Burke accepts her seat behind the desk. "Hello Fiora, it's nice to meet you," she says.

"What the fuck is this? Some kind of intervention?" I inquire.

"No, no. Nothing like that. I've just been checking up on the students closest to the latest incidents."

"Okay, but why me? Did Joey say something to you? Or O'Brien or Poppet?"

She shakes her head. "No one told me anything, I wanted to talk to you myself. Your name is Fiora Clairwater, and with the recent passing of Nebula Clairwater ... at best, you were a fan. At worst–"

"She was my mom," I finish for her.

"I am deeply sorry for your loss. Lots of people know of Nebula Clairwater, but what I would like to know is: who was Bailey Narvarro?"

An image of her as clear as rain as it appears in my head. Like a whole lifetime with her flashes before my eyes. Everything from my earliest memories with her as a child to the night before she died drinking together in the kitchen. "Well, she was my mom," I start off until I find myself at a loss for words.

Mrs. Burke nods. "How was she as a mom?"

"Well, she didn't really know how to do it. She had me when she was younger than I am now and had to give up everything just to have me. She did it all on her own too."

"Mothers sacrifice a lot for their children."

"Yeah, tell me about it. She gave up more than just *a lot*, but she never complained. Even when we were broke and homeless and struggling. She couldn't cook and whenever she tried it was a disaster, but we always had food. She always did what she thought was best for us, even if it was hard for her. Even still, she didn't complain. She always believed that things would just work themselves out, and I guess she was right."

"Did they work themselves out, or did she do it?"

I think about what Mom has done, including the deal with Atlus's father. "She made them happen."

Mrs. Burke smiles. "She sounds very strong."

"Yeah, she was."

"What do you think your mom would want from you if she were still here with us?"

"All she ever wanted was for me to graduate since she didn't get to, but I fucked that up last year. I just … didn't care. It's just a stupid piece of paper. But now … now I wish I had taken it more seriously so my mom could have seen that stupid piece of paper before she died."

"It's common to feel guilty after losing a loved one. Regretting some of the things you did or didn't do, but no one can predict the future. The best thing we can do for our loved ones is to live our lives to the fullest in their honor."

"Nah, I don't really care about that. I don't believe she's in the clouds with some racist bigot watching over me, or her soul is haunting me, or that she'll roll over in her grave. She's in a freezer somewhere right now, probably dissected and ripped apart with her organs in a bag."

"Y-You have quite the descriptive imagination. I can see how you're an author's daughter. That's alright. Not everyone is religious or spiritual. You don't have to do it for her, but do it for yourself. You can't go back and change the past to appease your guilt, but you can make it happen in the present. Like how your mom made things happen."

I point at her. "That's a good one."

She smiles. "Oh you like that? I'm glad. What advice would your mom give you?"

That causes me to chuckle lightly. "She was always telling me to choose my battles."

"That's some good advice."

"Yeah, it is."

I spend the rest of the afternoon in the office with Mrs. Burke. I'm about to leave when she calls out to me. "Oh Fiora, one last thing: everyone grieves differently. It's okay to feel however you're feeling, and whenever you wanna talk again, you know where to find me."

The bell to end the day rings, and I'm out the door.

Evening

What I do between leaving school and getting home is a blur. I drive around Blackridge to the sound of silence, and the next thing I know, the sun is setting. I pull into the garage and park beside Aunt Addie's Toyota Camry.

The TV is on when I get inside the house, but Aunt Addie raises the remote to turn it off when she sees me enter. "Fiora, where were you?"

I remove my backpack from my shoulders and hang my car keys on the hook mounted to the wall. "School."

"School got out hours ago. You were supposed to meet us at the funeral home."

"Well obviously I didn't. So, where is it?"

"Where's what?"

"The urn."

"It's still at the funeral home. It'll be returned to us once it's ready."

"You mean after Mom is cooked and burnt to ashes?"

Aunt Addie doesn't respond for a moment and catches her breath. "The memorial service is going to be on Saturday. Something small, just friends and family."

My hand is on the banister as I'm ready for this to be over with and go back to my room. Maybe I'll listen to some more music. "By *friends and family* you mean just us? Thanks, but no thanks. I have plans." I take a few steps up the stairs.

Aunt Addie scoffs. "What could you possibly be doing that's more important than your own mother's wake?"

I look over my shoulder at her sitting on the couch. "I'll figure something out." I get to my room and close the door behind me. The moment it clicks shut is the moment the tears are free to fall. I sit on the floor, my back against the bed frame, and hold my knees close to my chest.

The night passes on.

NOVEMBER 18 – SATURDAY

Evening

Figure something else out I did, for this weekend we're staying at the Nameless Hotel. I need to see this exhibit for myself.

"Enjoy your stay," the front desk clerk wishes and hands me three room keys. There's something else he reaches for behind the desk. "And here are your admission passes. Your time slot is at 8PM."

I accept the items and return to my friends waiting in the lobby. One room is for Joey and me so I pocket our key, another is for O'Brien and Cheese so I hand the key to her, then the last room is to be shared by Pandora and Poppet.

Poppet takes the key and does a little dance with the plastic card. "Sleep over, sleep over, sleep over!"

Our rooms are on the 6th floor again, and the elevator empties us to the hall. "Everyone be ready before 8," I instruct.

Poppet salutes. "Aye, aye, captain."

Cheese tilts her head. "Ready for what?"

"The exhibit!" I cry.

"You know Fi, we could always try to talk to your dead mom," Pandora says.

"Pandora, I'm not even joking. Do another stunt like that tonight and I'm kicking you right in your cunt."

She snorts. "Relax, I came unarmed. Halloween was insensitive of me, so I'm sorry I guess."

Joey scratches his head. "Geez, you flatter us with your sincerity."

I'm done with this conversation, so I hover the plastic card over the reader attached to the door. The light turns green, and the door is unlocked with a click.

The room may only have a single double bed, but it's more significant than the room the girls and I shared on Halloween, and it better be for the price I paid. There's the standard bathroom, dresser, and TV, but the view makes this room special. Large windows frame the back wall, presenting the coast of Blackridge. The gray fog and ocean stretch out far into the horizon.

"Wow," Joey says. "Blackridge almost looks ... pretty."

I reach out my hand to grab his and escort him deeper into the room. A couple of accent chairs are positioned in front of the windows, and I push him down to the cushion. His legs are spread, and I take my seat on his lap.

His hands cup my ass and give it a squeeze. "I like where this is going."

I kiss him and bite his bottom lip. "I want you to fuck me against the glass."

There's a cheeky smirk on his lips and a wink in his eye. "Yes ma'am."

* * *

There's just a few minutes until 8PM.

We pick our clothes off the floor and I sit against the edge of the bed as I secure the buttons in my cardigan. Joey finishes brushing his hair. "Hey, um ... are you sure you wanna do this?" he says.

"Do what?" I ask.

He sits down beside me. "You know, see the exhibit."

"Of course I do. If some fuckface is trying to make money off what happened to my mom, I need to see what they're saying about her."

"It's not just her, but your dad too. You barely know anything about the guy. Is this how you're gonna want to remember him? Once you see these things they don't just ... go away."

I reach over and place my hand atop his. "I'm a big girl, I can take it. I seem to remember you saying yourself that I can take whatever I want."

He scrunches his eyes and releases a breath through his nose. "D-Don't remind me of the cringey shit I say."

I slightly raise myself off the bed to kiss his cheek.

It's time to leave the room and we meet with the others in the hall. It's silent as we ride the elevator back down to the lobby.

The sign that once read COMING SOON has been replaced by a black curtain blocking off the section of the hotel. There's another sign reading WAIT HERE, where some takers already wait. It's a group of four women. One of them has a pair of wired headphones in her ear and speaks into the mic: "Blackridge is a small town tucked into the coast of Oregon with a population of no more than 2,000. It might seem like the perfect place for a summer get away, yet the locals know it as anything but. Blackridge is known to be casted in a constant state of fog, but what's most troubling is the deadly curse plaguing the small town. This is Unknown and Unseen and on today's episode, we're diving into the killer curse of Blackridge and where it all started 20 years ago."

The other women around her giggle when she finishes her recording. "That was so good!"

The woman recording loses her radio voice and giggles as well. "Right? I just came up with it on the top of my head!"

Joey reaches over and holds my hand. He lets me squeeze it as hard as I need to.

The black curtain is pulled to the side, and out comes a man wearing a black blazer and a white dress shirt underneath. His finger bounces as he counts everyone in line. "Perfect, everyone is here. Hello, everyone. My name is Aidan, and I will be your tour guide this evening. But of course, *Aidan* isn't actually my real name. You see, everyone in Blackridge must go by aliases for their own protection from the deadly curse of Elliot Vaugh." He reaches his hand past the black curtain, pulls out a top hat, and panders it around the line. "Come on everyone, pick out a name."

The group of outsiders are the first to aesthetically reach

their hands into the hat, each pulling out a metal name tag and attaching it to their shirts. They take turns announcing their new names:

"I'm Addison Gill!"

"I'm Angel Rogers!"

"I'm Danni Greer!"

"I'm Sam Ryan!"

Aidan approaches us, and our group is less eager to see which victim we've been assigned. Cheese is the first to reach in her hand and stir around the metal. She pulls one out. "Logan Clarke."

O'Brien goes next. "Jameson Cane."

When Poppet pulls hers, she's assigned Rene Martin and Pandora gets Caden Schmidt.

Fittingly, there are only two left. It's Joey's turn. "Tyler Newman," he reads out.

There's only one left, and it's mine: "Bailey Navarro."

Aidan places the now empty hat atop his head and holds open the black curtain. "Thank you everyone, and welcome to Seal Coast Community High School."

The group of women cheer as they step into the exhibit, while those of us behind can only drag our feet. The air gets more heavy with every step.

Past the black curtain is a thin hall with smoke effects covering our ankles. It's dimly lit with the only lights mounted against the wall, highlighting the framed portraits. There are ten portraits of students with red-colored Xs marking out their faces. The paint oozes off the photos like blood. There's nine of them, Jameson Cane, Caden Schmidt, Angel Rogers, Danni Greer, Logan Clarke, Sam Ryan, Rene Martin, and Addison Gill.

The only one left unscathed is that of Bailey Navarro.

I hold back the quiver in my lips staring at Mom's photo. She was so young and still so full of life. This poor girl smiling back at me had no clue what was in store for her and how it would all come crashing to an abrupt end. Then there's my dad, the man I never knew.

The group of women point at the portraits and then at their name tags stuck to their chests. "That's me!" they cry out.

I take a deep breath, squeezing Joey's hand harder.

"This is so sick," he growls under his breath.

Aidan begins the tour, guiding the group down the hall, but I stall, enchanted by the framed portraits.

"Hey, we should go or we'll be left behind," Joey says.

"Right," I say.

We regroup with the others further down the hall.

"Imagine it's an ominious day in, 2003," *Aidan* sets the scene, " and you're a student at Seal Coast Community High School. That afternoon, a shooter by the name of Elliot Vaughn came to the school with an AR-15, and a list of names. Here you can see that very list."

Aidan gestures to a sheet of glass on the wall. Encased inside is the very list Joey and I found online. Ten names are on the list, nine of which are crossed out. The paper is stained with dark, seeping drops of red.

The group of tourists use their phones to take pictures of themselves posing in front of the killer's list.

"Now, you may have noticed that one of these names is not like the others," Aidan points out. "For reasons unknown, Elliot failed to kill the beautiful Bailey Navarro before reaching his own demise by the hands of the police. But weeks later, also for reasons unknown, Bailey Narvarro passed away, thus giving birth to the curse of Blackridge ..."

Night

"God that really pissed me off," Joey growls when we return to our hotel room. "That dude was talking about the shooting like it was some campfire ghost story and not a real thing that killed real people. And those stupid podcasters. They had no respect at all. All they cared about were the views they're gonna get. If someone made some kind of sick exhibit like that of Keaton, I dunno what I'd do." I'm sitting on the bed's edge and he is sitting beside me. He holds my hand in his. "Um, sorry. This isn't about me. How are you?"

I look into his eyes and enjoy the warmth of his touch. "I'm fine. It's about what I was expecting."

Joey scratches the side of his head. "You know, I'm surprised. O'Brien and I were worried you'd start destroying things with bats or burn the place down or something."

I sigh and reach for my backpack by our feet. I bring it up to the bed and unzip it from the top. Inside is filled with both retail and illegal fireworks. "I thought about it, but what's it gonna accomplish? It's not gonna bring her back and it's not even gonna teach those fuckers a lesson. Hell, if anything pulling a stunt like that might just make them more money."

"Man, you're mature."

"It's not even that. I'm just ... choosing my battles." I lean over and rest my head on his shoulder. "Can we just go to bed and watch a movie or something?"

He wraps his arm around me and holds me close. "Of course."

My silent tears soak into his sweater.

NOVEMBER 19 – SUNDAY

Morning

The difference is night and day after pulling back the blackout curtains blocking the window, letting natural light into the hotel room.

Joey is sitting on the edge of the bed shifting through the laminated hotel menu. "Man, I'm starving. I've never ordered room service from a hotel before. Actually, I've never even been to a hotel until this year."

I sit down beside him. "Get whatever you want."

"But all this stuff is so expensive. Even just for some pancakes. You can get pancake mix from Nickels and Dimes and make it yourself for so much cheaper." He closes the menu and looks at me. "Wait, how are you paying for all of this without ..."

He trails off, so I finish for him: "My mom?"

"Well, yeah."

"I still have my credit card and once the lawyers figure everything out, Atlus and I are inheriting her estate. You're looking at a homeowner and millionaire before she's even 20."

"I–I don't know what to say to that."

"Don't say, just eat." I take the menu from his lap and open the front page to the breakfast menu. It's the typical hotel breakfast with different options of platters, omelets, and bagels, but nothing catches my eye. "Hey Joey, there actually is something I want you to say."

He hums and his cheeks glow red. "Don't you think it's a little soon for that?"

"Huh? What? No, I mean what you were gonna tell me."

"What I was gonna tell you?"

"Yes. After we left O'Brien's. About my mom's case. You said something about it was bothering you."

He scratches the side of his face. "Oh yeah, that. I did say that, huh?"

"You said it was too soon and that you'd tell me later. Well, it's later."

He releases a bated breath. "Yeah, yeah. It has been bothering me and I've been thinking a lot about it. Her case is different, and I don't think it's just 'cause she's a celebrity. But I don't think we can know for sure until a cause of death is released. If she wasn't shot, or at least by a different gun, then I think maybe she was killed by someone else. Someone who figured out the same thing we did. They found out she's the surviving student and probably thought her moving back to town jump started the curse, even though we know now it's not real."

My palms turn white as my nails dig into my flesh. "It always rounds back to that stupid fucking curse."

Joey wraps his arm around me, and I rest my head on his shoulder. He runs his fingers through my hair. "We'll get to the bottom of this. For your mom ... For Keaton ... For everyone who's had to die."

Afternoon

The lot of us check out of the hotel and Joey and Cheese have work today so I drop them off at Nickels and Dimes before going home. I turn onto Misty Lane and drive down the subdivision until I reach my house, where there's a car parked in the driveway. There's only one person I know rich and shallow enough to drive a Tesla: Chloe.

She's on the couch in the living room with Atlus and Aunt Addie. Chloe is pulling out a wooden block from the center of the Janga tower when she notices me entering the room. The tower collapses and Chloe jumps to her feet. "You stupid bitch."

She's changed her hair since the last time I saw her, a regular occurrence with Chloe like the seasons. It's cut shoulder length with a center part. One half is dyed black, while the other remains her natural blonde.

I'm constricted in her grip as she hugs me. Chloe stands at 5'8, making her several inches taller than me. "What are you doing here?" I ask when she lets go.

"I should be asking you that, you cunt. Of course I was gonna come to Nebbie's service. I loved her. Where the hell were you?"

"Something came up," I excuse.

Chloe tucks her hands in her pockets. "I get it. I felt the same way after my dad died. At least I had you, so I wanted to make sure I was here for you too."

"I mean, you could've texted or something."

She takes her hand out of her pocket to punch me in the shoulder with her boney knuckles. "I wanted it to be a surprise. But that's not the only reason why I came. I came to bring you home."

"Wh–What?"

"I came to bring you home. Ya know, to San Diego."

"Chlo, I'm sorry but I can't."

She furrows her brows and raises the corner of her lip. "Why not? All you do is bitch about how much you hate this place and now there's a killer on the loose. I'm giving you an out. Let's go home."

I shake my head and look past her to Atlus and Aunt Addie sitting on the couch. Their gazes are turned towards us, listening to our every word. "That's exactly why I can't go," I say. "Someone in this town murdered my mom and I haven't punched them in the fucking face yet."

NOVEMBER 20 – MONDAY

Evening

Today is the start of fall break for Seal Coast, but not for Promise Private Academy so Chloe left last night to make it on time. I'm in Atlus's room helping him pack. Now that it's been over a week since Mom died and since Aunt Addie has custody of him, she decided it's best they don't stay here any longer and move into her place.

All his things were in boxes when we moved here just a short while ago, and now it's time for them to go back. He doesn't bother to fold his clothes and tosses them into the cardboard box.

I take out the Breaking Benjamin shirt he tossed and fold it. "I bought you this, you dick."

"I don't care," he says and tosses another shirt.

There's a notification on my phone so I check that rather than folding his shirts:

MAY: My dad just got home if you wanna talk to him
FIORA: Cool shoot me the address
MAY: 2956 Misty Ln

I pause and make sure what I see on the screen is correct. The familiarity of the address is no coincidence. I'm out of Atlus's room, out the front door, and crossing the street to the next house over. May is the one to answer the door after I ring the doorbell. The look on her face tells me she's just as surprised to see me. "How did you get here so fast? Are you stalking me? I'll call ICE," she says.

I turn back to point at my house. "You stupid horse faced bitch, we've been neighbors this whole time."

She looks past me and at my house. "*You're* the new

neighbors? That's not possible. We don't let trash like you in this neighborhood. How have I never seen you? Or smelled you?"

"Remind me to kick your ass for that later. But we only ever go in and out through the garage."

She holds the door open. "Fine, whatever. Come in."

I step inside, and she closes the door behind me. We enter through the living room with the kitchen and dining space towards the other side of the wall. There's a recognizable figure sitting on a lounge chair using a single finger to scroll down the screen of a Kindle.

"Dad, she's here," May says before excusing herself up the nearby staircase.

Her father, Detective Angel, places his glasses and Kindle on the end table by his side. "Well, there's a familiar face."

I lazily throw up my hand to wave. "Hey Detective Angel. Or is it Mr. Calendar in your humble abode?"

"You can call me whatever you like. It doesn't really matter. Would you like a drink before our discussion?"

I notice the china cabinet in the open-concept dining area. "Copitas?"

It takes him a moment to process what I said, and he directs his gaze behind him. He turns back to me with a smile. "You must know your china."

"No, just Mexican."

He pulls himself from the lounge chair, groaning slightly. "I'll go get a couple of waters. Please, make yourself comfortable."

Making myself comfortable is impossible, but I sit on the couch and twiddle my thumbs.

Falco comes from the kitchen holding a piece of stiff pizza. He stares at me as he chews. "What are you doing here?"

"Business," I respond. Our informant has changed from one sibling to the other.

"How does your boyfriend's dick taste?"

"Wouldn't you know?"

His stance changes. His casual demeanor leaning against the wall straightens, and the anger radiating off him is enough to cook the cold pizza in his grip.

Detective Angels ends our exchange by carrying two glasses of water. "Son, go upstairs for a moment." Falco obediently complies while his father returns to the lounge chair. The glasses of water are set on the coffee table, and Detective Angels cups his hands atop his lap. "So, you wish to talk?"

I lean forward, slumping my back and shoulders. "It's been a week. You have to at least know something by now. There's been nothing new in the press and not a single phone call even though you said we'd be the first to know."

"What would you like to know?"

"I need to know how my mom died. More particularly, if she was shot."

He takes a moment to answer, breathing in and out through his nose. "We won't have an official cause of death until the autopsy is completed, which could take some time. But from what I could tell at the scene, no, she was not shot. Rather, her body showed signs of strangulation."

The image is evident in my head: Mom is scared and alone, and the only person by her side is some monster with something tight around her neck. Did she cry? "Sh-She was strangled?"

He nods. "We believe by hand. We've been unable to retrieve any DNA evidence off the body, meaning it was premeditated and likely by someone she knew who was able to lure her out into the night."

"Someone she knew? Yeah, 'cause that narrows it down."

"I'm sorry if that was not the information you were wanting to hear."

"Nah, nah, it's cool," I say despite it not being cool.

"When we get more information, you'll be the first to know."

I get up from the couch, the leather creaking as I stand. "Yeah, thanks."

Detective Angel escorts me to the door. He closes it behind

me and the sun has set by now, leaving me in the dark. Luckily, it's only a short walk across the street.

I stall under the streetlight and place my cell phone to my ear. It trills as I wait for an answer. "Hello?" Joey's voice answers. "So how'd it go?"

"It's exactly what you thought," I explain.

The sound of his breath sighs into the phone. "I was afraid of that. That makes us even further back than where we started."

"Are you still at Nickels and Dimes? I'll come meet you right now."

"No. I don't want you out by yourself in the middle of the night. You could get run off the road or snatched up in the parking lot. We'll talk tomorrow, okay?"

"Joey, I don't like the sound of that. It's not safe for you either. Someone was already murdered there."

"Yeah … yeah. I know. But you don't have to worry about me. I'm a big boy."

"This better not be the last thing you ever say to me."

"Well just in case it is, I know a lot of shit's been happening lately, but I'm really glad you moved to Blackridge. You're the first person in my life to ever make me feel … special."

"You are special, Joey. At least to me you are. I better see you tomorrow."

I get off the phone and have a short walk across the street to get home. Joey's theory about there being a second killer seems right, which means I have another night of list-making. Mom's killer has to be someone who knows her real name.

NOVEMBER 21 – TUESDAY

Morning

Joey and I pull into Bedrock's parking lot. "Do you remember Peggy? The short Black woman who sold us all those pumpkins for Halloween?" I ask.

"Yeah, I remember," Joey confirms. "But she's nice and a cute little old lady. There's no way it could be her, right? Th-That's like saying my grandma could do it."

"I specifically remember her calling my mom Ms. Navarro. We can't just ignore suspects 'cause we don't want it to be them, even Amanda."

"Yeah, yeah. You're right."

Peggy is behind the register when we enter the store's gardening section. She wears a green apron with smudges of dirt and places her hand against her chest at the sight of me. "Oh Fiora, my poor baby." She steps out from behind the register and greets me with open arms. We're about the same height, yet her build is much more frail as she holds me. "I am so sorry for your loss. Your mother was a great woman, a great woman."

"That's actually what we came to talk to you about," I say once she lets go. "How long have you known my mother? Did you go to school with her or anything?"

She laughs. "How old do you think I am? No ma'am, I wish I was that young. I didn't meet your mother until she started working here."

"But you've at least had to hear something. You know, around the name Navarro."

That's when the air changes, and Peggy nods. "Yes, that I have. I've heard a lot of things, but you don't get as old as I am by believing everything you hear."

I smile at her. "Thank you, Peggy."

"You come back anytime you want, even just to say hi." Her attention turns to Joey. "And you, I remember you from Halloween. You take care of her now, she's a gentle soul."

He nods. "I will, thank you."

The two of us leave the store and return to my car. "Guess we can cross Peggy off our list, at least for now," I declare.

"Where to next?" Joey asks.

"There's a hostess at Bread and Butter called *Emily* who not only recognized my mom, but was acting super weird about it."

"Ah, yeah. That sounds super suspicious."

Bread and Butter is primarily vacant at this hour. Students are supposed to be in school, and most adults are at work. Only a few gray hairs sit in the booths, nursing their coffees left over from the early bird morning rush.

A hostess stands at the podium and pulls out a couple of menus. "Two of you?"

"Um, we were actually looking to speak with Emily," Joey says.

"Oh, what for?"

"Well ..."

The hostess, Emily, gets a good look at me before her smile fades. Her eyes are like those of a deer in headlights. "I'm sorry, but if you're not here to eat, then I will have to ask you to leave."

Without a choice, Joey and I exit the diner. "Okay, but that was super suspicious," he says once we're out the door and out to the brisk fog.

"Oh yeah," I agree, "no way that bitch is getting taken off the list. We'll have to figure something else out and come back later."

Joey scratches the side of his head. "So what's the difference between a stakeout and flat out stalking?"

"Um, a badge and a gun?"

"Neither of which we have."

"Yeah, but Detective Angel does. The cops have nothing to go off yet so they have to look into any lead they can get, right?" I say.

"Well yeah, but they've also framed two innocent people already. Do we really want to risk a third? We're bound to run into people who are sketched out about your mom, even if they weren't the ones to run out and kill her."

"I mean, I don't know. We're just going off of nothing right now. But there is one more person I wanna talk to before you have to go to work."

"I just hope they're not as scary as that woman."

I pause to look at him. "W–We're looking for at least two killers, Joey. Of course they're going to be scary."

"Well, yeah. Okay. But who is it?"

"Pandora's dad. He's the one who you said has first hand experience with the shooting."

"Oh yeah, you're totally right. His auto shop isn't far from here. I'll give you directions."

We return to the car and with Joey's instructions, reach the auto garage. It's a small place with junk cars filling every inch of the yard. Many of them look as if they're impossible to fix. The garage itself is just that, nothing more, and the side of the building has a decal of a cartoon car with a dialogue box that says, "Wash me."

Joey and I get out of my car and approach the whirling machines.

A large man with dark skin, a bald head, and an oil-stained jumpsuit exits the garage. He whistles at the sight of us. "Now that's a nice car. Joey, how the hell can you afford that? Taking change from the register?"

Joey scratches the side of his head. "Um, no sir."

"It's my car," I explain.

Pandora's dad nods his head. His nametag claims his name is Harper. "Right, right. You're the girl who plays drums in Pandora's band. What can I do for ya?"

"I wanted to talk to you about 20 years ago–if that's okay."

He wipes his hands against a rag too dirty to do any good.

"Let's talk inside." He escorts us through the maze of junked cars until we reach the inside of the garage. It's cleared from the wreckage with a single vehicle elevated while someone works on it from below. Harper pulls up several metal folding chairs and we take our seats. "You know, you look just like her."

"So you know?" I ask.

He nods. "Yeah, I know. I'm sorry to hear what happened."

"Working at a garage, you have to hear a lot of things. Especially after my mom moved back to town."

"Oh yeah, I've heard it all. You hear a lot of things in a small town with nothing to do."

"But you don't believe it?"

He shakes his head. "It was disrespectful then and it's disrespectful now. And now, people are dying."

Joey and I exchange looks, and he nods. "We believe someone killed Neb–Bailey 'cause they thought she started the curse," he explains.

"Unfortunately, I can't say that's not what happened," Harper states. "Anyone with half a brain knows the curse has never been real, but most of the people in Blackridge don't even have two brain cells to rub together."

Joey snorts, and I wish I could laugh too. From what I've seen, I can't say I disagree.

"Thanks for talking with us," I say. "If you hear anything at all, can you let us know?"

He nods. "You should be careful too. With someone still out there, they might be looking for you next."

With those ominous words in the air, we leave the garage and return to the car to drop Joey off in time for his shift.

Afternoon

The house is empty. Never once has it been this quiet. Atlus isn't here, so I don't hear him playing games through our joined wall or even hear the sound of his sorrowful sobs. He took his dog to Aunt Addie's so Trash doesn't bark when I walk through the door. At home, all I have is Squeak and a black cat scurrying around the house doesn't make things any less ominous.

"She was fucking crazy, dude," I explain to Chloe on the phone about this morning's events.

"She totally did it. Have you punched her in the face yet?" Chloe asks.

"No. I was gonna but Joey said something about her possibly being *innocent* or something."

"Nah, fuck that and fuck that bitch."

A notification from Instagram appears on the status bar on my phone. I pull it down, and it's from the account E.L.L.IOT.VAUGHN. "Oh shit!" I instinctively shout out.

"What?" Chloe cries.

I'm at a loss for words as I press on the notification and I'm brought to my DM's where I can even deny or accept the request. What was sent is a video with the caption: Ask ur boyfriend how my dick tastes.

I shouldn't, I know I shouldn't, but I do. I press play on the video.

Joey is the subject, the camera up close to his face as he's on his knees performing oral sex on another guy. His eyes are closed, then he looks up and notices. "Wait, are you filming me?"

"Shut up and keep sucking," Falco's voice commands from off screen.

Joey obliges. "Just don't show anyone."

"Um, what the fuck is that?" Chloe asks before breaking out into laughter. "Bitch are you watching porn?"

I don't know how to explain. I don't want to explain.

"Take off your clothes," Falco's voice says, never showing his face yet filming Joey's every move. He listens to everything Falco tells him.

I can't watch. I press the bold red REPORT button and block the account. "Chloe, I gotta go," I say.

"No the fuck you don't. What was that?"

"I'll tell you later!"

"Bi–"

I don't let her finish and hang up.

I dial a group call for everyone in the Discord chat. Unsurprisingly, Joey is the only one who does not answer. If he's at work, does that mean he doesn't know?

"Was I the only one sent that video?" I ask to confirm.

Pandora raises a pierced brow. "Um, you mean Joey's sex tape?"

Poppet giggles. "Geez, knowing Joey the other person could be anyone."

Farrah is shaking her head. "Th–That was not something I ever needed to see."

"It's not a sex tape and it doesn't matter who it was!" I cry. "Wait no, it does matter! It's Falco and he needs to pay!"

Pandora nods. She's blunt and sometimes ruthless, but she's not cruel–not intentionally, at least. "Right. Revenge porn is a serious crime, and he sent it to Farrah who is still a minor. Joey needs to know about it, if he doesn't already."

Cheese tilts her head. "Amanda just texted me asking me to come to work. Says Joey won't come out of the bathroom."

"Fuck, okay. So he knows," I say. "Everyone meet at Nickels and Dimes. We have to be there for Joey."

* * *

We reach Nickels and Dimes within a few minute intervals and pass through the glass door together. It chimes when we enter and Amanda is behind the counter. She bobbles her head. "Oh thank God you're here. Joey ran to the bathroom and won't come out. Must be something he ate."

Cheese takes her place behind the counter while Pandora, Poppet, and I march down the aisle. At the end of the store are two metal doors with a sign that reads EMPLOYES ONLY. We push through, and in front of us is the closed and locked door to the bathroom.

Joey is sobbing when I press my ear against the door. I knock on it with the back of my knuckles. "Go away!" he cries.

"Joey, it's me."

"I–I don't wanna talk right now."

Pandora uses both fists to pound on the door with excessive force. "Joey, you need to press charges! Revenge porn is illegal!"

"Yeah!" Poppet agrees.

"Oh yeah, me against the son of the city's favorite detective," Joey rebuttals.

"Your lack of consent is literally on video," Poppet debates. "They can't defend that!"

"We both know that's damn well not true."

Pandora kicks at the door with her booted foot. "Damnit Joey, if you won't do it for yourself then do it for his next victim!"

I place a hand on Pandora's shoulder and pull her away from the door. "Pan, stop. If he's not ready, he's not ready."

"Sheesh, can you really blame him?" Poppet asks. "Just ask every single person who's ever been sexually assaulted ever."

I nod. "Right. You guys can go home if you want. I'll stay with him."

Night

The cement is hard and cold on my ass and the wall is dense against my back. I've been here for an ungodly amount of hours, hearing nothing but Joey crying from the other end of the door. Until finally, it opens. "What are you still doing here?" he asks. His voice is rough and raw, and his face red and puffy.

I stand up, the blood rushing back to my legs. "I wasn't gonna leave you."

"Why not? Everyone else does."

"I'm not everyone else."

He looks around the room. To the left is an open door leading to Amanda's office, and to the right is a pile of boxes. "Where's everyone else?"

"Th–They left."

Joey shrugs as he blows through his nose. "Figures. But I'm not going to the police."

I shake my head. "I won't ask you to. You wanna go home?"

He nods, and I hold his hand as we leave the back room.

It's Nickels and Dimes after hours with the store closed and Amanda and Cheese gone for the night. The lights are dim as we go down the aisle until reaching the glass front door. It's exceedingly dark outside with the heavy rain. "Ha, figures," Joey almost laughs.

We're soaked when we reach my car and I turn on the heater. Joey rests his head against the window as fast beads of water pelt against the glass. The wipers are at full speed as we start a silent drive to the trailer park.

I know the feeling, Joey. I've had several quiet drives home myself.

We reach the trailer parks and I park as close to his trailer as the mud and potholes will allow.

"Um, thanks. You know … for everything," Joey says before disappearing into the rain.

"Do you want me to come with you?"

He shakes his head. "No. I just need to be alone right now."

"Happy Thanksgiving," I wish him before he can close the door.

"Yeah … happy Thanksgiving."

NOVEMBER 23 – THURSDAY

Afternoon

Aunt Addie lives in a Tudor revival-style home on the outskirts of Blackridge. It's a small and quiet neighborhood, one of the first developed in the city, and where Mom grew up. Aunt Addie holds the door open and invites me inside, but upon entering, I feel as unwelcome as Mom felt the day she got kicked out–the day she told her own mother she was pregnant with me.

It's telltale that the place was inherited from an old and bitter woman. Everything from the hummels covered in dust to the family portraits that show plenty of Aunt Addie and none of Mom.

"So, how do you like living on your own?" Aunt Addie asks as we enter the foyer. "Are you finally feeling like an adult?"

"Oh you know, it's this and that," I disregard.

It's Thanksgiving, and the mouth-watering scent of a feast comes from the kitchen. Growing up, we never celebrated much with Mom, but the one tradition we had was Atlus cooking the holiday meals—one that is still being honored to this day.

Aunt Addie and I join him in the kitchen; he appears natural in his element in front of the stove, and beside him is someone I was not expecting to see until after the fall break. "Mr. Mark?" I ask.

He's busy fulfilling his duty as Atlus's taste tester but takes a moment away from licking the back of a batter-covered spoon to acknowledge me. "Fiora! So glad you could make it."

I squint at him. "Okay, but why are you here?"

Aunt Addie approaches his side, and he wraps an arm

around her shoulder. "Well, um ... I live here. We're together," he announces.

We've been unable to retrieve any DNA evidence off the body, meaning it was premeditated and likely by someone she knew who was able to lure her out into the night.

No, it can't possibly be ... Mr. Mark and his fucking gloves.

My brows crunch further. "Huh?"

"I thought the same fucking thing," Atlus says.

"We didn't want to tell you at first because we didn't want things to be awkward at school," Aunt Addie explains.

I snort, attempting to snap myself out of it, at least for tonight. If I am in the house of a killer, I can't let him know that I know. "I so knew it. I even asked if the guy you're fucking was another teacher."

Mr. Mark's face glows red behind his thick-framed glasses. "Hey–Hey, come on now. We're supposed to be celebrating and having a good time. Doesn't Atlus's cooking smell amazing? And it tastes even better."

He's not lying.

The teachers excuse themselves, leaving only Atlus and I in the kitchen. It's assuring to see him cooking again. "That smells good," I tell him.

"That's 'cause it is," he responds.

"How have you been?"

He's silent as he stirs the mac and cheese, slowly adding cheese until it melts and smoothly forms into a sauce. "Fine."

"Yeah, me too ... Um, I lost my mom too, ya know? So you can talk to me if you need to. Or, ya know. Come over sometime. It's no biggie."

He looks up from his pot at me. "Y–Yeah, thanks." There's a sparkle in his eye he wipes away with his sleeve.

Dishes are set on the table after dinner is completed. For the main course, Atlus prepared both a turkey and a spiral ham, both bursting with flavor. But it would not be Thanksgiving without the sides. There are all the classics: stuffing, rolls, mac and cheese, mashed potatoes, sweet potatoes, and green bean casserole. The table is so full of dishes that we struggle to find enough space to place our plates as we take our seats.

"Wait," Atlus declares. There can't possibly be something else he's missing, but he returns to the table with a framed photo of Mom. It's the most recognizable of her, the one that is on the back of all her books. The dishes must be too hot because the steam is getting into my eyes and making them water, same with Atlus as he places Mom's photo at the head of the table, making her the guest of honor this holiday.

Silently, I promise her I'll get to the bottom of her murder.

NOVEMBER 27 – MONDAY

Morning

"No fucking way am I going back there," Joey declares when I arrive at the trailer to pick him up for school. It's the first day back after fall break, and Seal Coast is bad enough without everyone gossiping about the horrible thing your ex did to you.

"I don't blame you," I tell him.

He leans against the doorframe. "You should stay here too. Let's hangout."

I shake my head. "We'll hangout after school. I have too much to do today."

Over the break I told Joey about Thanksgiving, including my newfound suspicions of the seeming inconspicuous Mr. Mark. "So what are you gonna do? You know, about Mr. Mark?" he asks.

I raise my shoulders. "I guess the first thing I have to find out is if he knew about my mom in the first place. He's kinda in between our generation and hers, so he might not know."

"Unless your aunt told him." Joey scratches the side of his head. "Man, I just can't wrap my head around it. Killing your girlfriend's sister then playing house with Atlus. That's just too cruel. Really think Mr. Mark is capable of that?"

I shrug again. "I dunno. Innocent dorky art teacher might seem like the perfect disguise for a secret evil mastermind."

Joey leans forward and kisses me on the forehead. "Just be careful, okay? Remember what Pandora's dad said. The person who killed your mom could be after you next."

"You don't have to worry about me. I'm a big girl."

* * *

With no Joey and no Atlus, I wait in the school's security line alone. The group of boys in front of me snicker at the sight of me and whisper into each other's ears. "Fucking spit it out," I challenge.

That riles the boys. "You're pretty hairless for a beard. Do you wax?" their leader teases.

"I will punch you in your stomach until you drop to your knees and slam your teeth into the fucking concrete."

"On my knees like your boyfriend?" That causes the boys to laugh and cheer, parading themselves for the only accomplishment they'll ever have in life: being worthless pieces of shit.

"Fiora!" a feminine voice calls out, one that previously only addressed me with insults. May cuts in line and joins me at my spot. Her lips have no gummy fake smile and her eyes are melancholy. "Um, Fiora ... I'm really sorry about what Falco did. I–I never told him to do that. Yeah, I've been horrible, but I'd never ask him to hurt Joey ... or April. I didn't even know he was the one behind that doxxing account. You have to believe me."

"Falco didn't do this 'cause of you," I explain. "I kinda mouthed off to him when I was at your place the other day."

Her lips raise just enough to expose her pink gums before dropping back down. "You do have a bad habit of that."

"It's only bad when it comes back to bite me in the ass."

"Isn't that most of the time?"

I release a sorrowful breath. "Yeah, pretty much."

We step further in line, inching closer to the security checkpoint.

"Um, so I'm assuming you've talked to him?" May asks.

I look at her. "No way. I never wanna see that piece of shit ever again."

"No, not Falco. I mean Joey. My dad has sorta been on damage control since the whole ... incident."

"Funny how your dad calls himself *Detective Angel* when he's nothing but a piece of shit like the rest of them. But no, you don't have to worry. Joey's too scared of the corruption, victim blaming, slut shaming, and biphobia to press any charges, if that's what you're worried about."

I'd assume someone as heartless and bitchy as May would be over the moon to hear her even more shitty brother will face no consequences for his actions, but instead, she holds her head down low as we take another step further up the line. She looks up at me. "I'm sorry. Falco needs to pay. He can't keep getting away with this. When I found out he was behind the doxxing page, I wanted to kill him myself."

"Did you ask him why he did it?" I inquire. "I mean, April was the first person posted. What the hell did he have against her? You two were–supposedly–friends."

"He saw how upset I was when I thought she was choosing you over me. He said he wanted to make people pay for hurting others."

I don't know if I want to laugh or spit. "He thinks he's some gracious vigilante of justice when he's nothing but a bullying asshole."

"He's a piece of shit," May says, finally something we can agree on. "If there's anything I can do, please tell me. April may have tied the knot, but as far as I'm concerned Falco murdered her."

It's our turn at security and the conversation pauses as they check out bags, wave us down with wands, and pass us through the metal detectors. May and I regroup on the other side of the gate. "Actually, there is something you can do," I tell her. "Principal Pal told the student council to report any and all instances of bullying, right? I'm on my way to go talk to him right now. Come with me. We'll tell him about all of this together."

The sullen look on her face lifts to one of fire. I never thought I'd find myself on the same side as May as we march through the administration office. We're like soldiers off to war with only a single objective in mind, ready to destroy anything that gets in the way. When we reach the principal's office, May hammers the door with enough brutality to cause any surrender. "Principal Pal, we need to talk to you," she declares.

"Come in," he announces from the other side. We enter the room, and Principal Pal sits at his desk while we sit across from it. "This is ... unlikely. What seems to be the problem?"

I'm offended that he has the audacity to ask such a thing. "It's about Falco," I start off. "You have to know what happened over the break. That's not only cyberbullying to the fullest extent, but it's a flat out sexual crime."

"He's also the one behind the doxxing page that bullied April!" May interjects.

Principal Pal releases a breath, his expression drained. "I'm sorry girls, but I have to tell you what I told McCarthy about that *page*. The school has done everything in its ability. Anything that happens outside of campus is not in our jurisdiction."

My feet are on the floor before I know it. "What? That's not what you said when I was suspended for giving out candles!"

"What you did was disruptive. The school has already placed rules against cell phones and all forms of gossip. After that, there is nothing we can do. Anything else is a matter for the police."

"Oh yeah, right. The police who have proven to be so competent while there's a fucking serial killer on the loose."

"Fiora, that's enough," Principal Pal declares. "I know you've been through a lot this year so I would hate to hand out another suspension, or even expulsion. My hands are tied. If something happens on campus, let me know and I will handle it. Other than that, you're dismissed."

May and I share looks of disbelief and disappointment before exiting the office. "That fucking fascist!" I cry once the door is shut behind our backs, and I hope it's loud enough for him to hear.

"I–I'm sorry," May says, and it's bewildering to hear a genuine expression of sympathy from someone so cruel.

The warning bell rings and we disperse to our lockers.

Third Period

Mr. Mark stands in front of the whiteboard, drawing a landscape piece with an erasable marker while dressed head to toe in his clear raincoat and blue nitrile gloves. "Mr. Mark. Or is it Uncle Mark now?" I greet him.

His eyes widen behind his glasses as he laughs shyly. "Haha, just Mr. Mark is okay. Guess we should have told you sooner, huh? But everything stays the same at school."

He attempts to return to his drawing on the board, but I have more to say. Who is Mr. Mark, and what business does he have with my family? "Why'd you start teaching at Seal Coast? Did you go to school here?" I ask.

Mr. Mark takes the hint and puts the cap back on the marker before placing it on the mantel. "Um, no. Actually, I went to Promise Private Academy in San Diego, like you did. That's what got your aunt and I talking in the first place. Small world, isn't it?"

"Get the fuck out."

He chuckles. "I would, but I have a class to teach."

"So then, why are you here?" I ask.

"Well, San Diego was a little much for me. I wanted something calmer so after I graduated I started applying for teaching jobs around Colorado, Washington, and of course, Oregon. I had a few offers, graduating from Promise opens lots of doors, but I found I liked Oregon the best. It's peaceful here … Well, it was."

It is time for the million-dollar question: "So, did you know about Bailey Navarro?" I ask.

Mr. Mark raises a brow and puckers his lips. "Who? I know *Addilynn* Navarro, of course."

If he's lying, he's good at it. "Bailey was my mom's name," I explain, "before she changed it."

He breathes out through his nose. "Oh, I'm so sorry. No, I

never met her. Would have loved to. I'm a big fan of her books, actually."

"So Aunt Addie never talked about her ever?"

"She talks about her sister, yes, but only referred to her as Nebula–or Nebbie. Never Bailey. I didn't know Nebula Clairwater and Bailey Navarro were one and the same until I saw it on the news. The bell for class rings and Mr. Mark looks back at the whiteboard. "Oh shoot, I didn't get to finish my drawing."

With class about to start, I sit at the usual table where Joey is missing.

"Why are you flirting with Mr. Mark?" Cheese asks after I'm seated beside her.

"Shut the fuck up."

After School

I have a key to Joey's trailer and help myself inside. The TV is on and Joey's grandma and her caretaker, Alice, are watching. "Hi Alice, hi Joey's Grandma," I greet.

Joey's grandma looks at me from the recliner chair with something dull and thick like vomit oozing from her chin. "Good morning, Keaton."

Alice has a bowl of oatmeal on her lap and feeds the older woman like a toddler. "That's Fiora, remember? Fi-or-a."

The older woman takes a long look at me, seemingly unable to comprehend what's in front of her.

"Um, is Joey here?" I break the silence.

Alice uses the spoon in her hand to point down the hall. "He's in his room. I think he's sick. I've barely seen him all day."

"Thanks."

Joey's room is dark inside with the lights off and curtains drawn, but lying on the mattress is a lump from under the pile of covers. I crawl onto the bed beside Joey and brush away his messy, fawn-colored hair. "Hi Miles," I whisper in his ears.

He shuffles and groans before opening his crusted eyes and looks at me. "I like when you call me Miles." He rubs his eyes and sits up, his back resting against the wall. "So, how did everything go?"

I sigh, hoping I could get away without being the one to tell him. "Exactly as you'd expect."

Joey's face drops and his gaze goes down to his lap. "Oh ..."

"Principal Pal won't do anything. Says it's out of his jurisdiction."

"Bet he wouldn't even care if I killed myself like April."

Those words lay heavy between us. What am I supposed to say, or possibly not say, to save a life? It seems I've been doing nothing but saying the wrong things and making countless mistakes. Except Joey isn't one of them. I reach over to grab his foot and place it in my lap. He's wearing a pair of black socks that I pull off to massage the soles of his feet. For a moment, neither of us says a word. His feet are large, and his toes are long, but his flesh is soft.

A light breaks through the dimness of the room.

"Your phone is ringing. You should answer it," Joey says. "It could be about your mom's case."

I answer, putting the phone on speaker. "Hello?"

"This is going to sound like a stupid question, but are you with Joey?" May's voice asks.

I look at him sitting beside me and his feet on my lap. "You're right, that is a stupid question."

"Fuck! I was hoping he was with Falco."

"Fuck you, cunt."

"No, not because of that. Falco's missing."

Joey sits up. "What?"

"Cappy just called me and said Falco never showed up for football practice," she explains.

Joey leans in to speak into the phone. "Falco wouldn't do that. Football is his life."

"I know, that's why I was hoping he was with you. I'm on my way back to the school right now. If he's not there my dad is filing a missing person's report."

"Keep us updated," I say.

"I will," she assures, and we hang up the phones.

NOVEMBER 28 – TUESDAY

Morning

For the umpteenth time, the students of Seal Coast Community High School are gathered in the gymnasium. A boy sitting on the bleachers' bench in front of us turns around to face us. He moves his hand back and forth in front of his mouth while sticking his tongue to his cheek.

Joey slumps back. "I so don't want to be here."

"At school or alive?" Cheese bluntly asks.

"Both."

"I'm surprised you are here," Pandora states.

"Well, I dunno. I feel like I kinda have to if I wanna learn anything new about the case … Now I wish I hadn't come."

Poppet wraps her arms around Joey's shoulders and squeezes. "Ignore the haters. We support you."

Joey sighs. "I'm–I'm used to it."

I'm holding Joey's hand as he squeezes and I want to spit in the face of the guy before us.

Principal Pal and several suits behind him stand in the center of the court. "Good morning everyone," he speaks into the microphone. "This year has been a rough one for everyone at Blackridge, and now more than ever is it important for us to come together as a community. One of our own is missing: Falco." He doesn't need to announce it. Falco's face has been plastered on the news and social media since last night. Even printed photos of him have been plastered on every wall and surface around town. "This is an ongoing investigation, and I would like to pass the mic to those in charge," he continues, handing the mic to one of the suits.

"Good morning. I'm Detective Angel and this is my partner

Detective Damien," he announces. "The first 24 hours is the most important in a missing persons investigation. The person we are looking for goes by the alias Falco. He is 18 years old, 6 feet tall, and 180 lbs. He has brown hair and brown eyes and is possibly either wearing a red T-shirt and jeans or his football jersey with the number 32. Any and all information is crucial. Please, everyone be vigilant. You could save a life."

The mic is returned to Principal Pal. "Rules have been strict on campus, and unfortunately I must announce there will be more. From now on, all students must be escorted to classes and extracurricular activities by a teacher or coach. No student is to be wandering the halls without an escort, including with a hall pass. And finally, clubs that do not have a coach or teacher supervisor, such as the student council, are hereby disbanded. It is unfortunate, but this is what is best for public interest to prevent any more tragedies. Teachers, you may escort your students back to their classes."

After School

Trying to get through today was like pulling teeth. Teachers and security are stationed in every hall, and it's impossible to even take a piss without Big Brother watching. The final bell has rung, and now students are being heard off campus like sheep. I'm taking my time as I wait for Joey. He's tall and easy to spot through a crowd.

"Come on, let's go, let's go!" the shepherds command.

It's slow pushing so many bodies past the foyer and through the main double doors. A whistle blows in my ear, yet I have nowhere else to go.

"She's with me," Ms. Hoyos explains to the security.

I look at her. "I am?"

"Yes. I thought we could do something together." The words she says should be inviting, yet the way they slip from her lips is stoic.

I look around the pool of bodies surrounding us. "Where's Atlus?"

"He went home with his girlfriend."

"Atlus has a girlfriend?"

"Yes, Farrah."

"Ha!" I exclaim louder than I should in a foyer filled with roving eyes. "I totally fucking knew it."

"Yes, I sent him away for your surprise."

My face scrunches. "My surprise? For what?"

"For your birthday coming up."

My birthday? That's right, I almost forgot with everything going on lately.

A taller Joey pushes through the crowd to join us. "Oh shit, it's your birthday? How old are you turning? 22? 23?"

I snort. "Shut up."

"Hello Joey," Ms. Hoyos says the same way she's been speaking. The robotic tone is almost reminiscent of McCarthy.

Joey waves. "Hi Ms. Hoyos. Um … good class today?"

Her lips raise in a way that twitches her face. "Thank you. Fiora, we should get going."

I give her a look. Something about this whole interaction tells me not to go with her, yet when she starts walking, my legs follow along.

"Better get ready for the surprise party I'm throwing for you next!" Joey's voice shouts behind my back.

The teachers' parking lot is at the back of the school with the buses and this is my first time seeing the inside of her 2008 Toyota Camry. It has cloth seats and not a single spec of dust on the dashboard. It's silent as she pulls out of the parking lot and turns at the light to enter the main road. I reach over to turn on the radio. The music barely has a second to play before Aunt Addie presses the same button, making the ride silent again. I squint my eyes at her. "Okay?"

There's something strange about her, even for Aunt Addie. Her back is straight, her eyes glued to the road, and her hands are at a perfect 9 and 3.

"Um, so where are we going?" I ask.

She doesn't look at me or seem to be blinking. "It's a surprise."

I can't take my eyes off her. That's why I don't see it coming …

NOVEMBER 29 – WEDNESDAY

Afternoon

Beep. Beep. Beep. Beep.

It's constant, and I wish I could turn it off, but it's not the obnoxious beeping of my morning alarm. My eyelids are heavy, seemingly impossible to lift. I do just the slightest bit, and the amount of white surrounding me is blinding. My consciousness comes and goes, but the beeping never ends, pulling me back. Opening my heavy eyes becomes a little easier upon every attempt. The blinding white takes shape, and the fluorescent lights burn a hole in my retinas. Crust holds my eyes shut like glue and I rub it away, making me increasingly aware of the IV pierced through my wrist. It's attached to a bag of clear, dripping liquid. The surface my body is laying on is stiff and uncomfortable while the blanket draped over my lap is thin and scratchy. I'm at a hospital.

"Hey, she's awake," a boy's voice says.

It takes a moment for my vision to focus on the other side of the room. A couple of seats rest against the white-painted walls, and in them are Atlus and Aunt Addie, the latter seemingly uninjured.

My body is stiff, yet I feel no pain. Whatever is in that drip must be the good stuff. "What happened?" I ask.

"There was a deer," Aunt Addie states matter-of-factly.

That's right, I remember now. We were driving down the main road through Blackridge, then the next thing I knew, we were facing oncoming traffic. I heard the horn of the vehicle before I felt the impact. "Yeah, 'cause swerving into oncoming traffic is totally the right move."

"I'm sorry. It was … reflexes. I'll do better next time."

"Better at what? Trying to kill me?"

There are two knocks on the door before a crowd of people enter. "Surprise!" There's Joey, Poppet, Pandora, Cheese, and O'Brien holding balloons and bearing gifts. They're obviously from the hospital gift shop, but it's the thought that counts.

Joey approaches my bedside and hands me a brown stuffed bear. It's holding a heart that reads GET WELL. "I wish we could throw you a better birthday party. We were waiting for you to wake up." Along with the bear, there's an envelope, and I open the unsealed flap. The front of the card has a black cat, and the inside is signed by everybody. Joey's handwriting even signed Squeak's name.

Aunt Addie rises from her seat. "I'll go tell the nurse you're awake." She makes haste to the door and it latches shut behind her.

Cheese approaches the machines I'm attached to and admires the bag of dripping clear liquid. Her reflection stares back at her as she tilts her head. "They gave you morphine? Tell them you have anxiety around cars now and they'll give you a Xanax prescription."

I raise my shoulders. "I dunno. Prolly. I feel great."

Pandora snickers. "You won't pretty soon."

"Right?" Poppet says. "When we heard about the accident we were surprised that you were alive, let alone the fact that you didn't even break a bone."

I make room on the bed for Joey to sit on the edge and notice how he hangs his head. I nudge his shoulder with my toes. "Hey, it takes more than that to kill me. I'm a fucking cockroach."

Atlus snorts. "Ain't that the fucking truth."

There's a gentle knock on the door. "Come in," I call out.

I expect the return of Aunt Addie or a nurse, but the door opens and in comes May. She meekly stands at the back of the room. "Oh, I didn't know everyone was here. I can come back later."

The others gawk at her like a deer in headlights. "It's cool," I assure her.

May takes several steps forward towards the bed, the air significantly heavy. "There's going to be a press announcement a little later, but they found Falco's body."

It's something we all suspected when the news broke that Falco was missing, but hearing the confirmation makes the air heavier. Someone else we know is dead, and I'm not.

"F–Falco's dead?" Joey asks.

May stoically nods.

"Good," Pandora blurts.

Poppet scoffs. "Panda! A time and a place."

"How is this not the time and place? He deserves whatever happened to him after what he did to Joey."

Silence fills the room, none of us able to oppose. Not even Falco's sister.

"His body was caught on one of the breakwaters at the pier," May goes on to explain. "It's pretty badly damaged from the water and fish, but we know it's him from his jersey. And you'd want to know this: he was shot in the head."

DECEMBER 1 – FRIDAY

FOUR AND COUNTING: ANOTHER
BODY FOUND IN BLACKRIDGE

BLACKRIDGE, Or. – Police are searching for the person responsible for the apparent shooting of 18-year-old Oregon football player, Jayden Burns, and supposedly dumped his body off the Blackridge pier.

Jayden Burns' family reported him missing Monday night after he failed to show up for football practice. His body was found a couple days later Wednesday morning.

This is allegedly the fourth victim in a string of murders across Blackridge and the second player from the Seal Coast Community High School football team.

Afternoon

"Do you have any questions?" the nurse asks after I return my hospital discharge papers.

"Um, yeah. My prescriptions," I say.

Aunt Addie displays a paper bag with a long receipt stapled to the front: "I picked up your Xanax for you." She's been surprisingly attentive since the accident. In the back of my mind, I may have thought she caused it on purpose, but now she just seems repentant by bringing me things to do and feeding Squeak back home for me.

"What about for pain?" I ask.

"Doctor says over the counter Advil as needed," the nurse explains.

I scoff. "What? That fucking quack! I'm in pain. I need Oxy."

She quickly flips through the paperwork and leaves the

room. It was worth a try, at least.

"Are you ready to go?" Aunt Addie asks.

I double check my bag to make sure I have everything. "Yeah, I'm ready. Where's Atlus?"

"I sent him to his girlfriend's for the night."

"Don't you think it's a little inappropriate for a fourteen year old to spend the night with his girlfriend?"

"No. Atlus is mature."

I squint my brows to the best of my ability after having my face assaulted by an airbag. "Um, okay. Where's Joey?"

"I sent him home."

"What? Why? I'm supposed to be going home with him."

"You're in too much pain to be spending the night with your boyfriend."

"That's not for you to decide. And Atlus is too young to be spending the night with a girlfriend. Mom lectured us a ton about safe sex, but that doesn't mean he has any business doing it."

Aunt Addie blinks several times. "Your car is still at the school so I'm bringing you home with me. So you can rest."

Without my car, I can't argue.

Night

Aunt Addie is right about me being in pain. Advil might be enough for the dull ache, but it does nothing for the black and blue. I stare at myself bare in the mirror, my body more bruise than woman. Surprisingly, the worst isn't on my right side where I was struck by the oncoming car. Across my chest is a thick and dark welt from the seatbelt, varying in colors from dark red, purple, black, and blue. None of my bones broke, yet my shoulder feels bound by pins and needles when I attempt to raise my cell phone to chin level. I take a photo of my reflection.

FIORA: >Sent attachment<
JOEY: That is the least sexy nude Ive never seen

FIORA: Did you just say your girlfriend isn't sexy?
JOEY: Youre a very sexy zombie
JOEY: How you feeling? They got you on the good stuff?
FIORA: No >:(
FIORA: I'm really tired though so I'm gonna go to bed
FIORA: Don't know if I'll be able to sleep though
JOEY: Did you listen to Cheese and get the xanax?
FIORA: Yeah
JOEY: Sounds like sweet dreams to me!
FIORA: Yeah, except I'm shacked up in my mom's old room
JOEY: Oh...
JOEY: Are you gonna be okay?
FIORA: Yeah I'll live
FIORA: Good night <3
JOEY: Good night <3

Mom's old bedroom is down the hall from the bathroom and it's exactly how she left it nearly 20 years ago. She wasn't allowed to take more than the clothes on her back the day she was kicked out. The wallpaper is blue and white stripes while the carpet hasn't been stepped on in years. Mom may have always been aloof, but she was neat and organized. The plants she used to have are long dead now, but her collection of books lives on. Of course a girl who would grow up to be a famous author would be a bookworm, and her overflowing bookcase shows it. She mostly read fantasy but dabbled in horror, romance, and mystery, just like her own writings. There's a desk with an old computer on it. I'm curious to know if it still works. I've never seen a monitor that big and bulky in real life; it's a relic of the past. Maybe some other day, I'll have the strength to do some more snooping and maybe even find some of Mom's earliest writings.

Her bed has a twin sized mattress and a black metal frame pressed up against the wall. I pull back the covers and attempt to get as comfortable as possible. My shoulder is screaming. I lay in the dark, the only light coming from my phone. It's as dim as it can go. My body may be tired, but I'm not sleepy. I scroll through the multitude of streaming apps until I find something to watch, something entertaining enough to get me through the night, yet also something I've seen so many times it won't matter if I fall asleep. A cowbell rings to start the theme song to *King of the Hill*.

Laying in Mom's old bed is weird. Between this and my aching body, I don't know if it'll get comfortable enough to sleep. The mattress reminds me of Joey's: filled with springs that press on all the wrong pressure points. Except, he's not here with me tonight to make it worth it. At least when he's with me, I can mostly lay on him. His skin is soft and warm, and I've gotten used to his natural scent without any cologne. It's been so long since Mom has slept here that it no longer smells like her and has been replaced by the musk of undisturbed dust.

Midnight

A line of light flickers on under the door, and footsteps come from down the hall. The bathroom is just a few feet away from Mom's old room, but the footsteps keep going and stop eerily close to the door. A shadow breaks through a section of the light and just stays there, silent and static.

If it weren't for the episode playing, I'd think time has stopped. Yet I know exactly how much is passing. It's an uncomfortable amount. The longer the shadow remains, the more its intent seeps under the door: bloodlust.

More footsteps are down the hall, heavier ones. A man yawns. "Addie? You coming back to bed?" Mr. Mark's voice asks.

"Yes," Aunt Addie replies, her vacant tone coming from directly behind the door.

"What are you doing?"

"I was bringing this pillow to Fiora. Make sure she's comfortable."

Mr. Mark yawns again before chuckling. "She's the type who'd let you know if she needed something. Come on, let's go back to bed."

The footsteps retreat together, and the lights flick off once further down the hall.

What the fuck, I mouth to myself. There's no way the car crash was an accident, and there's no way this intense sensation of fear is a coincidence. It's a warning.

I pause the episode to pull up Discord and send a warning of my own to the group chat:

FIORA: Ms. Hoyos is trying to kill me

DECEMBER 2 – SATURDAY

Morning

"Good morning, Ms. Hoyos. Good morning Mr. Mark. Is Fiora up yet?" Joey's voice is like a fresh breath of spring after an unbearable night.

"Good morning, Joey," Mr. Mark's voice greets. "She's still in her room. Down the hall to the left."

"Thanks."

I'm packed and ready to go when there's a knock on the door, and Joey enters Mom's childhood bedroom. "Get me the fuck out of here," I tell him. He scurries over to me and wraps his arms around me, lifting me from my feet. "Ow."

He places me back to the ground. "Oh, sorry. I don't know how I could have possibly forgot. Um, I got your message. What the fuck?"

"I'll tell you once you get me the fuck out of here."

He nods. "Right."

Joey carries my bag for me and we go to the kitchen where Mr. Mark and Aunt Addie sit at the breakfast nook. Their plates are bare with nothing left but crumbs and they nurse a couple mugs of coffee. Mr. Mark finishes bringing his mug to his lips and sits it on the table. "Oh, you guys leaving already? You don't want any breakfast? A cup of coffee?"

"Oh, um … no thanks, Mr. Mark," Joey declines. "There's an Uber waiting outside."

"You sure? I can drop you kids off wherever it is you're going."

"I'm sure," I say.

"Fiora, you need your rest," Aunt Addie says. She breathes, speaks, and eats like a human, yet the woman sitting in front of me seems anything but–especially if she did what I think she did.

I shake my head. "I'm good."

Mr. Mark chuckles. "Man, you Navarro women sure are built different. If I were in a car accident the other day I'd be in bed crying like a baby. But look at both of you. It's like nothing ever happened."

I wish I could say it's like it never happened. The bruising on my ribs and breastplate makes it hard to breathe, my neck is so stiff I feel I should be in a brace, and my right shoulder reminds me of O'Brien after he got shot.

After a few more excuses, Joey and I are out of the Tudor house and into the Honda Accord waiting by the curb. "Can you take us to 2958 Misty Lane, please?" Joey asks the stranger in the driver's seat.

"No," I interject, "take us to Seal Coast."

"School? But it's Saturday."

"Yeah, but my car is still in the parking lot."

"Oh yeah."

It's a silent drive with the stranger in the front seat as we drive down the main road that intersects Blackridge. Joey and I are the only ones here after we're dropped off at the student parking lot. I try to the best of my ability to toss Joey the car keys. "Do you mind driving?"

He has to dive to catch them due to my poor throw. "You mean the car that's push to start, has heated seats, a rear view camera, and costs more than my whole house? Nah, I don't think I'd mind."

Joey skips to the passenger side to open the door and help me inside. I hate feeling useless, but my body is so sore I feel my muscles have been replaced with pins and needles. He almost trips on his way to the driver's seat and takes his place. "Oh man, I've always wanted to do this." He presses the button and the engine starts.

He's so cute. "You know, I never took you as a car guy," I say.

"Why, 'cause I'm bisexual and don't have a dad?"

I snort and wince at the pain at the same time. "You got so excited when McCarthy finally let you drive the trailer for student council."

"I dunno, I can't explain it. I just think they're cool. So much of society revolves around cars and engines and stuff."

"Is that what you wanna get into after graduation? Some kind of engineering?"

His hands are on the steering wheel, but his excitement fades. "I–I dunno. I don't have the money for college or anything, so maybe I've been thinking about joining the airforce."

"Join any branch of military and I'm breaking up with you."

"Haha, yeah. I get it. I wouldn't do it 'cause I want to, that's for sure. We both know I'm gonna spend the rest of my life working at Nickels and Dimes anyways, so why bother trying?"

"Or you can quit and let me take care of you."

He chuckles grimly before changing the subject. "Um, I figured we'd stop by your place so you could feed your cat then pack some things. You shouldn't be alone at all right now. Not until something can be done about your crazy aunt."

"Wouldn't you rather stay at my place? You said yourself that just my car is worth more than your trailer."

He playfully rolls his eyes. "Well, when you put it that way."

It's a dank and misty drive through Blackridge until we reach Joey's trailer. Alice's car is parked in the yard and we find her inside making breakfast while Joey's grandma is fast asleep in the recliner. We exchange pleasantries before reaching Joey's room.

His school backpack is on the floor, and he dumps the components onto the mattress before packing. He brings things like his toothbrush and phone charger, then goes to the dresser with drawers dislodged from the tracks. "How many pairs of underwear do you think I'll need? One? Two?" he asks.

My body is so sore I take a moment to lower myself onto the mattress on the floor. Though the springs are so uncomfortable I'm better off standing. "You're gonna need more than that. I wasn't joking, you know?" I tell him.

He's holding a pair of black boxer briefs when he looks down at me. "About what?"

"Move in with me."

He takes a moment to fold the underwear in his hands before opening his mouth. "I don't wan–"

"Don't even finish that," I interrupt.

"I don't want you to get sick of me."

I fight through the aching of the right side of my body to stand to my feet. "I could never get sick of you, Joey. I want to see where our lives take us while we still have them. You're not joining the military, you're not gonna be stuck at Nickels and Dimes, and you're not gonna be stuck in this trailer. Alice thinks your grandma needs to be a facility. She doesn't even know who you are half the time. You're too smart and kind to just sit here and rot in Black-shit. Move on–move in with me."

He breathes out through his nose. "Yeah you say that now, but wait until you get to know me. You'll get sick of me ... just like all the others."

"I just told you I could never get sick of you. I want to get to know you more. I want you to move in with me 'cause I'm really starting to fall in love with you."

His eyes are glossy. "R–Really?"

"Yes, really. And I'm not just lying to you, or leading you on, tryna use you for your body, or whatever else is going on through that mind of yours."

"I–I love you too. Guess it wouldn't hurt to stay a little while and see how it goes, right?"

I nod. "Right."

So, Joey packs more things.

Afternoon

Just when it seems we're about finished in his room, Joey makes another stop at the dresser and admires the picture frame facing down. It's the smiling photo of him and Keaton. He turns to me. "D–Do you mind if I bring this? I've been meaning to bring this to Keaton's grave, but her family hates me."

"You can bring it," I tell him.

He smiles poignantly. "Why are you so awesome?"

"'Cause she meant a lot to you and I wouldn't want to take that away from you."

Joey packs the last thing into his bag and follows me down the hall and into the living room. His grandma is awake and watching TV while Alice is folding laundry. "Um, I'm gonna be staying with Fiora for a while," Joey announces.

His grandma looks over her frail shoulder and smiles. "Oh, that's lovely. Have fun and take lots of pictures."

"Pictures of what?"

Alice finishes what she's folding and places it in the basket with the other articles of clothing before getting up from the couch and gesturing us over to the side. We're out of earshot of the elderly Irish woman. "Joey, have you thought about what we talked about?" Alice asks.

Joey looks down at me and releases a breath. "Yeah, I think it's a good idea. Make sure she ends up somewhere good, okay? Not anywhere they'll let her get bed sores or anything."

Alice nods. "Of course. I'll take good care of her like I always have. You two take care of yourselves as well."

Joey and I exit the trailer and head to my car parked in the yard. The door unlocks when he touches the handle. "How are you feeling?" I ask.

"I dunno, a lot of things I guess," he answers.

The hatchback rises and Joey throws in his things. With an indefinite stay, he brought more than an overnight bag, including his guitar and bass.

We arrive at my house and park in the driveway. "Press that button right there," I instruct, and Joey presses on the remote clipped to the driver's side visor. The garage door rises and we pull inside.

It's so endearing to finally be home. I finally have my own bed, blankets, pillows, and now my own boyfriend. I wish I had my mom. I lay on the bed, and Joey lays beside me. Squeak joins us, jumping on the bed and purring.

"So, what happened last night?" Joey asks, and I explain. He's looking into my eyes, and I look back at his. They're exhausted. "That's so fucked up," he says. "And a pillow? Like the thing people use to smother other people to death with?"

I nod. Though Aunt Addie never entered the room, her bloodlust seeped under the door like a poison mist. "I think she killed my mom."

"Yeah, I think so too, even if I'm having a hard time wrapping my head around it. Shouldn't she of all people know the curse isn't real? Was that chance really worth murdering her own sister over?"

I shrug to the best of my ability. "I dunno. Probably. The more I think about it, the more it all makes sense. The day we move back to town there's that shooting at the mall. Then Lemming dies, Griffin and Keaton are murdered ... all this shit started the day we came here. She and my mom were pretty estranged. They hadn't talked in years until we moved back here. I guess in Aunt Addie's mind, she had to choose between her sister and her students."

Joey sighs. "Under any other circumstances, that might be noble. But this is just fucked up. Now that Falco's dead, she probably thinks the curse is still active as long as you're alive." I snuggle close to his chest and he holds me. His body is so warm, so comforting. "What are we gonna do now?" he asks.

I look up at him, my neck stiff like a rusted hinge. "Aren't you the one always saying we need evidence?"

He sighs wryly. "That pesky evidence, always getting in the way. What about Atlus? You think he's safe with her? Well ... as safe as he can be."

"I think he's fine for now. I mean, technically I survived the shooting too. Atlus has nothing to do with it, if that's what's really going through her mind. As long as I don't die before the killer is caught, Atlus should be fine."

"I won't let anything happen to you. Over my dead body."

I rest my head on his chest and he runs his fingers through my hair.

DECEMBER 4 – MONDAY

Second Period

"I don't want you alone at all today, not even for a single second," Joey said this morning before we parted ways to our separate classes. So far, things have been characteristically mundane, though I'm nervous as I report to second period.

Ms. Hoyos isn't here yet, so I take a seat at my usual desk. A few minutes later, O'Brien joins. "I didn't think you'd be back at school so soon after your accident," he comments.

"Yeah well, you know me. I'm real serious about graduating this year," I say.

He raises a bushy brow. "Is this something to do with your and Joey's investigation?"

"Yeah, more or less. How's it going with the football guys? Honestly, Joey and I thought it was Falco. But now …"

"Oh, yeah. The guys have been really upset about that. They're gonna dedicate the game this weekend in his and Griffin's honor."

It's only a moment away before class begins, yet there's no sign of Ms. Hoyos. There's a twisting in my stomach as I anticipate the inevitable, but it never arrives. The warning bell rings, and a young, short man enters the classroom wearing a suit and a bow tie. "Good morning class. I was told of your school's traditions so you may call me Mr. Del Rossi. I'll be filling in for Ms. Hoyos for the time being."

My hand raises. "Where's Ms. Hoyos?"

"She's not here today," he states the obvious and turns around to write his name on the whiteboard.

O'Brien and I exchange looks. What is she up to?

Third Period

O'Brien walks with me to third period and we split when I enter the classroom. Joey and Cheese are at our usual table while Mr. Mark draws on the whiteboard. He stops when he notices me. "Oh, Fiora. I wanted to talk to you for a second," he says.

I raise a brow and step closer. "What could I possibly have done in a *there are no wrong answers,* art class?"

Mr. Mark chuckles. "No, no. You haven't done anything wrong. I was just wondering if you've heard from your aunt today."

"No, she had a sub in class this morning. How do you not know where she is? You live with her."

"Yeah, but Atlus and I left early so he could make it to soccer practice. She said she would get here later, but clearly she hasn't. I'm worried with everything that's been going on lately, and I can't call her because of the cellphone ban."

I almost want to laugh if this isn't so serious. "No shit. Even teachers have to follow that bullshit rule?"

"Teachers gotta teach by example right?"

The bell rings, and I sit with Joey and Cheese at the table. I lean in towards him. "You heard that, right?"

"Yeah, it sounds serious. Right?" Joey says.

I scoff. "Wow, eavesdrop much?"

"Wh–What? I mean yeah I guess, but–"

"Relax, I'm just fucking with you. But yeah, it does sound serious."

Cheese tilts her head, her long hair dipping onto the table. "So the killer is now the killed?"

Joey scratches the side of his head. "We don't know that … yet. We won't be able to sneak out with all the security so we'll have to check it out after school."

After School

Without Aunt Addie, it's up to us to bring Atlus home, whatever that may entail. I'm still unable to drive because of the stiffness in my neck and arm, so Joey takes the wheel. He turns into the neighborhood teetering on the edge of the Blackridge border, and we drive down the line of Tudor houses. We reach a specific one with a 2017 Kia Sorento, Aunt Addie's rental car after the accident, parked in the driveway.

Joey slows down before pulling to the curb. "Is that her car?" I look at him and nod. "It … It looks like the engine is running," he says.

The car is still, yet the fumes foaming from the exhaust pipe mix with the surrounding fog.

The back door opens when Atlus attempts to exit my car.

"Wait!" Joey cries out. "Let me go first. W–We don't know what we might find."

With a skeptical look, Atlus closes his door while Joey opens his. We watch as he approaches the car and peers through the driver-side window.

A moment passes, and I get out of the car and join him at his side.

"Don't look," he tells me, yet I do anyway.

The engine is running and Aunt Addie's forehead rests on the steering wheel, her fingers still clasped to it. A hole is through her head and thick globs of blood are dried around the wound. Her large, wide-open eyes bulge from their sockets, and a deep, dark, dense pile of crimson rests in her lap.

This was more or less what I was expecting, but it's different seeing it with my own eyes. There's a sense of relief, along with a wavering sense of dread. Joey is right. Seeing a dead body changes you. "So, do we, like, call someone?" I ask.

Joey wanders to the other side of the car and inspects it from there. He's so lost in thought he doesn't hear me. "She was shot on this side of the head, making that side the exit wound, and none of the windows are broken. That means the killer was inside the car with her when she died. This could be the big break the case needs!"

"Okay, but do we call someone?" I ask again.

"Oh, yeah. We need to call the police."

I take my phone from my hoodie pouch and dial the number. It trills in my ear before the operator answers. "9-1-1, what's your emergency?"

"Hi, I'm at 548 Oak Avenue, Blackridge and there's a dead body. Her name is Addilynn Navarro. She's been shot."

"We'll send an officer out right away. Is there an immediate threat?"

I look around. The neighborhood is so peaceful, so quiet. Like no one knows a thing, and the killer has disappeared without a trace. "No," I answer and hang up. I sit down on the curb and Joey sits beside me. I look up at him. "This could be our big break?"

He looks down at me. "Oh, I did say that, huh?"

"Yeah, you almost seemed excited. So the killer was in the car with her?"

He nods. "Either he was in the car with her, or the car door was open. But both confirm that it was someone she knew. It almost seems like the killer got sloppy with this one. There has to be evidence left behind. If the cops weren't taking this case seriously before, there's no way they're not now after what happened to Falco."

"They still don't seem to be doing much."

"Well, it's hard to catch a killer when there's seemingly no motive," Joey explains "You know, it's easy when there's like jealousy, money, domestic violence. Common motives. Addie killed your mom then tried killing you. Her motive was obvious. But this killer, it seemed impossible to know until now. We were looking at this from completely the wrong angle. When you–"

Atlus comes scampering from the car parked on the curb.

"What's going on?"

The conversation cuts short and we both look at him. "Aunt Addie is dead," I announce, cutting no corners.

Atlus slowly inches closer to the car, and Joey reaches out for his hand. "Don't look," he tells the younger boy.

The neighborhood's serenity is sliced through by the shrieking of sirens when the entirety of Blackridge's city budget arrives on the scene. There's an ambulance, three black and white Dodge Chargers, and a black Chevrolet Suburban I know to be owned by Detective Angel. The uniforms rush out of their vehicles, most of which turn their attention to Aunt Addie's car, but the detectives approach the three of us sitting on the curb.

"Fiora, what happened?" Detective Angel inquires, his appearance disgruntled. His usual slicked-back hair is unkempt, and his suit jacket is wrinkled. Joey might have a point when he said the cops never cared until someone close to them became their target.

I explain what happened, though there's not much. We got out of school, came here, and found her body.

"We're going to need statements from all of you," Detective Damien explains.

The three of us are separated.

DECEMBER 5 – TUESDAY

Midnight

The three of us spent hours explaining the same things ad nauseam to the detectives until they finally let us go home. With Aunt Addie gone, Atlus is back at Misty Lane with me. He admires the withered plants in their pots. "You couldn't even keep Mom's plants alive for her? How useless are you?"

I scoff and roll my eyes. "Why, what's she gonna do? Haunt me?"

Atlus seems as annoyed as ever. I can see the gears working in his skull, trying to process everything he's been through. "Whatever. I'm going to bed. Come on, Trash." He and his mutt stomp up the steps and into his room.

I sit on the couch and run my fingers through my hair. Every time we take a step forward, we take four steps back.

"So, now what?" Joey asks, sitting beside me.

"Do you still have that note I gave you? You know, the one with all the killings. I think we have a few updates to make."

"Oh, yeah. Right. It's in my bag." He gets up from the couch and heads to my bedroom.

I wait until the door is shut before I grab my phone and dial a contact to make a call. It's late so I doubt he'll answer, but I can at least leave a message. The last thing I want is to talk to this bastard anyway. It trills several times until I get the automated message. Then, I wait for the beep. "Hi, Eric. This is Fiora. Don't delete this message, you're gonna like what I have to say." I take a deep breath, swallowing every ounce of my pride as I choose this battle. "I know about your arrangement with my mom. I'm sure you heard about what happened to her. Now that she's gone, I want you to know that I want to keep it going so I can keep custody of Atlus–here in Blackridge. You don't need to call me back. Just text me your response. Thanks, bye."

I hang up just as Joey skips down the stairs . He's admiring the crumbled note. "Man, your handwriting is awful. I was having a hard time reading this the first time." He sits down beside me.

"Oh shut up," I say playfully, reaching for the pen on the coffee table.

The facts:

- Holly McGuire–aka Lemming–died from a self-inflicted gunshot wound to the head the night of September 24th after posting a video to her Instagram story telling all of Blackridge her name.
- Zachary Moore–aka Griffin–was found dead in the locker room from a gunshot wound to the head by Falco the morning of October 10th, but he is assumed to have died the night of October 8th, after the football game that Sunday.
- Milena Freeman–aka Keaton–was found dead by a gunshot wound to the head by Joey on October 24th.
- Eloise Horton–aka April–died by suicide sometime between November 3rd and November 6th after her name was posted on the doxxing page.
- Jayden Burns–aka Falco–reported missing November 27th after missing football practice. His body was found November 29th believed to have been shot in the head then tossed off the pier

- Addilynn Navarro–aka Ms. Hoyos–was found dead by us December 4th after not showing up to school.. SHe was still in her car and had been shot in the head, seemingly by someone she knew

I admire the new additions to the note. I still don't notice anything about a pattern or a motive, but apparently, Joey does. "So, how were we looking at this wrong?" I ask him.

He scratches the side of his head. "Oh yeah. I almost completely forgot. After being questioned by the police so much again my brain is fried."

"Tell me about it," I agree. "Do you wanna wait until tomorrow?"

"No, let's do this now. We might have bigger fish to fry tomorrow. When you sent that Discord message, did you send it to anyone else? Even your friend Chloe?" I shake my head and Joey crosses his arms, seeming almost disappointed by that revelation yet also determined. Something about his stance tells me we're getting to the bottom of this–tonight. "Then that settles it," he says.

"Settles what?" I ask.

"The killer is closer than just someone everyone knows. They have to be one of our friends."

"Wh–What?"

"I've been spending this whole time wondering why Keaton had to die, and that's why I thought it was Falco. Her and Griffin were the first two victims, and I thought it made sense for Falco to be jealous. I mean, he was even behind the doxxing page that made April commit suicide and he had nothing to do with her." He shrugs. "Obviously, it's not Falco. This list is important, not 'cause of how the deaths connect to each other, but 'cause of what was going on in our friend group at the time. I still don't know why Griffin and Keaton were killed, but Falco and your aunt are pretty obvious. Falco 'cause of … you know what. And your aunt 'cause of that message you sent to the Discord group. This isn't just some serial killer, it's one of our friends acting as some kind of vigilante."

I hate how much he's saying makes sense. "Th–Then who is it?"

His lip quivers. "That … I'm not so sure. But if we go over these dates again, we might be able to narrow it down. Tonight." He passes the paper closer to him but struggles to read it. He takes his glasses from his pocket.

"Why don't you wear your glasses more?" I ask. "You look so cute in them."

He chuckles. "Ah, 'cause I get bullied enough at school without looking like a complete dork" He clears his throat. "Alright, so Griffin was most likely murdered on October 8th, the night of the pep rally. Who all of our friends were there?"

That was so long ago it takes a moment for me to recall. "Well, you weren't there."

He nods. "Right. I was at home that night."

"Pandora wasn't there, and McCarthy wasn't there even though she orchestrated the whole thing. Don't you think that's a little weird? Though, she was with me when Keaton was killed."

Joey crosses his arms. "A goody-two-shoes like McCarthy was never on my list to begin with."

I snort and smile. "McCarthy? A goody-two-shoes?"

Joey furrows his brows. "Um, yeah? Are we talking about the same McCarthy?"

"The student council president?"

"Yeah."

"Didn't you fuck her?"

Joey's jaw drops as he stares at me like he's tied to tracks and I'm an oncoming train. "That … that doesn't make her bad though."

"Do you even know why she fucked you?" I ask.

He scratches the side of his head. "Well, when a pretty girl throws herself at me I'm not gonna question it."

I throw my hands up and don't want to look at him. "God! I hate it when you remind me that you're a ... man–" for lack of a better word. "She knew that May liked you and only fucked you as some kind of mean girl dominance thing."

He arches his back and slumps his shoulders. "Why do people always have to be so messy?"

I lean against his shoulder and place my hand on his arm. "Well, look at us. We're analyzing our friends' every move to find out if they're serial killers or not."

Joey straightens up and gets back to business. "Yeah, you're right. If you think about it, pretty much everyone but you and Poppet can be suspects for that night, including me."

I squint at him. "Even you? But you weren't anywhere near the school that night."

He winks and smirks. "Well how do you know that? I could tell you anything, especially if I were a killer. And same with the others. Just 'cause they said they weren't there or said they were going home right after the game doesn't mean they actually did."

A thought suddenly hits me. "Oh! That's right. Cappy was throwing a party that night."

Joey crosses his arms. "Yeah, he always does after they win a game. Any clue who was there?" That's when we reach a dead end, and I shake my head. "Okay, maybe we can ask O'Brien later. He might know who was there ... but I don't think that'll help us much."

"How so this time?" I ask.

"Well, killing Griffin then going to Cappy's party to establish an alibi seems like something a killer would do."

I rub my hands down my face. "You watch too much true crime."

He chuckles, but his smile and laughter don't last. "Now ... Keaton. I was the most suspicious out of everybody."

I look into his big brown eyes behind the lens of his glasses. "You were already cleared for that. As far as I'm concerned you're not a suspect in any of this."

He smiles before leaning over to kiss me on the lips. His attention returns to the paper. "That was on October 24th."

"I was with McCarthy," I state, "then before we left to pick you up, I video chatted with O'Brien and he was at the hospital for his sister's cancer treatment."

Joey makes notes of his own on the back of the paper. "Anyone else?" I shake my head. "Okay, so that leaves Cheese and Pandora without any alibis."

"Out of those names, who is the most suspicious?"

He takes a moment to answer. "I really don't want to think that. And it's too early to tell. It could be either one of them. I mean, look at Cheese. She's really good at doing whatever she's told. What if there really is some mastermind pulling the strings behind the scene?"

"You mean like Mr. Mark?" I ask.

"Yeah."

"I think we can cross him off our list–at least for now. Right now, it seems like Aunt Addie was acting alone."

Joey nods and crosses his arms. "Yeah, I think you're right. And same with Cheese. She was already in jail when Keaton was murdered."

"So that just leaves Pandora, right?" Joey nods. "Okay, next was Falco. We were together," I say.

"Yeah, but what about everyone else?" he asks.

"I dunno."

"Then what about your aunt?" he asks. "Where was everyone when she died?"

"I dunno," I repeat.

Joey bites at his thumbnail as he intensely studies the paper. Something pops into his head the way he takes his finger away from his mouth and leans back on the couch. "I–It's Farrah."

"What?" I ask, making sure I heard him right. I almost want to laugh. "You mean 9th grade, not even 5 feet tall, dating my little brother, Farrah?"

He nods, and the sternness on his face tells me he's not joking. "Maybe not Farrah alone, but Cappy too. They're cousins. Wouldn't it make sense for her to tell him our gossip? We don't hangout with her much, but she is in the band's group chat."

"Okay, but what happened to us just talking about being Pandora?"

"Th–That's still not entirely out of the question, but I believe her when she says she doesn't care about any of this–or us. Except for the Falco thing, she cared a lot about that. But my gut thinks it's really onto something."

I think back to all my interactions with Farrah. I met her when she was crying after being bullied at school. Then we had fun playing together at the fundraiser–until it all turned to shit with what happened to Lemming. If anything, Farrah is the biggest victim in all of this. At least, that's what it seems.

"Wait," I say and reach for the paper. "Lemming died on November 24th, her funeral was on October 1st, then Griffin was murdered the next weekend, on October 10th."

Joey is looking at me. "Okay, and?"

"*And*, I was at the funeral and so was Griffin and his football buddies."

He crosses his arms. "Well it makes sense for them to be there. Lemming was Cappy's sister. That's kinda another reason why I suspect Farrah–or at least Farrah and Cappy. Cappy fits the profile we created."

"Yeah, I know that now, but that's not the point. Griffin had this thing where he'd try to guess my name as a way to flirt with me–"

"Man fuck that guy! Why is he always going after *my* girlfriends?"

"Joey, he's dead and we weren't together yet! But that's not the point. The point is that Griffin did that at the funeral and Farrah saw and got all pissed off. Said we shouldn't do that 'cause of the curse and how it had just killed Lemming."

Joey regains his composure. "And isn't she still insisting there was no gun when she found Lemming's body?" I nod. "This whole mystery is all 'cause of that stupid fucking gun.

Things sure would make a lot more sense if she took it. So if we can find it, it'll put this whole thing to rest, right?"

I nod. "Right."

Joey rubs his thumb against his bottom lip. "So Lemming commits suicide, and that much is confirmed by the police. After the investigation, the gun is returned to the family and Farrah and Cappy use it to kill Griffin after he upset Farrah at the funeral. Gregory gets blamed, then Farrah and Cappy use the same gun to murder Keaton, exonerating Gregory. Falco is next after posting that video, then your aunt is after that after she tried to kill you, but only after she already killed your mom … But wait, doesn't this mean that Gregory is in on all of this too?" he rubs his temples. "Ugh, all of this is hurting my head. Why can't I be smarter?"

I place my hand on his leg. "N–No, that all sounds right."

For the first time, it feels like we're starting to understand this mystery.

Morning

Thump thump. Thump thump. Thump thump.

My head rests on Joey's chest as I listen to his heartbeat. It's become my favorite sound–the sound of the living. I hear him breathing in and out through his nose and feel the warmth we've created under the blanket.

I pull my head up to kiss his neck.

Joey hums. "I love how frisky you are in the mornings," he says in his groggy voice.

I bring myself higher to whisper in his ear. "My body is still sore, but my mouth isn't."

Joey turns to kiss me. He wraps his arms around me but is gentle to the touch.

He says I'm frisky in the mornings when he's the one always with a case of morning wood. My hand explores the smoothness of his chest before exploring lower and slipping under the elastic of his pajama bottoms. His breathing grows heavy as I touch him. I'm as gentle with him as he is with me. I use a single finger to rub his tip, the only thing soft about him.

The stomping of heavy feet down the stairs pulls us apart like a cold shower. Body sore and vision blurry; my eyes eventually focus and Atlus is standing over us.

"So what, do you like live here now?" he asks.

Joey rubs his eyes and sits up. His glasses are resting on the coffee table. "I can leave if you want me to."

"I don't care," Atlus states and shuffles his feet. He's well dressed and hair groomed, much more put together in the days post Mom's death. "But did you do it? Did you kill Keaton?"

Joey shakes his head. "No."

"Then I'm over it."

"Oh, ah … thanks. Say, you're still friends with Kellan, right? Can you wait right here? There's something I want you to give him for me."

Atlus and I wait in the living room as Joey goes upstairs and enters my bedroom. When he returns, he's holding the framed photograph he brought from his trailer. He opens the back and removes the photo before ripping it in half. The half with Keaton he hands to Atlus. "She looks really pretty and happy in that picture. I thought her family should have it," Joey explains.

Atlus admires the ripped photo. "Yeah, she does. It's weird looking at pictures of people who are dead now."

I know the feeling. I hate the nights when I can't sleep and spend the late hours scrolling through the Instagram accounts that will never be updated again. This house may be mine now, but it's decorated with relics of Mom. "Do you wanna go to school?" I ask.

"I think I'd rather be there than here," Atlus answers.

"You didn't go to school for weeks after Mom died."

"Yeah well, that was Mom. I don't give a fuck about Aunt Addie. She was psycho."

Joey and I look at each other.

* * *

We detour from the student parking lot and instead get in the drop-off line. When it's our turn at the curb, only Atlus gets out. "We'll meet up with you later," I tell him from the passenger seat.

He brushes me off and turns his back to get in line for security.

Joey and I have somewhere else to go: The Tipsy Beaver. Lincoln is surprised to see us when he opens the door. "Joe, yous know I don't open 'til noon," he says.

"I know, and I'm sorry," Joey says. "You wouldn't still happen to have the security tapes from the day Keaton was killed, would you?"

"Of course I do. If I didn't I might have been in deep shit like yous were."

"Um, yeah … Would you mind if we looked at them?"

Lincoln shuffles. "I dunno. I know she meant a lot to yous, but I dunno if seeing those would do you any good. If the cops couldn't find anything then nobody can."

"Please, Lincoln. We just need to look for something real quick, then we'll be gone."

The man shuffles before relenting. "Alright, come on in." He holds the door open and escorts us to a back room behind the bar. It's dark with very little that's not trash. Empty chips, soda cans, and beer bottles. The only thing seemingly worth a damn is a TV old enough to be an antique. Lincoln bends over to grab a box buried in the clutter. "Here ya goes," he says. The inside is filled with VHSs, oversized cassettes older than Joey and I combined. "I'll leave yas to it." Lincoln escorts himself out of the cave.

Joey admires one of the plastic rectangles from front to back. "Wait, these aren't even labeled! How the hell are we supposed to even know which one we're looking for?"

"Want me to run over to Nickels and Dimes and get us some coffees?" I offer.

Joey already looks exhausted. "You'd be a lifesaver if you

did."

Evening

We've been here for hours, searching through tape after tape. We're looking for September 24th at around 5 PM, which should be easy enough to find … if the tapes were labeled.

An exhausted Joey rubs his temples. "This is taking forever."

The tape in the player is another dud, so I press the eject button and put it with the others. Somehow, we haven't made a single dent in the box. I grab the next tape and put it into the machine. A fuzzy grayscale video plays on the screen. I shake Joey's shoulders to garner his attention. "Wait Joey, this is it!"

He looks up. "Huh?"

The tape starts at midnight, so we fast-forward until later in the evening. The footage is only of the parking lot, and we watch as cars come and go. When it comes closer to the time we need, we slow down the video and watch carefully. "There!" Joey cries out and points at the TV.

Just before 5 o'clock, the image of a familiar 2008 Toyota Tundra, Cappy's truck, appears. The frames are choppy, and the vehicle disappears off-screen as quickly as it came.

We watch as the tape continues in a moment of silence. There's nothing left.

DECEMBER 8 – FRIDAY

Early Morning

Joey and I haven't been to school since Aunt Addie's murder. Everything feels so close, yet so far as we wait to make our move. What is our move? We haven't figured that out yet. We just know that if one of our friends is the Blackridge killer, we need to stay away and not give them another motive.

Another day we drop off Atlus at Seal Coast and go off on our own. "So, what now?" Joey asks, an expression that's seemingly becoming his motto.

"I wanna go to a hotel," I answer. It is my birthday, after all. "A nice one, not that piece of shit Nameless Hotel that can go fuck itself."

"A hotel? Like, all night? What about Atlus?"

"He's staying with Farrah tonight."

"Is … Is that really a good idea? You know, with everything …"

"Until we get some solid evidence, I think it's best we keep things how they are. If we tell Atlus or start snooping where we don't belong, he might become her next target. He's been spending almost every weekend over there anyway. Telling him he suddenly can't go over there would raise suspicions."

"Yeah, that's a good point. If she's only killing people she perceives as *bullies* then it's best to stay on her good side for now."

Griffin and Keaton as bullies? That's something I'll never be able to wrap my head around and will never stop pissing me off. Farrah–or whoever killed them–didn't know them, yet thought they had the right to take their lives. It can never be forgiven.

"What about this one?" I suggest and show Joey the phone. "Grand Major Hotel in Salem."

His eyes widen. "Holy shit. A night there is more than I make in a month."

Truth be told, I never look at the prices. "I can book a room online."

"Like, right now?"

"Yeah, why? Do you not want to go?"

"I didn't say that but ..."

"Then don't finish that sentence. Let's go. It'll be fun."

Afternoon

Oregon is a large state outside of dark and gloomy Blackridge, and I almost can't believe my eyes when we escape the fog and see the first glimpse of sunlight I've seen in months. Though, in the beginning of December, it's still just as cold when we get out of the car after an almost three-hour drive. I nearly can't believe it. This is what I have been missing. There are roads, buildings, and civilization while keeping the Oregon charm of being surrounded by woods. The trees are barren for the winter, but I can only imagine the green come spring.

"Look at that river!" I exclaim. The water is so blue and clear, unlike the coast of Blackridge.

"That's the Willamette River," Joey explains.

He's right. The hotel's ad said it overlooked the river, and here it is. The hotel is massive and taller than the trees. It's white and bright like everything else in the city, but all the windows make it more glass than stone.

Entering is very different from the rustic aesthetic of the Nameless Hotel. The floor is made of marble and reflects everything from the walls, decor, and patrons. There's a large chandelier hanging from the ceiling that has to be the size of a whale. It brightens the lobby, making the glow from the flooring almost blinding.

We approach the check-in counter, which is made of more black-reflecting marble and has several clerks behind it. They wear large smiles and suits. "Hello, welcome to the Grand Major Hotel. How may I help you?" we're greeted. The clerk smiles upon finishing the transaction and hands me the card keys. "Here you are, Mr. and Mrs. Clairwater. Please enjoy your stay."

I accept the keys, and Joey and I take the elevator to our room on the highest floor.

"Mr. and Mrs. Clairwater?" he asks.

I nudge him on the shoulder to my tender expense. "Yeah, I got us the honeymoon suite."

The elevator is made of glass so we watch the whole city as we climb higher and higher. And then when we get to the room, it's worth every penny.

At first, Joey is speechless. "Holy shit," he eventually says.

Red is appropriately the theme for the honeymoon suite. It matches the carpet and the comforter on the oversized bed, and chocolates nest on the pillow. The fireplace is already lit, eliminating any chill left in the air, and the balcony overlooks the crystal blue flowing river.

"Holy shit," Joey exclaims again, exploring the room. "Check out this bathroom! It's bigger than my whole bedroom!"

The floors and countertops are made of the same reflecting marble from the lobby. There's a special enclosed section for the toilet, while the bathtub takes up a large portion of the bathroom.

"I've never seen a tub this big in my life," Joey notes. "This is like a whole jacuzzi. Look! It is a jacuzzi. It even has jets."

I reach over to grab his hands. "Then wanna take off all your clothes and go for a dip?"

He leans down to kiss me. "Yes ma'am."

Lunchtime

"Are you hungry?" I ask after our bath. I doubt my skin has ever been so soft in my life.

Joey sits on the bed, bouncing up and down without a spring in sight. "I could eat."

"Alright, room service or fancy restaurant?"

"It's up to you. You're footing the bill." He stops bouncing. "Wow, that made me feel gross. You don't think I'm some kind of whore ... right?"

"Of course not. You're my boyfriend. Not my hooker. Plus, acts of service are my love language."

He gestures around the room. "Ha, I can tell. I'd say mine is quality time."

I smile ear to ear. "Yeah, I can tell. Let's go down to the restaurant."

The seventh floor of the Grand Major Hotel is grander than every shopping district in Blackridge combined. It's complete with shops, a fountain, and a restaurant. You usually need a reservation, but the Clairwater name opens many doors.

"I feel like I'm in a whole new world," Joey says as we're escorted to our table.

We're seated in a section away from the other patrons, divided by a fish tank built into the wall. It's quiet over here with nothing but the cackling from the fire in the modern hearth.

Joey whistles at the sight of the menu. "None of these have prices."

"This is the type of place where if you have to ask, you can't afford it," I say.

"Tsk, you're telling me."

"Don't worry about it. Just get whatever you want."

Joey shoots me a look and breathes out through his nose. "You've really never had to worry about money, huh?"

"Not since I was really little."

"And now with your mom's estate, you'll be set for life ..."

"Well I have to split it with Atlus, and there's taxes and

lawyer fees, but yeah. On top of Mom's worth from her books and the TV shows made out of them, she also had stocks, trusts, a hefty life insurance. She was a lot of things, but she knew how to turn a penny into a dollar and a buck into a grand. That kinda thing."

He places his menu flat on the cloth-covered table. "That's... wow. When we're just hanging out it's really easy to forget how rich you are."

"What can I say? I'm just sharing the wealth. Do you like calamari? Wanna order some for an appetizer?"

The change of subject causes a smirk on his face. "I'm actually allergic to shellfish."

I smile back at him. I love learning these little things about him. "Really?"

"Yeah. One time when I was 13, we were having this family reunion and it was pretty funny. Just a bunch of drunken Irish redheaded people. But while they were all getting shit faced I was at the table eating what I thought were the best onion rings I've ever had in my life. Until my throat started to close and lips went numb. I spent the rest of the night in the hospital and got a $45,000 bill for it."

"Holy shit," I say.

Okay, shellfish is out as an appetizer.

"What even is *foie gras*?" Joey asks, still admiring the menu.

"Duck liver," I explain.

"Liver? Why do rich people like taking poor foods and making them expensive?"

"I dunno. Probably to price out the poor people so they starve."

"I–I don't like how true that answer is."

We decide on an appetizer, main course, and dessert, giving us a feast worth a million dollars. We share Joey's first souffle.

"So, you asked about me, what about you?" he asks.

"You're gonna have to be a bit more specific," I say, finishing my bite.

"What are your plans after graduation? Well, not like you

need any ..."

I shrug. "I dunno. I never really thought about it. My mom always put a lot of pressure on me to graduate since she never got to, but I never cared. Like you said, I'm taken care of. I don't *need* to do anything."

"I get that," he says and takes another forkful. "If I wasn't so broke, I sure as hell wouldn't be spending my time outside of school as a cashier."

"What would you wanna do?"

"I dunno. I guess do what we have been doing," he answers. "Hangout with friends, probably be more serious about making music ... I guess being an auto mechanic would be pretty cool."

My lips curl into a smile. "See? I knew that's what you wanted to do. So, then just do it. Blackridge has a technical college, doesn't it? And I'm sure you could apprentice under Pandora's dad."

"You really always do have everything figured out, huh?" he teases. "But what about you? What would you possibly do with yourself while I'm busy?"

"I guess I wouldn't mind being a writer like my mom was." I wink. "Think I have any good stories to tell?"

"Ah, yeah. Like how we caught the serial killer of Blackridge. Um ... assuming we do and don't just end up looking like a couple of idiots."

My elbow is on the table and I rest my chin in my palm. "You know, you could always be auto mechanic by day, Detective O'Reilly by night."

He chuckles. "No way, I hate the cops. Especially now. They've barely done a thing for the case and were more than happy to frame me and Greg."

I hum. "What do you think happened to Greg? Do you really think he knows what Farrah and Cappy are up to?"

"I dunno. He could just be laying low after almost being framed for the murder. I can get how that feels. As for does he know what Farrah and Cappy are up to? ... I dunno about that either."

"I haven't seen him around, but I can't say I've been particularly keeping an eye out for him either," I say.

Joey crosses his arm. "That might be our next step: a stake out of our suspects so far."

The waiter scans the wallet app on my phone when it comes time to pay the bill. Before tucking it back in my pocket, I notice several missed calls from Atlus. He answers immediately when I call him back. "Finally, where the fuck are you?" he says.

"Somewhere," I answer. "Did something happen?"

"Well you and your boyfriend need to come pick me up."

"What? What happened to going home with Farrah?"

"We broke up."

"What?" I repeat, much louder and higher. "Why?"

"She's fucking crazy, and not the good kind."

Joey's facial expression shows he's thinking what I'm thinking: Atlus is in danger. "You're right, she is fucking crazy," I tell him. "You need to not be alone–ever. Go home with Mr. Mark if you have to."

"Mr. Mark is on a leave of absence, remember?" Atlus says. "His girlfriend was murdered and his house is a crime scene."

"You need to go find someone, now!"

"It's not that big of a deal, Fi. I'll just wait around until you get here."

Joey and I are already out of our seats and rushing through the lobby as I speak. "No, it is a big deal. We'll explain when we get there but we're 3 hours away."

"What the fuck are you doing 3 hours away?"

"Mind your fucking business! It doesn't matter. Just find someone. Your soccer friends, Kellan. Fuck, even Principal Pal if you have to. New rules say you can't be alone anyway. We'll be there as soon as we can!"

So much for date night.

Evening

It's well past after school by the time we reach Blackridge, and luckily, Atlus went home with Kellan. "You'd understand why I don't wanna go in there, right?" Joey says after I pull up to the curb of the Freeman residence.

I nod. "Yeah."

Get in, get out. That's all I'm going to do. I get to the door and ring the doorbell. Not long after that Atlus is ready to go and we're back in the car. "So?" is the first thing the smart ass says.

"Well ... Um ... You see..." Joey stalls.

There's no easy way to say it, so I rip off the bandaid: "Your girlfriend is fucking crazy and we think she's the Blackridge serial killer."

Atlus pauses, blank face like he's waiting for the punchline. "What? Yeah, I said she's crazy but I didn't say she's serial killer crazy. She's more like jealous of other girls and not giving me any space, crazy."

"Okay but like, have you ever thought about it?" I ask.

"What? No! Why would I?"

"Hey Atlus, where's Greg?" Joey asks.

Atlus furrows his brows. "Huh?"

"Greg, you know, Farrah's uncle. Don't he and Cappy live in the apartment across from hers?"

Atlus shrugs from the backseat, the seatbelt buckled across his chest. "I dunno."

My jaw drops. "You don't know? You're over there all the time."

"A girl invites me alone to her apartment, I'm not gonna ask where the adults are!"

"I mean, I get it," Joey says.

"Shut up, Joey," I don't mean to snap. "You said *adults*. Where's Farrah's dad?"

Atlus shrugs. "I dunno. I've never met him."

Joey and I exchange worried looks. "Putting it this way, can you see what we're talking about?" I ask.

"No," Atlus claims. "You're trying to say Farrah has killed all these people, including our own mom and aunt. She won't even kill the cockroaches in her room."

Something about that pisses me off.

"Farrah may not be the one pulling the trigger, but she's at the very least an informant," Joey explains. "We don't think Farrah killed your mom, but rather your aunt did."

"Then I told Farrah that I thought Aunt Addie was trying to kill me after the *accident*," I continue explaining. "Then a few days later, she's dead."

Atlus is shaking his head. His gears are running, but they're rusty and need oil. "None of that makes sense. Why would Aunt Addie kill Mom, and why would Farrah kill Aunt Addie?"

"Your aunt loved her students more than her family she barely knew," Joey states. "So when they started dying, she thought your mom was the cause and ... did what she did. I can imagine someone like that seeing one of her students and opening the car door for them, Then, that student shot her as revenge for your mom."

The scene playing out in my head the way Joey explains it. After seeing what we saw, I almost have no doubts.

Joey continues: "Griffin was killed in the locker room and had to have been killed by someone who was supposed to be there also. A week before his murder, Farrah got upset at him for something he said to Fiora. Then, Farrah must have seen a few instances of how Keaton treated me. I can remember a few instances myself where she was there."

I do too. Joey was looking for Keaton in the crowd at the fundraiser, and the band had to tell him that he deserved better. Then when school resumed after Griffin's murder, Farrah was in the cafeteria the day Keaton and I ditched him to go to the library.

"Falco is pretty self explanatory," Joey says, not going into more detail. He doesn't have to. "Then, there's your aunt. And now apparently the people who are supposed to be supervising Farrah and Cappy are missing but haven't been reported missing."

Atlus melts in his seat. "But ... But..." is all he can say. He has no rebuttal.

Joey presses his thumb against his lip. "If we can just find where they're hiding that gun, that'll prove everything."

"Have you seen any guns?" I ask. "Maybe a safe of them somewhere?"

Atlus shakes his head and then stops. "Wait, maybe..." He has our full attention as we wait for him to continue: "They have a deep freezer in the kitchen, but I've never seen what's in it. There's a padlock on it, which I thought weird. I asked about it before and Cappy said that's where they store the meat after hunting deer."

Joey furrows his brows. "Lots of people around here hunt deer, but there's no reason to put a lock on the freezer." An idea strikes. "That has to be where they've been hiding the gun this whole time! I mean, it makes sense. It's a small town. Lemming's investigation was probably wrapped up quickly as a suicide then the gun was returned to the family. They used the gun to murder Griffin and became the first suspects, but were able to clear Greg's name after killing Keaton while he was in jail. They've been making it seem like someone else somehow took the gun when it's just been hidden in some meat freezer!"

I'm still stuck on everything Atlus has said and the audacity of it all. "So, you were ignoring all of these obvious red flags just so you could get your dick wet?"

Atlus scoffs. "You have no stones to throw. Look who you're fucking."

"Hey!" Joey's voice cracks. "I thought we were over that."

"Yeah, we are. Kellan's family really liked that picture you gave them, so thanks."

Joey sighs. "Y–Yeah, no problem."

"So, what are you gonna do? Call the cops?" Atlus asks.

I shake my head. "Cops are useless. We're getting into that fucking freezer ourselves."

DECEMBER 9 – SATURDAY

Night

It's dim in my room, and the only light comes from the glow of the candles. They smell of strawberries and cream. "What are we doing?" Joey asks as he holds back my hair.

I take his dick out of my mouth and look up at him while still working him with my good hand. "I'm tryna make you cum. Why, do you not like it?"

"No, no. It feels really good. But … this whole thing is almost over, right? Then what happens to us?"

"*What happens to us*? Whatever we want."

"I just … I just don't want you to throw me away when I'm not useful to you anymore."

"Joey, I'm not gonna throw you away. We were friends before all of this even started and we're even closer now. We're gonna finish this and get justice for those close to us. Then, we move on." My phone lights up with a notification. "Oh, speak of the devil."

O'BRIEN: Seal Coast won

* * *

The Seal Coast football team vowed to be victorious in their fallen teammates' honors, and victorious they are. All that's left is to celebrate.

The last time I was at Pointe Grove Apartments was when I dropped off Farrah after we got our nails done. All I wanted was to cheer her up after her cousin committed suicide. I never thought soon after that, she would be responsible for several murders. Whether that's true or not, we'll find out tonight. Cappy throws parties after every victory, and though we skipped the game, Joey and I have an invitation courtesy of our plant, O'Brien.

We thought it best to conceal Atlus at the Nameless Hotel under the protection of Poppet and Pandora while the rest of Seal Coast is here tonight in honor of our fallen comrades. Joey, O'Brien and I take a moment to gather outside the apartment complex. We're far enough away from the music and crowd to hear our own thoughts.

O'Brien places a palm to his forehead and rests his back against a tree trunk, unable to maintain his footing as he comprehends our latest theory. "Wh–Why does that make sense? That can't make sense."

"That's what we're here to find out," I explain. "You guys just have to follow my lead and stick to the plan."

Joey scratches the side of his head. "So what exactly is this plan?"

"I'm gonna see what the hell is in that freezer," I vow. I flip my backpack around and reach inside, grabbing the bolt cutters. "You two are gonna cause a distraction and when no one's looking, I'm busting that shit open."

"Well, what kinda distraction? There's kinda a lot of people," Joey says.

"You two are gonna get into a fight."

"What?" They cry out in unison.

Joey gestures to O'Brien. "I'm not fighting him. Have you seen his arms? He's an athlete. He'd kick my ass."

"I've never been in a fight before," O'Brien admits, shuffling his feet.

"Dude, aren't you a trained boxer?"

"Yeah, but my mom won't let me compete. She doesn't want me getting punched in the face."

"You've already been shot. What's the worst that could happen?"

"Getting punched in the face."

There's a throbbing in my temples, and it's not from the music–at least not entirely. "You guys exhaust me. It's not a real fight. Just cause enough commotion to get everyone away from the kitchen."

"Why don't you just call the cops?" O'Brien asks. "I mean, surely they'd come for a noise complaint and underaged drinking, especially during a curfew."

"'Cause just having the cops here isn't enough," I explain. "They can't just go snooping without any kind of probable cause, and I'mma give it to them. We're gonna get in, get out, then call the cops. So are you two with me or not?" They both nod. "Alright, then let's fucking do this."

We start walking.

"Wait," Joey calls out. "O'Brien, you keep going. We'll catch up to you."

O'Brien goes towards the party while Joey and I remain by the woods. "What's up?" I ask. Joey lifts his shirt to expose the waistband of his jeans. Protruding through the denim is the unmistakable grip of a handgun. I take several steps back. "Whoa. What the fuck do you have that for?"

He offers it to me, keeping the muzzle pointing away from us. "I got it at the pawnshop. Take it. The safety is on, but it's loaded."

Right, like someone like me knows how to use a gun, let alone turn the safety off. "I'm not taking a gun," I state.

"Fi, do you not realize how dangerous this is? Think of all the people they've already killed."

"I'm not shooting a fourteen year old."

"Okay, but what about Cappy? If they find out we're onto them, then we're next. Just please, take it. I can't lose anyone close to me ever again."

I breathe through my nose and surrender. I accept the gun and store it in my backpack.

Together we walk towards the party, and the music gets louder with every step. Practically everyone from Seal Coast is here with so many people they're spilling out to the courtyard. We arrive at the perfect time with everyone already sloppy and drunk as we squeeze through the crowd and enter the building. Clusters of bodies loiter around the staircase with drinks in

hand as Joey and I push and shove our way up the steps to the third floor where Cappy's apartment is. The door is wide open and drunk people are spilling out from the inside.

Joey points to the apartment across the hall. "Look."

There's a flier pasted to the door, and we step closer to read the tiny print: EVICTION NOTICE.

"That's Farrah's apartment," I say. "So, where the hell is her dad?"

There are an abundance of holes in the stories Farrah has been telling, but tonight we're here to fill them. Who knows what's true and what's not. Was she really being bullied the day I found her crying in the hall? Was there really no gun the night she found Lemming's body? Did her mom really abandon her? Is she really the one putting hits out on our friends and having her cousin do the dirty work?

Joey and I enter Cappy's apartment and meet up with O'Brien, who sticks out like a silver-dyed thumb. He has a red plastic cup in hand and is grouped with the football guys.

I nudge Joey with my elbow. "Go."

"What am I supposed to do?" he asks.

"I already told you. Go over there and start a fight."

"But what if the football guys all jump me or something?"

"Then I'll kill them. Just go, I won't be long."

Joey pushes through the sea of drunken bodies to join O'Brien while I search for the kitchen. I've never been here before and it's hard to see where I'm going with so many heads in the way.

"Fiora!" a squeaky voice shouts over the music.

"Farrah? What are you doing here?" I ask despite it being a stupid question. Of course she's here.

She avoids eye contact and picks at her fingers. Could she really be the one responsible for so many of our friends' deaths? She's so tiny and helpless, that same little girl I found crying in the hall after being bullied–or so she claims. Too many instances align with her being responsible ... though, the same was said for Joey.

Farrah mumbles something I'm not able to hear over the music.

"What?" I shout.

"Is Atlus here?" she repeats significantly louder.

I shake my head. "No." Nor am I telling her where he is.

"He hasn't been answering any of my calls or texts."

"Just let him go, Farrah. People break up."

She looks up at me, those sapphire eyes of hers leaking tears. "If–If he's with another girl, you'd tell me, right?"

"Of course," I lie, "we're friends."

She wipes her soiled eyes on her sleeve.

"Y–You better watch your fucking mouth," I pinpoint Joey's voice through the commotion of the party.

"You–You watch your mouth," O'Brien cries.

The football guys surrounding them are gitty like school girls and reeking of booze like school girls. "You need to be careful around Joey's mouth, Brien, he might suck your dick," Cappy teases while the other jocks erupt into laughter.

You're going down tonight, fucker.

Joey delivers the first shove to O'Brien's chest, and then O'Brien shoves him back, causing Joey to take several steps backwards. He steps forward to deliver another shove, and the boys go back and forth.

"Fight! Fight! Fight!" the chanting starts, and that's my signal. A crowd of drunks stampede out the kitchen while I squeeze past the pressure to make an entrance.

The kitchen is where the fun is, and by that I mean booze. Several people leave their plastic cups on the counters, filled and unfilled, while a multitude of different types of liquor are on display. I help myself to a bit of liquid courage in the shape of a shot of vodka, and my eyes hone in on the freezer like the holy grail. It's the most prominent thing in a kitchen so small, sure enough with the capacity to fit at least several deer whole. Truly an overkill, even for the biggest of hunters. The color is supposed to be white porcelain, but the top has grown gray with dust. Keeping the lid immobile is a heavy-duty combination lock, though it will stand no chance against my bolt cutters.

I swing my backpack off my shoulders and get it unzipped. I'm almost surprised to see the gun Joey gave me and dig under it to get what I need: a pair of blue nitrile gloves inspired by Mr. Mark and the bolt cutters. I place the teeth of the pliers in the center of the steel wire and contract with all the pressure my body can muster. My right shoulder threatens to give out from the pain, but before it can, the wire surrenders instead.

The freezer is free to open, and without leaving a single print, I pull open the top. What I see is something I never could have prepared for or even imagined. It's something from a horror movie or an indie video game about bologna. Inside is the unmistakable form of a human body, perfectly preserved with pale flesh and frost stuck to his hardened, graying beard. His mouth is agape like he's screaming with no sound while his eyes are wide open, a bullet wound perfectly between them.

I can't help but stand still and blink my eyes as if every time they open and close, the scene before me will change. Nonetheless, the plan doesn't change. I'm not digging around that freezer to find the gun–if it's even in there. This is more than enough. I retrieve the last prop from my backpack for my reconnaissance: firecrackers. I purchased them to bring down the Nameless Hotel, but choosing my battles meant I could live to fight another day. I light the fuse and get the fuck out of here, joining the crowd rallied around Joey and O'Brien shouting, "Fight! Fight! Fight!" just to get interrupted by the sound of loud cracking and smoke filling the tiny apartment. Loud sirens blare as panic sets in.

I drift through the crowd like a current and we empty out of the apartment, pushing, shoving, and trampling anything in the way. I'm lucky I meet up with Joey and O'Brien when I do. "We need to get the fuck out of here," I shout, and we're not the only ones with that idea.

Underaged drinking, drinking and driving, drugs, and unbeknownst to the partygoers, the dead body of Greg

McGuire in the freezer will be a field day for the Blackridge County police, and here they come.

"Did you find the gun?" Joey asks.

"I'll explain later, we gotta go right fucking now," I say, and we hurry to my Ford Explorer.

The night fills with the spinning of red and blue as sirens close in.

DECEMBER 11 – MONDAY

BLACKRIDGE CURSE BROKEN: MAN CHARGED WITH MURDER AFTER TWO BODIES FOUND IN FREEZER

BLACKRIDGE, Or. – First responders arrived at Pointe Grove Apartments Saturday night for a suspected arson report and upon searching an apartment on the second floor, the frozen remains of Gregory McGuire, 41, and David McGuire, 39, were discovered in an open chest freezer. Both bodies had received gunshot wounds to the head.

A gun discovered at the residence underwent forensic ballistics and has been confirmed to be the weapon used in the murders of Zachary Moore, 18, Milena Freeman, 17, Jayden Burns, 18, and Addilynn Navarro, 28. A resident of the apartment, Cameron McGuire, 18, has been arrested for the murders while a minor child has been taken for a mental health evaluation.

After School

The lot of us who haven't killed anybody are at Nickels and Dimes when the news drops. Joey, Atlus, Poppet, Pandora, Cheese, and O'Brien are here.

Joey chuckles. "You know Fi, I had a feeling at some point this was gonna end at Nickels and Dimes."

"I–I still can't believe you guys were right," O'Brien gawks.

A part of me still can't believe it either. Though the article is right in my hand, it feels like a dream.

"That minor child must be Farrah," Cheese says with her yellow pigtails draped over her shoulders.

Joey scratches the side of his head. "You know, part of me wonders if she was just another victim in all of this. But no matter what, I can't forgive anyone who had any part in Keaton being murdered."

"Who knows what she said was true or not," Atlus says, and he's right. That's one of the things we may never know. At this point, I don't care; whatever puts an end to all of this. "She got close to me by saying she knows how it feels to have a dead mom," he continues.

"Her mom's not dead, she's on probation in Washington for drug trafficking," Joey says. "But I guess you can say whatever you want to the newbies in town and they'd have no way of knowing you're full of shit."

"I hope they don't let her out of the loony bin for a long time," Pandora states.

Joey folds his arms and nods. "Oh yeah. Whether she was responsible for the killings or not, she's gonna be seriously fucked up after all of this, if she wasn't at least a little bit already."

There's a melancholy grin on Poppet's face. "I really miss Griffin, but I'm glad he's going to get justice."

"We've been through hell and back in just a few months. Hey Fi, Attie, guess this means you can finally see what Black-shit has to offer since all of this started right after you moved here."

"What does Black-shit have to offer?" Atlus asks.

Joey winks and smirks. "Hmm, nothing."

The group laughs, ready to put an end to all of this and close this chapter. Rest in peace, Griffin, Keaton, and even Falco and Aunt Addie. Lemming and April, you won't be forgotten.

DECEMBER 24 – SUNDAY

Evening

Atlus is a brutal dictator in the kitchen, and a bead of nervous sweat forms on my brow when he walks up behind me. There's very little he trusts me with in the kitchen, though it's hard to fuck up making cookies. "Use a wooden spoon," he barks and hands me one from the drawer. Guess I stand corrected. I take the spoon and continue mixing the batter in the bowl. His attention turns to Joey flattening some dough with a rolling pin. "Stop! You need to put flour on the pin. See how the dough is sticking?"

"Sorry, Chef!" Joey panics and dusts flour atop the rolling pin.

The doorbell rings, and Atlus leaves his palace to answer the door. "Fi, the peanut gallery is here!" he calls out.

I cradle the bowl in my hand as I step out to the living room to greet everyone. There's Poppet, Pandora, Cheese, and O'Brien, all bearing gifts and goodies of their own.

Cheese holds up her own plate of sweet treats. "I made cookies."

"We're already making cookies. Better cookies," Atlus boldly states.

"Attie, don't even try having a dick measuring contest with Cheese 'cause you're not gonna win," I explain.

Joey joins us, the bottom of his shirt noticeably caked in white powder. "Oh trust me, you'll like Cheese's cookies. But only have a bite or you'll be seriously fucked up for the next few days."

I feel guilty for neglecting Mom's plants and letting them die, so in her honor, Atlus and I got a real tree for Christmas this year. We've never been a religious family, but something about the fresh smell of pine and a ham baking in the oven wraps me in a blanket of comfort and holiday bliss. Plus, I couldn't ask to be surrounded by better company. Attie, my boyfriend, and best friends I could never replace.

The furniture in the living room is pushed to the side so we can sit in a circle in front of the fireplace. It's my turn first, and Atlus is my victim. "Truth or dare."

"Dare," he states.

"I dare you to go into the kitchen and make yourself another plate."

"What, you tryna make me eat 'til I pop?"

"Just go do it, Ratatouille."

That makes Poppet snort and laugh as Atlus goes to the open-concept kitchen. He fills the plate with slices of ham, green beans, mashed potatoes, and gravy.

"Okay cool, so now put that in the blender, make a smoothie, and drink it," I instruct.

"What?" Atlus cries.

"You have to, that's the game."

I don't know what's more disgusting, the look of contempt he shoots at me or the smoothie he makes in the blender. The contents are thick and chunky and have turned green from the green beans. Atlus returns to the circle, drink in hand, and with a gust of bravery, he turns the drink bottoms up and chugs.

"Chug, chug, chug!" the group chants.

The Christmas dinner smoothie barely lessens with every move of this throat, contorting his face and making his best attempt to stomach down the chunky contents. He finishes, slams the glass onto the hardwood floor, and wipes his mouth on his sleeve. "You are not supposed to drink ham!"

"Then why'd you drink it then?" I ask.

Atlus shoots me a look that could kill.

There's a wicked grin on Joey's face. Everyone gets along now, but I know Joey appreciates the revenge for the times

Atlus treated him like a murderer. "Fi, truth or dare," he asks.

"Dare," I answer.

"I dare you to tell the truth about something."

"Hey, you can't do that!"

"Oh yes I can. You've mentioned being in jail before and that's why you're repeating your senior year. So tell me, whatcha do?"

Atlus chuckles, making me wish the dare I gave him was harsher, but I'm no loser.

"It was probably arson," O'Brien says and gets chuckles from around the room.

"Shut the fuck up, no it wasn't," I say. "My friend Chloe and I were trespassing and tagging walls then we got booked since we were 18. Our parents wouldn't bail us out, something about *learning a lesson*, and it takes a long as hell time in California to get a court date so we sat in jail until the charges were dropped."

"That's boring," Cheese says, as monotone as ever.

"Well what the fuck were you expecting? D.B. Cooper? Sorry I'm not actually the criminal you all take me for." Joey is leaning back with his arms stretched out and a smile on his face. "What?" I ask.

He puckers his lips and shakes his head. "Nothin'. Just imagining you in a cell and an orange jumpsuit."

"Shut the fuck up, Joey," Atlus defends my honor.

Poppet snorts and giggles. "Geez Fi, your brother is meaner than you are."

"I taught him well," I say. The doorbell rings and we look at each other in the circle. We're all here, so who could it be? I look at Atlus. "Did you invite anyone?"

He shakes his head.

Poppet throws her hand in the air. "Oh, it's my turn!"

The game goes on while I get up to answer the front door. It's pitch black outside with the pouring rain, so much for a white Christmas, and standing on the front porch is a soaking wet Farrah. Staring at her makes the cold night grow colder, and the chill fills my body in waves. "F–Farrah, what are you doing here?"

Her hand trembles as she reaches into the pouch of her hoodie and pulls out a gun. The barrel is aimed between my eyes, and her finger is locked to the trigger. "You–You ruined my life!" her high-pitched voice breaks through the rain. "Cappy never did anything wrong! He never killed anybody!"

I hold up both my hands so she can see them and try to remain calm, though my body's trembling betrays me. "I believe you," I lie. "Just put the gun down."

"Farrah, what the fuck are you doing?" Atlus's voice cries from behind me, though I never take my eyes from down the gun's barrel.

Farrah raises the gun over my shoulder, pointing it at Atlus. Then, the weapon lowers back down to me. Her finger is steady on the trigger, though the rest of her hand trembles. At any moment the gun could shoot, whether intentionally or not. "All I did is what you told me to," Farrah claims. "I stood up for people like you told me to."

There's so much I want to say, but it's staggering how a loaded gun can shut someone up. My mouth has gotten me in a lot of trouble, and this is the biggest so far.

As Farrah speaks, I notice a light through the second-story window of the house across the street. The curtain is pulled back, and May's figure looks out. There's a distance between us, but I know our eyes make contact. We communicate without words. She lifts her cell phone to her ear, and I sincerely hope she's calling her dad.

"You wouldn't be with Joey if it weren't for me," Farrah continues. "You wouldn't be alive without me."

"You're right, thank you." I have to swallow bile just to force out the words.

She's sopping wet with water dripping from every part of her body, yet the tears are still noticeable. "Then why? Why did you do it? Why did you set up Cappy? He never pulled a single trigger. He was too old and would get in trouble. It was me!

I did it! For you!" She waves her gun around heads, standing and waiting powerless, before placing it between my eyes. "I knew you liked Joey and Griffin and Keaton were only getting in the way. Your aunt caused that awful accident that could have killed you, and Falco sent that awful video of Joey. So why, Fiora? Why did you betray me? Bullies get what they deserve!" She raises the gun over my shoulder at Atlus. "And you. Why did you break up with me?"

"Are you seriously asking that? You're fucking crazy!" he cries.

Please Atlus, don't be stupid. This is literally life or death. She's already killed so many people, and with nothing left to lose, she'll kill us all.

My memory flashes to the night of the party, the night Farrah claims I betrayed her, when Joey handed me that gun. It's been hidden under my bed ever since, but it sure would be helpful right now. Instead, we're unarmed, and Farrah is dangerous.

Farrah's voice cracks. "C–Crazy? You think I'm crazy?"

Spinning bright lights of red and blue break through the dark and rainy night, and for once, being neighbors with a pig comes in handy. Both marked and unmarked vehicles fill Misty Lane, and the men and women in blue exit onto the scene.

The tables turn with guns pointed at Farrah. There's one of her and many of them. "Drop your weapon and step forward with your hands up," Detective Angel orders through a megaphone.

"No!" Farrah cries. "You can't make me!" Without a moment's hesitation, like her mind has been made up from the start, Farrah turns the gun to herself and pulls the trigger.

The bang is loud through what is usually a quiet neighborhood, and the buzzing in my ear is so intense I don't hear when Farrah's lifeless body falls to the pavement. Her eyes are open and rolled back to her skull while blood runs through the open wound. The crimson mixes with the rain and runs off to the road, finally putting an end to all of this.

JUNE 8 – SATURDAY

Afternoon

Many horrible things have happened in the past 10 months since moving to Blackridge. Two of our classmates died by suicide and won't be graduating with us. Three others were murdered. My mom was murdered by her sister, who in return was murdered by Farrah. Bad Omens collaborated with Poppy.

Putting on this cap and gown I never cared about is surreal, but if Mom could see me now, I know she'd be proud. This is the end of our high school days but the beginning of the rest of our lives moving on from this plague of tragedies. I gather with my friends and what's left of my family in the auditorium.

"Wait!" Poppet calls out and demands we come together in a huddle. We close together, and she extends her arm to fit us all in the frame. Then, she takes a picture with her cell phone.

"Hey, can you excuse me a sec?" I say and dismiss myself from the group.

Mr. Mark stands near the stage along with the rest of the faculty of Seal Coast. Mrs. Burke was helpful while here, but has since returned to Salem. "Mr. Mark," I call out.

He looks at me. In only a few months the attractive young man has aged considerably, adding lines to his face and more gray to his hair. After Aunt Addie's death, he took a leave of absence and has made himself scarce ever since. "Fiora, congratulations. You look beautiful. Just like … just like your sister."

The details surrounding the *why* of Aunt Addie's murder have been kept tight-lipped by Joey and myself. As far as the people of Blackridge are concerned, she was just another innocent victim. "Normally people tell me I look like my mother," I say.

Mr. Mark's face wrinkles when he smiles. "I bet you do. Your family is full of strong women. You've proved that this year. I just know you'll do great things with your life moving forward after all of this."

"What about you?"

"I–I think I'm going to move back to San Diego. Blackridge is a little too exciting for me."

I look over my shoulder at the group of friends I've made, including Chloe, who made the seventeen-hour drive just to get here. I return my attention to Mr. Mark. "Shit, you're telling me."

It comes time for the ceremony to start and we take our seats. Atlus sits to my left, and to my right is a framed picture of Mom.

Principal Pal takes the stage and stands behind the podium. He clears his throat and speaks into the microphone. "Good afternoon, seniors and loved ones of Seal Coast's senior class. The time has finally come. This has been a rough year for all of Blackridge but partially for its students. Many have lost friends and loved ones, though as life moves on, you gain more than you've lost and learn to cherish what you have. Today comes to an end of you being students, creating a new beginning for the rest of your lives. I wish each and every one of you nothing but success and happiness in whatever endeavors you precede.

"I bid you all a fare thee well on behalf of all remaining students and staff of Seal Coast Community High School. Now, please welcome to the stage your student council president and valedictorian, McCarthy."

Principal Pal steps away from the podium and McCarthy takes the stage. "Thank you, Principal Pal," she begins. "Like many of you, I have spent all my days here in Blackridge. We are a small but strong forgotten town with an endless plethora of unique individuals. When it comes to education, many emphasize the *school* in Seal Coast Community High School, but this year, we emphasized on the *community*. Where we could have despaired, we triumphed. Unfortunately, not everyone in our community could make it here today. I would like to take this moment to relish our fallen comrades' memories: Lemming, Griffin, Keaton, April, Falco, Ms. Hoyos, and Farrah. Let us cherish the days we're grateful to keep in their memories.

"Life is unfair and life is cruel, but us gathered here in this moment is proof that no path is set in stone, and after today, many more paths will be open. Let us take what we've learned to not only be better for ourselves, but better for our communities. Thank you."

There's applause after McCarthy exits the stage and Principal Pal returns. It's time to hand out the diplomas. "Fiora Clairwater," my name is called.

There has been applause for everyone called to the stand, but mine seems particularly loud. Maybe my friends are more obnoxious than the others, or perhaps I'm more focused on the company I've surrounded myself with. I do feel like we're part of a community.

Joey got me thinking more about the future, and I can't say I have any plans. But like McCarthy said, no paths are set in stone. I can have fun and heal now and decide what to do with the rest of my life later. I don't want to be a nepotism baby my whole life. Maybe Joey and I will go to university. Maybe I'll write a book about my unbelievable time at Seal Coast. But all of that is for the future, and today I take a step foreward in the present. I walk up to the stage, shake Principal Pal's hand, and accept the piece of paper.

Look Mom, I graduated. Just like you've always wanted me to.

Made in the USA
Columbia, SC
09 December 2024

48736576R00222